his ninth promise

A HAMMOND FAMILY FARM NOVEL

IVORY PEAKS ROMANCE
BOOK 9

LIZ ISAACSON

feel-good fiction

LIANA JOHNSON

one

Tucker Hammond couldn't stop laughing as he followed his older brother and uncle out of the farmhouse. Hunter and Uncle Wes had been sharing stories about their time as the CEO of the family company—Hammond Manufacturing Company. Hunt had run it for seventeen years, and Uncle Wes probably twenty-five.

And today, they were all heading into the city. Aunt Bree and Opal had some shopping and other wedding things to do; Tucker's only sister had just had her baby, and he was tagging along with Hunter and Uncle Wes to take lunch to everyone at Jane's house.

Tuck had come back to Ivory Peaks with his parents to see Jane and Cord's new son, and he'd been in town for less than twenty-four hours. Still, he'd thought of Bobbie Jo Hanks several times. If she hadn't gotten a new phone number, he could text her and find out if she had dinner plans.

For some reason, he hadn't. Tuck had been learning that just because he had a thought didn't mean he had to speak. Didn't mean he had to act on it.

No one had mentioned her. Not Hunt or Cord, nor Molly or Jane. So as Tuck left the homestead, he looked over to the stables, hoping to catch a glimpse of her. From this distance, she'd have to be literally walking toward him or crossing the pasture, and she wasn't doing either.

So he hitched his smile in place and listened as Hunt started a new story about staying late one night and accidentally asking three different people to order dinner in for those who'd had to work through the meal.

"You've never seen so much pizza," he said, his boisterous laugh filling the August sky. "Boxes and boxes of it."

"I could eat pizza for every meal," Tuck said.

"It's a favorite," Uncle Wes said. "But Jane requested the roast beef sandwich from Deli Harvest, so that's where we're going first."

"And then to Porky's, right?" Tuck asked. His mouth watered for the sloppy barbecue pulled pork sandwich, and he knew for a fact that Mike, Uncle Wes's son, Tucker's cousin, and the current CEO of HMC, had requested the same sandwich for his lunch.

"Right," Hunt said as he got in the passenger seat of Uncle Wes's truck. "You starving, little brother?"

Tuck grinned as he climbed into the backseat. "Always."

"Well, we've got a ways to go," Uncle Wes said, glancing

in the rearview mirror. "Lunch pick-up, driving to Jane's, another drive, more food pick-up, and then to the high rise downtown."

"He literally just ate two bowls of cereal inside," Hunt said. "He's fine."

"I'm fine," Tuck agreed. He tuned out the conversation as the drive started. He turned to his phone instead, where he'd been communicating with another manager in the rodeo about a cowboy who might potentially need a manager.

He'd met with Cole Walker, but he'd been working with a great manager named Leon Peters for only a couple of years. Tuck wasn't going to try to poach the man away, and he'd enjoyed his summer working with Blaze and Jem Young in their youth rodeo program.

He wasn't sure what the next step for him was, but he had faith in God that something would open up for him. He wasn't sure if that opportunity would present itself in Coral Canyon, or here in Ivory Peaks, or somewhere else completely.

He was trying to be patient, be open to all things, and keep his nose clean and his head down.

Since his parents were going to be staying in Ivory Peaks for a few months—until his cousin Opal married her fiancé Taggart Crow—Tuck would be here too. He'd moved into the generational house with his younger brother, because his old cabinmate had a new man living with him, so Tuck couldn't go back there.

He could've moved in with Hunter too, or even stayed with his parents, who were living in the foreman's cabin out in the cowboy community, away from the homestead. He'd opted for staying with Deacon, because it *wasn't* with the other cowboys.

He didn't want to stay on the family farm, plain and simple, and if he integrated himself into the community out there, it would be harder for him to leave. Tuck had already gone through that once a few months ago, and he didn't want to do it again.

Plus, you didn't want to run into Bobbie Jo.

He dismissed the thought almost as instantly as it had come into his mind. It might be true, but Tuck didn't trust himself to be alone with Bobbie Jo. "Especially after kissing her the way you did," he muttered.

The reason he'd given everyone was that he missed his brother, which wasn't untrue. Tuck did miss Deacon, and he actually admired how stalwart and steady his brother was. He knew what he wanted, and he got up every day and worked toward that thing.

Tuck felt blown about in the wind, the way a dandelion seed did after a child made a wish on it and sent it off to come true.

He'd always been a dreamer, and his daddy had spent the better part of the summer telling him it was okay to be who he was. That God had made him to be more spontaneous than Deacon, and that he could still make a good life for himself by dreaming and going after those dreams.

"We need help carrying everything," Hunt said, and Tuck pulled himself out of his head. He got out of the truck and went in with his family members to get the food they'd ordered for everyone out at Jane and Cord's new farm.

They'd moved completely onto the property now, and the house in the suburbs—where he'd lived with Jane before she and Cord tied the knot—had gone onto the market. Yes, she'd asked him if he'd wanted it. No, Tucker did not want a six-thousand-square-foot house in a neighborhood behind a gate.

What he really wanted was a big camper to tow around and live in while he moved from rodeo to rodeo with a really talented cowboy. He'd prayed and prayed for God to give him the talent in the saddle, but it simply hadn't happened yet. At this point, Tuck was pretty sure he wasn't going to be a rodeo champion.

He was great with a rope, and if he could find a partner with patience and deadly aim as the lead man, he might-could make a living in the rodeo. But so far, he hadn't been able to find that partner either.

Not since his last cowboy and best friend, Tarr, had retired officially.

He helped pick up the bags of food, and it all got put in the back of the truck with him. They then made the drive to Twilight Fields, the name of the farm Cord and Jane had bought. They hadn't renamed it, and a sense of shimmering sunshine and serenity passed over Tuck as Uncle Wes turned onto the dirt road that led toward seemingly only trees.

Tuck did like trees, and his mind wandered according to the rumbling of the tires. Maybe he could be a lumberjack or something. Did they travel and see different forests? What skills would he need, and would he have to go to college to get them?

Tuck did not like college or book learning very much.

"Tuck," Hunter said, and his loud voice startled Tucker.

"What?" he asked crossly. "I'm right here."

Hunter had already gotten out of the truck. "I've said your name three times." Hunter wore a frown that melted away as he slammed his door and pulled open Tuck's. "What are you thinkin' about?"

Tuck could absolutely not say *trees*. Not to his high-powered, super-CEO, older brother. "Nothing," he growled. "I'm coming." He twisted and reached for the bags of food he'd carried out of the restaurant.

Hunt watched him, but Tucker had been living with Daddy for the summer, and he knew how to withstand those dark-eyed looks that asked too many questions. He kept his head low, utilizing his cowboy hat to hide his eyes, as he went by.

Uncle Wes led the way inside, and everyone turned dark compared to his big personality. And right now, Tuck didn't mind living in the shadow of his magnetic uncle. He took the food into the kitchen so everyone at the farm would have something to eat, and then he skedaddled back to the living room, where the cutest baby in the whole wide world currently rested in a swing.

"Howdy, Clint," Tucker said as he moved toward the gently swinging infant. He was only a week old, and Tuck seriously didn't know how the little boy's head could fold into that ninety-degree angle.

"You can get him out," Jane said. "He needs to wake up now."

Tucker looked over to her, suddenly nervous though he'd held the baby already. "I can? Should I?"

"I'd love you forever if you'd hold him while I eat." She gave him a quick side-hug. "You guys are getting lunch somewhere else, right?"

"Yeah," Tucker said, looking back to the baby. They held such wonder for him, and he decided he could fumble around with Clint and learn how to deal with a newborn baby. So as Jane moved into the kitchen, Tucker moved over to the swing.

He switched it off and unclipped the safety belt around the still-getting-pudgy baby. "All right, buddy," he said. "Come see Uncle Tuck." He lifted the baby up, one hand sliding up behind his floppy head.

Clint made the cutest squeak and groan possible, and a shot of joy injected itself right into Tucker's heart. Then he cradled the baby against his chest and moved as slowly as he ever had—and that meant something for Tucker, who'd been hustling and bustling everywhere he went since the age of four.

The baby made a disgruntled noise, and Tuck went, "Shh, shh, shh." Then he remembered Jane wanted the baby to wake up. He honestly had no idea how to keep a baby awake, and he figured his sister knew that.

People talked and laughed in the other room, but Tuck ignored them. The noise of his family faded away, and all he could see and hear and smell was the perfect little boy in his arms. Tuck had never considered himself as a father, but the feelings running through him told him that perhaps Tuck should be looking for someone to call home, someone he could be a partner with throughout the whole of his life, and someone who could give him a perfect baby like Clint.

Of course, because his mind liked to torture his heart, an image of a pretty strawberry blonde came to the front of his thoughts. Bobbie Jo Hanks.

"Maybe I should just text her," he murmured to Clint. "What do you think, buddy? I mean, it's a text. She can ignore if she wants, right?"

Clint groaned again, and Tuck swore he heard the baby give him permission to text Bobbie Jo. He could do it from the truck, as Uncle Wes drove them from the small town life an hour from the city to the high rise building where Mike worked in downtown Denver.

"Ready, Tuck?" Hunter asked.

Cord followed him, and he finished wiping his mouth as he did. "I'll take him, Tuck."

Tucker easily eased Cord's son into his arms, noting how soft and paternal Cord had become in a single moment. He gazed at Clint with such love, and Tuck's heart sang for this to be his life too.

These thoughts half-surprised him and half-irritated him. He'd been working for months to find a cowboy to manage. Getting back his contacts in the rodeo—and Blaze and Jem Young were still *huge* in that arena—and mapping out what he wanted for the next few years of his life.

Fatherhood had been nowhere in the plan.

"Tucker," Hunter said, more wariness in his voice now.

"I'm coming," he said.

"You're really checked out today," Hunter said.

"He is?" Daddy asked.

Tucker threw a glare at his father, then one to Hunter. "I am not," he said. "Let's go."

"Waitin' on you," Hunter said with an over-exaggerated wave of his arm toward the front door. Tucker did his best not to stomp past everyone and out of the house, because he wasn't thirteen anymore.

He heard his father and Hunter start a conversation behind him, and he knew they were talking about him. Daddy would probably wait a while and then text, or he'd bring it up with Tucker the next time they were together.

Tuck rolled his eyes now, but he knew his daddy loved him, worried about him, and prayed over him constantly. So he didn't really mind talking to his father and spilling everything in his heart and mind.

He did his darndest to stay present, though he didn't care about the conversation happening in the front seat. He did care about getting his pulled pork sandwich, and he did care about getting up to Mike's office as quickly as possible to eat.

So he didn't have Hunter breathing down his back, Tuck stayed attentive through it all, and he carried his beloved sandwich and a huge cup of soda across the lobby and toward the elevator.

One more ride up a bunch of floors, then a walk down a long hall, and finally, *finally*, Tuck could eat. He was so anxious to get to the food—and to prove to Hunter that he didn't need to be prodded like an errant child—that the moment the elevator chimed its arrival, Tuck started toward it.

A voice he knew met his ears, and it took his eyes a moment to catch up to his memory. The prettiest woman in the world had her head tipped back as she laughed, and Tucker wanted to bathe in the sound of Bobbie Jo's voice.

Unfortunately, he'd been living in small-town Coral Canyon or Ivory Peaks for years, and he didn't frequent a lot of elevators. And double unfortunately, he'd already started moving onto the car.

He realized too late that etiquette dictated that he should've waited for the people already on the elevator to get off, and Bobbie Jo did exactly that.

And since she wasn't looking directly at Tucker, she didn't see him.

Everything in the world turned into slow motion. He tried to stop, but his long legs were between steps. He instinctively lifted his hand to block her or shield himself or something. Truth be told, his brain couldn't work that fast.

Bobbie Jo looked at him, and he caught a hint of surprised recognition a mere nanosecond before he ran straight into her with his cola cup.

Which exploded.

Brown liquid shot out of the top, dislodging the lid and sending fizzy soda in all directions. Tucker even got a few drops straight to the face.

And in a triple move of unfortunate, most of his Diet Coke spilled down the front of Bobbie Jo's pristine white scientific lab coat.

two

Bobbie Jo Hanks had a temper that fired like an automatic weapon when she got irritated. Or even when she just hadn't gotten enough sleep the night before.

And right now, as ice-cold cola seeped into her clothes and ran down her skin, a deadly combination of exhaustion and irritation made her go, "Tucker Hammond, what is wrong with you?"

Someone in the elevator had gasped. Someone else had cried out. Bobbie Jo took a step back, the brown puddle of liquid at her feet only adding to the nightmare unfolding in the elevator.

She held up both hands as if she'd dipped them in tar and looked at Tucker like he'd done the worst thing imaginable.

"I'm so sorry," he gushed. "I just got on, and I didn't—"

He cut off, his face turning a deeper shade of red with every passing moment. "What are you doing here?"

So not the time for this conversation.

"Tucker," Hunter Hammond said. "Brother, you're in the way. Let's let everyone get off this car. Uncle Wes went to get security."

Tucker spun toward his older brother. "Security? Why?"

"They'll close this car down," Hunter said matter-of-factly. Then he turned toward someone, laughed loudly, and drew the man into his chest for a hug. "Howdy, Earnest. We're gonna need maintenance and janitorial."

"Oh, ropin' and ridin'," Tucker muttered under his breath, and it almost made Bobbie Jo smile.

The elevator car started to emit an alarm, and he did get out of the way then. That allowed the people behind Bobbie Jo to get off the elevator, and she looked helplessly at Troy, a co-worker she'd been about to go to lunch with.

"I'll be at The Corner Bakery," he said. "I'll get you the soup and salad combo. Catch up to me when you're cleaned up." And off he went, leaving Bobbie Jo only a single step from leaving the elevator and getting her overdue midday meal.

Tucker stood in front of the doors so they couldn't close, and the high-pitched wail only bothered her further. She let out an exasperated sigh and looked over to the panel of buttons. She jabbed at the red one, the one she'd use if the elevator stalled or she needed help, and on the second try, she hit it.

A siren sounded, and Bobbie Jo cowered down as if fighter jets would soon be peppering the building with bullets.

"Great," Tucker yelled over the noise. "As if everyone wasn't already staring at us."

"Us?" She glared at him. "I think you mean me. You don't have cola all over you."

"Don't I?" He held up the ruined cup, which still dripped ominously with Diet Coke.

At least she assumed it was Diet Coke. She'd never known Tucker to drink anything else.

You might not know anything about him, she thought, and Bobbie Jo felt herself coming down out of the red zone. Thankfully, before either of them could say anything else, more people arrived.

A maintenance worker and a man with a mop, along with at least three of the men who stood at the front counter and took care of any problems with people coming and going in the lobby.

"Let's get you out of that puddle," the janitor said. "Maybe the showers, Mister Hammond?"

"Sure," Hunter and an older gentleman said in unison. Bobbie Jo didn't know him, but he bore the same long, sloped nose as Tucker and Hunter, so she assumed they were related. They both laughed while Tucker stood there with a brown paper bag and his half-crushed cup.

Hunter gestured to the older man. "We're both Mister Hammond. We both ran HMC."

"Oh." Bobbie Jo didn't know what else to say. "I don't need a shower. I don't have other clothes here." She looked over to Tucker, but he'd handed his cup off and ducked his head.

"We'll find you something," Hunter said jovially. "Come on, Bobbie Jo." He guided her out of the elevator, and the maintenance worker stepped onto it and silenced the alarm. "We've got full facilities on this level, and I can get you something new to wear for today. Unless you've moved closer? I can send someone to your place and get you something. Or you can just jet home really quick."

Of course he could do any number of things. Hunter had unlimited resources, and she had no doubt he had any number of minions who would run to her apartment and get her precisely what she dictated to them.

She glanced over to Tucker, her heartbeat doing strange flips and flops in her chest. She really wished her old cabin-mate had never called him the hottest cowboy in the country, because since she had, every time she looked at him, that was all she could think.

He'd cut his hair recently, if the clean-shaved look of his neck and up around his ears meant anything. He wore a cowboy hat indoors, which wasn't surprising, but only made her like him more. Blue jeans—standard for a cowboy. His shirt wasn't a polo or a button-up, but a plain old short-sleeved T-shirt, which meant he hadn't come in from the farm for lunch today.

The dark gray made him seem a bit more mysterious, as did the logo on the front—a B, J, and Y—as she had no idea what it meant.

He looked up at her, and their eyes met for a moment. Her

whole world changed in that moment, and Bobbie Jo didn't know how or why or even which way was up anymore. She only knew that Tucker Hammond had walked right back into her life, spilled a lot of cold cola down the front of her body, and then stood there looking like the surface of the sun.

"Bobbie Jo?" Hunter asked, and when she slid her gaze to his, she found him looking over to Tuck.

"I don't live close," she said. "I really can just...get a new lab coat."

"Tuck here will get you something." Hunter grinned with all he had as he nudged Bobbie Jo toward the Cowboy Who Hadn't Moved.

"What?" he barked. "I don't know how to do that. I didn't run this place."

"Mike's expecting us," Hunt said. "We've got some business to discuss with him."

The other Mister Hammond looked at Hunter, obviously confused. "He won't—"

"He is *starving*," Hunt said over him. "He's been texting me for twenty minutes." He still wore a smile akin to a clown, and Bobbie Jo's ire skyrocketed again.

"*I'm* starving," Tucker said. "I don't know where the shower facilities are, and I certainly don't have everyone in this building queueing up to get my autograph." He glared at Hunter. "You're embarrassing me."

Bobbie Jo's heart went out to Tucker, because he was a sweet, sweet man. Her lips tingled with the memory of kissing him. "I'm really okay," she said. "I'll just go get cleaned up in the restroom."

Hunter had fallen back a step, and he didn't say anything. The older man stood there too, obviously going to let someone else play this out.

Tucker said, "Me too. Let's go, Bobbie Jo. You two go on up without me. I know the way to Mike's office, at least." He stalked away from the situation, and Bobbie Jo decided not to dawdle.

She went after him, saying, "Tucker."

"Look, I'm really sorry," he said. "I just—my brother's been riding me all day, and I was just in a hurry to get upstairs and eat. I should've just waited to get on the elevator."

He had the longest legs ever, and Bobbie Jo jogged to catch up to him. "Hey," she said, her temper rising again. "Can you just *wait*?"

Tucker came to a complete stop now, and she nearly ran straight into his back. He turned, and if she hadn't stopped herself in time, his shoulder would've taken her out. "What?" he barked.

She blinked at him, trying to make the pieces of him line up. "I've never seen you in a bad mood."

He rolled his eyes. "Of course you have."

She actually smiled. "No, I don't think I have."

Tucker's square shoulders deflated. "Well, I guess there's a first time for everything." He dropped his chin, his right hand still gripping that brown bag. He looked up at her from beneath the brim of that sexy hat. "I really am sorry."

"Do you have the same phone number?" she asked.

He raised his head fully and stared openly at her. "Sure

do," he said easily. Then he swallowed, so maybe it wasn't as easy to say as she'd assumed.

Bobbie Jo wanted him to ask her out. Words streamed through her head, things she could say if she had more courage, if she wanted to know what he was doing here, on a Wednesday afternoon, at her new place of employment.

But she wanted *him* to ask her out. *Him* to ask if he could text her or call her. Maybe suggest dinner, so she could kiss him before they even got inside the restaurant.

He said nothing.

Maybe their kiss almost three months ago hadn't meant as much to him as it had her. Maybe she wasn't a good kisser, and men like Tucker probably had plenty of women to compare her to.

"Where you livin' now?" he asked.

"I've got a place up in Boulder," she said. "It's a cute little blue house with three bedrooms. I share with two other girls." She swallowed, not sure why she'd started rambling about where she lived.

"Boulder," he said. "That's still a commute."

"Everything is a commute to HMC," she said. "Unless you have the last name Hammond and can live in the building next door." She quirked her left eyebrow at him, almost daring him to contradict her.

He graced her with a smile. "You're right about that."

"Did you sign another cowboy?"

"Not yet," he said. "I did summer rodeo camp work in Coral Canyon, with a couple of big-name cowboys. Blaze and Jem Young."

Her eyes dropped to his chest. "Is that what the BJY is?"

"Yes, ma'am."

Her fingers stuck together, and she pried them apart. The soda had started to dry, and she really should get into the bathroom, get cleaned up, and get to The Corner Bakery. Troy would have her food, and he'd demand to know the story behind her knowing the Hammonds.

When Tucker didn't ask or offer anything else, Bobbie Jo took a breath. For a moment there, that single moment suspended in time with their eyes locked, she'd thought God had reunited them. That He'd brought Tucker back to the area specifically so they could have their second chance at something meaningful and lasting.

Maybe he's dating someone else.

The thought struck her like a ton of bricks being dropped on her head, and Bobbie Jo let out a frustrated breath. "Okay, well—"

"There you are, sweetheart."

Both she and Tucker turned toward the male voice, and she found another co-worker rushing toward her. Ben wore a semi-crazed, half-panicked look, and he lifted his arm as he approached her.

That was when the word *sweetheart* rang in her ears. "Ben—"

His arm landed around her shoulders, something he'd never done before. He tucked her into his side like he'd done it a thousand times, though. He grinned down at her like he was just so thrilled to see her.

"What—?"

"Who's this?" he asked, cutting her off. He definitely cooled as he looked at Tucker. "Is he that friend you said we might be able to double with?"

"What?" Bobbie Jo swung her attention to Tucker, who had both eyebrows sky-high now.

"Double with?" Tucker asked. He looked at Bobbie Jo. "He's your boyfriend?"

Bobbie Jo wanted to laugh, but her throat seemed to be full of sand with only a hint of saliva, and everything felt too thick.

Surely Tucker wouldn't buy that. Ben looked nothing like the type of man Bobbie Jo would ever, ever go out with. He wore *slacks*, for crying out loud. Tucker was a smart cowboy; he'd figure it out. He'd make a joke, laugh about the ridiculousness of her and Ben, something.

But things were moving so fast, and neither of them had time to say anything before Ben said, "Yeah, I'm her boyfriend. Who are you?"

three

Of course Bobbie Jo was dating someone. She was only the most beautiful woman on the planet. Tucker had kissed her three months ago as a *good-bye-until-we-meet-again* gesture, and he could admit he was surprised to see her standing next to some...some scientist in slacks with his arm awkwardly around her.

That kiss had skewed his world. He'd been walking sideways ever since, but it had obviously meant nothing to Bobbie Jo.

"We are not dating," she said, her cheeks taking on more and more pink. "Ben, what is wrong with you?" She stepped out from underneath his arm, and now the three of them made a triangle outside the restrooms on the first floor.

Tucker actually smiled because he liked those sassy words when they were aimed at someone else.

"Troy said you might need help," Ben hissed between his

teeth. He cut a look over to Tucker, who still wore that devilish grin.

Tucker couldn't wipe it away fast enough, and Bobbie Jo saw it too. Her frown deepened, and those pretty eyes narrowed.

"What are you grinning about?"

"Do you have any other fake boyfriends I should know about?"

She rolled her eyes. "Of course not, Tuck."

"What about real ones?" he asked.

Her eyes met his, and all the stars in heaven could be fueled by their chemistry.

"No," she said flatly.

Tuck's first inclination was to ask her out. He bit back the words and said instead, "Me either."

"No?" she asked. "You didn't find a girlfriend up in Coral Canyon?"

He shrugged, realizing he still had cola all over him when his shirt stuck to his skin. His stomach growled, and Tuck wished for the umpteenth time that he could time travel.

Then he could go back and act more like a gentleman when he first met Bobbie Jo. He wouldn't come on too strong, he wouldn't ask her out every other day, and he wouldn't tease her about her dentist boyfriend back in Oklahoma.

Oh, and he'd be able to erase the Diet Coke explosion too.

Sadly, God had not given Tuck the time travel capability, and he had to suffer in the situation he'd created.

"Well, I'm going to go clean up," he said. He lifted the bag with his sandwich in it. "And eat. I'm starving."

"Yes," Bobbie Jo blurted out almost over the top of his last word. "I'm hungry too."

That was his cue to walk away, but he didn't do it. Bobbie Jo didn't duck into the ladies' room either. And Ben stood there and studied Tuck like he was a new species never seen before on the earth.

"I heard you got a new number," he said, his feet automatically going into dance mode.

"Yeah," she said. "I had to...." She trailed off and looked over to Ben. "Will you go tell Troy I'm going to order something to my desk?" She indicated her clothes. "I still have to get cleaned up."

"Okay," Ben said. "I'm sure he ordered already, and we'll bring it to you."

A glorious smile filled her face, reaching all the way to those gorgeous green eyes.

"Thanks, Ben."

He left, and Bobbie Jo's smile turned off as if she'd flipped a switch. She focused on Tucker again, her gaze definitely hotter and more murderous than it had been a moment ago.

"I haven't even said anything," he said.

She considered him, her fire burning out fast. He'd missed that about her. He'd missed her up-down-hot-cold personality. He'd missed the sound of her voice.

He'd simply missed *her*.

"So...." he said. "I didn't get a new number. I'm going to be in the city for the next couple of weeks, helping Mikey here and playing errand boy at the farm."

She nodded, and he wished she'd blurt out something flirty or funny or just plain what weighed on her mind.

"If you need anything, you can text me."

She nodded again, and Tucker's cowboy boots took him a step closer to her. "You can text me?" he asked.

She swallowed and looked up at him. "Your number was saved in the cloud. I've got it."

He grinned at her, his pulse doing gallops through his chest and up around his ribs. "All right, then," he said. "I hope—"

"I need some clothes," she said, doing that blurty-thing he wanted. "Hunter said maybe someone could get me some?"

"Yeah, sure," Tucker said, though he didn't have the power to send anyone to Bobbie Jo's house to get her clothes.

"My co-workers are going to be back soon," she said, shooting a look toward the huge wall of glass doors leading into HMC. "I'll clean up the best I can, and then I'll text you my address."

"Okay," he said.

"It's...good to see you, Tuck." Bobbie Jo reached out and squeezed his forearm, and when she tried to pull her hand back, it didn't go.

Where she touched him, his skin ached and burned and fizzled all at the same time. He looked down at her hand as she tried again to get it to release. His skin and the hair on his arm pulled with the stickiness of the soda—probably the cherry syrup he'd ordered—and she finally freed her hand with a grunt.

"My word," she muttered as she moved swiftly past him. "Why can't anything go right between us?"

Tucker turned all the way around to watch her enter the restroom, wondering if she knew she'd spoken right out loud for him to hear. He grinned, ducked his head, and hurried into the men's room, a plan forming in his mind.

He didn't need to hurry upstairs and ask Mike or Hunter who to send to get Bobbie Jo's clothes.

He'd go get them himself. After all, then he'd be able to see her again, whether she texted him or not.

"Genius," he whispered to himself as he splashed water up his arms to get all the stickiness off.

Ten minutes later—who knew having one elevator shut down could cause so many people to pile up at one-thirty in the afternoon?—Tucker ducked into Mike's office. Hunter, Uncle Wes, and Mike all sat around a kidney-bean-shaped table, with Mike currently leaned back in his executive office chair, his feet up on the table as he grinned at his father.

He wore a suit to work every day, but he'd tossed his jacket somewhere. They all looked to Tucker as he finally sat down with his mashed lunch and soda-stained clothes.

"Hoo-boy," Hunt teased. "You're in a state."

"I just need to eat," he said as he pulled out the sandwich he'd been craving for hours now. "And I, uh—" He shot a glance over to Mike, who raised his eyebrows. "Bobbie Jo decided she did want new clothes, so I'm gonna head to her place and get them."

"*You're* going to?" Mike asked. "I've got people I can send."

"Oh, he likes Bobbie Jo," Hunter said, still teasing Tuck completely. "He's really asking if he can borrow a vehicle."

"Yep." Tucker nodded in an exaggerated way. "That's what I'm asking." His phone still hadn't gone off with her address, and as he chewed, he stewed over that. Uncle Wes said there were trucks down in the parking garage, and Mike said he'd call and let the attendant know Tucker would need the keys to one of them.

Done. Easy.

His phone chimed at the same time Hunter asked, "So are you going to go out with her?"

He practically dove onto his phone, because the message had come from a number he didn't have saved in his device. Bobbie Jo didn't identify herself, and the text was literally two lines of an address in Boulder.

"I'm not asking her out," Tucker said almost absently as he wiped his mouth and picked up his phone.

"No, he's going to go get her clothes so he can see her again," Mike said.

Tucker nodded enthusiastically again, his brain firing at him in so many different ways. He needed to get Bobbie Jo's favorite dessert. Her clothes. A vase of flowers. A red-check-ered cloth.... With those things, he could make a simple dessert picnic and maybe sit and chat with Bobbie Jo for a few minutes right here at HMC.

She loved picnics and eating outside, and he had access to the roof.... "Can I get on the roof?" he asked, looking up from his unsent message.

All three men in his family grinned back at him. "Yeah, sure," Mike said almost casually. "What are you thinking?"

"Does Bobbie Jo have access to the roof?"

"What floor is she on?"

Tucker looked over to Hunter. "Uh, she's a metallur-gical-ist." He grinned at his older brother, who burst out laughing. "She studies something about metals." He took another bite of his sandwich, because the clock ticked louder and louder with every passing second.

"Our metal-work is on the eighth floor," Mike said with a grin of his own. "So no, she won't have access to the roof."

"Classist," Tucker said.

"We open the roof to all employees for certain occasions," Mike said, almost in defense. "But it's only accessible to project managers and company officers year-round."

"I'm an errand boy," Tuck said. "I certainly don't qualify."

"You've got an in," Hunt said. "Now, keep eating so you don't miss your window to lure her up to the roof."

Tucker choked on his bite of sandwich. "Lure her on the roof? My word, Hunt, don't make me sound like a serial killer."

They all laughed again, and Tucker did practically inhale his sandwich, he accepted a can of Diet Coke from Mike, and he met his older brother's eyes. "Can you order the caramel cheesecake from The Corner Bakery for me?"

"For two?" Hunt asked, picking up his phone.

"Yes, sir."

"On it."

"Thanks, brother." Tucker left his trash behind, suddenly

in a hurry to get out to Boulder and back before Bobbie Jo decided the wait wasn't worth it.

That *he* wasn't worth it.

Getting the keys from the parking garage attendant took less than a minute, and Tucker navigated himself to Bobbie Jo's little blue house in Boulder without an issue. He peered through the windshield at the white shutters, and he could hear her exclaiming over them.

She loved old things, and small things, and fluffy things.

"And wearing clean clothes," he muttered to himself as he swung out of the truck. She and her roommates had hung a pumpkin sign on the door for the fall, and someone had put a pair of wicker chairs with thick cushions in the corner of the porch.

Tucker rang the doorbell, as Bobbie Jo hadn't given him any indication that he could just walk into her house and rummage through her dresser drawers. He pulled out his phone and sent her a text.

Will anyone be home at your place? And what do you want to wear?

He didn't want her to know he was the one standing on her front step to get her clothes, but she'd literally given him nothing.

My roommates work too, she said. *We have a number pad on the door. The code is 011710. I'm fine in jeans and a T-shirt. I probably have something laying on the recliner in my bedroom. It's the last one at the end of the hall, on the left.*

Got it, thanks, he sent, and he looked up to tap in the code she'd just given him. The keypad beeped as he did, and then the lock disengaged. He twisted the doorknob and stepped up and into the house, feeling very much like that serial killer he'd mentioned to his brother.

Especially when a woman screamed and rushed at him with something dark and long in her hands.

"Whoa, whoa, whoa!" Tucker yelled as he moved backward, stumbling back down the single step to the porch. "I'm here to get something for Bobbie Jo!"

He threw up both hands just as the dark-haired woman reached the doorway. He recognized the object in her hand as an umbrella, and he reached out and grabbed it from her before she could hit him with it.

His chest heaved as he tossed the umbrella over to the pair of chairs. "She got dirty at work and needs new clothes."

The woman grabbed onto the door and brought it almost all the way closed, so Tuck could only see half of her face through the gap. "Who are you?"

"Tucker Hammond," he said. "But I don't want her to know."

"You don't want her to know?" The woman narrowed her eyes, and Tucker wished he knew her name.

"I told her I'd send someone to get the clothes," he explained, his patience for this down near zero. "So no, I don't want her to know I came myself."

"I'm not going to let you in," she said. "I should call the cops."

"She gave me the code to the door," Tucker said, fumbling for his phone. "Look." He shoved his device toward her, and she looked at it for a long moment before her hand snaked

29

out and took it from him. She sucked the phone into the house, where it was darker on her side of the door, and looked at his phone.

He could've rammed the door with his shoulder and knocked her all the way down, but he said nothing as he backed up a step.

She finally raised her eyes to his again. "Jeans and a T-shirt," she said. "That's it." She thrust his phone back to him. "And I'll get them and bring them out to you."

"Fine," he said. "Could you not tell her I came? Just say, 'Some guy came to get your clothes. I gave them to him. Hope that was okay.' Okay?"

"Fine," she said back to him. Then the door slammed closed in his face, and the distinct sound of the sliding-closed deadbolt met his ears. "Dear Lord," he said as he breathed out all the air in his lungs.

"Please let this mystery roommate hurry with the clothes."

Because the clock was ticking, ticking, ticking, and Tucker didn't want to lose another moment when it came to Bobbie Jo.

four

Bobbie Jo kept trying to focus on the report that had come back from the lab that morning. But for the life of her, she couldn't. Running into Tucker had ruined her concentration completely. She kept imagining his gorgeous smile, that big dark brown cowboy hat, and the Southern twang of his voice—and then she couldn't remember what she'd read.

Or even looked at.

Or her own name.

So when her phone chimed, and she saw Cara's name on the screen, she picked up her device and said, "I'm going to take a break."

"Are they back with your clothes?" Troy asked, as his desk sat directly beside hers.

"Should be soon," she said. "I'm just gonna walk the floor." The eighth floor had an outdoor track, and when anyone needed a break, they went out there and walked. Bobbie Jo actually loved that about working in this high-rise building in the city—which were two things that squashed her cowgirl spirit.

She'd cleaned up the best she could in the restroom, but her clothes still felt sticky and uncomfortable. At least the lab coat covered most of the stains.

Once she'd left the office, she looked at Cara's text. *Some guy came to get some clothes for you. I hope you're okay. I gave him a pair of jeans and that T-shirt with the rainbow cat on it.*

Bobbie Jo smiled and tapped out. *Thank you, Cara. Why are you home?*

What happened at work? her roommate asked almost at the same time Bobbie Jo sent her text.

Someone spilled cola all over me, she tapped out.

Half-day training, Cara said. *And then we had the afternoon to implement, and we were allowed to come home, so I did.*

Ah, got it, Bobbie Jo said. *Sorry, I gave out the code to the door so they could get in and get my clothes.*

It's fine! I talked to him and gave him the clothes so he wouldn't be digging through your underwear drawer or anything.

Bobbie Jo giggled, sent her roommate a *thank you* text. She'd just pushed outside, the flaps on her lab coat getting grabbed immediately by the autumn wind, when her phone chimed again. She pulled it closed around her and folded her arms as she exercised her legs for a minute.

When she gained the corner, she checked her phone, the ground beneath her feet vanishing at the sight of Tucker's name on her phone. *Got your clothes. Meet me in the lobby? I have a surprise for you.*

Her heartbeat fluttered at the word *surprise*. What could Tucker possibly have planned in the last ninety minutes? "He's a billionaire," she reminded herself. He could've sent someone for her clothes, someone else to get the surprise he had planned, and a third person to do whatever else he wanted.

No matter what, she wanted to get out of her sticky clothes, and she took a deep breath, as if air alone could defend her against the magnetic Tucker Hammond.

On my way, she texted him while she waited for the elevator, and a couple of minutes later, she stepped out into the lobby again, her thoughts chasing each other like kids hopped up on sugar. "Don't get your hopes up, Bobbie Jo," she lectured herself in a whisper. She'd missed Tucker every day since he'd left Ivory Peaks in favor of another small town, in another state.

Despite the ultra-sparky kiss they'd shared three months ago, she'd made it clear she didn't want a long-distance relationship. Been there, done that, heart broken. And Tucker had made it clear that he felt suffocated in Ivory Peaks, at his family's farm.

Tucker certainly stuck out, what with his height and that sexy cowboy hat. He stood against the far wall, watching the elevator. She lifted her hand in a wave, and he tilted his head back, the cowboy version of *Hey, I see you, beautiful.*

At least for Tucker, and she'd totally added that *beautiful* out of pure—and pathetic—wishful thinking.

Her breath came quicker as she approached him, and she looked left and right like someone might jump out of the shadows and stop her from making contact with the cowboy.

"I got your clothes," he said, holding out a plastic grocery bag. "And I'm pretty sure your roommate has pulled all the still images of me on your front porch, and I've got a file with the Boulder PD now."

Surprise made Bobbie Jo yank the bag from him. "*You* drove to my house and got my clothes?"

"Yes, ma'am." He grinned at her and held up another bag. A great big one from The Corner Bakery, and Bobbie Jo leaned forward to try to smell what that thing held. Tucker reached into his pocket and pulled out his phone. "And my cousin just sent me the code for the *fancy* elevator that will take us to the roof."

Her eyebrows flew up. "The roof?" She'd never been up to the roof, as she'd only worked here for eight weeks, and only the upper-level management had access to the full amenities of the building. "What's in that bag?"

"The surprise," he said. "Do you have a few minutes?" He stepped past her and led her toward the elevator on the very end. An actual security guard stood there, and he merely nodded at Tucker when Bobbie Jo felt certain she'd have been wrestled to the ground.

The security guard pushed the button for Tucker as Bobbie Jo said, "Yeah, maybe twenty minutes or so."

"That's long enough for cheesecake," he said.

Bobbie Jo's mouth started to water, because she'd eaten cold soup and soggy grilled cheese for lunch. "Cheesecake?"

"Barrel racing," Tucker scoffed, his form of swearing. "I wasn't going to tell you that." He threw her a look from his milk chocolatey eyes. "I'm the worst at surprises."

The elevator car arrived, and he led the way onto it. Bobbie Jo joined him and feeling brave and slightly reckless, she slipped her hand into his. "I'm still surprised."

"Yeah?"

"And I love cheesecake," she said.

"Well, I knew that." He bumped her with his hip. "But it's still good to know that some things haven't changed."

Warmth filled her from head to toe, as if God Himself had draped her in a hug. Tears actually came to her eyes, and Bobbie Jo looked away as embarrassment filled her. The atmosphere in the car changed instantly, and Tucker looked over to her.

"I once again didn't say anything," he said.

"You actually have," she said, glad her voice didn't sound too nasally or pinched. "I...." She didn't know how to tell him how lonely she felt. "I really only talk about work," she said. "Or who's going to pay the utilities that month. I don't—hold hands." She squeezed his and somehow moved closer to him. "I don't—have very many people who are close to me. I doubt anyone in the office or either of my roommates knows that cheesecake is literally my favorite food."

Tucker gazed at her, a thoughtful look in his eyes. "Well, I do."

"Yeah," she said, unable to hold the intensity of his eyes. She looked up to the floor indicator, still in awe that she could get to twenty-four—where the CEO worked—and the roof. "You've always been very good at seeing me and listening to me, Tuck."

He cleared his throat, but he didn't say anything, and they rode the rest of the way to the roof in silence. She let him go first once the doors had opened, though she felt like a five-year-old on Christmas morning, trying to get to the presents under the tree before anyone else.

"Wow," she said as she looked up into the brilliant blue sky. "You know, I've heard rumors about this place."

"Yeah?" Tucker didn't seem that impressed by the raised flower beds holding rose bushes, then aspens, then mini Cindy-Lou-Who pine trees. Pops of color and metal sculptures peeked from around a tall hedge, and Bobbie Jo wanted to explore every square inch of this rooftop paradise.

"There's a walking path," Tucker said. "But...how do you feel about picnics?"

Her eyes widened, sure this handsome cowboy had not set up a picnic on this private corporate rooftop. "I love picnics," she said slowly.

Tucker's grin widened. "Good. Because I've got one all set up right over here." He led her through the maze of trees, flowers, and bushes closest to the elevators, and indicated a small building seemingly right in the middle of the roof. "You'll want to change first, I'm sure. Mike told me the restrooms up here were functioning, but that the water might be real cold."

Bobbie Jo stared at the bathroom, so many thoughts flying through her head. Was this...a date? The plastic bag in her hand crinkled, testifying that it absolutely was. *No*, her brain shrieked. *Cara got you the rainbow cat tee.* And she'd never wear that on a date—at least not a date with Tucker Hammond.

"Okay," she said. "I'll be right back."

"I'll be here," he said. "This place is a little crazy, and I don't want you to get lost."

Bobbie Jo hurried to the restroom, her mind whirling. As she changed into the clean clothes, she couldn't help wondering what Tucker was up to. Was this just a friendly gesture to make up for the soda incident? Or could it be something more?

"It's totally Tucker," she muttered to her reflection, and then she shoved her lab coat and her dirty clothes back into the plastic bag.

She emerged from the restroom a few minutes later, feeling much more comfortable in fresh jeans and a soft T-shirt. Tucker waited right where she'd left him, but he grinned at his phone now.

"Your family?" she asked. "Tarr?"

"My daddy," Tucker said, looking up. "He loves to send me memes he's made with his horses." But now, he shoved his phone in his back pocket, his complete attention on her. "Ready?"

Bobbie Jo nodded, falling into step beside him as they headed down the path away from the elevator. After a couple more turns, she caught sight of the walking track that clearly went around the gardens, and Tucker tugged her off the path and around to the far side of a hedge, where a big patch of shade waited.

A red-and-white checkered blanket had been spread out, with a vase of wildflowers waiting in the center. Tucker moved right over to it and set the big brown bag of cheesecake down, then turned toward her. "Surprise. It's a rooftop dessert picnic."

"Tucker," she breathed. "This is amazing."

He indicated she should sit, and Bobbie Jo did just that. He joined her, rubbing the back of his neck and looking uncharacteristically shy. "I'm glad you like it. I just thought... well, I've missed you, Bobbie Jo. And I selfishly wanted to see you for longer than five minutes in the lobby, when we're both covered in cola, and some guy thinks he needs to protect you from me by pretending to be your boyfriend."

Bobbie Jo's heart soared at his words. She smiled up at him. "Scientists, right?"

He chuckled, and all of the tension that had been hovering between them simply floated away, right up off the rooftop and into the Colorado atmosphere.

"Yeah," he said. "Scientists are the worst." He then unrolled the top of the bag, and his whole being seemed lit up from within. He exuded such a vibrant spirit, and Bobbie Jo really needed something exciting in her life right now. "So, this here's a caramel cheesecake."

And he lifted an entire cheesecake out of the bag. It had a plastic dome over the top of it, but Bobbie Jo could practically taste the golden caramel that had been pooled on the top and which dripped down the sides. Graham cracker crumbs looked like they'd been pressed on precisely and undisturbed as the cheesecake got boxed up.

He balanced the cheesecake on his knee as he folded the bag to make a placemat for the dessert. "How do you like working here?"

"It's good," she said, her voice pitching up slightly.

"Sounds like it."

"No, really," she insisted. "I'm just really new. I started the first week of June, and sometimes, I still can't find my way to my desk."

He smiled at her. "It's a big building." He lifted the dome off the cheesecake, and the sticky sweet scent of caramel punched her in the nose. "Do you miss the farm?"

"Every day."

Tucker paused, the big chef's knife hovering above the cake. "Really?"

"Yes, really." She smiled at him as a realization hit her. "You don't miss the farm."

"There are...certain aspects of the farm I miss." He focused on the cheesecake and cut straight down the middle of it. He made a few more long cuts, and then he slid the tip of the knife under a particularly bulky triangle of cheesecake and put it on a plate. "For you, Your Cheesecake Highness."

Bobbie Jo fed off his joy, and she took her cheesecake with a nod and a "Thank you, Tuck."

He handed her a plastic fork and started dishing himself a slice of cheesecake. If this was one of their previous conversations, his next words would've been a tease about how they'd have so much fun on a date, if only she wasn't dating that guy in Oklahoma.

Or he'd ask her to dinner.

Now, Tuck simply picked up his own plastic fork and dug into his cheesecake. "Does it smell like it's been laced with arsenic?" He nodded to her still untouched dessert.

"Arsenic is actually odorless," she said, pouring as much flirtation into her voice as possible.

Tucker tipped his head back and laughed, and Bobbie Jo so loved that sound. She did miss him terribly, and she could admit—only to herself—that when she thought about the things she missed at the Hammond Family Farm, Tucker always stood in the forefront.

And he wasn't making any moves to ask her out.

So she said, "So if you're not seeing anyone, and I'm not seeing anyone...." and let the words hang there, because she did not want to be the one to ask *him* on a date.

five

Tucker couldn't quite make eye contact with Bobbie Jo, though all kinds of fill-in-the-blank statements rushed through his mind.

She almost seemed like she *wanted* him to ask her out. But a mighty battle raged inside him. He'd already been over-eager in setting up this rooftop dessert picnic, and he didn't want to shoot himself in the foot further.

He wasn't super experienced with women, but he'd never had a problem talking to them. Even Bobbie Jo. So he drew in a deep breath, begged God for the right thing to say, and opened his mouth.

"I'm just not sure about things," he started, still searching for the next words.

"What do you mean?" Part of her shuttered off, and Tuck reached out and threaded his fingers through hers, paying close attention to the pops and zings and pleasure that shot through him. Yep, the spark still burned hot between them.

He raised his chin enough to be able to see her eyes. They flamed with fire, so she felt that pulsing energy between them too.

"I mean...you're living in the city and working in the city now, and I'm out at the farm. It's a long drive." He swallowed because he couldn't believe what he was saying. "It feels like long-distance."

"It's an hour."

"What time do you get off?"

"Five," she said.

"So it'll be six-thirty before you could get out to the farm, if you're going to come see me. And you have another hour back, and you're up early, and unless you've changed radically in the past three months...you go to bed at ten at the latest. So we get a couple of hours."

"And cowboys are up with the sun," she said with some measure of resignation.

"And I'm not planning on staying in Colorado, Bobbie Jo." He whispered the last bit, because he felt like he'd just fired fifteen shots, all of them aimed at his chest. Now his heart throbbed and thrashed around, bleeding through multiple holes.

"I know that," she said. "But you're here now." She squeezed his fingers, and he dang near jumped out of his skin. His eyes dropped to her mouth, but Tucker sternly told himself he would not kiss her. Not here on the rooftop, not before they'd gone on at least one date. "I don't know how long I'll be here, and then what?"

"Then maybe we just see," she said. "I'd like to go out with you." She raised her chin and glared—yes, glared—at him. "Look me straight in the eyes and tell me you don't want to go out with me."

Tucker allowed himself to smile, because he loved her sass and fire. She *lived* life and Tucker absolutely wouldn't lie to her. So he said, "I'm dying a terrible death every second we don't have a date set up."

"Then ask me out."

Tucker's mind moved fast, but he couldn't come up with a concrete, compelling reason why he couldn't go out with her. Tonight, for dinner, would work.

"Do you want to go to dinner with me sometime?" he asked.

Her face bloomed prettily, with a pink flush in her cheeks and those perfect, full lips curving upward into a smile. "Yeah," she said. "I'd like that."

"You're the one with a full-time job," he said. "I'm getting settled out on the farm and helping with the harvest for a little bit."

"That's full-time work," she said dryly. "But nice try." She picked up her phone and started swiping. "Oh, look at that. Every evening is wide open for the foreseeable future." She tossed her phone back onto the red-and-white-checkered blanket. "I guess that's what happens when you don't have a boyfriend or a social life."

Tucker burst out laughing, and he lunged at Bobbie Jo,

tackling her to the ground as she cried out and yelped and then dissolved into giggles in his arms.

He quieted and laid on his back and looked up into the bright blue sky. He sighed out all his breath and said, "You have friends. You could do something with that guy who came running in to save you from me."

"Yeah, Ben's a nice guy," she said. "What made you think he wasn't my boyfriend?"

"The slacks," Tucker said, and Bobbie Jo buried her head in his side as she laughed some more.

He took the opportunity to knead her closer and take a deep inhale of her hair. Still peaches and vanilla, and all of the unsettled pieces of Tucker's life calmed down.

"I'm so not into scientists," she said.

"Well, you did date that dentist once."

Bobbie Jo lifted her head and pushed herself up on her elbow. "Also a huge mistake." Her gaze dropped to his mouth too, and Tucker would pay any amount of money to know what she was thinking.

"Yeah," he said, his voice suddenly choked and tight. "Because you like cowboys."

"Yeah," she said. "I like cowboys."

"We could meet somewhere halfway," he said, and Bobbie Jo looked at him again. "I can also just stay here and run errands for Mike until you're done, and then we can go to dinner."

"How will you get back to Ivory Peaks?"

"The same way I got out to your place in Boulder." He

closed his eyes, so he wouldn't have to see her reaction to his next sentence. "Company truck."

"Oh, sure," she said as she settled back against his side. "I forgot for a second that you're a Hammond."

He chuckled. "Lucky you."

The mood changed between them, and Tucker wished he'd curbed his tongue.

"You're an excellent Hammond," Bobbie Jo murmured.

"Am I?"

"Of course you are."

"Sometimes it's easy to be forgotten when you're not a CEO or a farm owner or...anything really." A failure in the rodeo. Disinterested in the family business *and* the family ranch. A gypsy-hearted cowboy, with nowhere to call home.

Tucker didn't lack ambition; he'd simply jumped ship and found a different path to walk, and while it ran parallel to the other Hammond roads, he still had trouble merging sometimes.

Bobbie Jo let them lay in silence for a minute or two, and then she said, "I have to get back to my desk."

"Sure."

She exhaled heavily and sat up. She ran her hands through her hair while Tuck watched, how carefree and easy his life was sitting right in front of him.

"You should take the cheesecake to your co-workers," he said.

"Are you kidding?" She gave him a cutting look. "If you're going to give it away, I'm going to take it home and eat it for breakfast until it's gone."

He laughed again as he sat up and started repackaging the dessert so she could take it with her. She hadn't confirmed if they could go to dinner tonight or another evening, and Tucker didn't want to push the issue.

He packed everything up in record time, and she carried the vase of flowers in one hand, with the cheesecake in the other while Tucker led the way back to the elevator with her bag of soiled clothes.

He congratulated himself on keeping his lips to himself *and* saying what he truly thought as they rode down to the eighth floor, and when the car dinged, announcing their arrival, she looked over to him.

"You wanna meet me in the lobby at five?"

"Yes, ma'am." He nodded his cowboy hat at her and smiled her off the elevator.

"Bobbie Jo?" a woman asked. She peered past her to Tucker inside the car. "Is...? You're on the executive elevator."

Bobbie Jo started to answer as Tucker leaned forward and touched the button for the top floor. He could spill everything to Mike and Hunter, and they could help him figure out if starting something with Bobbie Jo when both of them knew he wouldn't be in Ivory Peaks for long would lose him his heart all over again.

* * *

Tucker woke to the sing-songy quality of his phone's alarm, and he rolled over in the soft, comfortable bed to silence it.

Sleep started to reclaim him, because he'd had a couple of

late nights and early mornings strung together, and he still felt tired.

Then his memory kicked at him, reminding him that he'd set his alarm for thirty minutes before he needed to be in the lobby of HMC to meet Bobbie Jo.

That got him up and out of bed, already searching for his jeans. Mike hadn't needed anything that afternoon, so after Hunter and Uncle Wes had left, Tucker had come next door to the high-rise building his family also owned, where he'd found an apartment filled with all the necessities for a nap, a shower, and a snack.

But Tucker had just needed the bed. He quickly redressed and headed into the bathroom to brush his teeth and check his hair.

He felt sure he could find a fresh shirt in the closet, but as he looked at himself in the mirror, he figured the gray, long-sleeved, button-up he'd put on this morning looked good enough.

Nervous energy filled him, and Tucker thought of the pure current that ran from him to Bobbie Jo whenever they were together.

Confidence filled him, because he'd kissed her before. He'd held her hand before. He still wanted to put forth a good impression and show her a good time, but he'd crashed and burned in far worse ways in the past.

It took several minutes for him to get down to the parking garage and through it, then through the back hallways that led to an elevator that went to the upper floors at HMC.

He had to go to the twelfth floor before he could exit the

private elevator and get on one that would deliver him to the lobby.

A woman met him outside the elevator, and Tucker tipped his hat at her. "Sorry," he said. "I'm no one important."

"No problem, Mister Hammond," she said, and she turned to return to her post. He'd learned that the secretaries got notified if the private, executive elevator was set to stop on their floor, and Tucker hated the lack of privacy for his movements around this building.

He supposed if he was someone important like Wes, or Hunter, or Mike, he'd have a great many things to do, and his time couldn't be wasted in transition. He'd probably want someone standing right outside the elevator door to get him to the right meeting or office as fast as possible.

As it was, he had to stand awkwardly with the group of actual HMC employees waiting for an elevator down to the lobby, as it was the end of the day and everyone was headed out.

Tucker didn't wear the same clothes as anyone else, and he hadn't felt so out of place in a long time.

He waited through three elevators before he could cram himself on with everyone else, and he stepped out into the lobby at HMC at five minutes past five.

People streamed out of the building, and Tuck felt like an island as he stopped and scanned the area for Bobbie Jo.

He found her over against the wall, where he'd been waiting for her earlier. He dodged through the business-people and scientists leaving the building and made it to her against the wall.

"My word," he said, breathing hard. "This is insane."

"You should see the sidewalks outside," she said. "We've started having staggered start and end times to help with the traffic."

"But you're nine to five?"

"All research departments are, yes," she said.

"Do you have a favorite place to eat?" he asked, still watching crowds of people leave the building. "Do you want to walk somewhere, or...? What do you do in this madness?"

She grinned up to him. "You're so not a city boy."

Tucker reached up and touched his cowboy hat. "Gee, I wonder what gave me away." He reached for her hand and easily took it in his.

"I ride the train out to a station, where I park," she said. "Then I drive out into the suburbs."

"I'm gonna follow your lead on this," he said. "I do have a truck we can drive somewhere. I'm willing to walk. Take a train." He looked down at her, creating a little pocket for just the two of them. "So you tell me, Bobbie Jo, and I'll do it."

Tucker felt like that could sum up his feelings and relationship between the two of them—whatever she wanted, he'd try to make possible.

Whether that made him pathetic or not, he wasn't sure, and right now, Tucker felt like he was right where he wanted to be.

six

Bobbie Jo had not planned for this Thursday night dinner with Tucker Hammond, and she couldn't seem to get her mind to settle on a restaurant where they could go.

HMC continued to empty, and that meant the bus stops and train stations would be filling up. Perhaps somewhere right here, right downtown Denver.

Most of those establishments were small, and she wasn't sure she wanted to eat with her knees touching his, and he'd have a hard time folding his over-six-foot-tall frame into a table or booth at one of her favorite chicken places.

"Burgers?" he asked in a murmur. "Mexican?" He held his phone in front of him, scrolling through options.

Bobbie Jo's heart beat hard for this gentle man, though nothing about him was really soft. He laughed loud and quick, and he had plenty of wit, and a neatly trimmed beard and beautiful eyes and everything about him appealed to her.

"How far is the Shrimp Palace?" she asked. "They have great surf and turf, and I love their butter garlic shrimp."

"Shrimp Palace," he muttered as he released her hand and tapped with both thumbs. "It's point-eight of a mile." He looked up at her. "Are we walking that?"

She shrugged one shoulder. "It's September, and the weather is usually pretty nice in the evening."

"I'm game." He tucked his phone into his back pocket and retook her hand. "I think I can get us there."

"Without looking?"

"It's west," he said. "And you'll steer me right once we get closer."

"That's putting a lot of stock in my ability to navigate," she said. "Have you forgotten our very first friendly confessional?"

"Absolutely I have not," he said as they left the building together. "That was one of the best days of my life."

"Your whole life?" she teased.

"Yeah," he said. "I mean, maybe after Tarr winning the National Championship, but it's right up there."

"Why's that?"

"Because I was with you," he said. "And we were just... talking. It was normal, and nice." He glanced over to her. "A great day."

The things Tucker said oozed with warmth and honey, chocolate and all good things, and Bobbie Jo did like talking to him. He had a way of making her feel safe, and heard, and perfectly cherished. Like talking to her? *That* was one of the best days of his life? Really?

But she believed him, because Tucker didn't have a disingenuous bone in his body.

"Maybe we should do another friendly confessional," he said.

"You think so?" She'd said plenty on the rooftop mere hours ago, and she wouldn't even know what to add.

"Sure," he said easily. "I'll go first: I had a great time in Coral Canyon this summer, working with two top rodeo champions. It was amazing, and I made a lot of good contacts."

"That's great, Tucker."

He beamed over to her, and she liked making him do that. "For me, uh." Bobbie Jo didn't know what to say. "I still really like tacos? I enjoy my job at HMC, and I like my roommates, so that's good. I found the house, and I put up an ad for some single female roommates, and I begged and begged God to give me some good ones." She thought of Cara and Jenny. "And you know what? He did."

"I'm glad," he said. "The one I met seemed pretty overprotective."

"Cara is great," she said. "She's been divorced; no kids; and she's a little wary of men. That's all."

"I *was* asking to come in and go into your bedroom to get some clothes."

"She told me you walked right in."

"You gave me the code and told me no one would be home."

Bobbie Jo grinned, enjoying the evening air and the big, tall trees running down the middle of the pedestrian mall in downtown Denver. "I do like the city."

"Two confessions," he said. "Wow."

"I don't want to live in the city," she said. "But I love working here. I love the vibe, the energy of it, but then I want to retreat somewhere quieter."

"I don't want to live anywhere," he said. "I like traveling around, seeing different places, meeting different people."

Bobbie Jo knew that about him, but to have him say it so right-out-loud gave her heart a little shock.

He really wasn't permanent here in the Denver area. *And he's been really honest and up-front about that,* she told herself. So she couldn't be upset about such a thing, nor surprised, but her heart hadn't gotten that memo, and it boomed at her in a loud, strange way.

"So...what would you do if you ever did have a wife and kids? Or do you not want those things? Wife and family? A place to call home."

All Bobbie Jo wanted was a place to call home. That was why she'd looked up the house rentals and signed her name to the whole lease. She wanted to feel like the place was hers.

Tucker didn't answer for several steps, and then he said, "I do want those things," in a really somber voice. "I guess I've just never thought that far ahead."

Something pinched in her lungs, and Bobbie Jo took a breath to try to dislodge it.

"I suppose I should," he said. "Because I sure do like you,

Bobbie Jo, and I do want to see— I held Clint this morning, and yeah, that baby is somethin' special."

"Okay," Bobbie Jo said, her voice pitching up strangely. "I mean, it's the first date." And she couldn't believe she even walked alongside him. "And I'm assuming Clint is Jane's baby."

"Yeah," Tucker said, drawing in a quick breath right after. "Yeah, he sure is. Was born last week. My parents came down, and I came with 'em. We're all staying through Opal and Tag's wedding."

"So Jane's delivery went well?"

"Seemed to," Tucker said. "It's not like I know anything about that."

Bobbie Jo smiled. "Yeah, cowboys never have to worry about delivering horses or cattle or goats or anything."

"That's not a baby," he said.

"It is so a baby." She laughed and nudged him with her body. "What is it if it's not a baby?"

He looked at her, pure puzzlement in his expression. "I mean—I guess it's a baby."

She pulled on his hand to get him to prepare to cross the street. "We have to go this way to the Shrimp Palace."

"It's just...human babies are so helpless. You deliver a calf, and bam. They're up on their feet, walking around. It's not the same at all."

"I suppose that's true." Bobbie Jo beamed up at him, feeling less like a storm cloud and more like glitter than she ever had. That meant something to her, because she'd always been the serious one in her family. She'd been the most upset when her parents had lost their farm in Oklahoma.

Her first instinct was to put her head down and get the job done. She didn't need a lot of friends, and in fact, she didn't even want them. But something about being with Tucker made a lot of her grumpy switches flip the other way.

"What are you smilin' about?" he asked, this time the grump coloring his voice.

"I don't know," she said, because she didn't. Maybe it was the perfect weather right now. Maybe the vibe of the city she'd mentioned earlier. Maybe the image of Tucker holding his week-old nephew.

Maybe just being with him.

He'd always brought much more color to her life, and Bobbie Jo simply breathed in this new vibrancy.

"You wanna come out to the farm this weekend?" he asked as they neared the Shrimp Palace. The bright lights of it flashed on the shady side of the street, and Bobbie Jo's stomach grumbled for as much seafood as she could give it.

"I'm not helping with the harvest," she said.

He laughed and leaned down to tap a kiss to her forehead. "I thought we could go horseback riding or something. It's such great weather right now, and Molly and Gloria have tons of new horses since the riding programs have really grown in the past couple of years."

She warmed at the fact that he'd just asked her on a second date when they hadn't even completed a first. "Sure," she said. "I think I remember the way out to the farm."

"Have you not been back?"

She shook her head. "Why would I go back? I don't work there anymore."

"I don't know," he said. "You were friends with Hattie and Molly and them. I thought maybe...I don't know, maybe you'd been back out to say hi or eat lunch or whatever."

Bobbie Jo's throat tightened, and she shook her head as Tucker reached for the door to the Shrimp Palace and opened it. He turned back to her to let her walk through first, and his eyebrows went up when he saw her face.

"What did I say?"

"Nothing," she managed to squeeze out through the narrow opening her throat had become.

"You've gone dull," he said. "And it's been a while since we've been face-to-face, but I recognize this."

"I'm fine, Tucker." She brushed by him and entered the Shrimp Palace, the scent of garlic, salt, and butter only encouraging her hunger to vocalize itself again.

"Yeah, I'd let you off the hook before," he said as he crowded in behind her. "Two, please," he told the woman approaching the stand, and she plucked two menus from the side of it.

"This way."

"But that was when we were just friends, and I didn't want you to be mad at me," Tucker continued as if they weren't in public at all.

Bobbie Jo increased her pace to keep up with the hostess, and she went around to the far side of the booth. She slid in and glanced at Tuck as he did the same on the other side. The hostess put down the menus and asked, "Water to start?"

"Does it have ice?" Tucker asked.

The woman looked like he'd just insulted her mother and said, "I can put ice in it."

"Then yes," he said, picking up a menu and handing it to Bobbie Jo.

"Ice water for me too," she said, taking the menu.

The hostess left, and while Tucker picked up the second menu, he didn't open it or look at it. "But I don't want you to shut down and go dull on me anymore. Not if we're going to do this." He gestured back and forth between the two of them with the tall menu. "So you have to tell me what I said wrong, and why."

"What if I don't want to right this second?"

He returned her glare and flipped open his menu. "I can give you a few minutes," he said as he lifted it to hide his face. "But if you really can't figure out how to tell me tonight, then I don't think you should come out to the farm this weekend."

Tucker lowered his menu and pinned her with that powerful gaze he owned. "Ain't nothing that hard to tell me."

"It's not you doing the telling."

"You act like I've never met you before."

"You act like everyone should be you."

He held her gaze for another moment, and then everything about him dropped. His shoulders slumped in, and he raised his menu again as he sighed. "Let me just look at this —did you know half of this is in Japanese?—and then we can figure it out."

"It's Chinese," Bobbie Jo said, just because she could. Then she buried herself behind her menu too, something shuttering and cold moving through her chest. She didn't like Tucker's ultimatum, nor the fact that he wanted to rush her into saying right out loud the things about herself she didn't like.

He was an open book. He had a quick smile and chuckle for everyone. He shone like the Christmas star on the darkest of nights.

Didn't mean everyone was like him, or had to be like him, or even could be like him. Bobbie Jo's anger stirred and stewed as she found her butter garlic shrimp and set aside her menu and looked over to Tucker.

He wore a slight frown between his eyebrows—which she found so cute—and her ire softened and started to blow away.

She slid to the end of the bench and quickly rounded the table to scoot in beside him. She pressed in close as he looked at her, another gloriously intimate pocket forming between them. "Okay, so this section is appetizers," she started. "Like calamari and single-serve sushi rolls. Down here, you have the steaks...."

Everything between them turned mushy and soft, and Tucker actually lifted his arm and put it around her, pulling her closer and closer and closer as she continued to detail the menu for him.

And Bobbie Jo knew she wanted to keep Tucker in her life. She wanted to go horseback riding with him desperately. So she'd tell him this thing about herself and pray it wouldn't be a strike against her.

seven

Bobbie Jo so didn't play fair. Tucker wanted to be irritated with her, and there she sat, the warmth of her body melding with his. He couldn't get her close enough, and he'd pulled her right into his chest.

"...so that's what I thought you'd like," she finished. She looked at him, and only a couple of inches separated them. His mind blanked, and he forgot why he'd gone salty with her.

"Ice water," a woman announced loudly, and he looked up to find a different woman there. "I can take your drink and appetizer orders." She smiled with all of her teeth, and Tucker felt inclined to return it.

"I'll have Diet Coke," he said.

"Same," Bobbie Jo said.

"Any starters?"

"We'd like the pork Bao buns," Bobbie Jo said, looking

from her to him and back to her. "Did you want anything else?" She returned her gaze to Tucker's, who shook his head.

"Great; I'll be right back with those Diet Cokes."

Bobbie Jo slipped away from him, and Tucker had no choice but to let her go. She resettled herself on the other side of the table again, and Tucker laid down his menu. He wasn't sure what to ask or say next. He'd been friends with Bobbie Jo for a couple of years now, and it wasn't like he had to ask her about her family—two younger siblings, a brother and a sister.

Her parents still lived in Oklahoma, and her dad now managed a supermarket. Her mom worked at an elementary school, and Tucker's memory failed on what her siblings did. She'd come to Denver to apply for a job at HMC, and when she'd hadn't been able to get one right away, she'd taken a position out at the farm.

She loved being outside, loved dogs, and loved horses. She'd wanted to be a farmer and take over her parents' place in Oklahoma, and as Tucker looked at the rainbow cat on the front of her T-shirt, he couldn't believe for a single second that she wanted a life in the city.

No, that job at HMC was temporary too, and she just didn't know it yet.

"I'm not good at making friends," she blurted out. "Okay? And once I move on, I just...move on. So no, I haven't kept in touch with Hattie or anyone out at the farm. I don't work there anymore."

"So that chapter of your life is just—over? Closed?"

"Yeah," she said. "It's kind of like that."

"But you dated Lawson for months after moving here," he said, his heartbeat starting to wail at him. She certainly hadn't closed that chapter the moment she'd crossed state lines, and he couldn't help wondering why.

Why hadn't she?

She could've easily drawn a heavy line in the sand and broken up with him. Then, she would've been free to go out with Tucker.

Maybe she didn't want to go out with you, he thought, and a new frown came to his mind, body, and soul.

"Yeah," she said, holding her head up high. "And it was a huge mistake. I'd moved on, and I should've broken up with him sooner."

"So you just move on now," he said. "Out of sight, out of mind." He folded his arms and looked at her, truly trying to understand. He'd known she didn't have tons of friends, but she'd *lived* with Hattie for years. They'd been close, at least from what he'd observed.

"It's not that simple." She reached up and ran her hands through her hair, gathering it into a ponytail at the nape of her neck. She released it and met his eyes. "I'm not heartless, Tucker, but I'm not...nurturing. I don't need a lot of friends. I don't know how to...maintain close relationships like that." She swallowed, and everything about her opened up and shone with vulnerability.

"I'm really not a very good friend," she said. "And yeah, I move on and leave people behind."

He nodded, though what she'd said fit with her personality, completely aligned with what he knew about her already. "Maybe you have a gypsy soul then too."

"I don't even know what that means."

They paused the conversation when the waitress returned with their colas, and they put in their orders. Tucker didn't want his first date with Bobbie Jo to be this. To be filled with heavy topics and her feeling bad. To be him questioning everything so soon.

So when the waitress walked away, he reached across the table and took Bobbie Jo's hands in his. "Let's shelve this for now, okay?"

"Are you serious?" she asked. "You literally just told me you wouldn't go out with me again if I didn't tell you everything tonight."

He grinned at her. "I like it when you're spicy."

She rolled her eyes, but when they came back to meet his, they held that edge of fiery desire. "You're impossible."

"I maybe just got irritated," he said. "Of course I want you to come out to the farm this weekend."

She tilted her head and considered him, and Tucker let her look. She should know when she got him, she got what she saw.

"I'm sorry," he said. "Really. I'm allowed to get irritated sometimes."

"What made you irritated?"

"That you went dull." He pulled his hands back. "You don't hide how you're feeling very well, and I knew I'd said something you didn't like."

"It's not you," she said with a sigh. "It's me."

"I won't push you into corners," he said.

"Maybe I need to be pushed into corners." Her eyes fired a challenge at him now, and Tucker really liked that too.

He'd worked with cowboys on the rodeo circuit like this too. They didn't want to be told what to do, or what to wear, or who they had to talk to at the pre-events and post-parties. But Tucker managed them with a firm hand, and in the end, they always thanked him for pushing them where they didn't want to go.

He didn't want to think of Bobbie Jo like one of his rodeo cowboys—she was so far from that, it wasn't even funny—but maybe it would help for the time being. So he picked up his glass of Diet Coke and took a long drink through the straw. He smacked his lips together and said, "I love that stuff so much."

Bobbie Jo softened and smiled and sipped her own drink. "I know you do."

"I just want to know everything about you," he said. "That's all. I get you have more walls than me." He leaned forward, his own intensity rising through him. "But I'm going to kick them down, because I don't want any walls between me and you."

Bobbie Jo blinked. She swallowed again. Said, "Fine."

"Fine," Tucker repeated. "Because that's what I want with my partner. An open relationship, where I get to be irritated with things when they irritate me, and you can be grumpy and sullen as long as I know why. And we just...get to know everything about each other, and it's all okay."

He took a deep breath. "I'm not perfect. You're not

perfect. But we get to be who we are with each other. You don't have to hide things from me."

"But maybe you won't like me once you know everything."

"Maybe I won't," he admitted. "But I'd rather know that now than in a few months when I'm already in love with you. Or after we're married. Then what?"

He shook his head, this thing very important to him. "I don't believe in hiding my flaws until after the wedding. I want you to know them all, see them all, experience them all before that. Then you'll know what you're getting when you get me."

There. He nodded, glad when his steak and lobster arrived in that moment, sparing him from further speaking. Bobbie Jo let the food distract her too, and she lifted a shrimp dripping with butter and visible chunks of softened, caramelized garlic.

"Look at this," she gushed. She bit into it, her eyes rolling back into her head in bliss. After she'd moaned, chewed, and swallowed, she looked at him again.

"I want you to know what you're getting when you get me too," she said. "My momma always told me I was an acquired taste, and well...I'm not sure I've ever thought someone would want to...acquire me."

"You've dated plenty," he said. "You have to know men find you downright gorgeous."

She smiled at him and shook her head, that pretty hair swinging back and forth. "No, Tucker, I don't know that."

"Well, you are," he said, and he cleared his throat as he

looked down at his own food. "And I like you." He cut off a piece of his steak and speared it with his fork. "And I just want to know everything about you. That's all."

"Such a small ask," she teased.

"That's why we date, sweetheart," he shot back. "And be honest about stuff while we do it."

She looked like she might argue again, and then she simply took another bite of her shrimp. "Okay, Tuck," she said quietly when she finished it. "And you have to know how incredibly handsome you are too, right?"

"No," he said. "I don't know that."

She grinned at him, all sparkle and no spice now. And oh, he loved this part of her too. "Well, you are." She made an over-exaggerated grinding noise in her throat, clearly mimicking him. "And I like you too."

* * *

A couple of days later, Tucker sat on the front porch of the generational house where he lived with Deacon. His brother had fried sausage, scrambled eggs, and perfected coffee for breakfast that morning, and their empty plates still sat on the table between them.

Deacon still nursed his cup of coffee when he glanced over to Tuck. He kept his hands moving over the leather strip in his hand, his attention still looking there, but his ears perked up to his younger brother.

"I need a new foreman," Deacon said in the same slow drawl his daddy had when he ran the farm.

Tucker looked over to him. "You do? Is Matt retiring?"

"He met with me last week." Deacon looked out over the field in front of them. It was their family garden plot, and Tucker had dug out plenty of potatoes just yesterday. "He wants to be done in the next few years."

"Hunter owns the farm," Tucker said as his blade went *wisp, wisp, wisp* over the leather to soften it. "He'll hire someone."

"Hunter wants me to do it," Deacon said. "I run the farm, Tuck."

And Deac would own it before too much longer too. Tuck knew that. He just didn't concern himself with the transitions and dates, because they didn't impact him. He'd always have a place here at the Hammond Family Farm in Ivory Peaks if he wanted it.

"Probably good for you," Tucker said. "Then you can get someone you like, who you work well with, who can stay on for a long time, like Matt's done."

"Yeah," Deacon said. He rocked back and forth a few more times, everything about him slow and calm this morning. He worked like a beast, though, and Tucker admired his younger brother for his steadiness and strength.

"I'm thinking of two people right now," he said. "Mission and...Tarr."

Tucker jerked his head up. "My Tarr?"

Deacon grinned at him. "He's yours? Are you two going to be making an announcement about your engagement I need to know about?"

Tucker glared at Deacon and rolled his eyes. "He's my

best friend." The only reason Tarr had come to Ivory Peaks was because of Tucker. "And he has enough money to buy his own farm if that's what he wants."

"And yet," Deacon said. "He hasn't."

No, he hadn't. Tucker stopped working on the strip of leather and surveyed the land in front of them too. He'd never minded growing up on the farm. It did have a keen sense of serenity to it, with flowing sunshine and the mountains right there but also in the distance.

"Matt has always had enough money to buy his own place," Deacon said. "He's never wanted to. Maybe Tarr's the same."

"Mission's been here way longer," Tucker said.

"He's also in his forties," Deacon said. "Which means I need another new foreman far sooner than I would with someone like Tarr."

"Tarr is thirty-four," Tucker said. "That's not that much younger than Mission."

"Mm."

They sat in companionable silence for several minutes, and the leather strip in Tucker's hand got softer and softer. He'd be able to twine this with several other pieces and make a nice belt for himself.

His phone chimed, and his pulse shot to the top of his mouth. "That'll be Bobbie Jo." He hoped. Deacon glanced over to him almost lazily as Tuck got the phone out of his pocket. Sure enough Bobbie Jo had texted: *I'm here. Should I just walk around the farmhouse to the generational house?*

Yeah, start this way, he sent. *I'll come meet you.* He set aside his leather-working tools and grinned at his brother. "Did you want to come riding with us?"

Deacon looked at him with a measure of disgust on his face. "Do I want to go riding with you and your brand-new girlfriend?" He scoffed. "I think I'll pass."

Tucker laughed, because yeah, he wouldn't want to do that with someone else either. "Yeah, all right. I'll see you later this afternoon."

"I'm sure I'll hear all about it," Deacon muttered. "As if I was there."

Tucker bounded down the steps like an overeager dog who hadn't seen his master in months, Deacon's comment not even bothering him. He did tend to talk everything out to anyone who would listen, and unfortunately, he lived with Deacon right now.

So that man was Deacon.

He went down the dirt path that wasn't really a road but could be driven on, and around the corner of the house. Bobbie Jo walked toward him in her cowgirl garb—blue jeans, those pretty cowgirl boots, and a button-up shirt in pink and purple plaid, and she'd added a hat and a pair of sunglasses to her look.

Cowgirl chic, and Tucker's heartbeat thrashed at him. "Hey." He jogged through the long grass his nephew would probably mow sometime today and swept the beautiful strawberry blonde into his arms. "Mm, it's so good to see you."

"It's only been one day," she said with a giggle. She

gripped him back in a hug too, Tuck noted. "And we've been texting non-stop."

"I don't think you know the definition of non-stop," Tuck teased as he stepped back. He laced his fingers through hers and grinned at her. "I need to text Molly, and she'll meet us over at the stables."

"There were a lot of cars out by the big red barn." Bobbie Jo looked that way, and Tucker did too.

"Oh, right," he said. "Horseback riding is still going. So she'll be out in the stables already." He led her back to the dirt path that ran between the pastures separating the family farm from the more commercial operation of Pony Power, and he sure enjoyed the sun on his face as they walked.

"How was the drive?" he asked. "Not bad on the weekend?"

"It's sixty-four minutes from my front door to yours," she said. "I timed it."

He laughed again, not caring that his voice came out too loud. "Of course you did."

"And no, traffic was nothing," she said. "There was a tiny slow-down through Elmer, as there's a great diner there with amazing eggs Benedict."

"Mm, we should go there," he said.

"They only take reservations on the weekend," she said. "As they only serve the eggs Benedict on the weekends."

"I'm not really a reservations kind of man," he said.

"You're joking," she deadpanned. "You don't like making plans? Who knew?" She squeezed his hand, but something inside Tuck squeezed too.

"And you can live with that?" he asked. "I know I'm spontaneous, and I like doing things based on how I feel."

"Yeah, it took me a while to figure that out, but now that I know, it's fine."

Tuck nodded, his throat still a tiny bit tight. "My daddy says, 'When you say you're coming, we don't really expect you until you get there.' Because I change my mind all the time."

"You've told me that before."

"It's important, though," he said. "I don't like making plans, because what if I *feel* like a huge all-meat omelet on the day we've made reservations for eggs Benedict?" He raised his eyebrows and looked over to her.

"I don't think I have a spontaneous bone in my body," she said. "I anticipate what's on the calendar, I guess. So I'd wake up ready for eggs Benedict, because I've been staring at the reservation for eggs Benedict all week."

"Right." Tuck watched the activity around the barn as it picked up. The riding lessons this morning were clearly for teens, as more and more groups returned, dismounted, and started brushing down their horses.

Cowboys came out of the doors between the huge administration barn—which doubled as a stable—and the true stables and started helping with the equines.

It sure seemed to him that he and Bobbie Jo were opposites in some things, something he'd never picked up on before.

Opposites attract, he thought as they reached the fencepost marking the end of the first field. An intersection ran in front of them, and Tuck continued on toward the stables. Ahead of him, the exercise circles sat dormant, as most of the horses on the farm got used for the riding lessons.

He enjoyed the peace and tranquility on the farm, but on his next step, something rose up into the air. A cry, then a scream, and then another.

Tucker slowed his movement even as his pulse sped, and he frantically searched for the cause of the trouble.

A couple of dogs barked, and he found the crowd getting pushed back, almost like a wave of water being sucked back into the ocean—except they'd been moved toward the barn.

"What's going on?" Bobbie Jo asked, and Tucker released her hand and jumped up on the fence so he could see better. He climbed up another rung and found the cattle dogs flat on the ground, barking, barking, barking at something that had come into the herd of horses.

Cowboys rushed to pull the horses back, and as his throat clogged with fear, a couple of riding horses—usually gentle and calm—reared up onto their back feet, shrilling out a warning as well.

Men yelled, and Tuck found Gloria and Molly both there, each of them with their hands raised.

He still couldn't see what had caused the ruckus, but his cowboy instincts told him it had to be an animal. A coyote who'd somehow found himself in the wrong place at the wrong time.

As he watched, everyone else disappeared. All the kids had been pushed back. The horses had been moved inside. Only Gloria, Molly, and the three farm dogs remained, and even so, Tucker stood on the second rung up and watched the women who ran the riding lessons fade into the stables, and the dogs turned tail and went into the barn, leaving nothing and no one outside.

His phone went off as profound fear bolted through him. He'd just seen the pointed ears, and he didn't need to wait to hear the howl of a wolf. He'd lived in the countryside for decades, and he knew the danger of wild animals.

"What is it?" Bobbie Jo asked as she climbed up on the first rung.

"Get up here," he said, reaching for her and pulling her up another step. "There's a wolf right down there."

eight

Molly Hammond's chest had turned to a stone. She ducked down the aisle between horse stalls, most of them holding far more occupants than usual.

"What's going on?" a cowboy asked.

"Was it really a wolf?"

"I didn't see it," another cowboy said. They continued to chatter as Molly ducked into the office at the back of the stable. Her lungs couldn't get enough air against the rock-hard cage of her ribs, and she sucked at the air, telling herself silently not to pass out.

She'd sent a text to everyone on the ranch. *EMERGENCY: Wolf spotted near stables. All personnel and visitors please shelter in place immediately. Do not approach. Text in your location and if you're safe or need help. Wait for further instructions.*

But even as she threw herself into her chair and slammed

her palm down on her mouse to wake the computer there, she knew not everyone on the farm right now was on that text string. Gray and Elise weren't, for one. They didn't live here anymore.

Hunter's parents could be outside somewhere, taking a walk, enjoying the September mid-morning sunshine. His uncle Wes and aunt Bree were staying at the farm for the next couple of months too, as they prepped for Opal's wedding.

She just needed to get the footage of the cameras outside the stable pulled up. Her phone chimed over and over and over, the beeps and notifications coming in on top of each other, as she did. But she couldn't answer, and her emotions wavered as tears filled her eyes.

"Please, God," she whimpered. She thought of her children who lived on this ranch. Her baby was only six years old, and a wolf could carry off her Clay without any problems at all.

She clicked as her phone rang, and she stabbed her phone to get her husband's call connected. "Hunter," she breathed. "There's a wolf between the barn and the stables. Came out of nowhere."

"Yeah," he said. "I got your text."

"I wouldn't joke about a wolf," she bit out at him. "I'm pulling up the cameras now, but it's been about a minute. I don't know where it went."

The images filled her screen, and it felt surreal and strange to see no movement where only a few minutes ago, there had been so much energy. So many people teeming.

"I see him." She clicked on the rectangle with the only

movement in it. "He's in the middle of the exercise ring." The wolf stood in the middle of all that dirt, almost near the mechanism that kept the horses moving around and around.

Its gray fur bristled as it swung its head left and right, and she let out a shuttering breath. "I've never seen one this close before. I have no idea where it came from." A nervous shimmer went down her spine, and she tore her eyes from the dangerous predator. "Tell me where the kids are."

"Ryder's the only one out," Hunter said. "He was getting the lawn mower going. He got your text, sweetheart, and he's safe in the equipment shed."

Molly wiped her tears. "Lisa, Char, and Clay are with you then?"

"Right here in my office," he said. "We're standing at the window, lookin' over to you, baby."

"Your parents?"

"Lisa texted them. Momma said they're in their cabin, and Wes and Bree hadn't left yet. They're safe."

Molly nodded though her husband couldn't see her. She hated the thought of her oldest out in the equipment shed alone, though Ryder was seventeen years old now. "I'm going to call Wildlife Management."

"Deacon said he did," Hunter said. "You're not looking at your phone."

"I ran to the office to look at the cameras." She pulled in a breath. "He's moving, Hunt. He's headed into the fields between the stables and the farm." She couldn't move the camera to see him once he left the range. "I'm going to lose him."

"Uh, Mols."

"What?" she barked out.

"Deacon's here. I'm gonna pass—"

"Tucker's in that field," Deacon said, interrupting him. "He and Bobbie Jo were on their way over to the stables for a ride."

Molly's heart fell all the way to the soles of her boots. She'd forgotten Tucker had asked if he could go riding with his long-time crush, Bobbie Jo. "The wolf is going that way," she whispered.

"I'm on the phone with him," Deacon said. "He and Bobbie Jo climbed up the fence."

"It's a seven-foot fence," Molly said, getting to her feet. She needed that wolf to go west, not north. If he'd just head for the mountains, he'd get off the ranch faster. Everyone she loved would be out of danger sooner.

"They're on top of it," Deacon said. "And yes, the wolf is now in the field kitty-corner to where they are. Tuck says...he's just walking along. Doesn't seem concerned about much of anything."

"What is it doing here?" Molly asked, once again feeling her emotions waver and shimmer.

"Looks like almost everyone's checked in," Hunter said, his voice further away. "Matt and Boone. Their kids. All the parents are in their cars or in the barn, Cosette said."

Molly looked out the back window, and the scenery that usually calmed her and showed her the power of God's glory only made more tears prick at her. She looked away from the mountains, which housed so many dangerous wild animals, and quickly scanned through the messages which had come in, relief washing over her as each person confirmed their location.

Mission: *In the garden shed with Tarr and Jake. Safe here.*

Matt: *The kids and I are at Boone's with his kids. Everyone accounted for.*

Hattie: *We made it back to our cabin: me, Millie, and Rose.*

Ryder: *In the equipment shed. I'm alone, but I'm safe with all the doors closed and locked.*

Cosette: *Parents are flooding in now. I'm sending a text to all of them to stay in their cars.*

Gloria: *Cowboys in the stables with me. Cosette, how are the teens over there?*

Cosette: *Texting their parents and scared, but no one's hurt too badly. A scraped palm or two from those who fell down in the scuffle to get inside.*

Molly looked away after that. The emergency text had worked. People had immediately gone into their sheltering protocols.

But again, Tucker didn't work here, and he wouldn't have gotten the text. He and Bobbie Jo just happened to be outside, too close to the wolf, to get to safety.

"Can you see Tucker?" she asked Hunter. If he stood at his office window and looked toward the stables, he should be able to see them on the fence.

"Yes, sweetheart, I can see them."

"And?"

"And they're holding real still, sitting back-to-back, with

their feet up on the top rung with them. They're fine for now."

"Can you see the wolf?"

"No, baby."

"It's right there, Daddy!" Lisa yelled, and Molly dang near jumped out of her skin.

"Yes, I see it now," Hunter said. "He's moving toward the far corner of that southwest field, Mols."

"Maybe he'll hit that road and just take it west."

"Maybe," Hunter said. "We're going to lose him."

"Tuck can see him," Deacon said. "He's moving away from them, Molly. It's going to be fine."

"It'll be fine when the wildlife officers arrive and secure the farm," she said.

"They're here," Hunter said. "Do you want to go with me or stay here with Deacon?"

"I'm going with you too," Deacon said in a growly voice. "This is my farm, Hunt."

"I guess we're all going," Hunter said good-naturedly, and one of their kids started to cry. Scuffling and shushing came through the line, and then Deacon said, "Hunter's going to stay with the kids, Molly. I've got his phone and mine with Tucker on the line, and I'll go talk to them."

"Thank you, Deacon. He's a big one. At least a hundred pounds."

"Okay, I'll tell them. Tuck, where is he now?" The doorbell chimed over the line, and Molly wished she could see through walls. She didn't have that superpower though, and she paced in the office instead. She listened to Deacon calmly explain the situation, listened to the questions from the wildlife officers, listened to her brother-in-law ask Tucker where the wolf was now.

"We'll go see if we can drive him back into the woods," the officers said, and Molly nodded. She didn't want the wolf killed. She still couldn't fathom why he'd shown up here, or how they hadn't noticed until he stood so close to people and horses.

Her adrenaline faded moment by moment, until Deacon said, "Molly, they've cleared Tucker and Bobbie Jo—they're back in the generational house and safe."

"Praise Jesus," she said, pure relief filling her. She wouldn't know how to go on if something happened to someone she loved on her watch.

"I'm gonna hang up," Deacon said. "The officers are at the end of the field, and they've got it from here."

"We'll stay in place until you tell us we can come out."

"Yep," he clipped out, and then he added, "I'll send the all-clear text when I can."

The call ended, and Molly left the office. There wasn't anything she could do from there, and she hurried back into the midst of the cowboys and gathered everyone around. Gloria wore pure nerves on her face, and she held up her phone.

"Matt says Tucker's out there."

"The Wildlife Department is here," she said. "They got Tucker and Bobbie Jo back to the generational house. Everyone else has checked in and is safe. They're securing the farm now." She'd have a lot more questions to answer once the officers had ensured that no human life was in danger.

Her composure felt thin and about to snap, but she looked over to Gloria. The woman was a rock for Molly, and she linked her arm through Gloria's. "I want to say a prayer."

Cowboy hats started coming off, and Molly reached up and removed hers too. "Will you say it?" she asked Gloria, because she didn't want to put her wavering emotions on full display for all the cowboys, and Gloria was so much better at maintaining hers.

"Of course," she said, and she took a deep breath. "Dear Lord." She paused, and every cell in Molly's body shook. "We thank Thee for watching out for us this morning. Thank You for sending dogs to warn us, and for providing easy access to shelter for almost everyone on the farm. Bless the wildlife officers out there; protect them and help them return safely."

She took another few moments, breathed in again, and added, "We bow to you in gratitude, with full hearts. Amen."

"Amen," echoed through the barn, and Molly pulled Gloria into a hug. Cowboys around them embraced too, and the atmosphere here started to settle. She still worried about all the teens and Cosette only a few yards away, locked behind other strong doors.

Her phone chimed, and she pulled it out to look at it. *I can see the officers carrying the wolf into the woods,* Tucker said. *Bobbie Jo says hi.*

Despite the continued tension of the situation, Molly couldn't help but smile. Leave it to Tucker to find a way to lighten the mood, even in a crisis.

"I'm going to run across to the admin building and see if we can't get some of the kids into their parents' cars," Molly said, showing Gloria her phone. "Tucker says the officers are moving the wolf."

Deacon texted right then: *Wolf is tranquilized and they're moving him out into the wild again. Anyone on the west side of the ranch should stay in place. Others can probably move to safer locations, especially if you're not somewhere with air conditioning.*

Molly's heart pumped hard at the thought of Ryder in the shed, and she quickly texted Hunter to go get him. *Do not let him make that journey alone, please*, she texted.

On the way, Hunter said, and Molly eased over to the door.

"I texted Cosette," Gloria said. "She's opening the barn door now." Gloria helped her open the door of the stable, and Molly took a deep breath.

Then she ran from one building to the next, the door closing right behind her. "All right," she said as cheerfully as she could. "Let's get you guys to your parents."

nine

Hunter Hammond leaned against the kitchen counter with a can of Diet Mountain Dew in his hand. Molly bustled around preparing lunch as if nothing had happened this morning. As if she hadn't grabbed onto Ryder an hour ago and held him so tightly while she whispered how much she loved him.

A wolf could put things in perspective, at least, and when Ryder's life might be in danger it didn't matter that he'd been dating Clementine Thatcher behind their backs for the past six months. Just when they'd thought they'd talked to him about girls and dating until everyone understood.

Hunter tried not to worry about his son, because he'd been a teenage boy once too. A senior in high school, no less, with a wide open future in front of him. And Clementine was super pretty, a good person, and kind to everyone. Hunter understood why Ryder liked the girl next door, to be sure.

The events of the morning still weighed heavily on his mind, but he let the gratitude sweep through him from top to bottom and side to side. Tuck had gone horseback riding with Bobbie Jo as their second date, and Hunt had invited them for lunch afterward.

Thus, Molly was currently browning beef for the tacos, as she claimed she could put together a quick meal at any time. When she had to do that, they ate a lot of tacos. Or taco salad. Or burritos with taco meat in them. Hunter happened to love meat, beans, cheese, and sour cream no matter if it was combined with chips for one meal, or flour tortillas for another.

"Need any help, sweetheart?" he asked, though he knew better than to get in Molly's way when she was in full hostess mode.

She flashed him a smile. "I've got it under control. Why don't you go make sure Lisa hasn't opened the bag of chips and started eating them?"

Hunter nodded and crossed through the kitchen to the family room. The huge dining table could seat fifteen at any given time, as Hunter hosted meals a few times every week. So his family, plus Tucker, Bobbie Jo, Tarr, Mission, and Deacon would fit just fine. He loved having people over, though he definitely found his center when he escaped to his office, just him and a pencil and his puzzle book. He did crosswords on his tablet before bed too, and Hunter could admit he got peopled out quickly now that he wasn't CEO anymore.

"The chips are safe," he called to Molly as Lisa looked up from her phone. "Who are you talkin' to?"

"Brandon," she said. "He's sending me pictures of the poster he's been working on." His fourteen-year-old looked up to him, and Hunter decided Lisa wouldn't know if a boy was flirting with her or not. "I'm writing the two-page paper to go with it. It's due Wednesday."

Hunter glanced at her phone, where a poster about the water cycle blinked back at him. "Great," he said, completely disinterested in such things. He found schoolwork—especially group work—to be so...trivial. Why did Lisa need to know about the water cycle when she'd probably train horses for a living?

The front door opened, and laughter filled the house. Hunter turned away from his kids on the couch, torn between the front hallway, where Tucker would bring his new girl-friend, and the back door, which had just opened.

Mission, Tarr, and Deacon entered there, the three of them talking right over the top of each other. With so many new voices in the room, Hunter couldn't make sense of any of them.

Tarr burst out laughing, and he shook his head. "You have no idea what you're saying," he said to Deacon, knocking him with his shoulder.

In a rare showing, Deacon grinned and he even laughed a little too. "I do too," he said. "I'm telling you, it was that dragon movie."

"Dude, there's no dragons in that movie." Mission, who was close to the same age as Hunter, swatted at Deacon's chest. "You're thinking of that one where he gives up his heart."

"That was a monkey heart," Deacon said, and Tarr and Mission both burst out laughing again.

"What's so funny in here?" Tucker asked, and everyone looked over to him. He'd left Ivory Peaks and the farm for the summer, and Hunter could admit it sure did his older-brother-heart good to see him back home.

Tuck wouldn't stay, Hunter knew that. At the same time, his gaze moved to the pretty woman at his side, and Hunter knew love had a strange way of changing a man's ambitions. Morphing the things he thought he wanted. Providing him a new path to trod, when he thought he'd figured out everything that needed figuring out.

"Tucker," Molly said, though she'd helped him and Bobbie Jo saddle their steeds. "Come in, come in. Hey Bobbie Jo." She leaned in and gave her a quick kiss on the cheek. "We're just having tacos."

"We always have tacos," Clay said as he entered the kitchen.

"Whiny boys don't eat," Molly said as she turned back to the six-year-old.

"Plus, we don't always have tacos." Hunter scooped his son into his arms and grinned at the little boy. "We had that corn soup last night."

"Yuck," Clay said with a big smile.

"Shh." Hunter glanced over to his wife. "And you liked the chicken, and that's not tacos."

Tucker and Bobbie Jo migrated over to Tarr and the

others, and Hunter watched the way Bobbie Jo stood right at his side, greeting the men she'd once worked with. Her hand sought Tuck's, and Hunter grinned widely as he watched his brother hold hands with the woman he'd liked for a while now.

It sure was good to see them finally exploring a relationship, though Hunter knew Tuck worried about it. He didn't want to stay in town, but as he'd said in Mike's office earlier this week, "I sure do like her, you guys."

He moved over to his brothers and their friends. "You two okay after sitting on that fence this morning?"

Tucker looked at him with a grin. "We're fine, Hunt."

"Speak for yourself," Bobbie Jo said as she nudged him. "I don't really sit on fences, nor have I ridden a horse for while. I'm a little sore." She laughed lightly, and the others did too.

"I bet you've never been on a date with a wolf-scare," Hunter said.

"Who has been?" Tarr asked.

"Heck, I'd take a wolf if I could get someone to go out with me," Mission said.

"I thought you were dating someone," Tucker said. "A... a...Rachelle." Tucker snapped his fingers. "I know you went out with her."

"He's been out with tons of women the past couple of years," Deacon said in that casual way he had.

"Thanks for selling me out, bro." Mission exhaled heavily, his face turning a bit red. "I'm just not having much luck is all."

"No wolves," Molly said as she handed Hunter the bag of shredded cheese. "Put that on the table, would you, baby?"

"Are we ready?" Tucker asked. "I could help, Mols."

She looked at Tucker, then Bobbie Jo. "Sure, Tuck. Come dice the tomatoes."

"Dice?" he repeated. "Molly is that just a fancy work for 'cut'? Why can't you just say cut?" He went with Molly over to the island and picked up the serrated knife. He said something else to her that Hunter couldn't catch, and his wife grinned at Tucker and nodded.

"How was your time in the garden shed?" he asked Tarr and Mission. "Did you almost boil to death out there?"

"It wasn't too bad," Mission said at the same time Tarr said, "Yeah, it was awful." They looked at one another, then burst out laughing. Tarr had super dark hair with rugged features, and Hunter wasn't sure why he wasn't dating anyone. Mission possessed plenty of good looks too, but he didn't normally interact so much with everyone. Tarr brought out the best of him, and Deacon had done a good thing by pairing them up.

His youngest brother had gone quiet, his eyes on his phone. His thumbs then flew as he answered someone about something, and Hunter caught the soft sigh that came out of his mouth.

"Everything okay, Deac?"

Deacon glanced up. "Yeah, I'm not gonna text all day, I swear."

"Hunter understands," Molly said. "Him being able to put

away his phone was the best thing about him not being the CEO."

He'd worked very hard to detach from work at home, but sometimes it had been impossible.

"All right," Molly called. "We're ready to eat. Girls, Clay, let's go." She glanced around. "Where's Ryder?"

"He was on the front porch when we came in," Tucker said. "I'll grab him." He jogged down the hallway, and Hunter watched him go. He knew exactly what Ryder was doing on the front porch: talking to Clementine.

Hunter exchanged a glance with his wife, who wore worry in her expression for that brief conversation, and then she turned and set a big bowl of shredded lettuce on the table.

Ryder returned to the room with Tucker, and everyone started lining up at the island. They'd get their meat and beans there, and then Molly had put all the toppings on the table. When he realized his wife was looking at him, Hunter cleared his throat.

"All right, Charlotte," he said in a loud voice. "Would you pray over lunch for us?"

His most emotional daughter nodded, suddenly not poking at Lisa to try to be the first in line for food. "Sure, Daddy."

"All right, we're gonna pray," Hunter said as Tuck and Ryder started to laugh about something. They sobered suddenly, big smiles still on their faces. "Go on, Char."

Cowboy hats got removed, and Hunter double-checked to make sure he wasn't wearing his. Molly didn't like it when her boys wore their hats indoors, and Hunter wasn't wearing a cowboy hat.

Then Char said, "Dear Heavenly Father, we're so grateful for this farm and our family."

Hunter's chest pinched whenever one of his kids expressed thanks for family. They lived a very busy life, with Molly's children equine therapy unit, and Hunter running the family company for the first seventeen years of his marriage, and now all the horseback riding lessons.

A very busy life.

A very good life, Hunter thought, and before he knew it, his precious daughter said, "Amen," and he found himself repeating it along with everyone else.

Tucker hooked his arm around Bobbie Jo, whispered something to her, and planted a kiss against the corner of her eyebrow. Hunter added a silent prayer to the one his daughter had uttered out loud that Tucker could find his brand of happily-ever-after too.

ten

Bobbie Jo paused at the thermostat just outside her bedroom and nudged it up a degree. She lived in Colorado in September, which meant she also pressed the "heat" button, knowing full-well she'd be switching it back to AC by mid-afternoon.

The weather had a seriously OCD personality in the fall, though it was her favorite month.

She then proceeded into the kitchen to make coffee. Cara didn't like having blinds open at night, so she systematically went around and closed them. And Bobbie Jo, every morning as the sun showed its face, moved around the house and opened them all again.

She smiled into the golden rays, appreciating that she could sleep in on the weekends, though she didn't quite get to ten or eleven the way Jenny did. Then again, she didn't work twelve-hour shifts on a construction site either, so Bobbie Jo tried not to judge how late her roommate slept.

The house sat in silence, and she enjoyed the moment to herself as she measured coffee grounds and filled the machine with water. She hadn't been able to stop thinking about Tucker Hammond since their horseback riding date yesterday.

Fine. She hadn't *stopped* thinking about Tucker since she'd met him—and that had happened a lot further back than just yesterday.

Her heartbeat shimmied at the thought of that wolf walking directly toward them. Tucker had issued instructions out of the corner of his mouth, and Bobbie Jo had felt equal parts afraid and safe at the same time.

A soft padding of feet behind her broke into her memories, and she turned to find Cara entering the kitchen in a cute tank-shorts pj set in pink.

"Morning," Bobbie Jo said as she turned to get down a mug.

"Morning." Cara yawned as she joined Bobbie Jo and got down the same mug she used every morning. Cara liked things a certain way, and she'd wash her mug, dry it, and put it back in the cupboard before she got dressed. She then loved her specialty coffees, and she'd drive through her favorite spot on the way to the elementary school where she worked.

The coffee started to percolate, and Cara opened the fridge and pulled out something she'd brought home as a leftover.

"Did you go out last night?" Bobbie Jo asked, settling at the island.

"Me and Gramps." She grinned over to Bobbie Jo and flipped open her container. "Not all of us have hot, new cowboy boyfriends."

Bobbie Jo couldn't contain her smile, and while she'd only lived with Cara and Jenny for a couple of months, they did know quite a bit about her life.

Surface stuff, she could admit, and that included that she hadn't dated since she and Lawson had broken up almost nine months ago now.

"So. How was your date?" Cara asked, punctuating the T-sound really strongly. She turned to fill her mug with coffee now that it had finished, and she did the same for Bobbie Jo.

Bobbie Jo had had girlfriends before, and she didn't mind talking about Tuck. "It was fun." She reached for a spoon and the sugar. She was probably the only person on the planet who didn't like cream in her coffee, but she would take plenty of the sweet stuff. "I'm a little sore from the horseback riding. Haven't been in a while."

"I'd be sore from sitting on a fence, tracking a wolf." Cara leaned against the counter, sipped her coffee slowly, and watched Bobbie Jo.

"It added some spice to the date."

Cara grinned. "Was there any other spicy bits during the date?"

"Oh, you mean the part where we ate lunch with his family?" Bobbie Jo rolled her eyes. "No, nothing spicy."

"He didn't kiss you before you left?"

"Nope." Bobbie Jo looked away now. "I mean...we've kissed before, and I'm not sure why he didn't, but he didn't."

"You're still new."

"Yeah." Bobbie Jo drew in a breath, then raised her mug to her lips too. "Are you going to church today?"

"Uh, I don't know."

Bobbie Jo nodded. "I think I'll go." She liked attending church when she had something heavy on her mind. Sometimes it felt like the pastor had prepared his sermon just for her ears, and she took another drink of her coffee and got to her feet. "I'll leave in about forty-five minutes, if you want to come with."

"Okay." Cara forked up a bite of her leftovers, and Bobbie Jo knew she wouldn't come to church with her. That was fine, as Bobbie Jo had done a lot of things solo in her life, and she could sit on a pew and listen to a lecture without a buddy.

Surprisingly, when Bobbie Jo re-entered the kitchen wearing a dark brown dress with brightly colored flowers splashed across it, Jenny reached for her purse and said, "Cara said you were going to church. Can I go with?"

"Yeah, sure," Bobbie Jo said, taking in the little black dress on the blonde bombshell. She knew she was going to church, didn't she? Not a night club.

Bobbie Jo said nothing, and she grabbed her bag too, so she'd have her ID and money should she need it for the quick drive to church and back. Jenny had gone on a date last night too, and Bobbie Jo let her dominate the conversation on the way to the service.

They walked in together, and Bobbie Jo chose a seat about

halfway back, on the side, and let Jenny have the aisle. The meeting started a couple of minutes later, and by then, Bobbie Jo had calmed her pulse and her thoughts sufficiently to be ready to hear the word of God.

She wasn't much of a singer, but she enjoyed listening to the choir perform the opening number, and then, finally Pastor Cartwright got behind the mic, his smile as big as the whole room, his broad chest, and his giant personality. "I love September in the Rocky Mountains," he started, and a relaxed smile moved through Bobbie Jo's whole soul. "The bite in the air in the morning, the warm sunshine over blue skies, the evidence of God's power and love in every leaf that changes color."

He gazed out at the crowd, and Bobbie Jo had never felt like he'd paid all that much attention to her. She came to church more often than she played hooky, and she'd met the pastor several times. And today, he seemed to look right at her.

"Autumn is such an amazing time to rejuvenate your testimony that God lives and loves you. I do it by keeping a nature journal for a couple of months—until the first permanent snow of the year."

Bobbie Jo had heard of gratitude journals, and travel journals, and food journals. Heck, even a record of her dreams.

But a nature journal? She hadn't heard of that, and she peered at the pastor intently.

"Every day," Pastor Cartwright continued. "I get outside and specifically try to find something that proves God is real. That He created this earth where we all live, and that He is the Master of all. I can see it in the way the sun rises and sets every day. I see it in the way the leaves fall in the autumn and renew in the spring. I see His vibrancy in the golds and oranges and crimsons we see here in the mountains."

Bobbie Jo thought of the Hammond Family Farm, and how green everything had been yesterday. She'd seen it after the harvest too, with dormant fields, and then through the winter, as it existed in shades of beige and gray.

"And I write a few sentences—it doesn't have to be much, my friends—about the absolutely stunning beauty of nature that I observed that day, and then why it reminded me of God. I have come to know Him better though this process, and I challenge each one of you to keep a nature journal this year."

Bobbie Jo wanted to stop by the office supply store on the way home and get herself a cute notebook for her nature moments. For the opportunity to get closer to God. To know Him better meant she'd know herself better, and Bobbie Jo did enjoy exercises such as these.

"It can be something simple. A nature moment, if you will," the pastor said. "And I advise that you do it for at least a month. The more you look for evidence that God exists, the easier it is to find it."

In her lap, her phone vibrated, and as the pastor moved on from his weekly challenge, she let her attention seep to her device.

Tuck had texted, and Bobbie Jo's face immediately felt a little hotter. *It's Pumpkin Days in Ivory Peaks next weekend. We've never been together. Want to go?*

Yes, absolutely Bobbie Jo wanted to go. Tuck had already texted her late last night, after she'd made the sixty-four minute drive back to her house from the farm, that he'd be outside helping with the harvest all week. Then, Mike and Gerty needed help on their farm too, and Tuck would be going there to get their hay in and their fields winterized too.

Saturday? she asked.

Yeah, Saturday, he confirmed. *You could come out to the farm and we'll go into town together, or I can meet you there.*

I'll come to the farm, Bobbie Jo told him, and then she tucked her phone away and attempted to focus on the rest of the sermon. Now that she knew when she'd see Tuck again, and with a plan to start her own nature journal this week, Bobbie Jo's spirit felt full and light at the same time.

Yes, it was going to be a great week.

By the time Bobbie Jo turned down the dirt road from the highway, the pine trees standing guard and concealing the farm from her, she was tired of the drive from Boulder. She'd only made it three times in eight days, and she could see how it would be tiring for her.

She'd gone with a casual outfit—jeans, boots, and a T-shirt with a pig on it that said "Body by Bacon." She'd brought along a sweatshirt with an embroidered pumpkin on the front, a gift from her mother.

The road curved, and Bobbie Jo carved her SUV along it. The big red barn came into view, then the pastures and fields, and then the farmhouse. Plenty more buildings extended past that, with the cowboy cabin community down the road and behind the family plots.

She'd lived here for over a year, and Bobbie Jo let the sting of missing reverberate through her.

Tuck's truck sat parked near the gravel path that led to the generational house, and she pulled in next to him. Excitement bounced through her, and she took one more drink of her water, then pocketed her thread wallet and grabbed her sweatshirt.

She'd barely gotten out of the car when she heard Tuck whistle. "Hey, gorgeous." He broke into a jog, and he swept her into his arms in the next moment. He smelled like the pine trees she'd driven past, and the crispness of a winter stream, and the strong, smoke-spice scent of his cologne.

He stepped back, pure light and energy pouring from him. "You ready to drown yourself in everything pumpkin?"

"So ready."

He took her hand and led her to his truck, where he opened the door and waited for her to climb in. When he got behind the wheel, he said, "My parents used to take us to Pumpkin Days every year."

"It feels a little early, I gotta admit," she said.

"For the big boy pumpkins, yes," he said. "They'll do a huge smash event as part of the town Halloween celebration. This is more for the sugar pumpkins you can bake with, as well as the smaller carving pumpkins."

"Oh, this is so I'll learn to bake you the perfect pumpkin

pie, isn't it?" Teasing and flirting with him came so naturally to her, and it never had before.

Tucker laughed. "I do love a good pumpkin pie with lots of whipped cream."

Yes, he'd told her that before. Bobbie Jo didn't like pumpkin pie at all, though she adored pumpkin chocolate chip cookies, pumpkin spice lattes, and pumpkin-flavored caramel.

"They sell a lot of apples and peaches in the Saturday farmer's markets too," he said. "My momma wants me to get a bushel of the freestone peaches. She and Aunt Bree are going to make freezer jam."

"Maybe I could try my momma's dinner roll recipe again," she said. "Homemade jam is best eaten on homemade bread."

"I'm not going to say no to homemade bread during harvest time," he said. "I swear, I still have hay shards in my hair." He even reached up and brushed his hand along the back of his neck.

"Did you have to do the overnight mowing?"

"No, thankfully," Tuck said. "Deacon did it, because he says he only sleeps four or five hours per night anyway."

"What will you do out at Gerty's next week?"

"Mow, bale, fix fences, field prep for next year." He glanced over to her. "It's only her, Tag, and Steele—well, and Opal, I guess—and they've got a decent sized operation."

"How big?" She watched him as he drove down the highway toward the town of Ivory Peaks. "It can't be as big as your place."

"Oh, eighty or ninety acres," he said. "Nothing like Deacon's place, no."

"Still sizable," Bobbie Jo said.

"How big was your farm in Oklahoma?" He glanced over to her, and Bobbie Jo fought against the ice immediately forming in her veins.

"Huge," she said. "Fifteen hundred acres of dairy cows and corn fields."

"Wow," he said. "That is huge."

"My brother tried to grow the biggest pumpkin in the country one year." She smiled over to Tuck, her familial memories so fond and so quick to come. "He missed it by six pounds."

"How big was it?"

"Six hundred and seven pounds," she said.

"That's incredible." Tuck reached over and took her hand in his. "Sounds like all you Hanks' are pretty special." He lifted her hand to his mouth and kissed the inside of her wrist.

Pure delight popped through her, and Bobbie Jo let herself slip a little bit. Slip toward liking Tuck more than she had before. Slip toward kissing him good-night tonight whether he made the first move or not.

Slip toward opening the door to falling in love with the non-permanent cowboy in Ivory Peaks, a mere sixty-four minutes from where Bobbie Jo lived.

eleven

Tucker watched as Bobbie Jo slid out of his truck, her boots hitting the packed dirt parking lot with a soft thud. He couldn't help the grin that pulled at his lips. The crisp autumn air filled his lungs, and the scent of sweet hay, dried corn stalks, and dust met his nose. The smell of roasted almonds and a hint of cotton candy from the vendor carts made his mouth water. Pumpkin Days was one of those small-town traditions that made Ivory Peaks feel like home, even though Tuck had never truly wanted to settle anywhere permanently.

Tuck rounded the truck to meet Bobbie Jo, and he found her straightening her "Body by Bacon" T-shirt, and the sight of that pig, coupled with her playful spirit, made him chuckle. "You look ready to dominate the fall festival scene." He reached her and hauled her right into his chest again.

He simply liked holding her, and while he hadn't quite

figured out how to kiss her yet, he wanted to. He simply didn't want to kiss her out on the farm and then send her on her way, and he hadn't planned a date where he came to her house and picked her up.

She hugged him while she giggled, and then she pulled away. "I feel like this is going to be a competitive date."

Tucker puffed out his chest and grinned. "They crown a Pumpkin King at this event, I'll have you know."

Bobbie Jo laughed, and the sound filled his chest with warmth. "Pumpkin King, huh? You sure you're not just trying to hide a pumpkin obsession?"

"Oh, I don't hide my obsessions," Tuck said, clasping her hand in his as they started toward the entrance. "There's just something about the smell of pumpkin spice in the air."

"You mean the taste of pumpkin spice in everything." She raised an eyebrow in challenge."

"You like it," he said. "Wasn't it you who made Hattie sick with the number of pumpkin chocolate chip cookies you made last year?"

"They're really good."

"Yeah, well, it's good in white chocolate and coffee and muffins, too."

"And lip balm, and body scrub, and candles, and...."

"And don't act like you don't like it." He gave her a knowing look and pulled his wallet out to pay for their entrance to the festival.

After he paid, they walked through the entrance gate, greeted by the sight of booths lining the dirt lane in front of them, all of them boasting something autumnal. A sidewalk went to the right that led to the pumpkin patch, and Tuck spotted a sign further down pointing to the left for the hayrides.

He wanted to do it all, experience everything, and he wanted Bobbie Jo at his side the whole time.

The festival buzzed with excitement that wound its way into Tuck's bloodstream. Children ran from attraction to attraction, pumpkins of every size and shape piled high in wagons for decoration and purchase, and laughter and chatter filled the air.

Somewhere in the distance, a country band played, and Tuck wanted to get something to eat and drink and just take it all in.

"Where to first?" Bobbie Jo asked as she stood beside him and scanned left and right.

"Should we get the quiz out of the way?"

"The quiz?"

He nodded to the sign right below the one pointing to the pumpkin patch. "Corn maze, Bobbie Jo. We can test our navigation skills."

She blinked at the sign and then Tuck. "You win already," she said. "No need to rub it in."

He grabbed her hand as she started to move toward the booths. "Come on, sweetheart," he said, tugging her back to his side. "We can do it together."

Bobbie Jo's eyes narrowed in mock suspicion. "By 'we,' you mean I'm going to get us completely lost, and you'll get to ride in and save the day?"

Tucker's laughter filled his whole soul as it flowed from

him. "I'll never let you get too far off-course, baby." He pressed a kiss to her forehead and took them toward the corn maze and pumpkin patch. "We can get some pumpkins to carve later."

"Lead on, Your Majesty."

Tucker sure did like her, even if she did go from hot to cold to worried about her sense of direction in less than three seconds. Tuck actually wanted to get lost with her, because then, yeah, maybe he'd be able to provide something for her that she couldn't do herself.

He swung his hand with Bobbie Jo's and asked, "Are you goin' home to Oklahoma for the holidays?"

"I don't know," Bobbie Jo said. "My mom and dad live in a tiny little house now, and there's not really anywhere for me to stay."

"Your siblings are still local?"

"Yeah," she said. "Mm hm. My brother is dating someone pretty seriously. My sister lives nearby, so they don't need somewhere to stay."

"Maybe you could stay with your brother or sister." Tuck glanced over to her. "Since Tag and Opal aren't getting married until November, my parents are staying all through Thanksgiving."

"So you'll be here through then too," she said.

"I mean, maybe," he said. "I haven't even tried to reach out to any of the contacts I got over the summer." Familiar frustration fired through him. He immediately bucked against it. "But, like my momma says, it's not now or never, Tuck."

And Momma was right, even if Tuck didn't want to admit it. He wasn't a rodeo star; he could manage and train others with talent for years and years to come.

"That's a good attitude," Bobbie Jo said as the corn maze came into sight.

"Would you want to work at HMC for...ever?" he asked.

"You make a job sound like a death sentence," Bobbie Jo said in her trademark deadpan. "But the answer is no. It's an office job, and I'm pretty sure I've told you I'm a country girl."

"So you want...what, exactly?"

"Promise not to laugh?"

Tucker's heart filled with cold blood. "Bobbie Jo, I have never laughed at you." He slowed and stopped right there in the path. "I promise I won't laugh."

She looked at him for a moment, searching his face. Tucker waited, because he didn't know how else to assure and reassure her.

"I want to have a goat farm."

Tucker sucked in a breath so he wouldn't laugh. He would take the fact that his natural instinct was to laugh, because he'd promised. "Wow," he said. "I didn't—you've never mentioned anything even remotely goat-related."

She grinned at him. "Well, now you know." She put her palm against his chest. "Can we not stand here in the open sun? Let's at least find some shade if you don't want to do the corn maze."

"Oh, we're doing the corn maze," Tuck said. "*You're* the one trying to get out of it."

"I would never," Bobbie Jo said.

At the booth, the attendant gave them a map, which Tucker promptly folded up and stuffed into his back pocket.

"I don't even get to look at that?" Bobbie Jo asked.

Tuck looked up at the tall stalks of sun-dried corn towering above them. Then at a trio of ten-year-olds as they ran by. "I think we'll be fine," he said. "Look, those children are doing this. We don't need no map."

Bobbie Jo crossed her arms, a teasing glint in her eyes. "All right, cowboy. Show me what you've got."

Tucker confidently strode into the maze, pulling her along with him. The walls of corn rose high above them, and the path ahead twisted and turned in different directions.

"I've got a feeling we go left here," he said, tugging her down a path that seemed promising.

They walked for a few minutes, the cornstalks rustling gently in the breeze. The sound of children's laughter echoed from somewhere deeper in the maze, but Tucker kept his focus straight ahead, determined to lead them out like he had some sort of internal compass.

Another turn, another dead end.

"Tuck," Bobbie Jo said slowly, a smile tugging at her lips. "Give me that map."

"I will not," he said. "When you reach a dead-end, you just turn back the way you came." He took the left turn instead of the right.

Another dead end.

Bobbie Jo laughed, and Tucker stopped, scratching the back of his head. "Okay, we have to go back *two* steps."

"You think?"

"Don't worry, I've got this," Tucker said, turning them around. He led them down a different path, but it wasn't long before they hit another dead end.

"Map me." Bobbie Jo held out her hand, and Tuck admitted defeat by pulling the folded map from his pocket and slapping it into her open palm.

"I was just testing your problem-solving skills."

"Right," she said, unfolding the map and smoothing it against his chest. His blood burned in his body as she studied it, and then she glanced up at him. "I don't even know how to read a map."

Tuck burst out laughing, and he covered her hands on his chest with his. "Let me see it, sweetheart." She let him take the map, and he glanced at it for a moment, easily seeing where he'd gone wrong.

"Okay, this way." He stuffed the map away again, the same way he had with his phone when they'd gone to the Shrimp Palace.

Right turn, another right turn, and then a left, and they met no dead ends. Tucker strode into the sunshine, both hands raised high. "And that's how you do it."

Bobbie Jo grinned and grinned, and Tucker felt his chest tighten in the best possible way. As he gazed at her, on the high from getting out of that maze, he could admit silently— to himself—that he wanted a lot more Septembers with her.

More corn mazes.

Many more Pumpkin Days festivals.

But in order to do that, Tuck would need to be in close proximity to Ivory Peaks.

Bobbie Jo's hand slipped up his arm, and her hand cupped his elbow. "Pumpkin toss?" she asked, and Tucker centered himself in this moment. The future confused him, and he'd never spent too much time thinking about it.

Bobbie Jo had blended up his life in only a week, and he didn't know whether he was coming or going anymore.

She led him across the path to the pumpkin toss, where the tiny sugar pumpkins were being used similar to beanbags. Big bullseyes had been spray-painted on the ground, with a bright orange center where tossers tried to get their pumpkins.

Participants of all ages hurled small pumpkins toward the bullseye, and Tucker and Bobbie Jo got moved down to the adult target.

"I am never going to hit that," Bobbie Jo said. She actually shaded her eyes to look into the distance, and the adult target spanned so wide, a flag had been planted in the middle of the bullseye.

She looked at him, and he looked a her, and with perfect timing from his growling stomach, he said, "Let's go find something for lunch."

Bobbie Jo sighed in what Tuck assumed was relief as she tossed her sugar pumpkin back in the pile. "Yeah," she said. "That sounds good. But I totally want to come back over here and get pumpkins for carving." She looked down the road, past the exit of the corn maze, where the huge sign advertised the you-pick pumpkin patch.

Tuck slung his arm around her shoulders and turned her back the way they'd come. "Lunch and shopping and whatever else you want, Bobbie Jo. We'll get pumpkins on the way out."

He beamed down at her, and he could totally see her on a goat farm somewhere. The real question was whether Tuck could see himself working it alongside her. Or coming home to her after a day of training his rodeo champions.

You have money, whispered through his mind. He didn't have to work at all. Not to get by on a day-to-day basis. He could start a rodeo training facility right here in Ivory Peaks, on a big piece of land that would be half training facilities, where his cowboys would come to him, and half goat farm for Bobbie Jo.

The fantasy bloomed right in front of him, and Tuck let it play out as equal parts hope, joy, and fear spread through him.

Sure, he thought. *A fantasy is nice. But how are you going to bring that to life?*

Tuck had no idea, and he'd never made a good decision on an empty stomach. So lunch first; life-changing decisions second.

twelve

The clouds seemed to be chasing the sun, and they cast playful shadows across the small deck off the back of Bobbie Jo's house. Tucker's laughter filled the air, mingling with the scraping sound of carving tools against the tough orange skin of pumpkins. The smell of fresh pumpkin innards, earthy and sweet, wafted up into the crisp autumn morning. Bobbie Jo wiped her hand on her apron, squinting at the face she'd just carved into her gourd.

"Mine certainly won't be winning any beauty contests," she muttered, holding up the grinning jack-o'-lantern for Tucker to inspect.

Totally normal.

Boring.

Triangle eyes. Round nose. Toothy grin. Honestly, it looked like an eight-year-old had carved her pumpkin.

Tucker leaned over from his spot on the small patio table,

elbow-deep in pumpkin guts, and gave her creation a critical once-over. His gorgeous smile spread slowly, his eyes twinkling with amusement. "I think it's got character. You know, the kind of face only a mother could love."

Bobbie Jo smirked, which really turned into a grimace. "You're not exactly working on a masterpiece yourself, cowboy."

Tucker pulled his pumpkin closer, so Bobbie Jo couldn't see it, and her curiosity kicked up a notch. "You'll see it when I'm finished," he said.

"I think I'm going to call mine," Bobbie Jo said, pushing herself up from the picnic table. "I'll go get the candles." She moved over to the sliding glass door but paused as she opened it. "How much longer do you think you'll need? Should I make our sandwiches right now?"

They'd become weekend daters, and Bobbie Jo had decided that was okay...for now. She saw him on Saturdays, usually for the whole day, and it felt like a pattern they'd fallen into.

He texted her a lot during the week, and this week, he'd messaged her on Wednesday about carving their pumpkins this morning and taking a hike for the rest of the day. In the glorious Rocky Mountains, a better time to hike didn't exist.

Bobbie Jo loved being outside, and she'd readily agreed to his suggestions for today's activities. Not only that, but Bobbie Jo didn't have to drive to him. He'd come to her.

"I'll be done in about five minutes," he said. "I can come make my own sandwich."

"I'll get started." Bobbie Jo ducked into the house, where

she found Cara slathering peanut butter onto a slice of toast. "Hey." She grinned at her roommate and gave her a quick side-hug. "What are you doing today?"

"Grading State reports," she said with a groan. "What about you and Tuck?"

"We're going hiking," she said. "I'm not sure where but Tuck knows. I'll ask him and text you and Jenny as a backup."

Cara nodded, because they both believed in taking care of one another, of always knowing where a roommate was and when they should be home.

Bobbie Jo set the candles on the edge of the counter, as she'd proudly display hers and Tucker's pumpkins on her porch. He'd said he didn't have anywhere to put them, and she might as well have them at her house. That was why they'd ended up here, in her backyard, carving pumpkins this morning.

She got out her own loaf of bread, and then the sliced turkey and ham, the cheese, the mayo and lettuce, and the box of sandwich bags. Tucker could eat, and Bobbie Jo made him three sandwiches before he came inside carrying her pumpkin.

Cara had vacated the kitchen, but she glanced over from where she'd set up camp on the couch in the living room. Bobbie Jo nodded over to her. "My roommate, Cara. The one who tried to attack you with an umbrella."

Tucker practically threw the pumpkin on the counter. "Sure, yeah, hey." He strode into the living room and shook her hand. "Great to meet you."

"We've met," Cara said.

"Properly," Tucker tacked on, and he glanced over to Bobbie Jo. She gestured for him to come help her.

"Get the chips and snacks you want," she said. "I have granola bars, string cheese, pretzels, all of that." She indicated the boxes and bags standing on the shelf in the open pantry.

"You've made three sandwiches?"

She laid out two more slices of bread. "Those are all yours, cowboy."

"Thanks, baby." He swept a kiss along her cheek, which sent sparks down to her toes. She felt like someone had plugged her in as she made her own turkey and provolone sandwich, then gathered several snacks for the hike and put them in a gallon-sized bag with Tucker's items.

"I'll put the pumpkins out front," Tuck said as the plastic bags rustled around in his hands. "I've got all the food in my pack." He put everything inside and zipped his bright red backpack closed.

"I've got sunscreen," Bobbie Jo said, reaching for her own bag she'd put on the dining room table. "Extra socks." She also had a visor and a travel first-aid kit in her backpack, which also held two liters of water in a plastic bladder with a straw attached.

Tuck had a similar setup, so they didn't need bottled water, and Bobbie Jo shouldered her pack as he came back in from the deck carrying his pumpkin.

Bobbie Jo sucked in a breath as she took in the artistic face on his gourd. "Tuck." She flicked her gaze up to his and then looked at his jack-o-lantern. He'd carved in beautiful arches for the eyebrows, which sat above oval eyes that somehow held plenty of character.

The mouth had been carved into an elegant O, with sharp, jagged, monster teeth around the whole rim done in the lighter flesh of the pumpkin. She'd just cut chunks out. He'd *sculpted* something amazing.

"You like it?"

"It's amazing," Bobbie Jo said. "It's going to look like a parent did yours and a child did mine." She wanted to be upset, but being back with Tuck these past couple of weeks had reminded her of how many talents he possessed. How thoughtful he was. How easily he laughed.

And she really liked how he sometimes looked at her like she was the only thing in the world that mattered.

"Be right back," he said, and he crossed through the kitchen and went down the hall to the front door. She cleared her throat and grabbed a windbreaker before also picking up his backpack and following him. "I'll text you, Cara."

"Okay," her roommate said in a distracted way.

Outside, Tucker placed the pumpkins and put the candles down inside. "We'll light them when we get back tonight," he said.

"Your backpack," she said, holding it out for him.

He took it, gave her a quick smile, and turned to head over to his truck. Always the cowboy gentleman, he opened the door for her, and Bobbie Jo put her pack on the floor before she climbed into the vehicle.

Tucker drove them west, away from Boulder and toward

the mountains. "It's maybe twenty minutes away," he said. "I can't believe you haven't done it."

"I just barely moved a couple of months ago," she said. "I'm tired on the weekend, Tuck."

He looked over to her, concern in his expression. "Too tired today?"

"No." She took his hand in hers. "You said it was an easy-moderate hike."

"Yeah," he said. "And we can go real slow, or turn back anytime we want."

Bobbie Jo leaned her head back against the headrest, and she smiled over to him. "I'll be fine."

"I want you to be able to take a nap if you want."

She enjoyed the warmth and size of his hand around hers. "I want to be right here, Tuck."

"Okay," he said, and he tightened his fingers around hers. The sun moved behind the clouds as they arrived at the trail-head, and Bobbie Jo looked up into the sky after she got down from his truck. She reached back to get her pack, and she put on her windbreaker first.

"Ready?" Tuck joined her on her side of the truck, and she nodded at him.

"It smells so good out here," she said, taking in the pungent pine tree smell which hung heavy in the air. "I just love it."

"I do too," Tuck said. He led them past the information signs and out into the woods, and Bobbie Jo did her best to keep up with his longer legs. They didn't speak, and Bobbie Jo really enjoyed the mountain stillness, the soft rustle of the leaves and pine boughs, the nearly-silent scuffs of their hiking boots on the hard-packed earth.

They'd probably gone a half-mile or so when the deafening roar of thunder cracked through the sky. Tucker stopped immediately, his gaze instantly in the sky. "It's going to hit us hard," he said.

Bobbie Jo stepped to his side, her heart pumping hard. The air felt moist now, and rain scented it though not a drop had fallen yet. "I think—"

The wind came barreling through the trees, and Bobbie Jo silenced her voice so she could listen to it coming closer and closer. It hit her square in the back, and she actually smiled when it did.

The rain followed, and she looked at Tuck as he looked at her. "Let's get under this tree," he said, and he pulled her off the path about ten feet to an enormous pine tree that might be able to provide some protection from the needling rain.

It arrived only two seconds later, and Bobbie Jo's pulse pounded in time with it. She peered out, not getting wet, but feeling all the shades of unease anyway. She shivered next to Tuck, and he met her gaze. "Cold, sweetheart?"

"Yeah," she whispered to match her volume to his. "It got cold really fast."

He pulled his sweatshirt off the strap of his backpack and handed it to her.

"Aren't you cold?"

"Nope."

"Okay, thanks," she said, pulling his hoodie over her head and right over her windbreaker and backpack too. It smelled like him—woodsy and warm, with a hint of spice and it made her feel like he'd wrapped her in his arms. She hugged it closer as the rain intensified, and then just as fast as it had started, it tapered.

"You want to keep going?" he asked. "It's probably another mile."

"I want to see it," she said. "I think we can make it."

"It's just a flat rock with names on it," he said.

Bobbie Jo laced her arm through his. "But those names represent a promise someone has made to someone else. It's... interesting. Sweet. I find it fascinating."

"What are you gonna promise?" He stepped out from beneath the pine tree, taking Bobbie Jo with him.

"Do people speak their promises out loud?"

"They're not wishes, sweetheart." He chuckled, and Bobbie Jo smiled too.

"Maybe I'm still thinking about it," she said, and she catalogued what the world smelled like now that it had just been washed clean. The scent of dust and water and pine and wood might make an amazing nature moment for her journaling.

"Great view from the rock," he said as they moved back into a single-file line on the trail. It hadn't rained for long, but the water hadn't soaked into the ground yet. It just puddled there, and Bobbie Jo kept her eyes on the ground, focusing so she wouldn't slip in any mud.

The aspens had turned positively golden, and Bobbie Jo had never seen so many hues and shades of that color. With the wind and rain, the leaves fluttered and fell to the ground like sheets of gold.

The tension of the week apart from Tuck melted away as she walked behind him, the steady rhythm of his footsteps matching hers. The beauty surrounding her couldn't be described, and Bobbie Jo paused to take a picture of the evergreen trees, the brownish-gray, rocky tips of the mountains, and all that gold.

She tilted her camera down and got one of Tucker walking among all that wonder and beauty, and she smiled at her device like she'd captured a great gift.

Tucker slowed and looked over his shoulder, then called, "Bobbie Jo?"

"Just taking a picture," she said, and she tucked her phone back in her pocket and hurried to catch up to him. She loved being outdoors, and with Tucker beside her, the world felt just a little brighter, a little richer with possibilities.

"The sky is scaring me," he admitted.

"How far away are we?" As much as she'd teased him in the corn maze, she trusted his sense of direction.

"Maybe another quarter-mile," he said. "Five minutes."

"We can do it." Bobbie Jo checked the sky too, and yes, it sure looked angry. Foaming, gray clouds, with an angry, whipping wind.

They started again, the pace a bit quicker now. The air held mist, and Bobbie Jo's breath came quicker and quicker. Then she took a step past a clump of pines, and an enormous, flat, gray rock spread before her. Tuck moved to the left, and they both stood there and stared at it.

"It's really huge," she said, not sure why this sight had rendered her mute. It just seemed so *big*. Huge. Grand.

No way a person could ever move it, and it had to be the work of the Lord, a crucial piece of His creations.

The trail continued around the rock, which literally looked like it had been placed as a picnic spot by a giant. Trees grew up all around it, and Bobbie Jo thought of all the promises that had been made here.

By Jarrod.

Lizzie.

Rockwell, with a heart.

This place held reverence, and Bobbie Jo felt it through every cell of her body. She thought of the promises she'd made in her life, and what they'd meant to her. She kept her promises, and she wanted to believe that everyone who'd hiked here, made a promise, and put their name down did too.

"The paint pens are in that small pocket," Tuck said, his voice barely louder than the mist. He turned his back on her, and Bobbie Jo unzipped his bag and pulled out the paint pens he'd bought.

"Will we be able to do it in the rain?"

"It's not raining right now," he said. "Let's pick a dry patch and do it."

Bobbie Jo didn't want to go too far out onto the rock, because parts of it did hold water, and she feared it could be slippery. So she walked behind Tuck as he circled up toward the top of the rock. He found a spot and knelt down to write his name in blue paint.

Bobbie Jo shook her paint pen, which boasted that it could write on metal, fabric, plastic, and more—hopefully rock—and got down next to Tuck. Her name got bled onto the rock in bright red, and she learned with the first letter that she needed to write it bigger than she'd anticipated.

Tuck's four letters went on quickly, but Bobbie Jo had twice that many letters, and she made the dot over her I into a heart. She sat back on her heels and looked at her name, thinking through her promise.

I promise to listen to Thee, she thought.

When she looked over to Tuck, he wore one of the more contemplative looks she'd ever seen. "What did you promise?"

He took her pen and capped it for her, then sighed. "I promised my parents I'd do them proud."

"That's beautiful," she murmured.

"I promised myself I'd work hard to find my own way."

"Oh, multiple promises," she said with a smile. She suddenly thought she should come up with another one. She'd never been blown about by the whims of others, though, so she wasn't sure what else to promise.

"And I promised God that I'd do whatever He told me to do." He got to his feet and extended his hand to help her do the same.

She put her hand in his and groaned as she straightened. "That's sort of like mine," she said. "I promised God I'd listen to Him. It's sort of the same."

"Listening can be hard sometimes," Tuck acknowledged. "The world is so loud."

Bobbie Jo put her arm around his waist and snuggled into him as they looked across the rock and down into the valley. "Not up here, though."

"No," he whispered. "It's not too loud up here."

The wind kicked up again, a gust that threatened to bring in another microburst of rain. But in that moment, with only trees and weather patterns around them, it felt like they were the only two people in the world.

She turned toward Tuck as he did the same to her. Bobbie Jo's pulse quickened as Tuck stared down at her, his eyes soft, his expression unreadable. For a moment, neither of them moved. The air between them buzzed with something unspoken, a certain excitement that had been building for weeks, maybe months, maybe since the moment they'd met.

The sun chose that moment to peek through the clouds again, casting a golden glow over everything. She smiled up at him and tucked herself into his arms. He held her close, and Bobbie Jo quickly made another promise.

I promise I'll be honest with myself—and with Tucker.

He stepped back and exhaled, and she glanced up at him. Their eyes met again, and Tuck's smile painted her life in such glorious colors. Tucker leaned in, his hand gently cupping her cheek, his breath falling softly against her lips.

Bobbie Jo yearned to kiss him again, experience the bubbling excitement of having another person care about her so much.

His kiss started out soft, tender, filled with all the things he felt but had managed to keep inside. Bobbie Jo's heart took flight as she melted into him, the simple press of his lips against hers sealing another promise between the two of them.

"I wasn't going to do that," he whispered, and then he kissed her again, moving deeper this time, his hand tangling up into her hair. The earth moved, and Bobbie Jo braced her feet, thinking for a moment that she'd fall down the mountain as Promise Rock cleaved away during the earthquake.

Then she realized that only *her* earth had moved, because of Tuck's kiss. And she really hoped he felt his current reality shattering and a brand-new one forming as she kissed him back.

thirteen

Tucker's whole world tilted once more, as if Bobbie Jo's touch had taken the ground out from under his feet. Her soft lips tasted like cherry lip balm mixed with autumn rain, and Tucker wasn't sure how his mind could work while kissing her.

The pressure of her body against his, the way her hands slid up around his neck and pulled him even closer—it felt all too perfect. Almost too good to be real.

But it was real. Absolutely real.

He'd finally—finally—kissed Bobbie Jo, and this time, no goodbye hung over them like a snake about to strike. This wasn't the kiss they'd shared months ago, when he hadn't known the next time he'd see her. This felt so different—full of promises. Full of hope.

And it terrified him.

Every nerve in his body fired at once, and yet, Tucker

floated outside his body. Like he had wings he never knew about. He deepened the kiss, trying to memorize every single part of this moment. His heart pounded in his chest so loudly it drowned out everything else—the wind, the leaves rustling, even the distant hum of the world below them. None of it mattered. Only Bobbie Jo mattered.

When he finally got control of himself, he pulled away and rested his forehead against hers, his eyes still closed. His heart hadn't stopped racing, and he wasn't sure it ever would.

"Wow," he whispered, his voice hoarse.

Bobbie Jo let out a small, breathy laugh. "Yeah. Wow."

He opened his eyes and found her staring up at him, her soft green eyes bright and beautiful. She looked a little dazed, and that made him grin. He knew that feeling all too well.

"I really didn't plan that," he murmured, his thumb brushing over her cheekbone. "The sun just came out, and I don't know. I wanted to."

"Same." She drew in a breath and looked past him, back across the rock and down the mountain. The clouds shifted again, and Tuck checked the sky.

"We should head back down," he said. He hadn't minded huddling under the pine boughs with Bobbie Jo, but he didn't like hiking in the muck and rain. On the way down, the sky continued to darken, and the air grew more and more biting.

Every step brought him closer to reality, and he didn't want to leave the mountains behind. Didn't want to leave this time with her, didn't want to step back into the real world where things weren't this simple. Where their differences—where his wandering heart—might complicate things.

With a sigh, Tucker finally led her past the trailhead signs, and she came to his side. The wind whipped across his face, and he bent his head to fight against it. "It's getting nasty."

She hurried to the passenger side, and he opened the door as the first drops of rain fell. He hustled around the hood and practically jumped behind the wheel. He swung his backpack over the console and dropped it on the back seat, the interior of the truck feeling damp and humid.

Bobbie Jo smiled at him, that same smile that made his heart do backflips, and she brushed her hair back. "We barely made it."

Tuck turned the key in the ignition, the truck rumbling to life beneath them. "I had a really great time today," he said, looking over at her. She'd shelved her inner grump, though Tuck didn't mind it so much.

"Me too," she said, her voice so genuine. "But I always do when I'm with you."

Tucker's grin widened, but before he could say anything flirty, or suggest another date, his phone buzzed from the console. He glanced down at it, and his stomach immediately flipped when he saw the name on the screen.

Jem Young—and his phone said he'd called three times in the past hour.

His heart kicked into overdrive again, but for a whole different reason this time.

"Do you mind if I take this?" he asked. "It's Jem Young."

He tried not to say the man's name as if he was a celebrity, but Jem kind of was.

"Sure, go ahead."

Tuck reached out and tapped the screen of the truck to connect the call. "Jem, hey."

"Hey, Tuck," Jem's upbeat-yet-husky voice came through the speaker, and Tuck immediately knew this wasn't a casual call. How, he wasn't sure, but Jem sounded half excited and half irritated. "Got a favor to ask."

"Yeah?" Tucker glanced at Bobbie Jo, who'd focused all her attention out the window, but she didn't fool him.

"I'm just wonderin' if you've signed up with anyone yet."

"No, sir," Tuck said, swallowing hard afterward. He really wanted to have this conversation in private. "I'm in Ivory Peaks through Opal's wedding anyway, and it seems like most people have their management through the end of the season."

He shifted in his seat, because he'd spoken true, and perhaps for the first time, he'd said out loud that he'd be in Ivory Peaks through the New Year. Maybe February or March, as a lot of cowboys took a couple of months off to recover and rejuvenate after the Nationals in Las Vegas.

"Right," Jem said. "Well, I got someone who wants you."

Tuck dang near drove him and Bobbie Jo right off the road. Bobbie Jo yelped, and Tuck righted the truck in the lane and glanced over to her. "Oh?"

"Rosie," Jem growled out. "She's ready to turn pro, and she wants you to manage her and help her train."

Tuck had seen Jem's daughter ride the barrels, and she

had a great horse and excellent command of the event. "How old is she?" he asked.

"Gonna be nineteen in February," Jem said. "She doesn't want to compete until next year. She just wants to get started with the professional training and earning points toward her professional licensure."

Tuck didn't know what to say. He took a moment to throw up a prayer to God, and with all the promises he'd just made up on the mountain, he knew the Lord would help him. "I've never managed a woman," Tuck said. "Gotta be honest about that."

And managing Rosie Young? Jem and Blaze were two of the biggest names in rodeo, even now that they'd been retired for over a decade. Still, the surname would be recognizable, and he'd be right there in the thick of everything with her.

This definitely meant a lot.

A whole lot.

But it also meant leaving Ivory Peaks. Rosie would most likely want to train in Wyoming, where she'd lived and grown up for years. Where her daddy and family lived. One of her cousins, Cash, had turned pro, and he trained out of Jackson Hole, and then he'd gone up to Montana.

So why can't Rosie come to Colorado? The thought rose from the depths of his mind and swirled around. If Rosie didn't want to compete until next year, maybe Tuck would have time to find a facility here.

He glanced over to Bobbie Jo, and then rubbed his forehead, the weight of the decision in front of him heavier than he knew how to carry.

"You're good with people," Jem said. "And Rosie's a little...."

"Just say it, Daddy," a woman said on Jem's end of the line. "I'm a little salty," she said louder. "That's what he's gonna say."

"And bossy," Jem shot at her.

"And headstrong," she said back, and Tuck grinned at their back-and-forth. "And always hungry."

Tuck laughed then, and he couldn't fault Rosie for that last one.

"Don't worry," Bobbie Jo said, sending pure surprise through Tuck. "Tucker is always hungry too."

"So you'll get along just great," Jem said.

"It would be an honor," Tuck said, but he didn't want to commit right this very second. "I'm gonna need to see some paperwork, and I need some time to work out a few things I've never dealt with before." Tuck had done business with big names before, and he sure was glad the words had come forward when he'd needed them.

"What events, Rosie? Just barrel racing?"

"I'm doing breakaway roping too," she said.

"She's real good with a rope," Jem said.

"All right," Tuck said, because he was real good with a rope too. It had been a while since he'd thought about training someone with a rope—working with teenagers in a summer program wasn't quite the same as managing the training of professional-level athletes—and he'd never done barrel racing before, as it was an all-female event.

132

"Could we meet up?" Rosie asked. "I could come to Colorado, or you could come up here."

"How are you gonna get to Colorado?" Jem asked, and Tuck once again grinned to himself.

"In a truck, Daddy," Rosie said, and beside him, Bobbie Jo giggled quietly. "I know how to drive, for crying out loud."

Tuck's gut twisted, because he truly could go to Coral Canyon, Wyoming, where Jem and Rosie lived, tomorrow. He didn't want to, though, because he'd rather go to church and then drive to Bobbie Jo's and kiss her again.

"I'm sure we can meet up," Tuck said, and he swallowed hard. "I'll need to do some research, Jem," he said after a beat. "Rosie, I've never dealt with barrel racing."

"I know, but you're so good," Rosie said. "I don't want to navigate it all myself, and my Daddy's got all these little kids here."

"Two little kids," Jem said. "And eleven is *not* a little kid."

"Skye is five," Rosie said. "She's little."

"Okay," Jem said, and he drew in a deep breath. "I'm sorry, Tuck, that you've got to listen to us bicker. I swear I've had normal conversations with my daughter."

Tucker laughed, and Bobbie Jo joined him. Neither Jem nor Rosie did, though, so Tuck cut his laughter short. "I'm driving right now, so I can't look at my schedule. Let me get on home, and then I'll hit you back."

"Sure thing," Jem drawled, and he and Rosie called goodbye.

"Talk soon," Tuck said, and he reached out and tapped the button on the screen to end the call. The resulting silence in the truck pressed down on him, and Tuck felt the same as he had while kissing Bobbie Jo—like he couldn't think.

"I liked her," Bobbie Jo said. "And Jem Young is one of the best rodeo cowboys in the world." She held up her phone, and Tuck glanced over to her as she continued to read from it. "Brother of Blaze Young, the Young Brothers compete in team roping events, and continually try to one-up the other for the biggest prizes and National Championship titles."

She looked over to him with wide eyes and lifted eyebrows. "And that's Jem's daughter."

"Yes, ma'am," Tuck said.

"This says Blaze's son is already a professional rodeo athlete, with two National Championships under his belt."

"Mm, that's right," Tuck said. "I told you I had some great contacts this summer."

"Yeah, the billionaire Young Brothers." She tucked her phone away and looked out her passenger window again.

"I think Blaze is the only one who's a billionaire," Tuck said coolly.

Bobbie Jo scoffed, and Tuck's skin turned into the wrong thing to have over his muscles. They'd never talked about his money, not exactly. She knew his family was rich—everyone in the greater Denver area knew that.

But having *family* money was entirely different than having personal money.

He didn't have to look at Bobbie Jo to know she wasn't happy. He could feel it radiating off her like heat from a campfire.

"Bobbie Jo," he said. "Talk to me."

She sighed and finally turned to face him, her eyes full of that fire he loved so much. "I just...I don't know what you want me to say."

His heart clenched. "I haven't even decided if I'm going to take her on."

"But you want to," she said, her voice laced with frustration. "You're practically bouncing in your seat. Tuck, you've been trying to get yourself back out there, and now you've got a star calling you."

He didn't deny it. "I don't even know if I'm qualified," he said. "Barrel racing is a women's event, and I've never managed or coached anyone through it."

The thought of leaving Ivory Peaks, leaving Bobbie Jo, walking away from what they'd just started to build....

Tuck wasn't sure how to do that.

He'd been upfront with her about his restless nature, about how he didn't want to settle down in any one place. But now, with her sitting next to him, looking at him like she wasn't sure if she could trust him to stick around, Tucker started wondering if maybe he'd been wrong all along.

Maybe settling down wasn't such a bad thing.

Could he see a future with her? Could he really imagine himself staying in Ivory Peaks, building a life here, with her?

The thought didn't scare him as much as it should have.

But it still had sharp teeth that sent blips of fear through him.

"I need to talk to my daddy," he said, and he sat up straight in his seat as he drove. "I know that's not the answer you want." He spoke fast now. "I don't have all the answers right now. I'm in limbo, and I know that's not what you want either."

"There's no wrong or right, Tuck," she murmured.

"Of course there is," he said, his frustration growing. He made a turn into her neighborhood, their time this afternoon coming to a close. He'd thought he'd stay and spend the whole day with her, but Jem's call had him itching to get back to the farm, talk to his father, and make a list of the pros and cons of taking on Rosie Young as a client.

She looked away, but not before he saw the fierce fire in her eyes, and the silence in the truck grew heavy.

Tuck's heart twisted painfully in his chest. He reached out, took her hand in his, and squeezed gently. "I'm not going anywhere just yet."

"I know," she whispered back, though her grip on his hand wasn't as tight as it had been before.

And there it was—the first crack in the foundation they'd been building.

Oh, and you should probably tell her you're a billionaire too, he thought, but he didn't want to add even more weight to the things that had already crashed into their perfect autumn day.

fourteen

Bobbie Jo stared out the window, the rhythmic hum of the truck's tires against the road doing little to calm the crackling tension in her chest. Her stomach growled, and she suddenly remembered the sandwiches she'd made. "We didn't eat," she said.

"Oh, my heck." Tucker slammed on the brakes, then seemed to realize he didn't need to avoid hitting a family of kittens. With his truck stopped right there in the middle of the road, he looked over to her, plenty of shock in his eyes. "I meant to eat on the mountain, but the rain distracted me."

The misty rain had cleared somewhat, and the storm wasn't nearly as bad down in the valley as it had been up in the mountains.

Her mind churned, stuck in the whirlpool of emotions that threatened to pull her under. She'd known Tucker was restless. That he wasn't the type to stay put for too long. That he wanted another cowboy to manage in the rodeo, that he loved traveling, that he loved being outside, with people he barely knew.

But knowing something, and hearing it, were two completely different things than being confronted with the reality of it. Of *feeling* it.

Bobbie Jo folded her arms across her stomach, trying to keep the growling at bay. Really, she just didn't want to let all of her poisonous thoughts come spewing out of her mouth. Tuck had left once before, and he hadn't been the one left behind, wondering if he'd ever come back.

She wasn't sure what they were doing if he wasn't permanent.

You're kissing him, she told herself. *And you knew he wanted to leave town again.*

She had, yes, and that only made the situation that much more maddening. She wouldn't keep seeing him when he left. She'd had a boyfriend in Oklahoma when she'd come here, and that long-distance relationship had ruined her when he'd finally ended it.

No, she would not be doing that again.

The thought made her stomach twist, and she reached for her water bottle, taking a sip to push the rising lump in her throat back down where it belonged.

"Hey, are you okay?" Tuck asked, his tone laced with concern.

Her thoughts scattered as she startled out of them. "Yeah, I'm...yeah, I'm okay." She didn't want to break-up with him, so she pressed her lips closed and looked over to him.

"I asked you about Anderson Park," he said, tilting his phone toward her. "It's just around the corner. Have you been there?"

She shook her head. "No." She wasn't sure she even wanted to be in public. "We can just eat on the back deck."

"Nope." Tuck dropped his phone into the cupholder, as he'd proven several times now that he only needed to look at a map for a moment before he knew where to go. "Let's go check out this park. I hope it's nice."

"It's a park in Boulder," Bobbie Jo said with a hint of acid riding the letters. "I'm sure it's nice."

Tuck navigated them around the corner, and then turned left, and sure enough, a big green space opened up. Bobbie Jo hadn't even known it sat there, but she could probably walk to it from her house in five minutes.

He pulled into the parking lot, where a big playground spread in front of them, with a splash pad to her right, and a block of pickleball courts to the left. With the cooler temperatures, plenty of people had come outdoors to enjoy the amenities, but Tuck managed to find a parking space.

He gathered his backpack while Bobbie Jo got out and stepped up onto the sidewalk. A big bank of trees sat on the other side of the soccer fields, and she figured that would get them away from the crowds and provide some shade.

"Ready?" Tuck joined her on the sidewalk, and she glanced over to him. She wasn't sure how to talk to him in this moment, and he didn't linger anyway. He led the way out onto the grass, and Bobbie Jo hurried to go with him.

After several steps, with the silence pressing down on

them, something inside her snapped. "I don't want our time together to be weird," she said.

Tuck grunted but didn't look at her.

A bit of relief moved through her. "I want to enjoy our time together. I mean, if it's all we get, we should try to make it good, right?"

"I'm going to be here through at least the New Year," he said. "Opal and Tag aren't getting married until November."

Bobbie Jo's strides lengthened as her irritation sparked. "November is not the New Year, Tuck."

"It's not tomorrow either," he said, glaring over to her. "And who wants to move to Wyoming in the winter?" He shook his head. "Not happening."

"It's not like winter here is great," she said, just because she could. But she really didn't want to argue with him, and she drew in a breath to calm herself.

Bobbie Jo caught his hand and squeezed, but she held her tongue. The trees around the park still held onto their leaves in brilliant shades of red, orange, and gold, the colors vibrant against the gray-blue sky.

She didn't think for a single second she possessed what it took to anchor Tuck in a single spot. Nothing about her was special, and the man possessed a big rope that he wanted to lasso the whole world with.

"Maybe I'm just too boring for you," she blurted out. "I mean—"

"You're not too boring," he barked at her. When he got frustrated, he walked faster, and Bobbie Jo had to practically run to keep up with him.

"Maybe it's not the right time."

"Maybe you shouldn't look so far into the future."

"Well, I don't know how to do that," she snapped.

Tuck slowed and softened. "I know, sweetheart." He released her hand and drew her against his side. "You want to know every step of the way before you take it."

Her insides shook as she nodded. "Yes, I do," she said. "I don't know how to think differently."

Her mind whispered that January was a solid three and a half months away, and people fell in love in that amount of time all the time. Not her, as it took forever for Bobbie Jo to truly let someone into her life, and that only reset her frustration.

They reached the edge of the trees, and Tuck took off his backpack and unzipped it. As she watched, he pulled out a blue-and-white plaid blanket and spread it on the ground. Tingles and warmth started in her fingertips as he added their sandwiches and snacks to the blanket and then looked over to her.

"Let's eat." He knelt down and then fell to sitting cross-legged as he picked up his first sandwich. "It's a picnic. I meant to surprise you with it at Promise Rock."

Bobbie Jo joined him, a small smile forming on her face. "This is great," she said. "Now I know this amazing park exists close to my house."

Tucker could eat his turkey and cheese sandwich in only a few bites, and he did that while Bobbie Jo sifted through the food and found her sandwich, as well as a bag of Cheetos. He wouldn't look at her, and Bobbie Jo had already blurted out two pretty major things.

A third would strike her out.

So she waited, because Tuck sure seemed to have something on his mind that she suspected would come out soon enough.

"I need to tell you something," he said right when she took her first bite of her turkey and provolone. She chewed, but she felt certain she wouldn't be able to swallow until Tuck had spoken.

"You've been to the farm," he said.

Surely he didn't need her to vocally confirm that, so she simply nodded.

He swallowed and reached for a bag of pretzels, which got violently ripped open. "You know my family has money."

Bobbie Jo managed to swallow her bite of sandwich. "Everyone in Colorado knows your family has money," she said. The Hammond name seemed to be everywhere, especially in the city.

"But did you know that *I* have money?" He kept his gaze on the trees a few yards away, and he threw back a handful of pretzels.

"You mean from your time in the rodeo?" She hadn't realized he'd ever been a champion. In fact, he'd told her he'd quit riding the circuit and turned to managing, because he couldn't make a living. But he did manage National champions, and surely they paid him a pretty penny for that.

"Sure, I could've lived on that," he said. "As long as I was working. This is...." He balled up the pretzel bag and tucked it into his empty sandwich bad. "Generational wealth. That's how my momma and daddy explained it."

Generational wealth.

Wealth?

Generational wealth! screamed through her head.

"How about you explain it to me too," she said.

He gave her a dirty, dry look that lasted only a heartbeat. "I mean, all Hammonds inherit two billion dollars when we turn twenty-one-years-old," he said. "It's generational wealth."

Tuck reached for another sandwich, and how he could do that so easily, so casually, Bobbie Jo didn't understand. Her throat tightened. She wasn't sure what she wanted him to say, to explain.

An inexplicable anger ran through her, and while she'd known life wasn't fair, she'd never been confronted with it so powerfully. A few truths managed to march across her mind in the still silence.

Tuck didn't need to work at all.

With his "generational wealth" he could do anything he wanted.

"We're tasked to do something good with the money," he said. "One of my uncles builds custom motorcycles for veterans. Another built a police dog training facility, and he donates dogs to departments all over the country."

He blew out his breath and took another bite of his sandwich. With the second one gone, he flicked a look in her direction, but his gaze didn't stick. "Opal's probably going to open a non-profit health clinic once she'd married and settled, and Hunt owns two non-profits, including Pony Power."

Shock ran through her in electric zips. "No one pays for the services there?"

"Some do," Tuck said. "Some don't, but it's a non-profit, sweetheart. That means Molly and Hunt don't profit from it."

"They just live on his generational wealth." She didn't mean to allow so much disgust taint her words.

Tuck swung his attention toward her. "You're upset."

"No," she said.

He tilted his head at her, his way of saying, *Yeah, right. It's cute how you think you can hide from me.*

Her chest heated as she breathed in, and she glared at him. "Fine, you know what? I'm upset about this."

Bobbie Jo took a deep breath, trying to calm the storm inside her. She didn't want to be mad at him, but the frustration still simmered under the surface. "It's...just...it feels so unfair," she said, her voice shaking. "My family lost everything, Tuck. We lost our ranch, the home where I grew up, everything. And you're here in Colorado sitting on your billions when people lose their whole lives in Oklahoma."

Just like usual, her words spilled out and stained things before she could stop them. As soon as they hit her eardrums, Bobbie Jo regretted them. She hadn't meant to bring up her family's struggles, but the bitterness she'd buried for so long bubbled right on the surface.

And looking at him, a wild sense of jealousy moved through her too. He hadn't taken a job in the city he didn't want simply because they paid well. If she was him, and had his family opportunities, she'd have her goat farm and be living her dreams.

Her throat had narrowed to the point that she couldn't even swallow her own saliva, and she really hated feeling like this about someone she should be happy for.

Tucker's face softened, and he dropped his gaze. "I'm sorry that happened to you, Bobbie Jo," he said. "I can't imagine what that must've been like."

"No, you can't." The anger behind her words faltered when she saw the pain in his eyes. She quickly reached for him, her mood all over the place since that blasted phone call. "I'm sorry. I shouldn't have said that."

Tuck stayed quiet, and he pulled his hand away from hers, giving her room to breathe. "I do have money. My own money. I'm still trying to figure out what I want my life to be, and how to make my parents proud." He shoved his second bag inside the first. "You've already done both of those, Bobbie Jo. Money doesn't solve everything. In fact, money doesn't really solve much."

It would've saved her family's farm, but Bobbie Jo bit the words back.

"I know it's unfair. I know I'm blessed. But I don't want you to think that's all I am—a bank account. A really handsome, lucky, blessed cowboy with too much money." He gave her a smile, but it carried more sadness than anything else.

Bobbie Jo's heart squeezed painfully in her chest. She'd known Tucker came from a wealthy family, but she hadn't really thought about what that meant for *him*—the load he might carry because of it.

She also had no idea how someone like her—someone who'd lost everything and had nothing—could build a life with someone like Tucker, who literally had the world in the palm of his hand.

But as she looked into his eyes, so full of sincerity and caring and adoration for her, she realized that maybe she was...wrong.

And oh, Bobbie Jo hated being wrong almost as much as she hated the injustices in the world.

So, like she did when she'd calmed enough to find the eye of the storm inside her, she tried to see the other side of the coin.

And on this side, Tuck was exactly who she needed in her life. Someone who didn't need to see the next step, but who woke up excited for the spontaneous possibilities of the day ahead of them. Someone who could whisk her away from the labs at HMC and give her the goat farm in the country.

Someone who morphed into more and more of a cowboy prince who could make all of her fairy tale dreams come true —partly because of who he was, and yes, partly because of the resources he possessed.

"I see more than a bank account," she said.

Tuck nodded, and he dropped his chin, hiding his eyes from her. "I promise we'll talk through everything every step of the way, okay?" He looked at her. "If you'll agree to that, then this won't be our last date."

"I don't want this to be our last date," she said, her heart-beat pumping hard now. "Is that a possibility?"

Tuck grinned and shook his head. "You should see your face right now."

Her worries crashed to the ground. "Tuck." She swatted at his chest, and he laughed as he dodged her hands. He grabbed them and pulled her toward him. Bobbie Jo held no power against him, and she easily slid into his lap.

"Promise me," he whispered. "That you'll give me the chance to talk through everything before you decide to break up with me."

She ran her fingers down the side of his face, feeling so comfortable and so safe in his embrace, against his chest, wearing his sweatshirt. "You're the one who just said you were going to make this our last date."

"Promise me," he insisted.

She looked into his eyes. "I promise."

"Good," he said. "Me too."

And that was a promise she'd grip until her dying breath.

fifteen

Tucker tugged at his collar, trying to loosen the tie that felt like a noose around his neck. He'd never been one for dressing up, even for the Sabbath Day. As a child, his momma would let him go in slacks and a white button-up, no tie. But he wasn't six years old anymore, and Tuck figured he could wear a tie for a couple of hours.

"Stop pulling at that." Deacon swatted his hand away from his throat as they headed for the front door of the generational house. "You're acting like this is your first time goin' to church."

"I just hate dressing like this," Tucker muttered under his breath, though he'd been worshipping weekly with his parents for months. It felt good to be back in Ivory Peaks, though, as he'd grown up listening to the same pastor preach from the same pulpit.

He expected the church to be the same—the creaky

wooden pews, the stained-glass windows casting colorful shadows on the floor, the faint smell of old hymnals and fresh flowers. The thought comforted him, and he followed Deacon out of the house and to the right when they usually went left.

Momma and Daddy had moved into one of the cowboy cabins for the next couple of months, and Tuck pushed down his cowboy hat and ignored the tension around his neck as he followed his brother toward the family sheds and farm buildings.

Once past those, he found Daddy coming down the steps from the cabin, with Momma right at his side. His knees weren't great anymore, and living somewhere with a lot of steps wasn't ideal. Their house in Coral Canyon didn't have any stairs beyond the two or three wide ones up to the front porch. Tuck had been living there with them for the past few months, and he had full and free rein of the basement, since Daddy wouldn't go down there.

"Hey," Deacon called, and both of their parents looked up. Momma's smile broadcasted her patience and love for everyone in her sight, and while she was over a dozen years younger than Daddy, her blonde hair had started to lose its color.

She radiated beauty, and Tuck relaxed a bit more. Momma and Daddy made it to the bottom of the steps, and Tuck moved in to hug his mother while Deacon took Daddy's arm and turned to help him to the truck.

"I'll drive us," Deacon said. "If you want."

"Yes, please," Daddy said, and he willingly climbed into

the backseat of his own truck. That would put Momma up front, and Tuck would get to ride with his father.

Perfect, he thought, because he wanted to talk to his daddy about a great many things. As he helped Momma into the truck and then went around to the other side to get in behind Deacon, the uncertainty swirling in his chest made everything feel so tight.

He'd had such a great time with Bobbie Jo yesterday, even though some of their conversations had been fairly intense. But she'd admitted a lot of things, and Tuck had chosen to go with how much money he had over spewing out the still-forming thoughts in his head about finding a big piece of land and pouring every ounce of energy he had into learning how to make it into a rodeo training facility for cowboys and cowgirls.

Something like that didn't exist on the scale Tuck was thinking, and as Deacon backed out of the driveway, Tuck shifted, buckled his belt, and looked over to his father.

Daddy had his head ducked slightly, so Tuck could barely see his father's eyes under the brim of his cowboy hat. "You were gone all day yesterday," he drawled.

"Yeah." Tuck threw a look up to his mother, not believing for a moment she wasn't listening. "I'm sleeping out at Mike's tonight too, since I'll be helping with their harvest this week."

"Mm." Daddy faced the front as Deacon rumbled down the road toward the highway.

"I wanted to talk to you," Tuck said.

"Yeah, I figured."

Tuck wasn't sure what gave him away when it came to his father. Maybe the fact that Tuck had never made a major—or minor—move without consulting with his daddy first. Usually both of his parents, actually.

"It's about Bobbie Jo," he said, as he'd never been shy about his feelings for her. "And my life." He sighed like the two would never reconcile. "Jem called me yesterday; Rosie wants me to be her manager."

That brought Daddy's eyes right back to his, and Momma gasped and turned around. "Tuck." She reached over the seat and squeezed his hand. "That's amazing news. She's just starting out, and you'd be really good for her."

"Sounds long-term," Daddy said. "Which you wanted."

Tuck couldn't argue with them on any of it. He swallowed, trying to find the core of his internal debate. The reason he'd gone to war with himself. Something.

"He really likes Bobbie Jo," Deacon said from the driver's seat. "And Bobbie Jo really wants somewhere fixed, permanent, stable. She wants a home. Tuck wants an adventure."

Irritation shot through Tuck, and he wanted to bark at his brother that he had no idea what he was talking about.

However, Deacon had just summed things up really well.

So he ducked his head and studied his fingers. "It wouldn't be fair to ask her to wait around while I chase my dreams, managing rodeo stars and moving from rodeo to rodeo, place to place."

"Tucker," Momma said in the kindest voice possible. But she didn't continue, and Deacon didn't jump in again either.

"Staying in one place has never been part of your plan," Daddy said.

"I mean," Tuck said. "No, but—but, I mean...maybe now I'm thinking about it."

"Managing Rosie is a huge opportunity," Daddy said.

"I know that, Dad." Tuck exhaled a slow breath, his gaze drifting out the window as the truck rolled past the pine trees guarding the farm. Deacon made it to the highway, and then it would only take ten more minutes to the chapel.

"Tell us what's on your mind," Momma said.

Daddy grinned at him and reached over to squeeze his hand too. "You've never been one to hold back."

Tuck flashed a grin too, but it didn't stay for longer than a moment. "I've been thinking about buying some land around here," he admitted, leaving out the part about how Bobbie Jo needed land for her goat farm. "And...setting up my own rodeo training facility."

He glanced at Momma, met Deacon's eyes in the rearview mirror, and cleared his throat. "You know, how Uncle Cy has that motorcycle shop, and he helps veterans, employs people, and also gets to do what he likes doing."

Daddy hummed again, and Momma nodded. Tuck loved how familiar it was to speak to them, to put things out of his head that weren't fully formed yet, and they'd help him take them and mold the ideas into something more tangible and real.

"Lotta research and work to get to where Uncle Cy is."

"I could go talk to him," Tuck said. "Or Uncle Ames. I

know he sells some of his dogs and donates others. He's not entirely non-profit."

"Hunt is."

"Right," Tuck said. "Maybe I could partner with the Justin Cowboy Crisis Fund or something."

"That's for injuries," Daddy said. "Opal probably could, if she gets her clinic open."

"Yeah." Tuck exhaled again, not sure how to do any of the things boiling in his mind. He'd never gone to college; book-learning bored him.

"I've never wanted the farm," Tuck said slowly as the outskirts of town came into view. "But that's not the same as not wanting somewhere of my own to call home."

Deacon didn't pipe up and say he'd always be welcome at the farm, because everyone knew Tuck could show up there at any time and find a bed and something to eat. But a home was so much more than a place to sleep and a cupboard with his favorite cereal in it.

"Maybe I need something that's mine," he said, and his thoughts stopped shouting at him.

"You've got the money to do it," Daddy said.

Tucker's throat tightened. Yeah, the money. He had more than enough to buy a lot of land, build the best facilities, all of it. His inheritance sat virtually untouched, and he'd used Hunter's investment wealth manager since he'd gotten his money almost seven years ago.

But it wasn't the money that scared him. It was the idea of staying in one place. Of settling.

Of the dream shifting.

Of becoming someone...different than who he'd always wanted to be.

"You think you could name one place as home?" Momma asked, almost as if reading his thoughts. "Really build a life here in Ivory Peaks?" She shook her head. "Or somewhere. It doesn't have to be here."

Goat farms can be anywhere, he thought, but Tuck kept it to himself.

Instead, he rubbed the back of his neck, his fingers brushing the collar of his shirt and migrating to where the tie sat knotted around his throat. "Maybe," he said quietly. "If Bobbie Jo's part of that life...."

"I need to meet this Bobbie Jo," Momma said with a smile.

"You know her, Momma," Deacon said, glancing over to her. "She lived with Hattie last year. Had that boyfriend back in Oklahoma." He tossed Tuck another look in the mirror, and Tuck gave his brother a nod.

"Oh, sure," Momma said. "She must not have the boyfriend anymore."

"No," Tuck said. "They broke up at the beginning of the year."

Deacon slowed and flipped on his blinker. He pulled into the parking lot at church, and Tuck looked over to his dad.

"Have you prayed about it?"

"No, sir," Tuck said honestly. "Not yet. It's all really new. Me and Bobbie Jo. Me and sticking around. This whole training facility thing. All of it is really new."

Daddy nodded, wisdom shining in his dark eyes. "Sure.

Well, you're a smart man with a good mind, a good gut, and a great heart. Listen to all of those things, and then take it all to God. He won't lead you wrong."

Tuck nodded now, and he suddenly wanted to head home so he could be by himself, so he could order his thoughts, so he could pray right now.

So it was probably a good thing that Deacon found a parking spot, and they all started spilling out of the vehicle. Sometimes Tuck needed to slow down and make a plan— something else he didn't enjoy doing.

His boots sounded hollow against the asphalt, and he went around the truck to help his parents. The four of them walked toward the church, and sure enough, everything shone out to him exactly as he remembered it.

Coming to church was a reverent affair, and Tuck basked in the silence as they went up the steps and inside. The familiar scent of old wood and the polish that went with it met his nose, and Tuck felt like he was relaxing into a hot shower.

He had always enjoyed attending church, even if sitting still had been a challenge for him as a child, and keeping his attention on the sermon had been nearly impossible as a teenager.

Tucker settled into the pew, his heart still heavy with thoughts of Bobbie Jo, goat farms, Rosie Young, Uncle Cy, and rodeo training facilities and grounds. And money. And Ivory Peaks, and how much he'd never wanted to live here permanently.

For now, he tried to push everything aside. He needed clarity and silence so he could organize his thoughts.

The sanctuary quieted as Pastor Cartwright stepped up to the pulpit, his presence commanding yet gentle as always. He'd aged, as he'd probably turned sixty by now, and he had graying hair and warm, kind eyes that seemed to see right into Tuck's soul.

"Good morning, my brothers and sisters," Pastor Cartwright started, his voice carrying through the room to anyone willing to hear. "Today, I want to talk about prayer."

Tuck shifted in his seat, glancing over at his daddy. Seriously, the man could be a pastor, though Tuck couldn't imagine him standing up in front of a congregation and giving a sermon.

"Prayer is one of the most powerful things we can do," the pastor continued, pacing slowly in front of the congregation. "It might feel useless sometimes. You might wonder if God hears you at all." He paused and looked out into the crowd. "Because what is one voice? With all God has going on, all the people on the planet, surely He doesn't hear you. Right?"

He took a couple of steps and faced them all again. "Wrong, my friends. That is wrong. I testify that God hears all prayers. All of mine. All of yours. All of hers, and all of his." He pointed left and right, his voice increasing in volume.

"You are not just one voice in a sea of millions. You're not. God *hears* you. You are important enough for Him to notice, for Him to hear. Your prayers are loud enough, even if they're whispered or even just streaming from your heart."

Tuck's chest tightened. He hadn't prayed as much lately

as he once had. Not really. He'd uttered a few words here and there, but he hadn't poured out his heart like he used to.

"One more thing," Pastor Cartwright said as he finally settled behind the pulpit. A microphone sat there, and he didn't have to project his voice now. "It doesn't take multiple voices to make God sit up and listen. All it takes is one. One voice. *Your* voice."

Tuck swallowed hard, his hands gripping each other. *One voice. His voice.* Did God really hear him? Did He really care what Tucker Hammond had to say?

Pastor Cartwright smiled, his eyes sweeping over the congregation. "Let me remind you of the Parable of the Lost Sheep. There was a shepherd who had a hundred sheep, but one day, he found one of them missing. Now, most would think, 'Well, he's still got ninety-nine sheep. What's one sheep?' But that's not how the Good Shepherd thinks."

Tucker's pulse quickened, his mind locking onto the story. He'd heard it a thousand times, but today, it felt different. Personal.

He hadn't realized how alone he'd felt until this moment, sitting in church, listening to the pastor talk about sheep.

"The shepherd left the ninety-nine behind," Pastor Cartwright continued. "And he went after that single lost sheep. He searched high and low until he found it. And when he did, he rejoiced. Because *every* single sheep matters to the Lord."

Tuck's throat tightened as the words sank in.

The pastor seemed to look right at him. "He rejoices when you pray to him, no matter how long it's been, no matter how far you've strayed. The one matters to Him—*you* matter to Him."

To Tuck's great surprise, tears burned in his eyes. True tears. He couldn't remember the last time he'd felt so seen, so loved, and so...heard.

Momma reached over and squeezed his forearm, and Tuck ducked his head to wipe his eyes. That broke the connection with Pastor Cartwright, and Tuck kept his chin low as he continued with, "God hears you, my friends. He hears every word, every cry, every plea. And He answers. It might not always be the answer we want, but He always answers. Sometimes it's yes, sometimes it's no, and sometimes it's 'wait.' But rest assured, He's always listening."

Tuck's chest ached as he stared down at his hands. He'd been so caught up in his own uncertainty, his own fears, that he hadn't taken the time to really pray. To really ask God for guidance.

Yes, everything coming at him in the past couple of weeks was new. But Tuck hadn't taken anything to the Lord.

Sitting right there in church, as the pastor continued to preach, Tuck closed his eyes, his fingers locked solidly together. *Lord, I don't know what to do. I don't know where I'm supposed to be, or what path I'm supposed to take. But I trust You. I trust that You'll guide me. Help me figure this out. Help me do what's right—for me, for Bobbie Jo, for my future. I'm listening, Lord.*

Nothing flooded his mind immediately, but Tuck could lift his head and focus on the sermon again. It ended a while later, and then, as the final hymn played and the congregation rose to their feet to sing it, a strange sense of peace washed over Tuck.

He didn't have all the answers yet. But for the first time in a long time, he felt like maybe, just maybe, he was on the right path by being here in Ivory Peaks, dating Bobbie Jo, and helping his family with whatever they needed.

It's not forever, Tuck, whispered through his mind, and he wasn't sure where those words had come from.

Oh, wait. Yes, he was.

God had heard—and answered—him.

sixteen

Bobbie Jo adjusted the rearview mirror as she navigated the winding country road, the radio playing Travis Tritt as loud as she could stand it. With the blasting music, she didn't have space to think too hard about where she was going.

She could only focus on the steps of driving.

She couldn't think about what she'd find when she arrived on the country property where billionaire Michael Hammond—oh, yeah, her *boss*—and his wife had a farm. In fact, Mike himself had *come to the eighth-floor metal-research lab* and *personally* invited her to tonight's dinner.

She wouldn't have said no even if she'd wanted to.

Thankfully, Tuck had already given her the heads-up about the dinner, and Bobbie Jo had stammered out an acceptance for the tall, dark, powerful cowboy who ran the company where she worked. Then she'd had to answer a billion questions from her friends and co-workers in the department, and she'd spent her lunch hour texting everything to Tuck.

He hadn't answered right away, because he'd been staying at Mike and Gerty's farm this week to help them get their harvest in. "But these Hammonds...." she muttered to herself as she navigated the next turn. "They don't even know who they are."

Because Mike Hammond was the CEO of the company. He could've sent a secretary to tell her about the dinner that night. He could've emailed her. He could've done nothing and trusted that his cousin would invite her if Tuck wanted her there.

And yet, he'd descended from his top-floor office to invite her himself.

"Wild," she said as she made the last turn off the paved road onto a dirt one. The country stillness infused into her bone marrow, and Bobbie Jo really wanted a small plot of land like this, far from the city while being close enough that she could go should she want a taste of that vibe.

Should she and Tuck want to go to a concert in the city. Or the Shrimp Palace. Or a staycation away from the goat farm.

She scoffed as she continued to take in the gorgeous scene in front of her. She wouldn't be surprised if a river ran through this property. It was absolutely picture-perfect, and Bobbie Jo's heart suddenly seemed to be sucked into a box, where it couldn't get any hope, any oxygen, nothing.

Fall was her favorite season, and she swore her blood was made of golds, oranges, and reds that mirrored the leaves on the trees. As Bobbie Jo took in the picturesque view, her heart swelled with a strange mixture of anticipation, joy, and uncertainty.

She once again hadn't seen Tuck since Saturday, and while this dinner brought them together a couple of days sooner than normal, she couldn't shake the nagging feeling that everything between them—despite their promises—felt suspended in midair, hovering between hope and the unknown.

A small smile tugged at her lips as she continued along the road, a big farmhouse sitting down another lane to the right. A stable and barn stood beyond that, and the road to the left seemed well-driven as well.

Bobbie Jo turned right and parked in front of the bright yellow farmhouse with the white railing on the porch. Several other vehicles had been parked out front, and her heartbeat thrashed like a fish out the water.

Being invited to Mike's farm was a big deal. Not only was he her boss at Hammond Manufacturing Company, but this dinner was also a family affair. She wasn't even close to being part of the Hammond Family—the very idea was laughable; she and Tuck had been dating for less than a month—but the invitation felt like she was being welcomed into the inner circle of the Hammond clan. Her vision turned white as a sheer wall of overwhelm hit her. She blinked, trying to get through the rushing, white water that had obscured her sight.

She'd felt like this when her parents had come home from the bank and told her and her siblings that they'd lost the farm. That they'd have to move. That everything she'd planned her life to be was suddenly gone.

Ripped away, as if a tsunami had washed across the whole continent to Oklahoma and wiped out everything she'd ever known.

Bobbie Jo sucked at the air and found she couldn't get enough. She put one hand on her chest and leaned her head over to simply try to get back to stasis.

"Hey." Someone opened her door, and Bobbie Jo turned that way, the addition of the fresh air so welcome. Frantic now, she clawed at her seatbelt so she could get out—*get out! Get out!*—of the SUV.

"Whoa, what's going on?"

Tuck's voice.

Bobbie Jo sobbed as the seatbelt finally released and she practically jumped from the vehicle. She sagged into Tuck's arms, and to his credit, he caught her easily, fluidly, perfectly.

"All right," he said. "It's okay." He stroked her hair as if he'd seen panic attacks every day of his life. Maybe he had.

Bobbie Jo had no idea why she'd spiraled. Or how it had happened so fast. She simply clung to him, her mind so full and flowing so fast, she couldn't catch anything there.

"Breathe with me, baby," he murmured, and his chest started to rise. Bobbie Jo did her best to mimic him, but her lungs couldn't hold as much as his. They started to ache and collapse, and she let them as another horrible noise came out of her mouth.

Her body felt so hot, and she suddenly couldn't be next to the human heat source that was Tuck. She pushed away from him, and thankfully, her vision worked. "I...I can't...." She walked away from him, from the trucks, from the farmhouse, from everything, as fast as she could.

"I'm coming after you," Tuck said, and Bobbie Jo could only hear his footsteps behind her. She focused on that, and then on taking in another lungful of air. Then another.

She went past the barn and the stables to the fence with a gate that stood open. A newly harvested field lay beyond that, and she simply came to a stop and looked into the horizon, the chilled evening wind brushing across her face and bare arms.

She shivered just as Tuck reached her, and she sank back into his warmth, now needing it. She twined her fingers on one hand with his, and fiddled with her necklace with the other. The symbol of her faith grounded her as her thoughts spiraled.

She had never imagined herself in this position, attending a family gathering for a family that wasn't hers. But the more time she spent with Tuck, the more she found herself picturing a future that involved him—a future that might even include a farm exactly like this, children and pets, and a life in a small town that was...permanent.

"I brought an apple pie," she whispered.

"I'm worried about you."

"I—don't know how to explain," she said. "I just got overwhelmed." To her left, the barn doors opened, and a cowboy exited, then another.

"Howdy-there," one of them called, and Tuck raised his hand in acknowledgement.

"They're coming this way," he murmured, and Bobbie Jo quickly released his hand and turned her back on everyone. She didn't wear much makeup, so she didn't worry too much about having black tracks down her face.

Still, she wiped her eyes, drew in a breath, and faced them with Tuck at her side.

"Tag," Tuck said, pulling Bobbie Jo against his side. "Steele. This is Bobbie Jo. Not sure you guys have met her." He beamed down at her, his concern carefully concealed beneath the sparkling stars in his eyes.

"I don't think so," Bobbie Jo said as she stuck out her hand. "It's great to meet you both." She shook Tag's hand, feeling right at-home with cowboys. It was billionaires and CEOs she didn't know how to be around. "You're marrying Tuck's cousin, right?"

Tag's whole being brightened. "Opal, yeah. Only six weeks now." He grinned at Tuck as Bobbie Jo shook Steele's hand.

They all turned toward the house as laughter and music floated through the air. Someone had opened the side door and let the party into the night, and the golden glow of the lights welcomed all to the farmhouse.

"I'm gonna run home and clean up," Steele said.

"Same," Tag said. "We'll be over in about twenty." He nodded to Tuck and Bobbie Jo, and the two cowboys left.

Tuck waited until they'd disappeared around the corner

of the barn before he turned toward her. "Do you need another minute? We don't have to go in at all."

"Of course we're going to go in." She couldn't quite get herself to look at him for longer than it took for her eyes to brush across his face. "It's a big celebration to finish the harvest."

"They'll survive without us."

"I want to meet Opal," she said. Though she'd lived at the Hammond Family Farm for over a year, Opal hadn't been there, and Bobbie Jo didn't attend family functions much there. Big farm gatherings, sure, but there had almost been an invisible line drawn between those with the last name of Hammond and those without it.

"Tuck-Tuck, Tuck-Tuck," a little voice came through the descending darkness. "Ope, Ope, Ope. Tuck-Tuck?"

"He's out here somewhere," a woman said in a kind voice. She wasn't placating or talking baby-talk to the little boy, and Bobbie Jo's heart filled with joy at the little boy's continued, "Tuck-Tuck. Tuck-Tuck." Then he yelled, "Tuck-Tuck! Where you?"

Tucker chuckled, and he leaned closer to Bobbie Jo. "That's West, Mike and Gerty's little boy. I'm his favorite, and I've been here less than a week. Everyone seems to be upset about it."

"You gave him candy, didn't you?"

"Hey, I know what little boys like."

"I'll call him, Westy," the woman said.

"I'm right here, Opal," Tuck said, and he took Bobbie Jo's

hand as he started back toward the lighted part of the farm. Both Opal—a gorgeous, petite, dark-haired woman who totally bore the Hammond nose and chin—and West, the half-blonde, half-dark boy at her knee faced him.

"Tuck-Tuck!" West ran toward him, and Tuck let his biggest, belliest laugh into the sky as he bent and scooped the little boy into his arms. The child squealed and laughed, and as Tuck held him in his arms high above the ground, West held out a small pumpkin. "Pump."

"Pump-*kin*," Tuck said, tapping the boy's nose. "Westy, look who came to eat with us." He grinned over to Bobbie Jo as she approached. Her fantasies had come to full fruition. A handsome cowboy on a quaint, perfect farm. The scent of horses and hay hanging in the autumn air.

The cutest little boy ever, who obviously came from someone light and someone dark.

"This here's Bobbie Jo," he said. "Remember I told you about her?"

He'd told a two-year-old about her? What had that conversation been like?

West shied into Tuck's chest, and he chuckled and said, "Oh, you can't be shy around her. She's the nicest."

Thinking fast, Bobbie Jo took the few remaining steps to her car and pulled open the passenger door. To her great relief, the paint pen she'd used at Promise Rock last weekend still stood there, and she grabbed it.

"Can I see your pumpkin?" She held out her hand, and West looked at it, then Tuck, and then her. He extended the pumpkin toward her, and she quickly drew on a pair of eyes, a tiny nose, and a great big smile.

"There." She turned it for him to see. "It's West in pumpkin form." She grinned at him, thrilled when the little boy's face stayed very still, then slowly lifted, then jetted straight to glowing. He looked at the pumpkin and took it from her.

He showed it to Tuck, as if he couldn't see it, and said, "Wessst. Wessst. Pump-Wessst."

"That's right, buddy." Tuck passed him and the pumpkin to Opal. "We're comin' in too. I'm just gonna get Bobbie Jo's apple pie."

Opal smiled at Bobbie Jo. "I don't think we've met. I'm Opal Hammond, Mike's sister. Tuck's cousin."

Tuck spun back to them. "Bobbie Jo, this is Opal."

"She just said that, cowboy." Bobbie Jo smiled at him and stepped forward to shake Opal's hand. "It's great to meet you and West."

"C'mon in. Food's almost done, and the cowboys will be over in a few minutes."

"Yeah, we just saw them," she said as Tuck ducked to get the pie off her passenger seat. She went with Opal, determined not to let herself spiral again. Seeing Tuck with that little boy in his arms....

Bobbie Jo now had a true-life vision of her fantasies, and she'd never get that image out of her head.

Inside the farmhouse, a long table had been set up in the kitchen as an extension of the island. Both held dishes, bowls, and platters of food, and an aroma of roasted meat, baked bread, and hearty vegetables filled the air.

Gerty, Mike's wife, had her blonde hair braided down her back, and Bobbie Jo paused in the doorway as she watched her four-thousand-dollar-suit-wearing boss bustle around the kitchen in a pair of jeans and a black polo.

"Right here?" he asked an older woman, and she nodded.

"Right there, Mikey."

He set down the rust-colored bowl in the spot indicated and looked up just as Tuck came in behind Bobbie Jo. She shifted out of the way, and he stopped beside her to close the door. "Bobbie Jo brought apple pie. Where do you want that, Carrie?"

"On the dessert end of the table, Tuck," the older woman said, and he veered over to the folding table. He set down her pie—which she'd paid her roommate to make for tonight's dinner—and turned back to her.

"Everyone, this is Bobbie Jo Hanks. She's my girlfriend, so it would be great if you didn't say or do anything to embarrass me."

"You'll do that just fine on your own," Gerty said with plenty of wit and a wide smile. She stepped past Tuck to Bobbie Jo. She drew her into a hug. "Good to see you again, Bobbie Jo. How's the job in the city?"

"Oh, uh." She cut a look over to Mike. "It's amazing. Just great. Yeah, I like it."

The house and everything in it paused, and then Gerty burst out laughing. "Oh, honey, he knows what it's like to work at HMC."

Mike too smiled and chuckled. He merely shook his head, and the door behind them opened again. Bobbie Jo moved out of the way, and thankfully, Tuck was right there to pull her past the table and into the living room as Tag and Steele joined them in the house.

"You okay? We can leave any time you want."

"I'm okay." She wrapped her arms around him. "I don't know—let's talk after, okay?"

He pressed a kiss to the corner of her eye and nodded just once. "It's so good to see you."

"You're just saying that because you finished the harvest early and we have tomorrow off."

"Even if that was true—which it's not—the fact remains that it's so good to see you." He touched his lips to hers just as Gerty yelled, "Okay, everyone. It's time to eat. Where'd my daddy go? Daddy?"

"Gamp!" West yelled. "Gamp-pa, Gamp-pa! Gamp-paaaa!"

"Westy, not so loud." Opal grinned at him as she chastised him, which did no good whatsoever.

Then Boone Whettstein came bustling down the hall. He clapped his hands together, and that set off a couple of toys. A Halloween song started blaring through the room, and it took Bobbie Jo a moment to find the skeleton bee-bopping as he sang.

"Keleton, Keleton." West strained to get down, and Opal practically dropped him as she set him on his feet. He ran toward the toy; a dog barked; the front door opened, and another woman walked in.

She carried a stack of dishes, and Boone moved to help his wife, Cosette. "Pies, pies, pies!" he boomed, and Gerty threw him a dirty look.

"Daddy, put down those pies and say a prayer for us."

"Yes, ma'am." He didn't seem ruffled by Gerty's saltiness toward him, and she bent to pick up her son.

"Baby, we're eating, and it's time for the prayer." She sat on the couch only a pace away from Bobbie Jo, and she helped her son fold his pudgy arms as cowboy hats got removed and adults bowed their heads and closed their eyes.

Bobbie Jo couldn't look away from West, with his scrunched up eyes and hunched-forward shoulders. Love filled her for this precious child she'd met ten minutes ago, and while she'd never considered herself overly maternal, she knew in that moment she wanted to have children.

The prayer ended, and Bobbie Jo took a deep breath and looked around the room. Gerty stood and with her son in her arms, she said, "Before we eat, Mike and I just want to thank all of you for helping us get our harvest in this year. It's such a busy time of year, and I could never do it myself." She nodded, her expression fierce. "Harvest bonuses for the cowboys are over on the counter, so be sure to get yours before you go."

Bobbie Jo didn't even want to know what a harvest bonus looked like for Gerty Hammond. She moved over to the food table and passed West to his father, and again, Bobbie Jo saw a brand new side of Mike that she hadn't before.

She'd only known him as the CEO businessman, though

Gerty had come to Pony Power and the farm where Bobbie Jo had worked.

"How was the drive?" Tuck asked as they joined the line.

"Not bad," she said. "The fall colors are beautiful right now. Almost gone, though. So much wind."

"Yeah, that's for sure." He paused, his gaze lingering on her before adding, "We should go for a drive tomorrow, after you sleep in. Get out of town for a bit, go grab some of those pie shakes I told you about, just...relax."

"Sounds perfect." Bobbie Jo smiled, her heart doing that funny little flip again. She met Gerty's grandparents, said hello to Cosette, and went through the line to get a sliced turkey and cheesy potato feast.

She'd expected the meal to be livelier, but though there were a lot of people in the farmhouse, the energy stayed low. People chatted easily, and Bobbie Jo got drawn into conversations as if she'd been out on this farm all week, helping to bring in the alfalfa.

She could see why Tuck loved his family so much—there was a sense of unity here, a bond that went deeper than blood. It was something she hadn't realized she'd been missing until this very moment.

And she wanted this life so much it hurt. Tuck put his hand on her knee and leaned in close. She ducked her head toward him too, liking everything about him, about the way he touched her, the way he created space for just the two of them, the way he seemed to know when something inside her had shifted.

"I'm headed to the dessert table," he said almost under his breath. "You want me to bring you anything?"

"Anything and everything that looks good," she said, and Tuck grinned as he pulled away. As he went to get their desserts, Bobbie Jo decidedly fell a little bit more in love with him, and in love with this cowboy way of life he could provide for her.

Now, she just needed to figure out how to keep his attention—and keep him in town—for long enough to see if her fantasies could become reality.

seventeen

Jane Behr stood on the back deck and gazed out over Twilight Fields, cradling her month-old baby, Clint, in her arms. The crisp October air tingled against her skin, and the scent of freshly harvested hay and dried corn husks filled her nose. For a moment, everything around her seemed to still. The farm, her farm now, stretched out before her in golden hues, the nearly-bare branches of the trees dancing in the gentle breeze. Everything seemed perfect, and for the first time in a long time, Jane felt settled. Grounded. Whole.

She looked down at Clint, swaddled snugly in a pale blue blanket with tiny pumpkins embroidered along the edges. Momma had made it, of course, as Jane's mother possessed exceptional skills behind a sewing machine. She'd be here later, as she came almost every day to see her new grandson.

That, or Jane took Clint to the farm where Momma and Daddy were living until Opal's wedding.

Clint's tiny chest rose and fell in calm, long, even breaths as he slept, his round little face tucked close to her heart. A soft smile tugged at her lips, and she hugged him gently, marveling at how small and yet oh-so-perfect he was.

Adjusting to life with a newborn had been hard. Harder than she'd expected, to be honest. But whenever she thought about it, a rush of gratitude filled her heart and made tears prick her eyes. This kind of hard broke her down and made her stronger. This kind of hard reminded her that she wasn't the same woman she'd been a year ago, that she could grow and change and be better.

She'd wanted to be a mother for so long, and she whispered, "Thank you, Lord," as the barn doors opened and her gorgeous cowboy-mechanic husband emerged. Cord loved Twilight Fields with his whole heart. No, they hadn't planted this year at all, so they hadn't had to bring in a harvest.

Cord planned to plant next spring, as the mechanic shop would be a couple of years old then, and Clint would have more months of life behind him, and things would be more settled.

She hoped.

Cord had just finished checking the last of their farm equipment in the barn, and she raised her eyebrows as he neared. "How'd it go?"

"Just fine, sweetheart." Everything about Cord called to Jane, and she smiled at him. Always so steady. Always the same. She loved that about him.

He reached her and bent down to kiss her. "I'm real dirty."

"Mm-hm." He kissed their baby boy, and then she shifted so he could move past her and go inside to finish washing up. He smelled like metal and grease and oil, and Jane loved that too.

He was just as handsome as the day she'd met him— maybe even more so now, with a baby in his arms every other moment and a whole farm to care for.

Cord had worked all day in the shop, then come back to the farm to feed the chickens they'd collected over the months, continue his mechanic work on his own machines, and now, he'd most likely throw something together for dinner. No matter how long his day had been, no matter how tired he felt, he always had time for her and Clint.

Inside, he rewashed his hands, getting more of the oily residue off his hands. He also claimed to absolutely hate the liquid pink soap he used in the barn and the shop, and he wanted his final wash to be with her "more luxurious" soaps.

"Looks like you got more Halloween decorations," he said.

Jane looked over to the dining room table where she'd been piling all the party prep items. "Plates, cups, napkins, and streamers today."

"No costumes?"

"Yours will be here tomorrow."

He grunted, and Jane bent to slide Clint into the bouncy seat she kept in the kitchen for when she worked here. "Come on," she teased. "You can be something besides a cowboy for one day."

"I dislike Halloween," he said, not for the first time.

She'd been planning for Halloween for weeks. Her first Halloween as a mom. It felt like such a big deal, even though Clint was too young to remember it. Still, she wanted his first costume to be something special.

"You'll have bigger muscles than you do now." She cuddled into him as he dried his hands.

He flashed her a grin. "Did you tell your parents?"

"They're going to come over on the day-of," she said. "Not for the party. Momma has something for him, of course."

"The costumes are gonna come in time," he said, taking her into his arms. "And we're gonna be the best superhero family in town."

Jane melted into his chest, a new measure of happiness filling her. "You'll be Mister Incredible in real life *and* in a costume."

"And Elastigirl can do anything." He touched his lips to hers and kissed her sweetly.

She loved the movie *The Incredibles*, and it had been like heavenly light pouring into her life when she'd decided they could dress up as a family. The baby's name was Jack-Jack, but they were going to call their son Clint-Clint.

Jane's heart fluttered at the thought of Clint's first Halloween, of showing him off to their family and friends at the Halloween party they were hosting right there at the farm next week. She couldn't wait to see everyone in their costumes. She'd even bought prizes for Best Costume, Most Original Costume, Best Make-up, and more.

"It's going to be a full house next weekend," she said, her

mind already racing with thoughts of decorations and food and the sheer joy of having her family here. They seemed to do so much at the family farm or Gerty's place, and she wanted her house to matter too.

"Are you ready for that?" Cord asked, his voice soft and teasing as he stepped back and opened the fridge. "You won't be able to make eyes at me and leave early." He raised his eyebrows at her and peered into the fridge. "Corn okay tonight?"

"I love corn," she said. "Clint's a newborn. He's our excuse if we need to end the party." She took a cob of corn from him and pulled down the husk. "Besides, it's not like we'll be doing anything too crazy. Just a family party. Lots of food, lots of laughs. Maybe a pumpkin carving contest or two."

"A pumpkin carving contest? Jane."

She laughed and shook her head. "No, I made that up. But we are having an apple cider bar, and I'll be giving awards for it."

"So I'll print up an award for your momma at the shop tomorrow." Cord chuckled, and Jane threw him a smile.

"I mean, probably." He wasn't wrong that her momma made the best apple cider and would probably win.

Cord chuckled, pressing a kiss to the top of her head. "Sounds perfect."

Jane sighed contentedly, watching him as they stood there together, shucking corn. "I love you, Cord," she said.

"I love you endlessly, sweetheart."

* * *

A week later, Jane stood in the kitchen, holding Clint in his bright red baby superhero costume as she surveyed the spread of food laid out on the dining room table. The family Halloween party had started an hour ago, and her family—the animals—had torn through the food.

Laughter, conversation, and the occasional shriek of delight from one of the kids filled the house, and Jane smiled into all of it.

"Argh, Matey," Hunter said as he came into the dining room. Molly had gone all out, as usual, with carefully coordinated costumes for the whole family, including pirate hats with the big, flowing feathers, real leather eyepatches, and billowy pants that tucked into knee-high boots.

Hunter wore his costume well, and all of their children had dressed the perfect part of a pirate family as well. "Got any of that hot chicken dip left?"

Jane pointed down the table and bounced Clint as he fussed. He'd been Mister Cries-A-Lot in the past couple of days, and she thought he was cutting his first tooth. "It was in that green leaf-shaped bowl."

Hunter moved down the table and lifted the appointed bowl. "Dang, it's gone."

"Momma made it," Jane said. "I'm sure she'll give you the recipe."

Clint let out a wail that so wasn't fitting a superhero baby who could do any number of things. Jane looked down at him, equally frustrated that he was making the party hard and worried that he wasn't happy.

Hunter started loading a bowl with another type of dip,

and Jane went out into the living room to see if Cord could get Clint to go to sleep. Then she'd just take him down the hall to his bedroom, and she might be able to be a good hostess for her family.

But Cord held West on one knee and Clay on the other. Ryder had crowded in around him, and Tuck bent over the back of the couch. The five of them watched something on Cord's phone, and Jane couldn't be mad about the scene in front of her.

Everyone loved Cord, and she turned, nearly running into Bobbie Jo, Tucker's new girlfriend. "Oh, I'm sorry," she said. "I swear I was less awkward when I was pregnant."

"Can I take him?" Bobbie Jo asked just as Clint let out a dissatisfied wail. Then Bobbie Jo simply took the baby from Jane, smiled at her, and added, "Does he need to be changed or fed?"

"I'll make him a bottle, but he should be fine," Jane said. "He's fussy tonight."

One of Hunter's girls came over with a ring and said, "Uncle Cord said he might want to bite this." She handed the bright blue ring to Bobbie Jo, who held it up to Clint's mouth. He glommed onto it as if he'd never had anything to eat, and Jane frowned at all the slobber coming from his mouth.

"I'll get him a bottle and try to put him to bed."

"I'll do it." Bobbie Jo followed her into the kitchen, where the party noise continued, just at a lower decibel. "I need a little break from the party anyway."

Jane cast her a look as she opened the fridge and pulled out a bag of her breastmilk. "You sure?"

Bobbie Jo had dressed up as a mad scientist, complete with her white lab coat and her hair sticking up all crazy, like she'd just stuck her finger in a light socket. "I'm sure." She glanced toward the living room. "It's been a busy week at work too."

"I bet." Jane heated up the milk quickly and fixed Clint's bottle while he continued to gum the blue ring. She handed the bottle to Bobbie Jo, and said, "His room is the last one on the left."

Bobbie Jo grinned and left the kitchen, ducked away from the party, and went down the hallway.

Jane sighed, wishing she didn't feel so relieved. But the truth stared her in the face—being a mother was hard work. She got no break, and Clint couldn't talk to her and tell her what he needed.

"Jane, Cord's askin' if you need him." Deacon, in all his white-sailor-suit glory, entered the kitchen and reached for the bag of sweet onion potato chips next to her on the counter.

"No." Jane folded her arms, suddenly unsure about going back to her own party. "Bobbie Jo took Clint down the hall to put him to bed."

Deacon crunched through his chips. "She's great, isn't she?" His voice dropped in volume, and he checked over his shoulder.

Jane didn't talk to her brothers about their girlfriends—or the lack thereof, in Deacon's case. She didn't want to close the door on that, so she casually asked, "Is there anyone you'd ask out?"

"I don't know," Deacon said with a big sigh. "There's not a lot of women on the farm, and I don't see how I can date anyone there anyway. I'm their boss."

"Yeah, that's a tough spot to be in," Jane agreed. "Trav and Poppy met at that speed-dating thing."

Deacon gave her a glare that could curdle blood.

Jane laughed, and she turned away from Deacon to get out a cold can of soda. "Okay, so not speed dating. Maybe church?"

"Mission's been, uh, using an app," Deacon said. "I signed up."

"You signed up for a dating app?" Jane didn't mean to sound so incredulous, nor did she mean to spin back to him so violently.

"Okay, we're done talkin' about this." Deacon tossed down the bag of chips and stalked back to the party.

Jane moved to the edge of the living room and watched her loved ones. Tuck had dressed as a rodeo clown for the party, complete with a painted face and colorful overalls, and she pulled out her phone to start making notes for her costume contest winners.

Mike and Gerty—who also steadfastly refused to dress up—had come with West, who was dressed as a little skeleton, proudly carrying around his toy "keleton" and making it dance for everyone who even looked his way for two seconds.

Gerty had brought a platter of caramel apples her grandmother had made, already sliced up for easy eating, and Mike had contributed by bringing several cases of soda and a cooler full of ice.

Opal and Tag had come too, though their costumes were a little more laid-back. Opal was dressed as a witch, complete with a pointy hat and a broomstick, and Tag had come as a cowboy—a real shocker. But Jane smiled, because she knew Halloween wasn't for everyone.

She marked down Tuck for Best Make-up, and Lindsay Whettstein, who'd once owned this farm, for Most Creative Costume. She'd dressed all in green, and then she wore a huge headdress with the golden petals of a sunflower.

Charlotte, Hunter's youngest daughter, would get Best Voice to Match a Costume, and Jane enjoyed looking around the room and making up awards for every person there.

Cord came up beside her, placing a hand on the small of her back. "You okay?" he asked, his voice low and full of love. She hadn't even noticed him leaving the party.

Jane smiled, nodding as she looked up at him. "Yeah," she said. "Britt is going to get...." She looked back out to the white-blonde girl who reminded her of herself forty pounds ago.

"Best Movie-Inspired Costume?" Cord suggested, and Jane giggled as she typed it into her phone, for Britt had shown up wearing the same type of shower and curtain that the main character had in *The Karate Kid*.

"Maybe that one should go to us," Cord said as he put his arm around her. "I mean, my muscles and chest are *huge*."

Jane burst out laughing, which drew the attention of some of her friends and family, and Cord nudged her to get out there and party it up with them.

So Jane did exactly that, and she sidled up to Tuck, who asked, "You seen Bobbie Jo?"

"Yeah." Jane bumped him with her hip. "She's feeding Clint and putting him to bed."

Tuck looked over his shoulder toward the mouth of the hallway.

"She's pretty amazing," Jane said. "I'm glad you two are finally dating."

"Yeah," Tuck said, though he was clearly distracted. "Me too."

"Is it serious?" Jane asked, thinking he'd probably say the truth in this moment. Tuck never held much back anyway.

So when he looked her dead in the eye, Jane got the full power of her younger brother. And he didn't blink, or swallow, or blush, or stutter when he said, "Yeah, it's serious."

Of course it was, and Jane couldn't very well tease someone who wouldn't deny his feelings. So she said, "Okay, well, I'm going to give her the Best Hair award. Do you think she'll like that?"

eighteen

Opal Hammond looked at her reflection in the ornate, full-length mirror, her breath catching in her throat. Her wedding dress, a custom creation worth more than she cared to admit, shimmered in the soft light filtering through the window beyond her.

The gown cascaded around her in layers of delicate silk and tulle, each fold a masterpiece of craftsmanship. Gems lined every hem, covering the stitches where different panels of fabric connected. The bodice, adorned with intricate bead-work that sparkled like the stars she loved so much, hugged her upper body and hips, while the train flared and trailed behind her.

When she walked in the dress, she felt as if she floated on clouds. Extravagant and breathtaking, the dress made her feel like her life had become a dream

And today, it was, for today was her wedding day.

A day she felt like she'd been waiting on for *such* a long time.

Around her, her momma moved, fixing the collar on Aunt Elise's dress, and then zipping up the back of Molly's gorgeous pantsuit.

Her dear Jane pulled the sleeves down on her pretty autumnal-themed dress. Opal had chosen chocolate brown, ivory, and burnt orange as her colors, with a hint of pink champagne in there, and her mother's dress looked like she'd be crowned after the nuptials today.

Gerty and Allison had gone to check on the flowers, as Opal hadn't seen her florist yet this afternoon, and she needed her bouquet before she could walk down the aisle.

Opal blinked back the tears threatening to spill from her eyes as her mother joined her in front of the mirror. She smoothed back an errant piece of her dark hair, streaked with silver and pulled back into an elegant chignon, and smiled at Opal.

"Ready for this?"

Opal nodded, her voice gone on vacation. She drew a breath and cleared her throat, and said, "I love your dress."

Momma looked down at the pretty, sequin-covered garment as if she didn't know what she'd just stepped into. All of the women she'd invited to help her get ready had come to the bride's room in the luxurious lodge and event center Opal had booked for the wedding.

She and Tag would be married in the largest outdoor barn, which had been decorated precisely to Opal's specifications, and then they'd jet off on a tropical vacation that would give them some relief from the encroaching winter temperatures. When they returned, life would go on at the farm, with Tag continuing to be the foreman and Opal continuing to help with West.

She'd made more headway on her health clinic idea, but she hadn't found the perfect piece of land yet. She knew God would provide exactly what she needed, exactly when she needed it, though—a lesson and truth she'd learned over the past few years of watching everyone around her achieve the things she wanted in her own life too.

And today, she'd be taking that first step toward the future she'd been dreaming of since she was a little girl.

"You're too inside your head, dear." Her mother's warm smile shone with a hint of pride as she put her arm around Opal.

Opal blinked, coming out of her thoughts. "Maybe," she said.

"Are you nervous?" Momma asked, moving to smooth a few strands of Opal's hair that still sat perfectly in place, secured in the intricate updo Molly and Jane had helped her with before she stepped into her dress.

Opal swallowed the lump in her throat. "Not really." She turned back to the mirror, her fingers grazing the beaded edge of her bodice. "Just...introspective."

She'd been so busy planning every detail of this day, looking for the perfect dress, combing through addresses for the invitations, that she hadn't let herself fully feel it until now. But with her mother standing beside her, it all hit her at once.

She was *getting married*. To the love of her life.

"All right," Gerty announced as she strode into the room. "We've got flowers." She beamed like she'd grown and harvested them herself as she moved out of the way so Alli could enter the room too. Then Gerty closed the door, already chattering about how she and Allison had to "tromp all over" the whole lodge looking for the floral delivery man.

"You'd think they'd never had to deliver flowers for a wedding here." Gerty exhaled as she arrived in front of Opal. "I've seen this dress before, but it steals my breath every time."

Opal eased into Gerty's arms, as she'd passed off the bucket of blooms she'd carried into the room. "I love you, Gerty," Opal whispered.

Gerty wasn't the most emotional or touchy-feely woman in the world, but she loved deep. She simply showed it in other ways besides saying it out loud. So when she said, "You are my favorite person, Opal," it meant so much. She stepped back and held Opal by her sequined shoulders. "I love you so much, and I'm so glad you and Tag will be so close to us."

"Yes," Alli said. "I'm jealous about that."

Opal grinned over to her too. "Ooh, tell Ethan to move back here," she said as she moved to hug her other sister-in-law. Allison and Ethan lived with their two kids back East, where Ethan had a really good job—not that he even needed one of those.

"I'm still working on him," Alli promised as she bent to hug Opal.

Molly, Jane, and Aunt Elise joined them in front of the

mirror, and Aunt Elise started handing out corsages. Chatter broke out as they slid them over their wrists, and a debate broke out over whether or not the blooms should be on the inside or outside of the wrist.

Allison had brought a second bucket, and it held Opal's bouquet, so she moved a couple of steps away from the ongoing discussion and lifted it out. Alli joined her, and she adjusted one of the flowers in the arrangement. She smiled softly, and Opal missed her powerfully in this moment.

"Saw your daddy outside," she said as she looked up. "Pacing."

"He's just glad he's lived this long," Opal said, and she was only half-joking. Daddy had turned eighty this year, and she could lose him at any time. Her chest seized, but she'd been through this before. She knew people didn't live forever, and she thanked God standing right there in the bride's room that her daddy had been given enough time on the earth to walk her down the aisle.

"It's almost time," Momma said now that everyone had decided to wear their wrist corsages with the flowers on the outside.

"Perfect timing," Opal said, grinning around at everyone. "I need all of you over here." Her heart swelled with gratitude for the women surrounding her. Each one had played such an important role in her life, and she loved them all so much.

"You're going to look like a movie star when you walk down that aisle," Jane said, stepping closer to pin the veil in Opal's hair. "Tag isn't going to know what hit him."

Opal laughed, her nerves rising up as the women

continued to fuss over her. "He's seen me in everything from flannel shirts to muck boots. I'm not sure a fancy dress is going to be that shocking."

Plus, he'd seen her in one of those too, and Opal smiled internally as she thought about their Valentine's date several months ago, and the glittery black dress she'd worn then.

"Oh, trust me," Molly said, her eyes sparkling with mischief. "That man looks at you like you hung the moon. He's going to lose his mind when he sees you walk down that aisle."

Opal's heart fluttered at the thought. She knew Tag loved her—he'd promised her the stars, after all—but hearing her loved ones say it out loud made the reality of it even sweeter.

"Okay," Aunt Elise said as Momma went to the door and opened it a couple of inches. "We're going to clear out, and your daddy is going to come in. He'll get you where you need to go." Aunt Elise looked at her with all the love of a mother, and Opal had grown up close to all of her aunts and uncles, and they'd all made the trip from Wyoming to be here with her and Tag today.

Tag's family had come from wherever they lived—his twin brothers from Texas, his momma from Alabama and his daddy from Kentucky. Opal had met them all, and they were lovely people.

The room emptied of women, save her, and then Daddy ducked into the room. Her breath caught, because she loved her father with every fiber of every cell in her body. She moved toward him, taking the small steps her wedding dress required.

"Daddy." Her voice cracked, and she did everything she could not to cry, for she didn't want to ruin her makeup.

Opal's breath caught, and she looked at her reflection one more time. Her makeup was flawless, her hair perfectly pinned, her dress a work of art.

"You're a shining star," Daddy said, his smile wide and wonderful and full of wisdom as he approached. He opened his arms and swept her into them, and Opal sank into the strength and warmth of her father's embrace.

"Not just any star," Daddy murmured. "The brightest one in the sky." He pulled back, everything about him big. His personality, his grin, his broad chest and shoulders.

"Thank you, Daddy," she murmured.

He offered her his arm. "I have been told I'll never be forgiven if you're even five seconds late to the altar."

Opal linked her arm through his and glanced out the window, where the afternoon light faded fast. Her wedding theme—stars and constellations—had been Tag's way of keeping his promise: To rope the stars for her.

Tonight, they'd say their vows under that sea of twinkling stars, both real and decor, and Opal couldn't imagine a more perfect setting to begin her forever with Tag.

Daddy cleared his throat, his voice thick with emotion. "You ready to do this, sweetheart?"

Opal nodded, her heart pounding in her chest at the term of endearment Tag would've used there. *Honeybee. Honey Bear. Honey-love.*

"I'm ready."

The walk from the bride's room to the barn felt like something out of a fairy tale. The path, lined with lanterns that flickered in the dusk, wound through the trees, and by the time they reached the open doors of the barn, Opal felt like this part of the world had been coated in magic.

Her father's arm stayed steady around hers, and she glanced up at him, her heart full of love for this man who had always been her rock. "Are *you* ready, Daddy?"

Daddy reached up and wiped his eyes. "So ready," he promised her. "I'm so happy for you and Tag." He pressed a kiss to her hairline.

Opal's eyes drifted closed as she smiled. The emotion of the moment seemed to sting the very air around her. "I love you, Daddy."

"I love you too, Opal." He looked toward the double-wide entrance of the barn and took the last couple of steps.

The music shifted, and the sound of violins and guitars filled the air. The guests started to stand as a murmur moved through the crowd, and Opal caught her first glimpse of the wedding venue in person. Momma and Molly had sent pictures when they'd walked through earlier, but Opal hadn't seen it with her own eyes yet.

Rows of white chairs lined the aisle, each one draped with fall flowers in that pale pink and burnt orange and twinkling lights. Star-shaped lanterns hung from the rafters and showered down colored light. White, ivory, champagne, teal, mint, sky, lavender.

The soft, dreamy glow flowed over the space, charming the old barn wood into looking like a million bucks. The tables sat ready for dinner, which followed the ceremony, with silver and white, with the seven-tier wedding cake over in the corner.

Opal could barely take it all in, and then Daddy ducked his head. "Opal, look." He nodded with his oversized cowboy hat toward the end of the aisle, where, beneath an archway of flowers and lights, stood Tag.

Her breath caught in her throat at the sight of him. Tall, rugged, and impossibly handsome in a deep, rich, dark tuxedo and a matching cowboy hat, Tag stood with his hands clasped in front of him, his eyes locked on her as if she were the only person in the world.

And in that moment, Opal knew that for him, she always had been.

As she and her father began their walk down the aisle, everything else faded away. The guests, the music, the decorations—it all melted into the background as her gaze stuck and stayed on Tag's. The love and pure adoration in his eyes made her heart soar, and she felt sure only she saw the small shift of his feet.

She didn't need a rock concert the way Hunt had, with all the men in their family dancing down the aisle. She seriously doubted her father could move like that anyway.

All she needed was the amazing cowboy now reaching for her.

Daddy lifted her hand to his lips and kissed the back of it, squeezed it between both of his hands, and placed it in Tag's. "You two be good to each other," he said, and Opal nodded along with Tag. Then Daddy moved to sit on the end of the front row, beside Momma, Ethan and Alli and their kids, and Mike, Gerty, and West.

"Ope," West said in a faux whisper, and her attention turned away from Tag and to the little boy. Gerty bent her head over his, obviously shushing him. "I say hi." He leaned around his mother and waved, and Opal almost burst into tears.

She waved back to West and then faced Tag again. Her heart skipped a beat as she stood beside the man she wanted to spend the rest of her life with, and they faced the pastor together.

"You look like you stepped down from the stars," Tag whispered, his voice low and full of emotion.

Opal smiled, squeezing his hand as tears filled her eyes. "You roped them for me."

nineteen

Taggart Crow could barely feel his own hands, what with the way his heart thundered in his chest, and how he shifted his stance for what felt like the hundredth time. *Opal's here*, he told himself, the very real presence of her at his side.

Still, he planted his palms against his abdomen just to make sure they weren't too sweaty, and he cast a quick glance over his shoulder to where his family sat in the first row. His parents, though they weren't together anymore, sat side-by-side, with his daddy grinning like a fool, and his momma wiping her eyes with a tissue.

The twins, Sawyer and Flint, both gave Tag a thumbs-up, and somehow that relaxed him. As he faced the altar and the pastor on the other side of it, his gaze swept past Opal.

His lovely Opal.

The guests surrounding them—so many people he'd never met before, because of her family's influence and presence in the community—faded into the background, their murmured voices nothing but white noise as he focused on the moment that had finally arrived.

"Taggart and Opal," Pastor Cartwright said in his deep, easy-going, soothing voice.

But Tag couldn't completely shake the nerves that knotted in his stomach. He wasn't a man who got nervous easily, not when it came to wrangling cattle or fixing a broken fence, but something about standing here, in front of all these people, with all the Hammonds in the room, churned his insides like butter.

Just when he'd thought he'd come to terms with Opal being a Hammond.

You have, he told himself. *She's just a person, and she loves you.*

And in fact, in that moment, Opal leaned into him, tilting her head back to get closer to his ear. He leaned down, the brim of his cowboy hat tapping against the side of her face. "Are you all right, baby?" she asked.

"Yes, honey-love."

So Opal was wealthy, influential, and powerful. She came from a billionaire family with deep roots in tradition, and while Tag had worked hard to be the best cowboy he could be, he couldn't help but feel a little inadequate at times.

Scratch that—he felt downright out of place standing here at his own wedding. His Alabama drawl wasn't as sharp these days, no, but his fingers still bore roughness from years of ranch work, and his family...well, they weren't the Hammonds.

Not even close.

He blinked, and realized the pastor had started the ceremony without him. Tag swallowed hard and adjusted his cowboy hat in a show of nerves.

"Marriage is such an amazing thing," the pastor said, and Tag cleared his throat. Everything had turned hot, and his head swam.

"Hey, so I just need a second," someone said.

Tag turned toward the male voice and found both of his brothers on their feet. Murmurs ran through the crowd, and Sawyer nodded respectfully to Opal and the pastor and then faced the crowd. "We just need Tag for thirty seconds."

"Sawyer," Tag said, but Flint had gone behind him, and he took Tag's arm and said, "Walk with me. Just for a second."

"I'm getting married," Tag said.

"Yeah, and we're all here for it but you." Flint cut him a steely look out of the corner of his eye. He turned around just as Mike arrived at Opal's side, and she looked like someone had thrown lightning bolts into the barn.

"Where you at?" Flint asked as Sawyer caught up to them, only about ten yards from the altar. Thankfully, shadows prevailed in this part of the barn, and Tag hoped they'd work to conceal him from the prying eyes of the crowd behind him.

"I'm right here," Tag said.

"You were *not* present," Sawyer said. "Are you just nervous?"

"You love this woman, don't you?" Flint asked, and Tag looked back and forth between the twins, their questions coming too fast for him.

"Of course I do," he said.

"Then *show up* for your own wedding," Flint said. "Get out of your head. She loves you."

"A lot," Sawyer said. "She's here, and she's ready, and you're up there clearing your throat and dancing like you might start runnin'."

"I'm not going to run."

"All right," Flint said. "I believe that's our time, and I'm pretty sure Momma is going to use a butter knife to fillet the muscles from my bones tonight." He cleared his throat this time. "So, we best get this groom back to his bride." He once again linked his arm through Tag's, and this time, he turned him around and the three of them walked back to the altar.

"Sorry, Opal," Flint said as Mike made room for Tag at her side.

"Ma'am," Sawyer said, and Opal, in her infinite goodness, smiled at them and ducked her head.

She looked at him while Sawyer gave a quick apology speech to the crowd. "Taggart," she whispered.

"I'm okay," he said. "I was just...lost there for a second, and the twins didn't want me to miss my own wedding."

Her gorgeous eyes searched his. "Lost...?"

"I love you," he said, bending his head to touch his forehead to hers. "I simply spiraled for a few minutes, but I want to be yours, and I want you to be mine, and I'm sorry I—I'm right here. Right now."

"Okay, honey," she drawled, her lips tipping up into a smile. He loved kissing her grin, and he did that while the crowd noise behind them rose.

Pastor Cartwright cleared his throat, and Tag came right back to this moment in time. He smiled as he broke his tender kiss with Opal—who still wasn't his wife—and quickly turned back to the audience. "Sorry, y'all. I just needed a second."

He faced the pastor again. "Sorry, Pastor. We're totally ready now."

Opal nodded and the pastor smiled politely and patiently.

"All right," he said. "I think you're really going to enjoy marriage, Tag."

"I intend to," he said.

Pastor Cartwright chuckled. "I think it's one of the greatest things God has given to his children. The ability to build a life *with* someone instead of having to face the uncertainties, the pressures, the ultimate lows all alone." He smiled at Tag and Opal, but also out to the crowd.

"And it's not just the bad things we need help weathering, but who here loves getting good news and keeping it to themselves? Who earns something amazing, or watches something incredible happen in their lives, and just...moves on like it was nothing?

"God has given us each other to celebrate with as well, and that's my counsel to you, Taggart, and you, Opal, today, as you choose each other, and choose to spend your time building something that is bigger than either of you could be alone—be there for each other in all things."

Tag nodded, and behind him, someone said, "Amen, pastor." Probably one of the twins, which made Tag smile.

"Choose each other through all of life's trials and joys. Build a partnership and commit to going on a journey where you'll walk side-by-side, supporting one another, growing in faith together, and building a life that honors God."

Tag squeezed Opal's hand, the gravity of the moment settling over him. This had suddenly become more than just a wedding.

This was a holy promise, a commitment to love Opal through everything—good times and bad, wealth or poverty, health or sickness.

He didn't fear the hard work it would take, and for the first time today, that nervous knot in his gut unwound completely.

He was ready.

The pastor smiled at them both, and then he spoke the words Tag had been waiting for. "Taggart David Crow, do you take Opal Marie Hammond to be your lawfully wedded wife, to have and to hold, in sickness and in health, for richer or poorer, as long as you both shall live?"

His voice, steady and full of certainty, filled the barn as he said, "I sure do."

The pastor turned to Opal, and Tag's heartbeat did that thundering and lightning action again. "And do you, Opal Marie Hammond, take Taggart David Crow to be your lawfully wedded husband, to have and to hold, in sickness and in health, for richer or poorer, as long as you both shall live?"

"I do." Opal didn't hesitate in the slightest. Her voice didn't waver. She'd become his anchor in a stormy sea, the one person he wanted to wade through life with, his other half that made him so completely whole.

A soft murmur rippled through the guests, and Pastor Cartwright smiled. "Then, by the power vested in me by the state of Colorado and our Almighty God, I now pronounce you husband and wife. Tag, you may kiss your bride."

Tag didn't need to be told twice.

He pulled Opal into his arms and kissed her, every bit of love, gratitude, and joy pouring into that moment. He heard the applause and the cheers around them, but all he could focus on was her—his honeybee, his wife.

They pulled apart, both smiling ear to ear, and Tag took her hand as they turned to face the guests. The barn erupted into applause, and for a moment, Tag felt like he stood on top of the world.

Opal leaned close to him, her voice barely audible as she said above the cheers, "I love you, Tag."

He kissed her temple, his heart so full it could burst. He owed Flint and Sawyer their favorite treat for recognizing he'd gone somewhere else and pulling him back.

"I love you too, honeybee."

Her mother arrived and pulled Opal into a hug, and Tag got engulfed by the big bear of man that was Opal's daddy. "I couldn't have picked anyone better for her, Tag."

"Thank you, Wes." Tag clapped him on the back and

stepped back, everything full of light and love now. As he continued to hug Hammonds, friends, and his brothers, his gaze never strayed too far from his new bride, and Tag knew one thing for certain—he'd just roped the brightest star in the sky.

And he was never letting go.

twenty

Mission Redbay stood at the edge of the dance floor, his hands stuffed deep into the pockets of his church pants. He watched as couples twirled and laughed with one another, the soft glow from the star-shaped lanterns casting a warm, multi-colored light over the dance floor in this high-end barn.

He just wanted to leave, but he'd come with Tarr, his cabinmate—and a total extrovert.

Huge mistake, Mission thought, as he stood on the opposite end of the scale when it came to socializing. Mission had been around people for hours now, and part of his soul felt like it was turning dryer and blacker by the moment.

He leaned against one of the wooden beams, out of the way and hopefully out of sight. The last thing he needed was Tuck or Tarr coming over to drag him out onto the dance floor. He'd always gotten more by observing than being in the fray.

Now, he watched the newlyweds swaying in the center of the dance floor, completely absorbed in each other. Tag's hands rested on Opal's waist as they moved to the soft country melody, their foreheads pressed together in a quiet moment despite the noise and movement around them.

Mission managed to smile, albeit internally, at the sight. He'd once been jealous of Tag, thinking he'd missed his opportunity at true love and happiness, but he knew now that he and Opal weren't meant to be. God had been kind and patient with Mission's pleadings, though He hadn't given him someone to have to hold quite yet.

He'd told God he'd just turned forty-three, just in case the Lord had forgotten. He lifted a glass of lemon-lime spritzer to his lips, his thoughts shouting at him that he wasn't getting any younger.

Loneliness weighed heavier and heavier on him with each passing day where he messaged and messaged with women... who then didn't want to meet. Didn't want to go out.

He'd dated a woman named Rachelle for a couple of months, but things had fizzled quickly between them. Mission wasn't even sure what he was looking for anymore. He just knew he hadn't found it yet.

A nudge at his side pulled him from his thoughts. Tarr Olson, his cabinmate and a good friend, eased up beside him, holding two glasses of bright pink punch. He passed one to Mission.

"You got that look on your face again," Tarr said, lifting

his pink punch to his mouth. "The one that says you're thinking too hard."

Mission simply held his drink. "Maybe I am." He took a sip of his punch and let the sweet, fruity taste linger on his tongue.

"There are plenty of women here," Tarr said.

"Yep." Mission didn't have to elaborate. Tarr had dated one of the cowgirls on the farm earlier this year, but Hattie had left to finish college. He'd gone out with someone else, like it was no big deal. Mission didn't know how to date casually. Heck, he didn't know how to do anything in a casual way.

Mission scanned the room again. The barn burst at the seams, as expected at any Hammond family event. Hunter and Molly danced nearby with their kids sitting at a table out of the way, a deck of cards in front of them.

Tuck and Bobbie Jo acted like they were the pair that had been united in holy matrimony today, as Tuck didn't allow even an inch of room between his body and hers as they danced on the far side of the floor. Bobbie Jo pulled back and grinned up to Tuck, which somehow made Mission's heart twist and ache at the same time.

He simply wanted someone to hold like that. Someone to say something to that would light up her face the way Bobbie Jo's was.

"Look at you," Tarr teased, his Texan drawl thickening. "You're about two seconds away from writing country songs about lost love and broken hearts."

Mission chuckled, though he did love writing country

music songs. "I don't think the world's ready for that kind of misery."

Tarr laughed, then nudged Mission again, this time sweeping his arm across the area in front of them. "Pick someone, Mission. Go dance. It's not a marriage proposal."

Mission growled, something he'd perfected in his four-plus decades of life.

"What about that new vet technician?" Tarr asked. "I danced with her a bit ago, and she seemed nice."

"She's blonde," Mission said, knowing exactly who Tarr meant. "Plus, she doesn't like me much."

"Why wouldn't she like you?" Tarr asked with mock surprise. "You're so sunny and talkative."

Mission rolled his eyes. "I'm ready to go."

"Mm, nope. One dance, Mish, and we can go."

Mission glared at Tarr, who only smiled back at him, drained his punch, and said, "I'm going to go find someone to dance with. When you've put in your dance, you come get me." With that, he walked away, and Mission suddenly understood how irritating it could be to be around a perpetual optimist all the time.

Tuck had told Mission that about Tarr, and he'd been dead-on. Tarr didn't get ruffled at too much, and everything seemed easy for him.

Kristie Higgins crossed in front of him as she got up from a table and moved to put her dishes on one of the return trays. A slight breeze came from the open door, and it caught her blonde hair—Mission so wasn't into blondes—and she reached up to tuck it back away.

She wore a light blue dress that seemed to move around her body like smoky water, and Mission could admit she possessed some prettiness. She didn't work at the farm, but she'd been coming out all summer to work with the horses at Pony Power, which he did too.

But no, she didn't particularly like him.

Mission wasn't sure why, and he wasn't an expert in women or anything, but he could read a room extremely well. He really wanted to leave, so he threw back another swallow of punch, practically slammed down the glass, and pushed away from the post. "Now, or you're never leaving this blasted wedding," he muttered to himself.

As he edged along the dance floor, he told himself to take the murderous glare off his face. He tried to replace it with a smile, but he felt like a dang fool, and that gesture dropped off his face too.

He lingered near the table Kristie had vacated, and she slowed as she saw him standing there. "Heya, Kris," he said casually. Well, as casually as Mission ever did.

She stopped and folded her arms. See? She so didn't like him. "Mission."

For some reason, something tugged strangely in his chest. Dressed in a simple but elegant dress, her blonde hair falling in loose waves around her shoulders, she made everything around her seem brighter somehow.

Her blue eyes narrowed. "Did you want to sit here?"

"No," he said, looking down at the table as the song ended, and the people on the dance floor clapped. He automatically did the same, glancing out at his friends. Some people streamed off the dance floor, while others stayed. They chatted in groups and pairs, and Mission swallowed. His throat stuck together, because he just needed another song to start, and in three minutes, he could be walking out the door.

The man Opal had hired to call the dance belted into the mic, "All right, everyone. It's time to get out on the floor with the bride and groom! They don't want a single inch of spare space, and some of y'all have been hiding in the shadows all night."

In that moment, the shadowy recesses of the barn— where the tables had been pushed to make room for the dance—got flooded with light.

Those on the dance floor started gesturing to those who weren't, and Mission watched as teenagers, children, and adults moved by him and Kris and onto the dance floor.

"Do you want to dance?" The words didn't choke him, and Mission counted that as a win.

Kris's pretty blue eyes widened. "With you?"

"No, with the broom I left back on the farm," he shot back before he could stop himself. A slow smirk tugged at the corner of his mouth, but the way Kris narrowed her eyes erased it.

"Come on!" the caller bellowed into the mic. "Everyone onto the dance floor!"

Mission just needed to get out of here. Fast. Before he could move, Tuck appeared in front of him. "Come on, Mission," he said, reaching for him with a goofy grin on his face. He looked over to Kris. "You too, cowgirl. Come on."

She melted for Tuck, which only annoyed Mission further. Tuck was like a giant star, and he pulled Mission with him onto the dance floor the way gravity pulled everything to the ground.

"Dance with Bobbie Jo, Mission," Tuck said, and he turned to Kris. "Will you dance with me, my lady?"

Kris giggled, which only set Mission's irritation on fire, and he took Bobbie Jo into his arms.

"Howdy, Mission."

"Bobbie Jo." The song started, thankfully, and Tarr had not specified that Mission had to pick someone who was single and who Mission didn't know. So Bobbie Jo so counted, and he was absolutely leaving after this.

He'd moved back and forth with Bobbie Jo a couple of times when Tuck expertly spun her out of Mission's arms, replacing the taken strawberry blonde with an available regular blonde.

Kris.

She stood stiffly in his arms, and her eyes danced away from his and didn't return. Mission managed to move with her, and he wasn't sure why his skin popped and sizzled all up and down his body. The heat of her hands on his shoulders seemed to melt through his shirt, and he wouldn't be surprised if he found red prints on his skin when he got home.

She said nothing, and Mission flailed for something to ask her. He came up with, "Did you finish that technician certification you were workin' on?"

Kris pulled away slightly so she could look at him. Her

blue eyes showed her shock, and her tone mimicked it when she asked, "You knew I was working toward a certificate?"

"Yes, ma'am," he murmured. "Dentistry, I think it was."

"Yes," she said. "It was."

He raised his eyebrows. "Did you finish it?"

"Yes."

He nodded, recognizing the end of a conversation. He didn't even try to think of something else to say, and when the song finally ended, he felt like he'd been in a bright spotlight for a solid year. He backed up the moment he could without being rude, and he nodded to her. "Thank you for dancin' with me."

Kris regarded him for a moment, then she nodded too, turned on her heel, and walked away without so much as a backward glance.

He stood there for a moment, shoving his hands in his pockets, watching her go. Then, with a low growl, he too spun, but he sought the exit. He spotted Tarr on the way, which only made life better. He strode toward him and said, "I danced with someone, and we're leaving."

Tarr blinked at him, another glass of punch in his hand as he flirted with a pretty brunette. "You did? I didn't see you."

"Now," Mission said as he brushed by Tarr, his goal the exit. He didn't know what he'd done to make Kristie Higgins dislike him, and right now, he didn't care.

He just wanted to go home.

* * *

A few days later, Mission found himself heading toward Deacon Hammond's office on the Hammond Family Farm. The cool November air bit at the skin behind his ears and along the back of his neck, and he adjusted the collar of his jacket as he ducked into the red administration building and kept on down the hall. When he reached the door, he wasn't surprised to find it closed.

Deacon kept it closed in the afternoon, as the teens and kids came for their equine therapy and horseback riding lessons, which meant Mission had to stop and knock.

"Come on in," Deacon's voice called from inside.

Mission pushed open the door and stepped into the office, the familiar scent of leather and wood filling the space. Deacon sat behind his desk, a stack of papers in front of him, but he looked up with a smile—well, as much as Deacon smiled—as Mission entered.

"Hey, Mission." Deacon jumped to his feet and came around the desk, extending his hand. "Good to see you."

"Good to see you too," Mission replied, shaking Deacon's hand before sitting in the chair opposite his desk.

"Thanks for coming over." Deacon settled back into his seat, folding his hands in front of him.

"I was just out in the stable." Mission hooked his thumb like he didn't mean the family stable. Mission had been working at the family farm for so long, he did chores on both sides of the line: for the Hammond family and for Pony Power. Today, he'd happened to be going over the schedule with Matt for the holidays, as Thanksgiving loomed on the horizon.

"I wanted to talk to you about something."

Mission's brows lifted in curiosity, and his pulse jackhammered in his chest a couple of times. He didn't think he'd get fired, as he couldn't quite taste that vibe, but something hung in the air. He'd felt like this before, when his life had blown up and he'd landed in the softest, best place possible—this farm.

Deacon cleared his throat, his expression turning serious, and that only increased Mission's nerves. "You've been with the farm for what, seventeen years now?"

"Eighteen come February," Mission said, still wondering where this conversation would end up. Did they have a cap on the number of years a cowboy could work here? Where would he even go next?

Everything about the Hammond Family Farm had saved him, and Mission couldn't imagine a life anywhere else. At least not a life worth living.

Deacon smiled. "That's a long time. You've been a good cowboy, Mission. Reliable. Hardworking. We've always been able to count on you."

Mission shifted in his seat, his mind spinning in a dozen different directions. "I appreciate that, Deac."

Deacon leaned forward slightly, his eyes locking on Mission's. "Matt's planning to retire soon. Maybe sometime next year. He's been a great leader for almost twenty-five years, and we're going to need someone to take over as foreman when he steps down."

Mission sat up a little straighter. "You're looking for a new foreman?"

Deacon nodded, his expression somewhat hooded. "Matt's been talking about it for a while, but he's actually serious now." He tapped a stack on his desk. "He turned in his paperwork, and he's ready to train someone to take over. We've been thinking about who would be the right fit for the job, and...well, I think that person is you."

Mission blinked, his mind racing to process what Deacon had just said. Him? The new foreman?

He'd never expected this, and his past shouted at him, told him he absolutely could not accept this job. Sure, he'd been with the farm for nearly two decades, but he'd enjoyed his role as one of the cowhands, the man who'd do whatever was asked of him, head down, mouth shut, no questions asked.

Nothing to see here.

"You want me to be the foreman?" Mission's voice barely broke a whisper.

Deacon smiled, nodding. When Mission didn't return his smile, Deacon turned serious again. He tilted his head, obviously feasting on the nervous, negative vibes pouring from Mission.

"You've earned it, Mission. You've put in the time, you know this farm inside and out, and you've got the respect of the other hands. Matt's ready to start training you, if you're interested."

Mission's first instinct was to leave. Flee. Get out. He took a breath and anchored himself to the chair in Deacon's office. "I'm...I'm honored," he said. "Truly. I don't know what to say."

He wasn't sure what Deacon knew, as Mission had joined the farm so long ago, the man in front of him had been a ten-year-old.

"I'm sensing a *but*," Deacon said.

Mission folded his arms, but he couldn't get out of this conversation. "I've never wanted a leadership role."

"You'd be great at it." Deacon leaned back in his chair and copied Mission's stance. "You don't have to accept right now. Take some time to think about it. But I think you'd be great at it, Mission."

Mission nodded, his mind still reeling. "I'll think about it," he said, because he could at least do that. What he really needed to do was call his grandfather and then get down on his knees. God sure had surprised him with this, as Mission had not seen this coming.

Matt retiring, sure. Mission getting the foreman job?

Absolutely not.

Deacon stood, and Mission got to his feet too. They shook hands over the desk, and Deacon asked, "You're still coming to Thanksgiving dinner next week?"

"Yes, sir," Mission said.

Deacon's smile appeared for a moment. "You don't have to call me sir." He shifted some papers on his desk for no reason. "Is your granddad coming?"

"Yes," Mission said. "Travis and Poppy know." The Thatchers were hosting all the Hammonds at the farm next door this year, and Mission sure did love Travis, his wife Poppy, and their kids.

"Sure," Deacon said. "Well, let me know when you know, or if you have any questions."

Mission reached up and pulled his hat down as he nodded. Then he left the office, stepping out into the cool November air with a nest of snakes in his gut.

"Foreman," he scoffed. "Real funny, Lord."

There was no way he could be foreman.

Not again.

twenty-one

Travis Thatcher hurried through the gate from the farm to the backyard, then he took the back steps up to the deck three at a time. He hated running late, but farm work couldn't be predicted. The scent of freshly baked bread and salty brown gravy met his nose as he pulled open the back door on the farmhouse where he lived with his wife and three kids.

"I'm so sorry," he gushed at Poppy, the auburn-haired woman who'd stolen his heart and taken very, very good care of it these past seventeen years.

"You're late," she said.

"Your goats got out," he threw back at her, attaching a smile to the words.

Poppy sighed and shook her head. "What else is new?"

Travis stepped over to the sink, where she stood peeling cucumbers. He touched a kiss to her cheek and pulled the faucet over toward him so he could wash up. "What am I doing when I'm cleaned up?"

"I need you to carve the meats," Poppy said. "Steele's only three minutes out, and the Hammonds should be here any second."

"Okay," Travis said, sudsing up quickly. "We don't have to have the food ready to go the moment everyone walks in."

Poppy pursed her lips in response, her way of saying, *Yes, we do* without saying it.

Outside the window, the sky blazed in various shades of blue, in a unique way that made him pause and thank God for the blessings in his life. The newly remodeled farmhouse stood strong and solid around him, filled with the scent of good food, good company, and amazing faith.

"Where are the kids?"

"Welcoming committee," Poppy said, finally smiling at him. She moved away to arrange the veggie tray, and Trav dried his hands quickly and turned to the island he and Tarr Olson had installed in the house only a couple of months ago.

Poppy had lived here for years before Trav had found her and fallen in love with her, and they'd been slowly updating everything from irrigation systems, to goat pens, to bedrooms, since. And this summer, the house had finally been finished.

"He's here!" Annie yelled from the front door, which immediately slammed again. Trav chuckled as he picked up the carving knife and went after the ham first. Steele was Poppy's biological son and Trav's stepson, and he'd gone to work for Gerty on her farm at the beginning of the year.

He'd really settled down, something Trav thanked God for every single time he prayed. He hadn't been happy here, and while he did basically the same work on the slightly bigger farm ten miles down the road, he sure seemed better now. Happier.

In fact, the front door opened just as Trav laid the final piece of sliced ham on the platter, and in walked Steele, surrounded by his siblings. They all laughed, and then Clementine started telling him about Dorothy, the old mule that still came running every time anyone went outside.

Steele glowed now, and Trav dang near dropped to his knees in gratitude. For a while there, he and Poppy had thought they'd lose him. To what, Trav didn't know and he hadn't wanted to find out.

He looked past the teenagers haranguing him and grinned at Travis. "Hey, Daddy," he said. His gaze swept the enormous kitchen, and pure joy burst from Steele when he saw his mother. "Momma."

He ran the last few steps to her and engulfed her in a hug. She laughed with him, and Trav's heart seemed to grow and grow and grow as it filled and filled and filled with love.

"Clementine," he said as the girl reached for a roll that had been placed in a basket with a pumpkin-y cloth. "Not yet."

His fifteen-year-old pulled her hand back, a sheepish look coming immediately to her face. "Sorry, Daddy."

"When are we eatin'?" Hawk whined as he climbed up on a barstool. "There's so much food here, and I'm starving."

"Sure you are," Trav said as he turned to the sink to wash

the knife of the candy-coating on the ham. "The Hammonds will be here soon. Why don't you guys take your welcoming committee back outside for them?"

He turned back to his kids just as Annie, his mischievous thirteen-year-old put something in her mouth. "Annie," he growled.

"It was a grape tomato," she said.

"I want a grape tomato," Hawk said. Trav supposed he could be grateful his kids would eat vegetables, but right now, he just wanted them away from the feast.

"I'll go welcome the Hammonds," Clementine said, and she turned and headed for the front door.

Trav watched her retreating back, dark clouds of unrest billowing in his soul. Of course Clementine would volunteer to go welcome everyone to the farm. She and Ryder Hammond had something going on between them—and had for years.

What, Trav wasn't quite sure. Poppy talked to their daughter about boys, and dating, and all that. Constantly. She kept Trav updated on what he needed to know, and they'd had a couple of formal sit-downs with the three of them to make sure Clementine understood she was only fifteen years old, and the age of child brides had passed long ago.

Heck, Ryder was only seventeen and in the middle of his senior year.

Trav had no idea what the boy would do with his life, but he suspected it would have something to do with the high-rise buildings in downtown Denver. Mike Hammond ran the worth-billions family company right now, and he'd only been at the helm for a few years.

But Hunter, Ryder's daddy, had done it for almost two decades. None of the Hammonds who lived in Wyoming seemed interested in coming to Colorado and doing anything with HMC, and Trav knew from his decades-long friendship with Hunt that they wanted the CEO to be a Hammond.

And with Mike's son only pushing two, the next logical choice would be Ryder.

"Sweetheart, you can't carve a turkey with your eyes," Poppy said as she came to his side. "Where's your mind?"

"On Clementine goin' to welcome Ryder to the farm."

Poppy looked toward the front door too, and Trav sliced the knife through the turkey to get his job done. "Hawk, Annie, go outside with Clementine. The Hammonds will be here any second."

"Yes, Momma," Annie said as she turned away from the counter, but Hawk whined, "I'm *starving*, Momma."

Poppy gave him a fierce glare—and a cucumber boat— and said, "Eat that. Now, go on."

Hawk went, and Trav loved his kids from the inside out. He truly did. He simply worried over them too. Annie couldn't seem to focus on school to do better than a C+ in any subject, and Clementine had her head in the clouds if a boy even crossed her mind.

Hawk, who'd just turned ten years old, was probably his best bet for the one who'd take over this farm one day, as he ran everywhere he went, and he could be kept happy as long as they didn't run out of food.

Poppy leaned into him for just a moment, her body relaxing against his. "They're okay."

"She's kissing him," Trav muttered back as Steele joined them at the island.

"You need any help, Momma?" he asked.

Poppy straightened. "Yes, baby. Go put the dogs away. With everyone coming, it's just too much."

Steele met Trav's eyes for a moment, and then nodded. He left to do what his mother had asked, and Poppy turned to Travis. "Kissing is pretty innocent."

"Not when the boy is two years older than you," Trav said, moving from the white meat to the dark. Thankfully, he and Poppy couldn't continue their old argument, as the door opened, and it seemed like all the life, all the oxygen, the entire party, entered when Hunter and Molly did.

Tucker strode in after them, and he had his hand secured in Bobbie Jo Hanks's. Trav put down the knife, wiped his hands on a towel, and went to greet them.

"Hey, Trav." Hunter pulled him into a hug, then moved to Poppy to do the same. "Thanks so much for having us for lunch."

"Of course," Trav said. Poppy loved to cook and bake, and they'd been feeding cowboys from the Hammond Family Farm for years and years. One of his best friends—Cord Behr—wasn't coming this year, and Trav's heart wailed for only a moment.

Cord had Jane now, and while all of Jane's brothers were coming here for Thanksgiving dinner this year, she and her family were going to Gerty and Mike's.

"Tuck," Travis said, stepping in to hug him. "It's good to see you again, brother." He grinned as he stepped back. "Bobbie Jo." He tipped his hat at her.

"Hi, Travis," she said, shooting a glance over to Tuck that said a lot. "Thanks for having me."

"Yeah, I'd heard you two started dating." He grinned and grinned, because while he didn't live and work at the farm next door anymore, he heard all the news, all the gossip, everything. And Tucker had liked Bobbie Jo for a long time now.

He turned and gestured to the house, which had been decorated for autumn and Thanksgiving all month. The dining room held two long tables, already set, with golden candlesticks standing among fall foliage. "Come on in."

They moved by him, but Trav stayed near the door, as Tarr, Mission, and Deacon had just walked in. He opened his arms to all three of them, catching smiles on all of their faces as the four of them squished together in a hug. "Welcome, guys," he said with a laugh. "Happy Thanksgiving."

"Happy Thanksgiving," Tarr said, and Mission and Deacon nodded along. That didn't surprise Trav at all. Mission and Deacon generally didn't stand out in a crowd by speaking up. Neither smiled much. But Tarr...Tarr was the complete opposite of that, and he laughed heartily as he moved over to Poppy.

"Hey, hey," he said as he hugged Trav's wife. "I deliberately skipped breakfast just so I could eat more of your good cookin'."

Poppy grinned and laughed, because she loved being complimented on her cooking. Who wouldn't?

Stepping out onto the porch, Trav found all the kids. Hawk ran in circles around Clay, Hunter's youngest. The boys laughed, and Trav grinned at them. The older kids—Ryder, Lisa, and Charlotte had gathered with Trav's teens, and his smile faltered when he found Clementine brushing something off Ryder's collar in an intimate way.

No one in their huddle seemed to think anything of it, but the starry-eyed look on Ryder's face told Trav all he needed to know.

Clementine then reached back and tightened her ponytail, flicking a glance to the porch. When she saw him there, she shaded her eyes. "Is Momma ready?"

"Yep," Trav called to her. "C'mon, y'all. Come inside and find a place to sit."

The kids started moving into the house as the crunching of tires came down the lane. Trav grinned and waved at Matthew Whettstein and his wife Gloria, who rode in the passenger seat of the truck. Another vehicle followed, and Trav went down the steps after all the kids had gone up them.

Gloria got out of the truck carrying a pie, and Trav took a couple more steps and took it from her. "You didn't have to bring pie. I'm pretty sure Poppy made ten." He grinned at her and swept a kiss along her cheek.

"Cosette made it," Gloria said. "Which I'm sure everyone will appreciate." She moved to close her door and receive her girls from the truck.

"Annie and Clementine are inside," Trav said to Alma and

Roxanne. Roxy, the oldest, was the same age as Ryder—a senior in high school. Trav knew she'd be going to Colorado State to do equine studies, as she had a real good head on her shoulders and got good grades in school.

"Thanks, Trav," she said with a smile. Alma was the same age as Annie, with Clementine in the middle of them all, and Trav had stood outside the tent with those four girls in it in his backyard and listened to them talk and giggle in the dark. It had fed his father's soul, and he loved Matt's girls.

Keith Whettstein, Matt's oldest from his first marriage, came around the front of his truck with a, "Howdy, Trav," before he opened the door for his wife, Lindsay.

"Howdy," Trav said to them. He turned to Matt, grinning, shook his hand, and pulled him into a hug. "Hey, brother."

"Happy Thanksgiving," Matt said.

Britt and Lars also dropped down from Keith's truck, and Trav simply looked at them with new eyes. He'd known them as children, and to see them all grown up, married, living amazing lives...they weren't even his kids, and yet, they were.

Enough to make his eyes misty, for sure.

"Happy Thanksgiving, Travis," Britt said, not an ounce of stutter in her voice. She wore a cream-colored dress with falling autumn leaves all over it, and she carried a scented candle in her hands.

"All right, y'all," Poppy called from the doorway, her voice carrying over the laughter and conversation. "It's time to eat. Trav, come on, baby."

Travis let Keith and Lindsay, Britt and Lars, and Matt and Gloria go ahead of him. He lingered outside for just a moment, because it would take several minutes to get everyone settled at the table, and he wouldn't incur the wrath of his wife if he took ten seconds to pray.

He took a deep breath, the cool air filling his lungs, and closed his eyes in a quick prayer of gratitude. "Lord," he whispered as he tipped his head back and looked up into the purest blue sky imaginable. His cowboy hat slid from his head, and he didn't care one whit.

"Thank you for this family, for this life, and for bringing everyone here safely. We are so blessed, and I pray You'll continue to guide us, protect us, and fill our lives with Your love and grace. Amen."

"Daddy!" Hawk called. "What you doin'?"

Trav looked to the porch, where his son stood, and he chuckled as he bent to swipe his hat off the lawn. Thankfully, it hadn't snowed and stuck yet, but Trav knew those days would be here soon enough. "Nothing, bud," he said as he hurried toward Hawk and the house.

"Momma wants you to lead us in the gratitude garland, and she won't let me have a marker unless you help me."

Trav laughed as he went up the front steps now the way he had the back—several at a time. He swooped Hawk into his arms and said, "Well, let's get goin'. We don't want Momma to be mad at us."

He'd forgotten about the gratitude garland, but he loved the white strips of paper Poppy would have ready. They'd all write down the things they were grateful for, link the strips together into a chain, and revisit them every day from now until the New Year.

"There he is," Poppy said when Trav entered the farm-house. Sure enough, she had the permanent markers and pure white papers ready. "Tell 'em, baby."

He grinned around at everyone who'd come to celebrate this Thanksgiving with him and his family, and he let the silence settle on them, hoping they could each feel the love and spirit he did.

Then he said, "Okay, the gratitude garland is real simple...."

twenty-two

"Yeah." Tuck let loose with a loud string of laughter as he drove along the highway toward Boulder. "That's great, Jem."

"Gabe approved the contract, finally," Jem said next, while the remnants of Tuck's laughter still echoed over the phone line. "We'll get it signed tonight and sent to you."

Tuck's pulse vibrated in a strange way, and he paused for a moment, trying to hear the word of the Lord. Instead of getting yet another confirmation, Tuck had the distinct thought that he'd already received his answer, and he didn't need to keep questioning it.

In fact, God didn't want to have to tell him over and over —and *over*—about something that He'd already revealed.

So Tuck said, "Great, thanks. I'll get it signed and sent back."

A loud squeal came through the line, and Rosie said,

"Thank you so much, Tuck. I'm so excited we'll get to work together."

Tuck grinned, because it felt good to be wanted. "Yeah," he said. "You're just excited to get out of the Wyoming winter and go to Texas in January."

"That too," she said with a laugh.

"How's the search for land going?" Jem asked. "Because you know, there's lots of that up here...."

Tuck blew out his breath, because the search for land hadn't been going as well as he'd have liked. "It's going okay," he said.

"Your momma and daddy are up here," Jem said, and didn't Tuck know it. Not only that, but his parents lived in Coral Canyon alone. Uncle Wes and Aunt Bree did too, while their three children lived elsewhere.

Most of Tuck's cousins from Uncle Cy and Uncle Ames had stayed in the area, but being close to family had been hung in Tuck's mind, and it would not leave. He knew God had put it there, and Tuck had been struggling with the Lord over it.

"I've got some cousins up there," Tuck said, though it sounded like a flimsy excuse even to his own ears. Uncle Colt and Aunt Annie lived in Coral Canyon too, and his parents had help if they needed it.

And as they'd been getting older and older, they definitely needed it.

Thus, Tuck had been getting stung over and over—and over—about where he should be long-term. It felt right to build a training facility in Ivory Peaks on some days, and others, Tuck felt like he could buy an RV and he and Bobbie Jo could travel as easily as he did alone.

And at times like these, the idea of moving north to Coral Canyon and building his training facility there felt like the right thing to do. Then *he* could help his parents as they continued to age.

Jane and Cord had planted their roots pretty deeply here, as had Hunter and Deacon. That only left Tuck, and he strongly disliked how things seemed to hinge on him.

"All right," he said to Jem. "I'll get it signed, and you know what?"

"What?" Jem and Rosie asked together.

"Send me some listings up there. I've been looking for at least fifty acres here." Tuck shifted in his seat, and he thought of Tag and how the man had shifted and shimmied as he tried to contain his nerves at his wedding.

Tuck felt the same way right now. "Seventy-five is better."

"No problem," Jem drawled, as if he'd been looking for land in Tuck's behalf. "That's a lot for a training facility."

"Yeah, well, it's going to be a multi-purpose piece of land."

"You'll live on it?"

"Yes," Tuck said, and he cleared his throat. "Bobbie Jo wants a goat farm."

Jem started to chuckle, the sound growing into a full-blown laugh as the seconds went by. For some reason, it irritated Tuck, though he'd been open and honest about his feelings for Bobbie Jo to anyone who asked.

He glanced over to the two dozen red roses, the picnic

basket, and the professional wrapped gift riding shotgun. "I have to go," he said into Jem's laughter.

"Daddy, be nice," Rosie said. "It's sweet that Tuck likes Bobbie Jo."

"He more than likes her, baby."

"I'm still on the phone," Tuck practically yelled, and he rolled his eyes, and then his whole head. "I'm hanging up."

"Great," Rosie said. "Now he's hanging up on us. 'Bye, Tuck! Thank you so much!"

"Yes, thanks," Jem said. "We'll be in touch soon."

"Yeah," Tuck said, and he let Jem end the call while he bickered with his daughter about how he *was* being nice.

Tuck gripped the steering wheel as he thought about Jem's reaction. "No wonder you haven't mentioned the goat farm to anyone else yet."

And he hadn't. Not to Hunt, who'd been going with him to look at plots of land. Not Mike, who he'd spent last week with as he acted as a second assistant during a very busy time at HMC.

Heck, he hadn't even told Bobbie Jo yet. She knew he'd decided to take on Rosie as a client, but he hadn't even mentioned anything about the training facility yet, let alone how Tuck was imagining a piece of land where he walked out his front door to the training facility, and she could walk out the back to the goat farm.

"So there's that to get out," he muttered to himself as he made a turn to go deeper into town. "And you want to throw Coral Canyon at her too?" He shook his head. "That's not gonna go over well, cowboy."

Bobbie Jo needed to be fed changes and possibilities in small bites, which she then chewed on for a while before she came to peace with them. She lived life at a slower pace than Tuck, though she was the one living and working in the city.

He'd already started planning her birthday weekend in San Antonio, as he and Rosie would be down in Texas training when Bobbie Jo turned thirty. In this instance, money could solve a lot of problems, and since Tuck had some major talent in managing a person's travel and accommodations, he'd started working on this for Bobbie Jo.

"Lotsa secrets," he said to himself as he turned down Bobbie Jo's street. She'd called that morning to say she was sick and wouldn't be going to work. She'd cancelled their date before lunchtime, but that had only spurred Tuck to find a way to stay in without being overbearing.

He pulled into her driveway alongside her SUV, and he gathered everything he'd gotten for tonight, checked his phone for a delivery time on the food, and got out of his truck. "Seven minutes," he muttered to himself as he rounded the hood of the truck and jogged up to her front door.

He knocked instead of ringing the doorbell, and he leaned in and said, "It's Tucker, for Bobbie Jo."

Her roommate—Jenny, the one he'd only met a handful of times—pulled open the door and put one hand on her bony hip. She'd obviously been home from work for a while, as she wore a pair of shorts with bright red hearts all over them and a light blue tank top. He smiled at her when he wanted to tell her it was *December*.

"She's not feeling well," Jenny said instead of hello.

"I know." Tuck grinned even wider and reached into the grocery sack he'd brought with him. "I got you...some Nerds ropes." He brandished two of them and watched as Jenny's face lit up like a Christmas tree.

She took them and stepped back, and Tuck wasn't going to be ashamed for using candy to get past the gatekeepers at Bobbie Jo's house. He moved into the house, and Jenny closed the door behind him. A small, formal living room sat to his left, somewhere his mother or grandmother would've put a piano and a love seat, maybe a couple of chairs, so they could entertain guests without inviting them all the way back into the main living area of the house.

The three women who lived here barely used this room, as it only held a single, lumpy couch Tuck had tried sitting on once. It only took once to realize what a massive mistake he'd made.

He went down the short hall past the formal living room and the coat closet, where the house then opened up to a kitchen, a dining area, and the living room. A baking show blared on the TV and he nodded to Cara and raised his eyebrows.

"Bobbie Jo," Cara said as she looked over to the other couch. "Tuck's here."

"Tuck's here?" Bobbie Jo sounded like she'd swallowed a toad, and she lifted herself up to show him she hadn't moved from the couch all day. Surprise widened her eyes, and a flush climbed into her face. "What are you doing here?"

She sat all the way up, dislodging the blanket on her legs, and ran her fingers through her hair. "I swear I cancelled."

"You did." He lifted the flowers and basket. "I ordered dinner for you ladies, and it'll be here in five minutes. I don't have to stay, but I thought I could set up a picnic for y'all." He looked at Cara, who smiled kindly at him.

Jenny walked past him to the dining room table and started moving items there. "You can set up the picnic right here, cowboy," she said around a mouthful of candy.

Bobbie Jo got to her feet, and she wore a pair of dark green sweatpants with a cream-colored sweatshirt with a watercolor turkey on it. "A picnic?" Stars shone in her eyes as she came around the couch. "What did you order?"

"I hope it's that double-pickle chicken sandwich," Cara said. She set aside what looked like a big basket of yarn and got to her feet too. "Is it that, Tucker?"

"No, ma'am." He nodded and smiled at her. "It's winter-time, and I figured everyone in the world likes soup in the winter." He scanned the three women, all of them looking at him. "And bread?"

"There it is," Jenny said.

Bobbie Jo grinned at him as she drew closer, and while he'd been with her around her roommates, he wasn't sure he could simply draw her into his arms and kiss her. She was sick, besides, so he didn't really want to get those germs.

"You ordered from Toasted Crumb." She snaked her hands up his chest and around to the back of his neck, and the most natural thing for him was to take her into his arms and hold her close like they might start slow-dancing.

"Yes," he murmured. "You mentioned you liked their

hearty winter stew, and it just came onto the menu this week."

She gazed up at him, and Tuck tried not to simply slide into her gaze and fall all the way in love with her. "I said that...." She titled her head. "Last winter, Tuck."

He had no idea when she'd said it. He just knew she liked the winter stew at Toasted Crumb, and he figured if he couldn't take her to get something delicious to eat, he could have it sent here.

Cara cleared her throat, and Tuck stepped away from Bobbie Jo. Heat rose through his body, and he ducked his head as he moved past her to get the table set up as a picnic. He took out the red-and-white checkered tablecloth and spread it over the cleared surface. Then he set out matching napkins, but he left the plastic cups and utensils in the basket. They wouldn't need those, and he went into the kitchen to get a vase for the flowers.

He cut the rubber band on the roses and arranged them in the vase, then turned to set those in the middle of the table. Jenny sat on the arm of the couch, eating the last of her second Nerds rope, and Cara and Bobbie Jo had disappeared.

The doorbell rang, and Jenny looked at him like he could earn his keep and be the butler. "It's probably the food," he said, and he took the opportunity to move away from her. He wasn't sure why she didn't seem to like him, and according to Bobbie Jo, she liked him fine.

He opened the door to find two huge paper bags waiting on the porch, and he called, "Thanks, man," to the guy already walking back to his car.

"Sure thing," the delivery driver called, and Tuck stepped out of the house to collect the food. Back in the kitchen, Cara joined him and helped him un-bag the bread, the soups, and the salads he'd ordered, and he carefully set his aside to take with him.

He'd been hoping he might get an invite to stay and eat dinner, but it wouldn't kill him to drive away and leave Bobbie Jo to eat and go to bed early. *Driving away to Texas might kill you though*, he thought, and Tuck didn't know what to do with things like this when they crept into his mind.

"Bobbie Jo went to change," Cara said.

"She didn't need to do that." He cut a look over to her out of the corner of his eye. "Plus, I got her something to change into."

"Of course you did." Cara smiled and went into the kitchen and opened the fridge.

Tuck picked up the gift he'd brought, and with everything else out of the way, he just needed to hand this off, breathe in the scent of Bobbie Jo's hair, and he could be on his way. He turned toward the mouth of the hallway that led down to the bedrooms and found her coming toward him.

She'd kept the pants but put on a long-sleeved tee with the words "Feeling Good" on it, and she'd pulled her hair up into a ponytail. "I got you this," he said, extending the present toward her.

She took it, her smile genuine and bright. "Who wrapped this for you?"

"I'm offended," he teased.

She flipped the present over and looked up at him. "Borgman's." Her eyebrows went up. "What is this?"

"Open it."

She pulled back the purple paper to reveal a new pajama set, and Tuck sure hoped the clothes were the right size. "You said you just want to be comfortable when you're sick, and you barely get dressed. So." He nodded to the pjs. "I figured a new pair wouldn't hurt."

Her gaze blazed at him, and Tuck sure wished she was well and they were alone, because he'd sure like to kiss her right now.

"These have goats on them," she said, glancing back at the pjs and then to him.

"You're very observant, Doctor Hanks," he teased. He pulled her close again, this time sliding his lips across her check so he could position his mouth at her ear. "I sure do like you, Bobbie Jo. I hope you feel better quickly."

Tuck stepped back, ready to go. He'd stooped to get his picnic basket and his roast beef sandwich with the chorizo sausage soup. "Okay, so—"

"You're not going to stay?" Bobbie Jo asked.

Tuck didn't need to make her beg, and he straightened and looked at her, then Cara and Jenny, both of whom had sat down at the table and started eating, apparently knowing which food had been ordered for them.

"I can stay," he said, and he told himself he'd call his momma on the way home and find out how he could stave off a cold before it truly got hold in him.

He needed to talk to her and Daddy about buying land in Coral Canyon anyway.

"Come on, then," Bobbie Jo said, and Tuck shelved all his thoughts about the rodeo training facility, buying land in another state, and anything to do with goat farms.

He couldn't talk about any of it in front of Bobbie Jo's roommates anyway, and he just wanted to enjoy his soup-er picnic with her.

They could talk later, though he told himself not to spend too much time waiting for the perfect opportunity. He, of all people, knew such a thing didn't exist, and he'd be better off to get everything out so Bobbie Jo could run through it all.

Soon, he promised himself—and her. *Really soon.*

twenty-three

Bobbie Jo hadn't realized laying on the couch in her own home could be so comforting. Of course, she'd stuffed herself with winter stew and sourdough bread—with plenty of butter—and then curled into Tuck's warm body.

He'd covered her with a blanket, and she kept her eyes closed as he stroked her hair absently. He'd moved in a pattern for a bit, and then a message would come in on his phone, and he'd text for a minute.

She knew he was talking to his parents, as his mother had called, and he'd said he'd text with her instead.

"Did you sign the contract with Rosie?" she whispered. The TV played something Cara had put on, but then her roommates had gone down the hall to their bedrooms, leaving Tuck and Bobbie Jo alone in the family room.

"They're sending it," he murmured back. "I spoke to them on the way here tonight."

Bobbie Jo didn't know what else to say. She sensed that Tuck had plenty on his mind, but he'd kept a lot of it to himself. "Will you talk to me?" she asked.

He moved, and Bobbie Jo opened her eyes and tilted her head back to look up at him. "I put my phone away," he said. "What's on your mind?"

"I want to know what's on yours," she said.

Tuck had removed his cowboy hat, and she found him equally as attractive without it as she did with it. He looked away from her, then sighed as he swept his gaze across the living room.

"I'm meeting them in San Antonio the first week of January," he said. "There's a great training facility there, and...I want to build one here." He pulled in a sharp breath. "Or somewhere."

Bobbie Jo's nerves danced at her, and she took several long seconds to absorb what he'd said. "You want to build a training facility...here?"

Tuck looked down at her, and he definitely seemed darker now than usual. His half-dark, half-light features turned deep in the winter night, with only a single lamp to illuminate his features.

"Can you just close your eyes again?"

Bobbie Jo did what he wanted, and he stroked her hair off her forehead again.

"I'm just going to say it all, and I want you to think about it."

"Okay," she whispered.

"I've been looking at plots of land here in Ivory Peaks," he said, his voice as quiet as before. No matter what Tuck did, it happened with intensity, and he never said anything that didn't hide some deeper truth beneath the words.

So a plot of land? He was looking to build a training facility here in Ivory Peaks, so he could be...permanent here in Ivory Peaks.

"I want a big place," he said next. "Where we can build a big house so you can have all the dogs you want, and I—"

"You're the one who wants dogs," Bobbie Jo said, her eyes opening and looking up at her handsome boyfriend.

He grinned at her. "So we can have a big house where I get all the dogs I want, and I can walk down the lane to the training facility to work with my clients. Heck, it could be big enough that they could live on-site."

"Like your family farm."

"Sort of," he said. "But less alfalfa, no crops at all in fact, and in the back, instead of all those cowboy cabins, there's this really amazing goat farm."

Bobbie Jo sucked in a breath. The picture he'd just painted had to be a result of a frenzied, drugged-up mind. She *had* just taken a pretty major decongestant.

"That will take a while to build, obviously," Tuck said, his voice still set on Serious, and Bobbie Jo let her eyes drift closed again. She needed quiet and space to think through this. "And I'm just going to throw it all out there, and then we can talk about it."

Bobbie Jo nodded faintly against his lap.

"God's been real cagey about where this place should be. I've become more and more...aware of how old my parents are getting, and I've been having these...pulls to Coral Canyon...." His voice trailed off then, and Bobbie Jo let the silence drape over the both of them.

Tuck wasn't exactly impulsive, but he definitely had more spontaneous genes than Bobbie Jo. Her brain whirred and whirred, and all she could see in her mind's eye was a beautiful, two-story, white farmhouse with loads of gorgeous land surrounding it.

She didn't see a commute to a train station, and then a ride into the city. She wasn't wearing a white lab coat as she put in long hours each day. The blue sky shone above her, with plenty of room to see the stars at night, and spread picnic blankets over emerald green grass whenever she and Tuck got the urge to do so.

A smile formed on her face, and Tuck moved his hand to cover it lightly. "What are you smilin' about?"

She started to laugh, and she pushed against his hand to get it away from her mouth. "You'll have to wash that," she said as she giggled around the words. She pushed herself up to sit beside him, and she turned to face him.

His smile, which usually lasted a lot longer than hers, slipped first, and oh, Bobbie Jo didn't like that. Hers straightened too, and she reached over and ran her fingers through his hair now. "You're heavy," she said. "Carrying heavy things."

He looked back at her, then nodded, and dropped his eyes to his now-empty hands. "Yeah, these feel like big life decisions, and you know what? This is embarrassing, but I haven't had to do this very often."

He glanced over to her and then looked away again. "I graduated from high school, which was easy for me. I knew I wasn't college-bound, that I wanted to be in the rodeo. I did that for a while, and I wasn't bad, but it was clear I wasn't going to be a big winner. But since I was entrenched in that world, it wasn't hard to find someone to manage. That world is so fluid, you know?"

No, Bobbie Jo didn't know, but Tuck didn't let his mouth run away from him like this very often, and she simply wanted him to continue.

"And I met Tarr, and he'd just lost his manager to marriage, if you can believe that." He scoffed, smiled, and shook his head all at the same time. "We rode together for five years, and I'm still really bummed that he decided not to go back to the saddle."

"I know you are, sweetheart." Bobbie Jo didn't express her feelings nearly as well as Tuck, but the term of endearment had come out of her mouth easily. "But you've got Rosie now, and she's going to be a huge star—thanks to you."

"We'll see." He smiled over to her then, and while it was definitely Tuck's smile, this one held sadness in the upturned corners of his mouth. He reached for her hand and cradled it in both of his. "Your turn to tell me what's on your mind."

"I'm...thinking I really liked how you used the pronoun 'we' in some of those sentences." Bobbie Jo leaned toward him, and Tuck closed the distance between them too.

Then he pulled back quickly. "Wait." His eyes dropped to her mouth. "You're sick."

Bobbie Jo started to straighten again, but Tuck's hand shot out and slid up the back of her neck. "Worth the risk," he muttered, and when he touched his lips to hers, Bobbie Jo swore she heard a choir of angels singing.

She also suddenly understood how much easier it was to say what truly lingered in her mind when she didn't have to look him straight in the eyes. She didn't kiss him for long, and she broke the kiss and tucked her forehead against his throat. The faint bumping of his pulse touched her temple, and she whispered, "I'm scared, Tuck."

"Of what?"

"This feels really fast to me," she said. "And you're talking about completely changing your plans. Doing something I've never heard you talk about doing. And for what?" She did lift her head then. "For me?"

"Yeah," he said, searching her eyes. "For you. What's wrong with that?"

"It's...." She'd never had anyone sacrifice much for her before, and Bobbie Jo didn't feel worthy of it.

"Do you love your job at HMC so much that you wouldn't quit?" he asked.

"No," she whispered. He'd said a lot tonight, in only a few minutes, with just a few sentences. Perhaps she could do the same. "Tuck, I only took that job, well, there's a few reasons."

He opened his arm and pulled her against his side. "Tell me," he murmured.

"One, that's the reason I came to Colorado, and I wanted

to prove to my parents that I hadn't just run away because we lost the farm."

Tuck said nothing, but the comforting press of him beside her told her he'd heard her.

"Two, I didn't want to stay at the farm without you," she whispered. "It felt too...scary. Too big. Too...something."

"Okay."

"And three, I did go to school for five years to get my degree, and I figured I might as well use it at least once in my life."

He chuckled, his warm, big hand sliding up and down her forearm in a nice way. "Would any of those reasons keep you from quitting?"

Bobbie Jo took a moment to think about it. Really think. "I suppose not," she finally said.

"Then maybe you could come to Texas with me and Rosie."

Bobbie Jo shot up then, her eyes wide and already searching his. He grinned at her and said, "Or maybe not."

"That's in less than a month."

"Sure is," he said.

Her heartbeat thrashed around in her chest, because she couldn't up and leave this house, her job, everything in less than a month. It sounded like something desperate people did, and Bobbie Jo wasn't desperate.

Tuck reached out and smoothed her hair back, tucking it behind her ear. "Will you break-up with me when I leave?"

"Why would I?"

"You told me you wouldn't do the long-distance thing again."

She had said that. But she couldn't even consider breaking up with him. "I guess things change," she said.

"People change," Tuck said with a big sigh. "I don't know what I'm doing, Bobbie Jo. I really don't. My momma just told me tonight it's time to stop treading water."

"What does that mean?"

Instead of explaining it, Tuck reached under her thigh and pulled out his phone. "Lord only knows." He gave her a wry look as he handed her the device. "I'd love to see what you think."

Tuck didn't have a lock code on his phone, and Bobbie Jo tapped over to his texts easily. He had been talking to his momma tonight, and as she looked at his messages, she realized both of his parents were on the group text.

She scrolled back up, until she found the timestamp for tonight. Tuck did talk to his parents a lot, and Bobbie Jo found that sweet and endearing.

I want to come up there for Christmas, he'd said. *I'll talk to Bobbie Jo about it. Could you host us?*

We'd love to, his mother had said.

You're always welcome here, Tuck. His daddy had added a boat emoji, followed by a fish. *Maybe we can go ice fishing.*

I've actually been thinking about moving up there.

Bobbie Jo's lungs seized. He really had been stewing on it if he'd told his parents already. A small part of her bristled that they'd known before her, and she reminded herself all of these conversations were happening on the same evening.

Moving up here? his mom asked. *Why in the world would you move up here?*

To be closer to you guys, Tuck said. *It's this feeling, this urge, almost a prompting from God.*

Tuck, we're fine up here, his dad said. *We just moved here ourselves.*

We miss you kids, his mom said. *But you get to go live your life however you want. You don't need to worry about us.*

So I'm to ignore the Lord?

Tuck, is this just part of you trying to figure out what you're supposed to do about Rosie? his dad asked. *Or how to keep Bobbie Jo with you?*

Maybe, he said. *I don't honestly know.*

Baby, you've been treading water for a while now, his mom said. *It's time to sink or swim.*

The conversation ended there, and Bobbie Jo looked up. "Well?" he asked.

"I don't know." She gave him the phone and hugged her arms around herself.

He sighed as he looked at the phone. "I do feel like I've been treading water." He turned his phone over and set it on the couch on the other side of his leg. His eyes wandered and then came back to hers. "But since we started dating, I feel more grounded. I feel like even if there was this huge wave that came at me and hit me, I'd be okay. I might go under, but you'd dive in and pull me back out." He whispered the last few words, and his gaze flitted away.

Bobbie Jo reached over and laced her fingers with his. "I would," she said.

Tuck nodded. "So maybe she's saying it's time to stop just letting time go by and start making plans. I've got to swim toward something, not just stay where I am and wish someone would come save me."

"Or rejoin the rodeo."

Tuck drew in a sharp breath, held it, and then blew it out. "I mean, you're not wrong. I just didn't realize Tarr had put me in such a holding pattern."

"And I'm keeping you there." She gently pulled her hand away.

"No," Tuck said. "You're not, sweetheart."

"But I kind of am." She drew in a breath too, this evening so unlike what she'd pictured when she'd called in sick this morning and then cancelled dinner with Tuck. "I don't mean to be, but I kind of am."

"Then maybe both of us just need to jump in. See if we sink or swim."

"Yeah," Bobbie Jo said. "Maybe we do." But neither one of them volunteered to be the first to take that plunge, and Bobbie Jo simply folded herself back into his embrace and let the pictures he'd painted for her that night swim through her.

And wow, drifting with Tuck at her side, and visions of the life they could have together sure felt good.

Now, she just had to figure out if she was floating...or drowning.

twenty-four

Tuck pulled up to the stop sign and looked left and right. "I'm not sure...."

"This says right," Mike said, peering that way and then looking at his phone.

"And I've got left," Hunt said from the backseat.

Tuck had brought them both along today, and the property he'd found on the north side of Denver—further out than where Keith had moved to a couple of years ago—spanned over a hundred acres. The pictures had been taken in the spring, and Tuck could see the fields of green for miles and miles.

Right now, though, all he saw in front of him was a T-junction with a brown field across from him and the road going in two different directions to the left and right.

It honestly mirrored his life, and while he'd finally told Bobbie Jo everything that had been swirling and curling in his head for the past couple of months, he still didn't feel any closer to knowing if he should stay in the Denver area or not.

All of his siblings, plus Tarr, would be leaving for the Christmas holidays in Coral Canyon in a couple of weeks, and Tuck had been pleading with the Lord to let him know where he should be once he got there.

Meanwhile, he'd been doing his best to swim right here in Ivory Peaks—though he'd brought his truck to a stop in a small community called Deerfield.

"Maybe it's right in front of us," Mike finally said, "And you can get there going either direction."

"I'm gonna go right," Tuck said, and he swung his vehicle that way. He'd only barely started to accelerate when his truck said, "Coming online," in a cool, female, robotic voice.

"It's left up here about another mile," Mike said.

"I'm rerouting," Hunt said. A moment later, he added, "Yep, Mikey's right."

Tuck found it comical that all three of them had pulled up the address of this farm, but his nerves shouted at him about what he might find here.

The house looked enormous according to the pictures. Of course, anything more than a couple of bedrooms seemed enormous to Tuck, and he cast a look behind him to Tarr, who'd stayed silent all this time.

His best friend in the whole world gave him a half-smile and went back to looking out his window.

Tuck had wanted him along, because together, they could decide if the facilities at this farm could be converted into what Tuck needed to train and manage his rodeo stars from right here in Colorado.

It currently sat on the market as a residential and agricultural property, and Tuck would have to see if he could even run a business from here. He didn't want to go the non-profit route, because he couldn't imagine who would give him money to train rodeo cowboys and cowgirls. He'd started to do a little research, and everything inside him had been so knotted, he'd quit.

No, non-profit wasn't the route for him.

"I see it," Mike said, and Tuck nodded, because he did too. He made the left turn from paved road to dirt, and he noted someone took good care of this lane even if it wasn't asphalt.

They trundled along, the country music filling the cab of his truck, until the road arced east again.

Tuck followed it, noting all the farmland. He swallowed, and his tongue felt like a slab of wood in his mouth. "This is good for the goat farming," he managed to say.

"If you buy this place, Gerty is going to rake me over the coals." Mike chuckled. "She'll want to know why I didn't see it."

Tuck glanced over to his cousin, his heart doing a little tap dance in his chest. "You guys have had your farm for a few years now."

"You've met Gerty, right?" Mike grinned at him.

Tuck relaxed, his muscles physically softening as he breathed out and then laughed with the others in the truck. "She loves her farm."

"It's perfect for her," Mike agreed.

"You've got a huge barn coming up on your left," Hunt said, and Tuck focused his eyes out the windshield again. Sure enough, a great big barn done in light brown wood—so not the same as the working barn on normal farms and ranches in the area—stood on the left side of the road.

Darker brown shutters flanked the windows, and Tuck suspected the same thing Hunt said: "That is an arena, my friend."

Tuck looked over to Mike. "Good for barrel racing, at the very least."

He didn't normally work with more than one client at a time, and they booked time at a facility based on what they needed. Most of that was determined by any animals they might need, but Rosie would bring her own horse with her to run the barrels, and that only left cattle for the break-away roping.

And she doesn't have to compete in that right away, he reminded himself.

In truth, Tuck's dreams had started to grow in the past couple of months as a combined farm for him and Bobbie Jo had been on his mind day and night.

Perhaps he could rent the facility to managers and rodeo stars. They'd come to him, instead of him finding them.

That would take a partnership with the National Rodeo Association, and that research had *not* bored Tuck. It could be done, and Tuck already had a meeting set up with Warren Walker for when he would be in Coral Canyon.

His father's connections were endless, and he'd done a

contract for the Walker brothers as they'd bought their ranch in Dog Valley, a small town north of Coral Canyon.

And the Bucking Bull Ranch trained and sold rodeo animals to men just like Tuck.

Everyone in the world knew who Wyatt Walker was, and all four of his children now lived and worked at Bucking Bull Ranch, and to Tuck, they were simply another piece in the thousand-piece monstrosity he was trying to put together.

Tarr whistled from the backseat. "This place is pristine, Tuck."

"Lotta money here," Mikey added.

Tuck had shown them all the listing. The farm had been on the market for months now, and as Tuck gazed around, he knew why.

Money.

He shifted in his seat, because not even twenty million would put a dent in the amount of money he had available to him.

"This could be the new Hammond Family Compound," Hunt said. "Look, there's a house right there I'm pretty sure Molly and I could live in with all of our kids."

Tuck saw it. And the stables that, according to the online listing, held fifty horses. And the enormous pasture beyond that.

"Wonder who lives there," Tarr said mildly, which almost caused Tuck to laugh.

But if he started, he wouldn't stop, and Tuck didn't want to spiral into maniacal cackles.

"Release your hold, brother." Mike reached over and put his hand over Tuck's on the steering wheel.

Their eyes met, and Tuck said, "I'm so nervous."

"Why?" Mike searched his face, but Tuck didn't know how to answer him.

"I don't know."

"It's because—well, I'll phrase it as a question," Hunt said. "Is it because you can see yourself here?"

"Of course he can see himself here," Tarr said. "It's the best thing he's looked at, ever. Heck, I can see myself here, and I'm not even the one looking."

Tuck once again glanced in the rearview mirror, words streaming across the back of his throat. Things he wanted to talk to Tarr about. Things like having him come work for the facility, for Tuck, once he got his training operation off the ground.

Tarr was *so* good with a horse and a rope, and he could be a rodeo manager just like Tuck. With the two of them, they could attract some great clients, and Tuck saw a building with offices and desks, so he could employ more managers, secretaries who only handled travel, those who managed endorsements, all of it.

"I can see myself here," Tuck admitted, spotting the blue truck up ahead. "There's Galen."

The real estate agent had said he'd park his truck on the road that led to the private family estate—he'd legit used the word "estate"—and Tuck could follow him to the house and private farm buildings before they looked at anything on this side of the property.

Tuck slowed and let Galen pull out before he made the turn; then, he simply followed him down the road.

"It could easily be converted," Tarr said, voicing what Tuck had suspected and hoped for. Prayed for, even.

"They're already boarding a billion horses here," Tarr continued, though no one had affirmed him. "And housing shows in that arena." His words carried a hint of frustration, and Tuck wasn't sure what that was about.

But with Tarr, he'd find out. He always did.

The family land appeared about five minutes later, and thankfully, no one else had any comments about the farm along the way. Tuck finally eased his truck to a stop beside Galen's, and all four of them spilled out of it.

The real estate agent wore a huge cowboy hat, which made Tuck trust him more for some reason. "No trouble finding it?" he asked as he extended his hand to shake Tuck's.

"That T-junction is confusing," Tuck said.

"Yeah, the public entrance to the barn is left," Galen said. "But the main entrance for cowboys and the family is right. I thought I texted you that."

"Could have," Tuck said, because his phone had overwhelmed him the past few days, and the only messages he'd read and responded to had been Bobbie Jo's. He hadn't told her about this place—*yet*, he added in his head—because he really wanted to make decisions for his life without any outside influences.

Ridiculous, probably, but his thought process nonetheless.

Tuck needed a future for *Tuck*, regardless of whether things with Bobbie Jo worked out or not.

But, the only reason Tuck had started down this road was because of Bobbie Jo and her need for a home, for something permanent.

Everything flowed in a strange circle, but Tuck always came back to him needing his own future.

And he wanted to be a rodeo manager, *and* a husband, a father, an uncle, a nephew, a cousin, a good son.

His heartbeat got stuck in his veins as he and Galen turned to the homestead together. The real estate agent swept one hand toward the grand property while Tuck tried to figure out how to get his pulse to function properly.

This place sat about an hour closer to Coral Canyon than the family farm did, but it would still take a whole day of travel to get to his parents should he need to.

"Seven bedrooms," Galen said. "Nine baths. Mother-in-law suite, with a fully landscaped and mature outdoor living space."

Tuck had seen the pictures of this place, and honestly, it did not look like somewhere a twenty-seven-year-old single cowboy would live.

People struggled and toiled and labored to get to this house. Tuck had simply been born with the right last name.

His privilege streamed through him, and he held his head high as he said a silent prayer to have the spirit of the Lord with him, whispering to him about this property.

Do I belong here, Lord? he asked as he went up the steps to the front porch, a wraparound feature of the house that Bobbie Jo would love.

Tell me if this is where my life is, he thought. *Give me a clear mind to see truth, to feel the future, to be brave enough to take whatever steps necessary to be on the path Thou would have me on.*

He didn't want to miss a message from God because of his anxiety, and he stepped into the house ahead of everyone except Galen, who talked about the front door and how they'd had it handcrafted from the wood on the original barn here on the property.

Hunt asked why the family who owned the farm and boarding stable was selling it, but all Tuck could see was the picture of three tween girls, grinning for all they were worth as they leaned over their show goats.

Goats.

"Clive Hallowell passed," Galen said as Tuck looked at the blue eyes of those girls, who couldn't be more than ten or eleven years old.

"The man had seven daughters," Galen said with a chuckle. "His wife's been gone for a decade, and all of the ladies live somewhere else, except one."

"She didn't want this place?" Mike asked. "Because it's incredible."

"She—it's a personal issue," Galen said. "Something with the assets, and she doesn't want this one to her name."

Tuck finally swung his attention to Galen, not quite understanding. But Hunt said, "She must be getting a divorce or something."

"And I heard there was no prenup," Galen said. "But that's not important. All you boys need to know is that they're not selling because it's haunted or every irrigation pipe under the ground is broken."

He laughed, and everyone but Tuck joined in. Tarr slung his arm around Tuck's shoulders and leaned in close. "Dude, cowboy, you need to lighten up. *Look* at this place."

Tuck turned toward his friend, some of the nervous energy blazing through him trickling out. A smile came to his face, and he ignored Tarr's raised eyebrows as he faced the framed picture of some of the Hallowell girls.

"Yeah," he said. "I see it."

And he loved it. He wanted it. So now he just needed to figure out if the Lord saw it and wanted him to have it. And if so...how to tell Bobbie Jo.

twenty-five

Bobbie Jo rode in the passenger seat of Tuck's truck, with Tarr and Deacon in the back. None of them had spoken since they'd crossed the state line into Wyoming and Bobbie Jo had said, "Another state for my bucket list."

That had sparked a whole conversation with Tuck about the existence of such a list, and then they'd all settled into silence.

But no, Bobbie Jo had never been to Wyoming. Or Idaho, or Montana, or Utah. She'd grown up in Oklahoma, and then she'd come to Colorado for a job.

Farmers didn't exactly take lavish family vacations all over the world, and the best she'd ever done in the world of travel was going to Florida to visit her grandparents one winter.

That had been her only experience on an airplane, and Bobbie Jo folded her arms to try to keep the inadequacies inside. They ate her alive from the inside out, but she'd rather not talk about any of it in front of Tuck's brother and best friend.

Heck, talking about them with Tuck made her nauseous, and thankfully, they'd simply been enjoying the first snowfall in the city, and then all the holiday festivities in small-town Boulder and Ivory Peaks.

And now Coral Canyon, a place Tuck had spent his summers growing up. All of his uncles and their families lived here, and he'd been ridiculously excited about coming for the Christmas holiday.

She'd just seen a sign that said they only had thirty more miles to go, and Tuck reached over and took her hand in his. She turned her attention to him, expecting him to ask her something. Instead, he simply smiled at her in that easy, cowboy way he had—and it still lit her up inside.

She returned it, because she wanted to enjoy Christmas— and Tuck.

She'd been coaching herself not to be afraid of the future, and she took in a deep breath through her nose to do so right now.

She was healthy and whole, and the entire world sat in front of her. Plenty of people wished for such a thing, and Bobbie Jo wasn't going to act ungrateful for the gifts God had given her.

As Tuck turned his attention back out the windshield,

Bobbie Jo wondered if part of her blessings included Tucker Hammond.

Of course they do.

The words simply entered her mind, but they didn't sound like her. Goose flesh broke out on her arms, and she pulled her hand back so she could put on her sweatshirt.

"Cold, baby?" Tuck murmured, and Bobbie Jo nodded, though the prickles on her skin hadn't come from the temperature.

He reached to turn up the heat, and she pulled her sweatshirt on as the voice of God reverberated through her whole soul.

Yes, Tucker Hammond was a gift, and Bobbie Jo wanted to appreciate him for who and what he was.

By the time they passed the "Welcome to Coral Canyon" sign, Bobbie Jo had taken more pictures of the Teton Mountains than humanly possible.

"Here we are," Tuck announced through the truck. "Tarr, wake up, brother."

"About time," Deacon grumbled.

Tuck twisted to look at his younger brother. "You dyin'?"

"My legs are so stiff," he complained.

"Holy—look at the mountains." Tarr had been asleep for all of Bobbie Jo's exclamations, and she smiled back to him.

"I got so many pictures."

He smiled kindly at her. "I forgot you've never been here."

Bobbie Jo returned her attention to the front, because she didn't want to miss a moment of his quaint small town.

"Ah," Tuck said. "Feels like coming home."

"Does it?" Tarr asked, and Tuck cut a quick look over to her. Her chest tightened too, and she honestly wasn't sure what to think or feel.

A few weeks ago, Tuck had mentioned his parents living here alone, and that perhaps he should be looking to build a rodeo training facility here.

As she watched the stores and shops pass, with the cutest Main Street possible, Bobbie Jo could see herself living here with him.

Those thoughts terrified her, because they felt so far into the future, and perhaps she shouldn't be thinking or imagining that far ahead.

Still, she and Tucker had been dating for almost four months now, and she'd liked him for far longer than that. He'd had a crush on her too, and in truth, Bobbie Jo, had known the cowboy and his heart of gold, his hardworking spirit, and his honorable intentions for a year and a half now.

And that wasn't moving too fast.

Who cares if it is anyway? she asked herself. She didn't have her momma harping on her to make sure she took her time to make sure she knew Tuck was the one for her. She only had herself, and how she felt, and those feelings hadn't led her too far astray in the past.

So maybe she just had to keep trusting herself—and trusting Tuck—and until the future arrived, she could fantasize about it.

When they pulled up to Tuck's parent's house, he said, "Looks like June is here."

And he didn't sound happy about that.

"Yep," Deacon said, and then he bolted from the truck, obviously on a mission.

"He has to go to the bathroom," Tarr said, and the rest of them took much longer getting out.

Elise Hammond came out onto the porch, pulling a black sweater jacket tighter around herself. She wore jeans with that, her hair down, and a smile that could probably light the whole town.

Tarr laughed as he jogged up the front sidewalk and took her right into his arms. He lifted her right up off her feet, then leaned in and kissed her cheek as he said hello.

Tuck looked like he wanted to do the same thing, but he waited for Bobbie Jo near the front bumper.

"Do we need to get our stuff?" Bobbie Jo asked as Tarr went inside the house.

"My dad'll come out," Tuck said as he drew her hand to his lips and kissed it. "You've met my parents before, remember?"

"As an employee on the farm," she said, still eyeing Elise like she might turn into a rattlesnake and strike.

"Well, now you'll get to do it as my girlfriend." Tuck grinned at her and took her up the walk and the low, squat steps to his mother.

"Hey, Momma." He hugged her tightly too, and Bobbie Jo's throat narrowed as she watched them. He too kissed her cheek and then he stood beside her as he indicated Bobbie Jo.

"You remember Bobbie Jo Hanks."

"Thank you for having me," she said.

"Oh, please." Elise grinned at her and stepped into her arms. "I feel like I've known you forever. You don't need to be formal with me."

Bobbie Jo didn't hug a lot of people. Just Tuck in the past few months, in fact, and it sure felt nice to have this female, maternal embrace.

"Now come on," Elise said. "It's freezing out here, and Daddy has the hot chocolate and cookies ready. Oh, and June came over to tell us about her new boyfriend."

Tuck's eyes gleamed like shined silver as his mother went by him, but he kept his gaze on Bobbie Jo. "I told you it would be nothing."

"Well, it was something to me," she said, the warmth Elise had shown her still sinking into her muscles and bones.

"Who's June?" Bobbie Jo asked.

"My cousin," Tuck said. "One of Uncle Ames's girls."

Bobbie Jo nodded, and she wondered why he'd been a bit standoffish when he'd seen her truck outside.

"Hot chocolate and cookies," Tuck whispered as he ushered her into the house. "I swear my parents aren't robots."

Bobbie Jo giggled, suddenly thrilled to be here, on a real Christmas holiday, with her boyfriend. New town. New state. But the same Hammond goodness.

Bobbie Jo could walk with her hand in Tuck's forever, despite the biting wind that kept trying to snake its way down her collar.

The scent of cinnamon and chocolate hung in the air on Main Street, and they'd escaped his house to have breakfast downtown this Christmas Eve morning, and they'd already ducked into a couple of shops to look for some small gifts for his family for Christmas morning.

"Let's go in here," Tuck said, tugging her toward a shop that looked like it sold boots and hats.

"Baby, I think you have enough of this kind of stuff." She grinned at him but went with him without question. She wanted to be with him, and not just on this Christmas Eve shopping trip.

"Maybe you need a new hat," he said over his shoulder as they left behind the chilly outdoors in favor of the leather-scented heated interior of the shop.

They were busier than Bobbie Jo expected a luxury leather shop and hattery to be on Christmas Eve, as a lot of the products in here had to be special-ordered to fit.

"I have a hat," she said as he moved over to the women's side of the store.

"When's the last time you wore it?'

"Well, I mean, it's been a while," she admitted.

He scanned the wall of cowgirl hats once and then twice, obviously looking for something specific. What, she didn't know. She normally bought whatever was on sale at the Boot Barn, and she didn't need high-end felt and custom leather banding.

She saw several hats she liked, but she made no move to get any of them down. Tuck finally selected one and turned to her with a face full of a smile.

"Let's try this one." He handed it to her, and Bobbie Jo took it, marveling at the weight and quality of it. As she looked at it, she really liked the dark brown color, with the deep purple eggplant banding around the upper part of the hat.

As she turned it over, she caught sight of the handwritten price tag, and she dang near dropped the hat.

"Tuck, I can't afford this." She tried to hand it back to him, but he backed up a step.

"That's why it's called a gift, sweetheart."

She cocked her head at him. "You expect me to believe that you brought me home for Christmas, and you don't already have a present for me?"

"A person can get more than one gift," Tuck said coolly, pocketing his hands. "Try it on, at least."

He nodded to her, and Bobbie Jo continued to stare at him. Finally, when she saw that his stubborn streak had kicked in, she sighed like he was the most insufferable cowboy in the world and stuffed the hat on her head.

She knew instantly that she currently wore the nicest hat she'd ever had the pleasure to put on her head, and Tuck moved out of the way so she could see herself in the mirror.

He moved to stand beside her and then behind her. "I was going to wait to tell you, but I think you're going to need a hat like this, sweetheart."

"Yeah?" she whispered, looking at herself with his taller

body a half-step behind her. Her eyes finally moved from the beauty of it to the beauty of him. "Why's that?"

He leaned down, only the top of his cowboy hat showing in the mirror as he whispered, "I bought a farm, and I want you to come work it with me."

Bobbie Jo sucked in a breath. "Tucker, you didn't."

"It's not final yet." He lifted his head and gripped both of her shoulders in his palms. "I think you'll like it, but here's the thing: it's a Christmas present to myself. It's not for you."

He wore a very serious expression, and Bobbie Jo turned away from the mirror to face him. "Good," she said. "Because I'd be very angry if you bought me a farm for Christmas."

He grinned at her. "Mike bought Gerty her farm for her birthday."

"Also not a suitable birthday gift," Bobbie Jo said.

He nodded to the hat. "Is that a suitable Christmas gift?"

"Yes," she said, though she didn't like the idea of him spending almost four figures on a cowgirl hat she'd likely never wear.

"All right, well, I think that's the sexiest thing I've ever seen you wear, and I'd like to get it for you."

Bobbie Jo reached up and swept the hat from her head. She handed it back to him while she tried to remember how to swallow.

He paid for the hat while Bobbie Jo pretended to look at belts she'd buy, knowing she'd never spend six hundred dollars on a belt. A *belt*.

"Ready," he said as he went past her and, and Bobbie Jo hurried after him. Outside, the cold air slapped against her tongue and lungs, and she didn't care. She took gulp after gulp of it, trying to find her center again.

"Will you show me this farm you bought?" she finally asked.

"I want to go in the bookstore," he said.

"Tucker."

"Yes," he said. "I'll show you the farm after I give it to myself tomorrow."

"When did you buy it?"

A bell on the door of the bookshop chimed when Tuck opened it, and he gave her a pointed look as she slipped by him. So he wouldn't answer. Fine. She could wait until tomorrow, when he gave himself the farm for Christmas.

She loved the scent of paper and ink, of storytelling and the imagination, and of far away lands. The window had been decorated like Santa's village, and the display case inside held a dozen prominently displayed children's books for any parent who needed a last-minute gift.

"Welcome to Becks Books," a boy said, and he wore a big black cowboy hat and a smile. "My name's OJ, and if you tell me what you're looking for, I can steer you to the right aisle."

He couldn't be more than twelve or thirteen, and Bobbie Jo grinned at him.

"Howdy, OJ," Tuck said, and the boy looked at him. "Remember me?"

OJ's face brightened with surprise. "Tucker!" He threw himself into the older cowboy's arms, and added, "You would not *believe* how much snow is in the mountains. Have you been here long? Maybe you went hiking already."

Tuck laughed as he stepped back. "We're not crazy, OJ," he said. "Who goes hiking in the winter?"

"My uncle Luke loves it," OJ said. "He took me ice caving last weekend, and it was *awesome*."

Bobbie Jo couldn't help but feed off his enthusiasm.

"That's great, bud," Tuck said. He pulled in a breath and looked around. "I'd like a recipe book for my momma, but not one of those mass-produced ones, and my aunt Bree said your momma curated one from the ladies at church, got it all bound, and is sellin' 'em here."

"Yeah, sure," OJ said easily. "They're back here by the register." He turned to go back that way, and Tuck and Bobbie Jo went with him.

Bobbie Jo didn't spend a lot of time reading, but she loved stationery and pens with her whole heart. She got detoured by those things, and before she knew it, she had several new stickers for her water bottle at work, a couple of journals, and three packs of gel pens. One for her, and the other two for her roommates back in Boulder.

"Oh, you're not ready," Tuck teased when he found her. He carried a pink plastic bag with his momma's cookbook in it, and Bobbie Jo looked at him with new shininess in her blood.

"Look at these stickers, Tuck. They say Coral Canyon on them."

"My daughter designs those," a woman said. "Howdy, Tuck. OJ said you were here."

"Georgia," Tuck said as he leaned in to hug her lightly. He indicated Bobbie Jo. "This is my girlfriend, Bobbie Jo." He grinned and grinned. "Bobbie Jo, Georgia owns the shop, and she's married to Otis Young. You know, from that album I played for you on the way up."

Bobbie Jo's heartbeat crashed against her breastbone. "Country-Quad-Otis-Young?"

Georgia laughed and said, "They're retired, Tuck."

"They still made thirteen awesome albums," he said. "And Bobbie Jo had only listened to the first one. I had to play *Glory Road* for her."

"I'm sure," Georgia said dryly.

"They're really great," Bobbie Jo said.

Georgia smiled kindly at her. "Will we see you guys for Bryce's birthday?"

"Did you know it's my birthday?" OJ asked. "I'm thirteen today."

Georgia smoothed back his hair. "You sure are, buddy. And working at the shop." She looked over to Tuck and Bobbie Jo. "We're headed out to Tex's after this. Another whole family party."

"They're *exhausting*," OJ said, clearly repeating something he'd heard someone older than him say plenty of times.

Bobbie Jo burst out laughing, because he was so cute, and he reminded her so much of Tuck. She could just see him as a child this age, blurting things out, chattering away to anyone who would listen about ice caving, all of it.

Georgia didn't correct him, or chastise him, and Tuck quieted first. Then he said, "The Youngs are a huge family," by way of explanation. "You think the Hammonds have big family parties? You ain't seen nothing."

Georgia grinned at them both as the bell on the door jingled again. "Come on Thursday. Then you'll see." She turned to go greet the customer, and Bobbie Jo went with OJ to check out with her stationery purchases.

He chit-chatted about the coffee shop down the street, and how his aunt Codi had a dog-washing bus, and that his family really was huge.

"We have our New Year's Eve parties in the furniture store." He bagged up all of her purchases and handed them back to her. "Will you be here then?"

"Oh, I—no," she said. "Plus, we can't just come to all your parties."

"Sure you can," OJ said with all the innocence of a child. "Everyone else does."

Bobbie Jo grinned at him and said, "I guess we'll see. If the birthday party in a couple of days is too *exhausting*, maybe we won't want to come to the furniture store New Year's Eve party."

OJ laughed. "Maybe not."

"I sure enjoyed meeting you, OJ." Bobbie Jo took her bag and headed for the front sidewalk, where Tuck waited for her.

"Ready, baby?" he asked as she came out of the store.

"Can we really go to Bryce's birthday party in a couple of days?" she asked, casting a look over her shoulder.

"Yeah," Tuck said. "I'm sure we can. My parents are friends with all the Youngs. My momma will know about it."

He put his arm around her and said, "Okay, it's time for second breakfast, and there's a great doughnut shop just down here...."

Bobbie Jo laughed, because Tuck could never get enough to eat, and hey, she liked doughnuts too.

Really, she liked *Tuck*, and she wanted to be wherever he was. So maybe, just maybe, the hat box he carried with her new cowgirl hat would definitely be used at some point in the future.

twenty-six

Tuck usually rose with the sun, but on Christmas morning, he reverted to the little boy he'd been growing up.

He woke while darkness still covered Wyoming, a giddiness inside him that only came on certain days each year.

He cast a quick look down the hall toward the guest room where Bobbie Jo slept. She was an early riser too, but Tuck didn't think he should tiptoe down there and rap on her door. He'd never seen her first thing in the morning, but he didn't think she'd be a bundle of pleasantness at this hour.

He grinned just thinking about it, though, because he'd sure like to see her first thing in the morning.

He cleared his throat as he turned away and strode down the hall and into the kitchen.

Finding his father at the kitchen table, a newspaper and a

cup of coffee in front of him, didn't shock Tuck in the slightest.

"Merry Christmas, Daddy." Tuck went right over to him and leaned down to hug him.

"Mm, morning, Tucker." Daddy embraced him back, and Tuck sure did like being home for Christmas.

"Momma's making lunch at one," he said. "There's coffee and stuff for breakfast."

"She won't care if I make scrambled eggs?"

"If you add cheese, she'll eat the whole pan." Daddy smiled, and Tuck returned the gesture before he turned back to the gourmet kitchen. Momma did like to cook and bake, and Hunt had found this house for them that suited them perfectly.

Hunter and Molly had their own house here in Coral Canyon, and as Tuck started cracking eggs and whisking in milk, salt, and pepper, he had the distinct thought that he could also purchase a house here in Coral Canyon should he want to. Perhaps he could work part of the year here, with certain athletes, and then they could be in Colorado too.

"Then why'd you buy that farm?" he asked himself under the sound of the whisk scraping the bowl. That place needed around-the-clock, all-year care, and he couldn't leave a farm and over a dozen buildings, not to mention the animals he'd have, for months at a time.

He cut off a pat of butter and put it in the pan, then started the flame under it. He pulled the shredded cheese out of the fridge, as well as a little baggie of real bacon bits, deciding on the spot to make an omelet-type scramble this morning.

"Morning," Deacon said as he came to Tuck's side. "What else do you need? I could make French toast." He flipped open the lid on the egg carton. "If there's enough eggs."

"Momma has millions of eggs," Tuck said. "Ask Daddy if we have enough. She might need them for that chocolate pie."

"The chocolate pies are done," Momma herself said. "They're in the fridge in the garage." She grinned in the kind, loving, maternal way she had and hugged Deacon with, "Oh, my baby. How are you this morning?"

"Just fine, Momma," he said. "Merry Christmas."

"Merry Christmas," she said, and then she moved over to Tuck. "I like it when you make breakfast."

She hugged him too, and he told her Merry Christmas before he turned to pour the eggs into the hot pan.

"I'm gonna make French toast," Deacon said. "Will the eggs be okay?"

"Just fine," Tuck said, turning down the flame. "It's better if the French toast is hot anyway."

"I'll heat up the syrup," Momma said. "Hunt and Molly and the kids will be here about ten to do presents, but we don't have to wait for them. They're opening presents at their house first."

"We don't have much anyway," Daddy said, and Tuck's heart flipped over. He had a lot to tell the people he loved, as he hadn't even mentioned the farm to his parents yet. Hunt knew, of course, but Tuck had sworn him to secrecy.

He and Deacon finished up breakfast, and Bobbie Jo still hadn't come down the hall. He didn't want her to feel left out, so he washed his hands real quick and then said, "I'll go check on her. Start without me."

"Deac, can you pause to pray?" Daddy asked.

Deacon turned from the stove as Tuck jogged toward the hall and said, "Yep."

Tuck slowed as he neared Bobbie Jo's door. He knocked quietly, and then twisted the doorknob. He peered into the crack that opened wider with every passing moment and asked, "Sweetheart?"

She lay in bed, utterly serene and still, her chest rising and falling softly beneath his momma's puffy blankets.

Tuck paused and watched her, because her beauty absolutely stole his breath right out of his lungs.

As he gazed at her, Tuck knew, on some level, he'd fallen in love with Bobbie Jo Hanks. He'd started to stitch together plans for a life—a real life—he could give her, and a new, bubbling excitement ran through his veins as a smile took over his mouth.

"Bobbie Jo, baby." He stepped closer to the bed, not sure how close to get.

She stirred, and Tuck added, "Breakfast is ready."

Her eyes opened, and it took a couple of seconds for her to focus. When she saw him there, she sucked in a breath and flinched away from him.

He chuckled and practically fell on top of her, the soft bed catching his free-fall. "Hey, baby."

"Tucker," she gasped as he crowded right into the bed with her. "What—what time is it?"

"Oh, like seven," he said. "We're eating, and I didn't want you to feel bad you missed it."

She pulled the covers up to her chin, keeping them between them, and Tuck smiled and smiled at her. "Merry Christmas, sweetheart." He touched his lips to hers, enjoying this slow, Christmas-morning kiss.

Bobbie Jo kissed him back, but she didn't go on too long. "Smells like cinnamon."

"French toast," he whispered, his mouth easily sliding down to her neck. Oh, he could taste her skin for a long time, but he pulled away. "I'll give you a minute to get ready."

Tuck rolled away from her and got to his feet. He forced himself to walk away from her, though her bedroom smelled like flowers and powder and fresh cotton.

He cleared his throat as he left her bedroom, pulling the door closed behind him. In the kitchen, he said, "She's gonna be a minute," as he picked up a plate and started loading it with eggs and French toast.

Bobbie Jo came out five minutes later, her cheeks holding a bit of pink as she took them in, all seated at the dining room table.

"Hey, baby." Tuck got up and went to help her get breakfast. "There's lots, and I can heat up your eggs real quick."

"It's fine, Tuck."

He put the syrup bottle in the microwave anyway, because she could at least pour something hot over her French toast.

She took a big scoop of eggs. "I should've known you'd be up early."

"It's Christmas," Tuck said by way of explanation. He couldn't stop the smile spreading across his face. "Don't you love Christmas?"

"Sure," Bobbie Jo said. "I also like sleeping in on vacation." She grinned at him, and the microwave beeped to signal the syrup had heated. Tuck got it out for her, then left her to finish getting her meal together.

She joined them a few seconds later, glancing around at everyone. "Sorry I'm late."

"There's no schedule on Christmas," Momma said kindly. She threw a look over to Tuck, but they'd been in Coral Canyon for a couple of days now, and he didn't need to referee every conversation between his parents and his girlfriend.

So he said nothing as Momma asked, "What are your folks doing today, Bobbie Jo?"

"My brother and his girlfriend are doing Christmas with them," she said, and Tuck simply listened to them talk about the holidays, her family traditions, and what she'd liked as a kid.

He and Deac cleaned up the dishes and leftovers from breakfast, and then Tuck looked over to the Christmas tree. "Should we open presents?"

Daddy clapped his hands together a couple of times, as if he were the little boy about to unwrap all his hopes and dreams. "Yes, let's do it." He led the way into the living room and pulled the armchair closer to the tree. Plenty of gifts rested underneath, because Momma and Daddy loved their grandchildren and had bought Hunt's kids a lot of presents.

"Okay," Daddy said, and then the front door opened with, "We're here."

Jane came down the hall with her chubby four-month-old in her arms, and Cord followed her with three boxes of doughnuts.

"Oh, good, we didn't miss the presents," Jane said. "Clint's so little, and we're in the rental, and I wasn't sure how early to come over."

Momma took Clint from her, cooing at him as the baby flapped his arms. "Never too early," she said. "We just finished breakfast, but we can make more if you're hungry."

"We had breakfast," Cord said. "Got these yesterday from Faith Young, so they should still be good this morning."

The scent of maple, chocolate, and yeast filled Tuck's nose, and he wasn't going to say no to a doughnut, despite the presents beneath the tree that called to him.

Everyone got their coffee and doughnuts, and then Daddy finally handed the first gift to Cord. "Here you go, son."

Cord grinned at Daddy and started unwrapping the red-and-white -striped package. He pulled out a canvas bag, glanced at Momma, and unzipped the bag. "Oh, it's a beard-care kit." He grinned at the contents and pulled out a tin. "I love this beard balm."

Daddy smiled at him and handed Jane a gift. She unwrapped a new skirt, and Daddy handed Bobbie Jo a present. It wasn't the one Tuck had brought for her, nor the hat he'd bought yesterday, and his pulse thumped wildly in his veins as Bobbie Jo thanked his parents and started unwrapping her gift.

He couldn't look away from her as she opened the lid on the box and lifted out a crocheted scarf, and then a matching hat. The colors of teal, cream, and salmon seemed so like her, and she looked up with a bit of awe in her eyes.

"I made them," Momma said. "We lived in Colorado, and it's cold there."

"I love them," she said sincerely. "Thank you so much." She looked over to Tuck and tucked her hair, that pretty flush in her face making him reach for her hand. He squeezed it as Daddy said, "Tuck."

He took his present and opened a new pair of cowboy boots. "Yes," he exclaimed. "I love these." He'd been padding around the house in his socked feet, and he pulled on his boots as Daddy gave Momma a present. Around and around they went, until Tuck's gifts started getting passed out.

Daddy opened a new packet of pencils, the kind he liked to use for crossword puzzles, and Momma exclaimed over her tea set.

Deacon grinned and clapped Tuck on the back as they hugged over his new pocketknife, and Jane and Cord showed each other all the things he'd put together in their "date night" box, including the coupon that said he'd babysit his nephew.

Bobbie Jo opened her cowgirl hat, and then, the small jewelry box made an appearance. He swallowed hard, because he maybe hadn't planned this moment very well.

She lifted out a horseshoe pendant, with diamonds studded all along the bottom curve.

"Tuck," she gasped again. Her wide, full-moon-eyes met his. "This is gorgeous."

He stood to help her put it on, and as her hair fell, she said, "I love it."

He nodded, his voice stuck somewhere down inside him, something that didn't happen to him very often.

He then opened her gift for him, which was a brown-leather-bound journal with the word *Thoughts* on the front.

He grinned over to her. "Thank you. I've been thinking of starting a journal." He cast a quick look at Bobbie Jo, who'd been writing in her nature journal for a while now.

"Oh, yeah?" Momma asked, drawing his attention. "You used to skip English because you hated the writing."

Tuck looked over to her, surprised she'd sell him out this way. Her eyes sparkled with teasing, and Tuck scoffed. "Well, I'm not fifteen anymore, Momma."

"The rest of these are for Hunt and Molly." Daddy started to rise, and Tuck cleared his throat.

Daddy looked at him once he'd straightened, and Tuck nodded to the tree. "That envelope is for me."

Daddy turned to the Christmas tree, which was a live blue spruce that filled the whole corner of the living room. He found the envelope Tuck had put there, and he took it from the boughs and looked at it.

"Who's it for?"

"Me." He cleared his throat again and got to his feet. "It's a present from me to me."

Jane wore a worried expression on her face as Tuck took the envelope from his father and turned to go back to his seat.

He couldn't predict how anyone in this room would react to the papers and color photos in this envelope, and he reminded himself that no one had to agree with him.

Momma and Daddy lived here, and Tuck looked around at everyone. Daddy had sat back down, and he half-chuckled and half-exhaled shakily.

"I've thought a lot about what I want," he said, still not sure about his permanent residence in Colorado.

He met his mother's gaze and then looked into his daddy's deep, dark eyes. Questions lived there, and Tuck knew in that moment that he didn't need to build his life here to be close to them.

He wasn't their only child, nor their only support, and Tuck took a deep breath and flipped over the envelope to open it.

"So I bought myself something," he said. He pulled out the first page and unfolded it. Another big breath, and he held it up, the aerial picture of the farm facing everyone in the room.

"I bought this farm and training facility in Deerfield. It's north of Denver, and it's...." He trailed off as he pulled out the next picture.

"It's got great training facilities for my cowboys and cowgirls, and—" His voice stuck in his throat, and he couldn't get himself to look over to Bobbie Jo.

"Wow," Cord said, taking the picture. "This is amazing, Tuck."

"Do you live on-site?" Jane asked, and Tuck found the awareness to pull out another picture, this one of the house.

"Yes," he said. "Yep. There's an embarrassingly big house on the property. It's got lots of extra bedrooms, so you guys can come stay with me anytime, and the property is this multi-functional thing. Lots of parking for people, and Tarr's going to come work with me, to build the clientele of the facility."

He swallowed, realizing how many words he'd said. And he had more to say.

"The other half of the property is a big farm." He pulled out the last sheet of paper and extended it toward Bobbie Jo. "A hundred and ten acres, and I can plant it or...." He'd come this far, and Tuck had never tried to hide anything, from anyone.

So he cleared his nerves away one last time and held his head high as he said, "We can put as many goats on it as you want."

twenty-seven

Bobbie Jo stared at the glorious picture in her hands. It didn't feel real. Her hands had somehow been detached from her body, and yet she felt the paper against her skin and the heat from the furnace filling the house.

Tuck's parents asked him questions, and he said he'd bought the farm and would be taking possession of it in the middle of January.

Jane passed her the picture of the house, and again, Bobbie Jo could only stare at it. At least ten of her tiny blue house could fit inside, and all she could hear was the word *goats*.

She'd told him once—one time—that she wanted a goat farm. She didn't think he'd actually buy a property where she could have that.

You should have, she told herself sternly. She knew Tuck

had money—so much money—and she knew he was the sweetest man she'd ever met.

"You're not saying anything," he said.

Bobbie Jo looked up at him, realizing everyone had gotten up from their places in the living room, and Elise and Jane had gone into the kitchen to start making Christmas lunch.

Deacon and Gray and Cord had moved over to the fireplace to light the fire, using the Christmas wrapping paper to get the logs to catch the flame.

Only she and Tuck remained in the living room, and he sat beside her as he exhaled.

"I don't—you bought me a goat farm."

"No," he said quickly. In a barky voice. "No, I bought a training facility for myself. It has nothing to do with you."

"Tuck." Bobbie Jo exhaled. "That is such a lie." She could be bold too. "You were going to move to Texas in a couple of weeks. Now you're not. *That* has something to do with me."

"I'm still going to Texas for a couple of months," he said quietly. "Rosie and I are going to start there while Tarr gets us moved onto the farm and starts recruiting other trainees."

"You've...you haven't told me any of this."

"I wanted it to be a surprise," he said. "And truthfully, I wasn't sure if I'd made the right decision or not. See, I've been trying to decide if I should be in Colorado or here, closer to my parents."

"I—I know," she said lamely, because she had known that. "I still want to have a voice in all of your ideas. I want to riddle through all the things with you."

"But you don't want the goat farm." He gently took the

papers from her and encapsulated her hand in his. "Because you can't reason through all the things with me if you don't also want the goat farm. It doesn't work both ways."

"This feels—I don't know how I feel."

"Are you mad?'

"Mad isn't the right word," she said, not sure how to explain it. She felt...left out.

And completely inadequate to be Tuck's girlfriend.

She didn't know how to tell him that, though, and she didn't want to ruin the holidays. With tears filling her eyes, she looked at him. "Will you take me to see it?"

"Of course." He hauled her into his chest and held her close. "I didn't mean to make you cry."

"I'm just overwhelmed," she whispered, but she wasn't sure if he heard her or not.

She needed more time to understand what ran through her. She needed to be alone to pace back and forth and talk out loud to herself.

She needed to figure out if she loved Tucker Hammond and could let him make all of her dreams come true.

* * *

"They've been up here for a couple of years now," Tuck said as he navigated himself and Bobbie Jo through the winter mountain landscape.

"I'm not sure the road will be open," she said, her worry openly coming through in her voice.

"Warren said it would be," Tuck said. "I've been texting him, baby." He cut her a look out of the side of his eye.

Things between them had definitely been less of him steamrolling her in her bed when he woke her for breakfast and more tension, glances that she couldn't read, and Tuck talking with his parents instead of her.

At the same time, she hadn't exactly been open to hearing about everything, despite what she'd told him on Christmas morning.

Only a couple of days had passed since then, and it was Bryce Young's birthday party tonight.

That was why Tuck had planned to visit Bucking Bull Ranch this afternoon. One, the sun was warmest and brightest in the afternoon, and two, they could stop by Bryce's farm on the way back to Coral Canyon for the party.

"Tuck, we left Dog Valley behind a long time ago."

"Like, fifteen minutes," he said. "It's right here, Bobbie Jo." He flipped on his blinker and slowed to make the left turn from the lonely stretch of highway to a path carved between two snowbanks.

If anyone else came down this road toward them, they'd have nowhere to go, but Tuck didn't seem worried at all.

They rumbled along the frosted dirt road, and Bobbie Jo crossed her arms to match her legs. She wasn't sure why this trip to Bucking Bull Ranch made her nervous, only that it did.

Tuck had learned of the Walker brothers and their rodeo animal training ranch from his father. Their daddy was the famous Wyatt Walker, and his four children lived on the ranch up here in Wyoming, where they'd spent their summers, the same way Tuck had.

Cole Walker, the youngest brother, still rode in the rodeo, and Tuck wanted to find out about his manager, as well as purchasing training animals for his farm-facility in Deerfield.

Bobbie Jo could still barely believe he'd bought a twenty-million-dollar farm an hour from downtown Denver.

Not that it mattered how far from the HMC high rise the farm sat. If she and Tuck got married, she'd become the matriarch of one-hundred-ten acres, a nine-bedroom house, and as many goats as she wanted.

It seemed like a dream come true, and yet Bobbie Jo had been resisting it. Why, she wasn't sure.

Tuck had taken the pictures from her and slid them back into the envelope, saying they'd talk about it all later. Hunter and Molly had arrived with their family, and Bobbie Jo had retreated to her room to shower and get dressed so she could look more presentable for Christmas Day lunch.

She could admit she really liked all the Hammonds. Heck, she really liked Tuck.

She wasn't sure why she thought she'd have to labor and work a dead, dry piece of land, carefully cultivating it back to a Garden of Eden, alongside her husband until they could enjoy the fruits of their hard work.

That farm he'd bought…it already waited as the perfect Garden of Eden, and Bobbie Jo would never admit to Tuck that she'd dreamt of walking through those green fields in the summertime, her goats trotting along beside her.

They'd be animals, she reminded herself. *Not pets.*

Of course, if she told Tuck she just wanted goats for pets, he'd let her do that too. She could sew picnic blankets and plan lunches for when he came in from that amazing training facility, and that life seemed to grow and expand and enlarge as she sat in his truck.

Tuck went down the left fork of the road, and a big gray rambler came into view. "Okay," he said. "This is the house."

"Do they all live here together?"

"Cole's not here," Tuck said. "He trains in Vegas. Warren and Harrison share the house. Rachel is their younger sister and the manager of the ranch. She has her own house too... somewhere."

Tuck brought the truck to a stop and looked at the front door. "She and Warren are meeting me—us."

Another quick glance. Another unreadable look. A rise in tension in the air.

"All right," Bobbie Jo said with an exhale. "Let's go in, then." She unbuckled her seatbelt and opened her door. Tuck followed her out of the truck, and she reached for his hand as they went up the front sidewalk that had been cleared and salted.

A yellow sticky note on the door said, *Tuck, come on in. The doorbell doesn't work and*

It trailed off as the note was small, and Warren had started out with letters that were too big.

Tuck got the message, though, and he knocked a few times before opening the door and walking in. "Hey," he called. "It's Tucker and Bobbie Jo."

She liked that he included her, and some of the tightness

in her chest released. He had not pushed her for a different reaction than the one she'd given him on Christmas Day, and Bobbie Jo squeezed his hand as they stepped up into the house.

"Hey," a man called. "Come on back. We're in the kitchen." A cowboy appeared at the end of the hall before they'd gone very far, and Bobbie Jo took in the polished wood floors, the two-tone paint on the walls and trim, the family picture of the Walkers: "The Rodeo King" Wyatt and his wife, a petite blonde woman, with their children. They varied in height, but almost all of them had blonde hair.

The shortest cowboy looked like he might start spitting bullets while the rest of the family smiled in a happy, joyous way.

"Hey, brother." Warren laughed as he reached Tuck and pulled him into a hug. "You found it."

"Bobbie Jo was worried for a bit," Tuck said, and he turned back to her. "This is her. Bobbie Jo Hanks. My girl-friend." He spoke in short sentences with all the teasing tenderness he usually did when introducing her, and Bobbie Jo put a big smile on her face.

"It's so great to meet you." She shook Warren's hand firmly. "Your house is beautiful."

"That's because my mother left this morning." Warren laughed and gestured for them to follow him back into the kitchen. They did, and a wide, bright room opened up, where Bobbie Jo would like to spend a lot of time.

Someone had put out blue, silver, and white placemats with snowflakes on them to mark the spots on the dining room table, and a white flower display of poinsettias took up the middle of it.

A blonde woman turned from the stovetop wearing an oven mitt, and she said, "Hey, everyone. I've got cookies here."

Bobbie Jo fed off the energy here, her spirits lifting up as the woman came closer. "I'm Rachel Walker." She couldn't be older that her early or mid-twenties, and she had more freckles across her face than the family photo had shown.

"It's great to meet you." She shook her hand, and then Rachel turned to Tuck. Her slight shoulders went up and then down in a quick breath and release. "So, you got that farm."

Tuck grinned for all he was worth, and in that moment, Bobbie Jo saw how much the farm meant to Tuck.

He absolutely had bought something to keep her in his life, and Bobbie Jo didn't want to be ungrateful about that. So while Tuck laughed about being served cookies and milk, she pulled out her phone and sent him a quick text.

I want to talk about the farm, and how many goats it'll hold, and what you see for us once you move there. When you're ready.

He'd told her they could talk when *she* was ready, as he always seemed to have his words right on the tip of his tongue.

She sent the text and shoved her phone away. He wouldn't get it right away, because Tuck didn't care about his device when he was with people. He'd give Warren and Rachel all of his attention—and Bobbie Jo would too.

She wanted to give her opinion on anything he wanted

her to, though she didn't know anything about what it took to train a rodeo star or what animals were needed to do that.

But she was Tucker Hammond's girlfriend, and she didn't want to break up over the purchase of a farm. She just needed to find her way through this confusing path to that glorious green field with all those goats.

Please, Dear God, she prayed. *I need to figure this out so I don't lose what could be the best thing in my life.*

She thought of the family farm in Oklahoma, and how she would've fought for it no matter the cost. She'd wanted it that badly.

So did she want Tuck that badly too?

Bobbie Jo thought she knew the answer, but she was simply too afraid to admit it, so she took a chocolate chip cookie and a glass of milk and settled down to listen to Tuck and Warren talk business.

Because she wanted to be involved in Tuck's life, and that included building his rodeo training facility.

twenty-eight

Bryce Young enjoyed his birthday more than any other day of the year. Well, maybe not when he got to surprise his wife with all *her* favorite things on *her* birthday, and now that they had a little boy together, watching him experience so much of life for the first time brought Bryce immeasurable joy he hadn't known a man could feel.

In fact, as he came down the hall from his shower, he found Matt toddling toward him with a piece of cheese in his hand, saying, "Dad, Dad, Dad, chee, chee, chee."

Bryce chuckled as he swooped the boy into his arms. Matt shrieked, and they laughed together before Matt took an overly big bite of the half-piece of string cheese Codi had obviously given him.

"I'm just getting the crust stuffed now," she said. "Then

this one will go in the oven, and people should start arriving any moment."

As if on cue, the back sliding door opened, and Reggie Avery walked in. He wore a puffy vest over a long-sleeved shirt, a cowboy hat, and his blue jeans as he said, "Kassie's putting the horses in the barn."

"How did Chiquita do?" Bryce asked as he went to half-hug Reggie. "Did she drag that hoof?"

"Hard to tell in the snow, but she made it without stopping and refusing to go on, so progress."

That was progress with the horse they'd adopted over eight months ago and had been working to rehab since. Bryce didn't normally keep horses for that long without adding them to their permanent stable, but Bryce couldn't take on any more permanent residents right now.

The Rising Sun Ranch was full, and he was hoping to sell at least a dozen horses at the New Year's auction he'd arranged for next week.

Including Chiquita, because while she couldn't really be a working horse for a farm, ranch, or the police department, she could be someone's pride and joy. They could ride her on easy trails or around their land.

So he'd added her to the list of horses that would be available at the auction, and he'd been praying that she'd be strong enough to show well when the time came.

"Reg-Reg," Matt said with the soft-G sound, and Bryce passed the little boy to Reggie.

Codi slid the pizza in the oven as Kassie opened the door and said, "Go in, baby. Hurry up now; it's cold."

A little girl wearing a full-blown pink snowsuit waddled into the farmhouse, and Bryce bent to help little Livvy out of her bulky clothes. She'd been born a month after Matt, and Bryce loved raising his son alongside his best friend's daughter.

Livvy babbled something Bryce couldn't understand, but Kassie said, "Yeah, Aunt Codi will get you a snack, baby."

And sure enough, Codi came around the corner and bent down while Bryce got the pink suit off the little girl's arms. "Here you go, baby." She held out the other half of Matt's cheese stick, and Livvy took it in her chubby fingers.

"Momma, chee-ze," she said, and she got some of the S-sound on there where Matt never did. He could say a few things that Bryce understood, but as a two-year-old, he still said a lot of nonsense that Bryce didn't comprehend.

"We're walking in," someone called from the front door, and Bryce straightened and turned that way. His daddy came under the archway, a huge box in his arms that had been wrapped in bright blue plaid paper.

"Happy birthday," Daddy practically bellowed, and he set the present on the couch and grabbed onto Bryce. He laughed as he hugged his father.

"We have the cake," Melissa, Bryce's half-sister said, and from there, the family continued to parade into the farm-house. Pizzas got sliced, and bagged salads got made, and before Bryce knew it, there was standing-room-only for his birthday party.

Once they said a prayer, he blew out the candles, and the food and cake got served, the kids would go into his office, where he and Codi had put a big-screen TV and lots of bean bags and blankets.

They had cousins and kids out to the farm all the time, and Bryce had actually been thinking of building another structure, like a kid's barn, so he'd have more room for the kids when they hosted big parties like this at his farm.

Usually, someone with a bigger house hosted, or they rented somewhere to have their parties. But in the winter, between Christmas and New Year's, Bryce had just wanted something simple, and his Momma and Aunt Georgia would come out and help Codi get the house put back together tomorrow.

"Look at this cheese!" OJ yelled as he pulled one of the pieces off the stuffed crust pizza.

"Bud, we're prayin' first," Uncle Otis said, but OJ's enthusiasm for the ooey gooey cheese didn't wane one bit.

"Oh, right," OJ said, and he plunked the piece of piece onto his paper plate and looked at his daddy with big eyes. "Ready."

Every eye came to Bryce then, as it was his house and his party, but Codi came to his side and twined her fingers through his. "Abby is going to pray for us," she said. "And then Kassie is going to light the candles on Bryce's cake, and then you can get the pizza and cake you want." She looked over to OJ, who gave her a thumbs-up, none of his shine diminishing.

Bryce loved that about him—he just took the criticism and correction and moved on with his life.

His mom came to his other side, and Bryce took her hand

in his free one as she bowed her head. He should remove his cowboy hat, but with both of his hands were occupied, he simply closed his eyes and let the spirit of God flow through him.

"Dear God," Momma said. "We're grateful to be gathered here as family and friends to celebrate having Bryce with us for another year."

He smiled, because he'd tried not to make a big deal about his birthdays in the past, but his parents wouldn't hear of it. Daddy had said he'd spent too many years away from Bryce on his birthday, and Momma had said that as he got older, he should celebrate that he'd lived another year, made it through the tough times, the good times, and everything in between.

"We're grateful for those who've spent time and energy preparing food, and we're grateful for nice houses that have good furnaces, and please bless all here with an extra touch of kindness in their hearts and a willing spirit to work."

Bryce squeezed Codi's hand, because she was one of the hardest-working people he knew. Even while nine months pregnant with their son, she'd gotten up every day, gotten dressed, and gone out on the ranch to work.

He usually just prayed right out loud when the thoughts struck, but he'd gotten better at keeping them between him and the Lord if necessary. So he prayed silently, *Thank you, God, for my good wife. And my little boy, and all of those who have loved us through so much.*

Bryce missed the rest of the prayer, only tuning back in when Momma said, "In Jesus name, amen."

"Amen," Bryce chorused along with everyone else, and then pure chaos descended on the table and counter in the farmhouse. He positioned himself next to the trays of pizza, and he started asking each kid who came through the line what they wanted.

"Cheese, pepperoni, or meat and veggie," he said over and over, putting the pieces on the plates everyone requested.

When one tray emptied, someone brought over another one. Aunt Georgia, or Codi, or Kassie, and Bryce thanked them every time.

Finally, the crowd thinned, and Bryce picked up his own plate just as the doorbell rang. He exchanged a glance with Codi, who said, "It might be a neighbor."

Bryce took his empty plate with him as he hurried to the front door, because no one should have to stand outside in this weather for very long. He pulled open the door to find Gray and Elise Hammond standing there.

Happiness filled Bryce's every cell. "Oh, my goodness. Hey." He stepped into them and hugged them, noting they weren't alone. "Come in, come in."

He went back into the house and opened the door wider. Gray and Elise entered, as did Deacon, their youngest son—someone Bryce had met several times as a much younger man—and a man Bryce only knew because he had two uncles who'd once rode in the rodeo. Tarr Olson.

"Hey, it's great to see you again," he said, as he shook Deacon's hand. "And you're Tarr."

"Guilty," the man said, a good air around him.

"Tuck and Bobbie Jo are coming," Gray said. "I hope that's

okay. Hunt wanted to, but Molly came down with a head cold this morning."

"Sure, sure," Bryce said. "Anyone's welcome. I'm sure you can take some food and cake to Hunt and his family."

As he started to close the door, headlights cut across the darkness, and Bryce let the Hammonds go in while he waited for whoever had just pulled up. He closed the door almost all the way, because while his momma had prayed for a good furnace, he didn't want to tempt God to make it go out.

A few minutes later, when Bryce heard footsteps coming up the steps to the porch, he pulled the door open all the way again. Graham and Laney Whittaker carried too many presents, as well as plenty of smiles and wishes of "Happy birthday, Bryce."

He loved them like his own parents, as they'd been *so* good to him over the years. So kind and so forgiving, and so willing to take OJ whenever they could.

They'd just gone by when another couple approached. Again, Bryce hadn't seen Tucker Hammond for a while, but he still recognized the shape of his face and the trademarked smile that shone into the night.

"Bryce," Tucker said as he jogged up the steps. "Happy birthday, man." He clapped him on the back a couple of times and stepped back. "I hope it's okay we're here," he said, falling back to his girlfriend's side.

"Of course," Bryce said in an easy way. If he got upset every time someone came by the house that he wasn't expecting, he'd live in a perpetual state of irritation.

"This is Bobbie Jo," Tuck said, beaming at the pretty

strawberry blonde at his side. "We've been dating for a few months now."

"That's phenomenal." Bryce grinned at them both. "Come in and get some pizza. Looks like there's still seats out here, or I'm sure there will be some on the deck."

"Outside?" Bobbie Jo asked, throwing a panicked look to Tuck.

"We pull some plastic closed and heat it," Bryce said, gesturing them back into the kitchen. "Come on. Come eat."

He led the way back into the kitchen, loaded up his own plate with food, and then a second one with birthday cake. Since he could never make up his mind between chocolate and vanilla, Abby always made a checkerboard cake for him with both.

"I helped this year," Pippa said, and Bryce grinned over to his youngest sister.

"Is that right?" He picked up a plastic fork. "Which part did you do, firecracker?"

Daddy had started calling Pip that a couple of years ago, because she had all the redheaded genes of her momma, and she never held back a thought.

"I cut the cake."

"With a real knife?"

"With a real knife." She grinned at him as she picked off a piece of pepperoni from her pizza. "Momma marked it with the pattern, and I cut all the chocolate cake."

"Then you lay it all together."

"Yeppers."

Bryce grinned at her and put a piece of cake on her plate. "Go find North and share your cake."

"Yes, sir," Pippa said in her sassy tone, and Bryce smiled her out of the kitchen.

He went to take a seat at the big picnic table outside, because Codi had gone that way, and he wanted to sit beside his wife on his birthday.

His parents had gone out there, as had Graham and Laney, Uncle Trace and Aunt Ev, and all of the Hammonds.

"Lord, please let there be a place for me," he prayed out loud as he approached the table.

"Right here, baby," Codi said, scooting closer to Laney. "There's room."

"Only if I shave off a leg." He eyed the tiny space, and he knew the kids would make room for him in the office-slash-TV-room.

"There's room," Laney said, and she moved down too. "We can move down."

"Where's Matt? I can go sit by him."

"Belle and Harry took him," Codi said. "Baby, sit down and eat."

Everyone had shuffled around enough now that Bryce could fold himself at the picnic table, so he swung his leg over the bench seat and sat.

"So Tuck," he said. "I heard you're taking on Rosie." He took a bite of pizza and looked over to the other cowboy.

"Yep," Tuck said. "You make it sound like I might regret it."

"He's not going to regret it," Graham said.

"Regret what?" Uncle Blaze asked as he came out onto the deck too. He held a single piece of pizza in his hand, no plate in sight.

"Takin' on Rosie," Bryce said.

"Oh, yeah, he's gonna regret it," Blaze said with a grin. "Rosie is so ready for the rodeo, though."

"I can't wait to work with her," Tuck said. "We're meetin' in San Antonio for a couple of months, and then we'll be back at my place in Ivory Peaks. I mean." He shrugged, his demeanor so good, though Bryce caught him flicking a look over to Bobbie Jo. "It's not Ivory Peaks, but a great place I just bought north of the city."

Bryce cut a look down the table to Tuck's daddy, who gave nothing away, as usual. Gray Hammond had always been one cool cat, and while the Hammonds weren't as big as the Youngs, they had a pretty amazing family that seemed just as loud and boisterous as Bryce's.

"Bryce."

He turned toward the sliding glass door to find Rosie herself standing there. "The kids want you to come open your presents now."

"I just got my pizza," he said.

Rosie cocked her hip. "I'll hold them off as long as I can, but you know how they get."

"They've eaten two whole cakes," Daddy said. "Just gonna throw that out there."

"It's *my* birthday," Bryce said. "And I want ten minutes to eat." He took another bite of pizza while Uncle Blaze said he'd go help Rosie with the kids.

"You better eat fast," Codi said as the sliding glass door slid shut. "Just enough to not be starving, because the moment even one of them starts a chant...." She shrugged like she didn't care what happened next, but Bryce had seen the consequences of it.

And he couldn't let the kids get to chanting his name to come back inside and open his presents. So he forked off a huge bite of cake and put the whole thing in his mouth.

Codi giggled, and Laney got up and said she'd go help with the kids too. Then his momma said she'd go get all the presents on the table so he could open them in the big living room.

He ate fast, but he had reinforcements helping with his cousins, so he didn't hurry.

Until the sliding glass door opened again, and he heard, "Bryce! Bryce! Bryce!" coming from inside.

And then he tipped his head back and said, "Lord, I love my family. Thank you for another year on earth with them."

twenty-nine

Tuck stamped his feet as he went up the steps to the generational house where he'd be living for only three more days. He slapped his gloves against the post there to get the snow and ice off.

His heavy pants and coat suddenly felt too hot now that he had slowed down. He had a lot of packing to do this afternoon, and Bobbie Jo would be by later for dinner. She said she'd drive out from the city and help him go through some of his things.

Then, of course, he'd see her again in a few days when he loaded up his truck and headed south to San Antonio. He wasn't sad about the better weather in Texas, but he didn't know what to do with the way his heart shriveled in his chest every time he thought about leaving Ivory Peaks, leaving his family farm, leaving his best friend to deal with the place in Deerfield, and leaving Bobbie Jo.

The real problem was Bobbie Jo, he knew, but he hadn't figured out a way past that yet.

He hadn't taken her to Deerfield, as they'd only been home from Coral Canyon for two days and snow had been falling since. She'd had to go back to work, and Tuck had been watching the weather to see if they could go by the farm before he left.

"If you can't," he muttered to himself. "That's just one more thing for Tarr to handle."

He didn't want his best friend to handle that, though he was thrilled that Tarr had told Matt that he would be quitting at the Hammond family farm to work Tuck's farm in Deerfield in the winter.

There wasn't a lot to do, but Tarr was a professional rodeo champion, and he wanted to go through all the equipment and facilities to see what they had and what they needed to bring in order to be a real training facility for champions.

Tuck had been managing rodeo careers for six years, but he'd only worked with two people. He had a lot of contacts in the rodeo still, and landing Rosie Young was a *huge* deal. Her cousin, Cash, had just won everything in Vegas during the National Championships for the third time.

Still, Tuck knew that a lot of rodeo success came from pure talent, and the training and management could make up the difference, but it couldn't make Rosie a better horseman. If that were true, *he* would be the national champion still riding the rodeo circuit.

He pushed all these thoughts away as he reached for the doorknob and entered his house. He expected to find it empty, warm, and waiting for him. It was two of those three things, but the gorgeous Bobbie Jo turned from the dining room table against the far wall.

She clasped her hands together in what Tuck knew to be a nervous gesture and said, "You're back early."

"I don't think I'm the one who's early, sweetheart," he said as he toed the door closed and sat on the bench Deacon had put there to remove their boots.

She came toward him. "You said you weren't going to pack until tonight."

He glanced up at her and then went back to his boots. "Do you really think I want to spend my time with you packing?"

She sighed as she sat down on the bench beside him, barely enough room for the two of them. "I was trying to surprise you."

"I'm surprised."

She laced her arm through his, and that got Tuck to look at her. "Really," he said. "I'm surprised." He leaned over and kissed her, sure glad that he could do so without a flutter of nerves, too much tension, or worrying that she'd slap him.

She seemed to like him a lot too, and Tuck wished he could see what the next couple of months would be like for them. He pulled away slightly and ducked his head until his forehead touched hers.

"The roads weren't too bad?" he asked.

"I worked half a day," she whispered. "It was sunny when I left. The plows have been out."

"Mm," he said, enjoying this peaceful feeling between them. They'd been kayaking down a fairly serene river until the last few weeks, as things had gotten more serious between them, and he'd made decisions for his life that he hoped would keep her with him.

"Supposed to be real nice on Friday," he said. "Maybe we can go to the farm then."

"All right," she said. "Are you going to shower or anything?"

He grinned and pulled away. "Are you saying I stink?"

She actually giggled, which so wasn't like her usually grumpy self, but at the same time, it totally was, as Bobbie Jo had many facets, each of which Tuck really liked and wanted to know more about.

"No," she said. "I'm hoping that I can finish my surprise while you're down the hall."

He looked past her toward the dining room table, and Bobbie Jo leaned forward, cutting off his view. "Don't look," she said. And *there* came that fiery, sassy side he loved so much.

"What are you doing over there?" he asked.

"It's a surprise."

He chuckled. He unzipped his coat and got to his feet. He hung the jacket on a peg over the bench and said, "I'm gonna go shower."

"I'll walk you past the dining room table," Bobbie Jo said.

He laughed, then grabbed onto her in the wild way Tuck had sometimes. She laughed with him, and as the moment sobered, he reached up and tucked her hair behind her ear.

"I sure am gonna miss you when I'm in San Antonio," he said.

"Yes, you are." She tipped her head back to receive his kiss. She didn't let him go on too long before she added, "Besides, I've heard a rumor."

"Oh, boy," Tuck said, pulling away completely. "Walk me past this dining room table as you tell me about this rumor."

He gave her a look out of the corner of his eye, his heart pounding as he took the first step toward the hall.

"Someone told me that you have a surprise for me too."

"Who?" he demanded.

"Oh, I'm not going to give away my sources," she said.

"Well, then I can neither confirm nor deny the rumor of this surprise." He'd only told a few people about the weekend he had planned in San Antonio for him and Bobbie Jo in just three more weeks.

He'd then planned to fly home for Valentine's Day, and then he'd be back at Deerfield by the first week of March. Hopefully.

So her source has to be Deacon, Hunter, Mike, or Tarr, he thought, and he didn't think any of them would talk to her. They had no real reason to talk to her very often, and Tarr and Hunt would never even cross her path.

"So it has to be Mikey," he mused out loud. "Did he call you up to his office to tell you what I had planned?"

She laughed and shook her head. "No. It wasn't him."

"Wasn't him?" Tuck asked as she lifted her hand and placed it next to his eyes on the left as they moved past the dining room table. "And you take your surprises really seriously."

"*I* take my surprises really seriously?" She paused at the

mouth of the hall and cocked her hip, putting one hand on it. "Tell me about the surprise you have planned."

"I will not," he said. "I don't even have anything."

Bobbie Jo's face bloomed into a glorious smile. "You're not a good liar, Tuck."

"Praise the heavens for that," he tossed at her. "I'm gonna go shower. How long do you need to finish your surprise?" It took every ounce of willpower he had not to look over at the table, but he managed to keep his gaze locked on Bobbie Jo's.

"Fifteen minutes?" she guessed.

"I suppose I can spend fifteen minutes in the shower," he said. "I'll be right back."

He turned and went down the hall, very aware of Bobbie Jo's eyes on his back as he did. He set a timer for fifteen minutes because he'd never taken that long to shower, get dressed, and head back into the kitchen after work. And though he had come in early, his stomach still growled for something to eat.

He did take longer in the shower. He brushed his teeth, combed his hair, and put fresh clothes on.

When the alarm went off, he left the only bedroom in the house, which he shared with his younger brother, a wave of gratitude filling him that he would be able to afford a short-term rental with more space in San Antonio. And then, of course, he had that monstrosity of a house in Deerfield, and soon enough, he'd feel completely overwhelmed by the space around him.

The moment he stepped into the hall, he smelled the evidence of food, and Tuck's stomach roared at him again.

He moved in socked feet to the end of the hall and stopped. Bobbie Jo sat at the table now, her attention on her phone, her legs crossed, and a picnic blanket spread across the dining room table. Love burst through him with every beat of his heart, every red or white square he drank in, and Tuck wondered how he would walk away from her and drive to San Antonio without telling her.

It's too soon, a voice whispered in his head. She hadn't reacted well to the purchase of the farm, and she hadn't believed for a single minute that he had bought it for himself and not her. He wasn't sure how he would feel and what he would do if he told her he loved her, and she didn't say it back.

Of course, he didn't want her to say it back unless she felt it and it was true, and he wasn't sure she would do that at this point.

Bobbie Jo didn't look up from her phone as she said, "I can hear you breathing over there."

Tuck rolled his eyes as he came around the corner. "You can not."

She looked up, her eyebrows raised in clear challenge. "You were there, weren't you?"

"You heard me walking," he said. "I'm like a gorilla."

She grinned at him and got to her feet. "Surprise," she said, indicating the picnic she had set out for them on the dining room table. "Deacon is going to eat over at Hunter's tonight, so we have the place to ourselves until around nine."

"You've been texting my younger brother?" Tuck asked in mock shock.

Bobbie Jo grinned at him, came toward him, and placed both of her hands against his chest. "I have to do something to keep up with you."

"It's not a competition, sweetheart," he said.

"It better not be," she said. "Because I'm always losing."

"Hey." He took her face in both of his hands. "Do you really feel like that?"

"Yes," she whispered, the moment suddenly turning tense and vulnerable between them.

"Tell me more." The words came out semi-demanding, though his tone had been soft.

"I just—I don't know." She turned away, breaking the connection. "It's store-bought fried chicken, so don't be all excited. But Cara made the rolls, and I put together those coconut crispie treats you like."

"Bobbie Jo," he said, following her over to the table. She'd laid out plastic plates and silverware from a real picnic basket, and all of the food sat beside it, complete with iced tea and pink lemonade.

"I'll make coffee," she said. "It's still early enough for that, right?" She sent him a nervous look and then darted into the kitchen. Tuck didn't want this night to be made of nerves—or anything but fried chicken and kissing.

"This is amazing," he said as she started measuring grounds for coffee. He took in the mashed potatoes and corn-on-the-cob, along with the homemade rolls and Deac's jam. "Where'd you get this?"

"Silverado's," she said as she came closer to him again. "We love their fried chicken. Have you ever been there?"

"No," he said. "It looks amazing." He hooked his arm around her waist and pulled her flush against him. "Why do you feel like you're losing?"

"I don't really think I have to spell it out."

"Maybe just start with the first letter," he said.

She gave him a dry, scathing look that somehow sent his hormones into overdrive and said, "It starts with a B and has to do with how much money you have." Then she turned and walked back into the kitchen to get coffee mugs.

Tuck stood there next to the picnic, his own inadequacies at how he'd come to be so rich running through him.

He finally took a seat next to where she'd been sitting, as the dining room table had been pushed up against the windows and could only be used on the ends and one side. He filled her plate with food and then his, and by that time, she'd returned with the coffee.

"I can't erase my money," he said, something dangerous and frothy rising through him. "And I'd gladly spend every dime on you if it would make you happy."

"It's not about that," she said.

"What's it about?" he asked. "You don't want someone to take care of you? You don't want the person who loves you to buy you what you want?" He pulled in a breath, nowhere near as loud as Bobbie Jo's.

"Tucker," she said in a warning tone.

"Forget it," he said. "I get it. Hunter had this problem. Mikey had this problem. Heck, even Jane had this problem. I think Tag and Opal did too. It's a conversation we *need* to have.

"I get it. I'm rich. I have money. I'm going to be able to buy whatever we want for the rest of our lives, Bobbie Jo, and if you can't handle that, that's fine. We should break-up now."

He pushed his plate toward her with his knuckles, a violent movement. "I didn't mean—" Something raged inside him, though, and he didn't know how to calm it.

"I don't want to break up," she said.

"What *do* you want?"

"I'm just working through how to feel like I'm not using you."

"I don't feel like you're using me," he said.

"But *I* do." She reached over and took his hand in hers, cradling it in one, then the other, and then both at the same time.

"It's a lot to take in, you know."

"The money?"

"Of course the money," she said. "Your family, how wonderful they are, how big they are, how giving and generous they are. When you don't come from that, Tuck, it's a completely different way of living, and I know you don't get it. You don't even see it. You don't even know *how* to see it, and that's not your fault."

It kind of felt like it was his fault, but Tucker didn't say that. He simply kept his head down and enjoyed the way she stroked her fingers across his.

"It's just a lot for me," she said.

"Okay," Tucker said. "I'm not asking you to marry me tomorrow."

"I know," she whispered.

"If you don't want to see the farm, it's fine."

"I want to see it."

"I'll sell it if you want me to." He looked at her, everything suddenly wide open between them. "Bobbie Jo, baby, I'll do *anything* for you. I *want* you in my life. I bought a place here to *keep* you in my life. I bought a place where you could have goats, because that's what you wanted. But if you don't, that's okay too. I just want you, and I just want you to be happy."

Tears filled her eyes, which only made Tucker feel worse. He couldn't stand watching her cry, so he pulled her into his chest and held her tight.

The roller coaster of the past ten minutes of conversation overwhelmed him, and then Bobbie Jo said, "I want to keep you in my life too, Tuck," and everything inside him settled.

He could wait for Bobbie Jo to get to a place where she could understand who he was and what he could do. Gertie had been mad about Mike buying her a farm too, but they'd worked through it. And since it sure seemed like neither Tucker nor Bobbie Jo wanted to break up, he prayed for a softening of her heart and for understanding to come into her mind.

And for more time that they could be together until they could be together forever.

"All right," Bobbie Jo said as she picked up a backpack and handed it to him. "That's everything you own."

Tucker put the pack over one shoulder and surveyed the generational house where he'd lived for the past four months. Bobbie Jo and Molly had cleaned the kitchen after breakfast, and he, Deacon, and Hunter had packed everything into the back of his truck, covered with a tarp and tied down. They'd all gone back to the farmhouse, and Tuck would go there too to get a cooler full of food from Molly for his drive south.

It would take him two days to get to San Antonio. He was staying somewhere in New Mexico tonight. "I don't feel old enough to be doing this," he said.

Bobbie Jo wore somber eyes as she nodded. "You've left home before."

"Yeah."

"You're really good at making plans and attending to details," she reminded him.

He nodded again and swallowed. "Yeah, I am."

"I would love for there to be one thing you're not good at," she said, grinning at him, and that got Tucker to bring his eyes to hers.

"What does that mean?"

"I would like you to be really bad at saying goodbye."

She reached up and cradled his face in one hand, and Tucker felt sure that the Earth would shatter.

"I don't want to say goodbye," he said.

"You're just going somewhere else for a little while," she said. "It's not forever, and I'll see you soon."

He reached up and covered her hand with his and then

lowered his arm as he twined his fingers through hers. "For your birthday," he said.

Her eyebrows went up. "Is that the surprise?"

"I don't think you do super well with surprises, sweetheart," he said, leaning on his wit to cover his emotion. "So I think I'll just give you a hint that we're definitely going to see each other for your birthday."

She smiled at him in the gentle, kind way that Bobbie Jo had when he got beneath her salty and prickly exterior. "I can't wait, Tuck." She leaned in and kissed him. It seemed totally unfair that Bobbie Jo was so good at saying goodbye when he wasn't.

At the same time, Tuck knew he needed to be in San Antonio for the next couple of months. As he'd been doing for the past month since he'd first looked at the farm in Deerfield, he told himself over and over, *You're coming back here. You're coming back here. You're coming back here.*

You're coming back home.

thirty

Rosie Young rode in the backseat of her daddy's truck, so many people she loved with her—her momma rode up front, though Sunny was her stepmom, and her two half-siblings rode in the back with her: Ladd and Skye.

Her younger sister had fallen asleep an hour ago, and Ladd played something on his tablet while Rosie's nerves continued to rise through her body. When she got nervous like this, her leg would shake, and then Daddy would know something was wrong.

Of course, something was wrong.

Rosie was nineteen years old and leaving Coral Canyon in the rearview mirror. She was going to live in an apartment with a *stranger*—a woman she'd never met before who was five years older than her—and she'd train for the professional rodeo circuit, which she'd never competed in before.

"This is a bad idea," she said right out loud.

"I told you not to get sushi in the Texas Panhandle," her daddy deadpanned.

"I mean moving," she practically yelled at him. Daddy didn't flinch at all because he'd known Rosie her whole life, and he knew when to bark back at her, when to make her come sit down in his office and talk to her, and when to leave her alone to rage and rant.

He also was extraordinarily good at holding her as she curled into his chest and told him all the things she was scared about, about everything that made her nervous, and every care that brought worry to her soul.

Sunny turned and looked at her, worry in her eyes, which only made Rosie's double.

"You're gonna be fine," Daddy said. "You traveled the circuit last year as an amateur."

"I did," she said. "And as a spectator. I didn't *ride*."

"Well, you're going to ride this year," Daddy said, and he glanced at her in the rearview mirror. As weak and fragile as she felt, she couldn't hold his gaze for long, but she couldn't silence his voice as he said, "Rosie-babe, you gotta figure out how to deal with these nerves. They ain't gonna go anywhere."

"I know, Daddy," she said crossly. "I've been nervous before, and I'll ride just fine in the pro circuit."

"It's different," he said, and he'd been saying that a lot.

"That doesn't help," she said, as she told him many times before. All it did was double her nerves.

She'd lived in Las Vegas for the first few years of her life with her mom, and then Daddy had gotten full custody of her and her older brother, Cole, and they'd gone to live with him in Coral Canyon when Rosie was only six.

She'd known nothing else for the last thirteen years, and she'd been surrounded by people who loved her, cheered for her, and championed her no matter what—no matter if she won, no matter if she lost, no matter if she threw up before-hand, no matter if she scratched because she couldn't get out on the horse—no matter what. That's what the Youngs did, and none of them would be in Texas.

None of them would be in Texas.

She'd brought both her horses with her, and she suddenly just wanted to be out in the field with them, so she could tell them all of her cares, all of her worries, all of her concerns, and let the sky swallow them whole and let Jesus carry them on his shoulders.

Rosie, at only one-hundred-and-five pounds, certainly couldn't do it.

"It's going to be okay, baby," Sunny said, as she reached over the seat and squeezed Rosie's arm. "You're going to be okay. You're ready for this." Her blue eyes shone with confidence and hope, and Rosie nodded at her in tight little bursts.

"Okay," she said. "I am. I am ready for this."

"You're going nowhere on the amateur circuit," Daddy said. "You've won that thing too many times."

Rosie didn't argue with him. She was barely old enough to be pro, so she certainly hadn't won the amateur circuit too many times—*two* times, exactly.

"Besides, Tucker's already here," Daddy said. "He checked on your room, and it's great."

"It's a private room," Sunny said, reminding Rosie of all the things that they had arranged for her in San Antonio. A couple of months after that, Tuck wanted to return to a farm he had bought in the Denver area. Rosie didn't care. She just wanted to ride.

She wanted to be a rodeo champion.

Tuck said he had on-site facilities in Colorado where she could live, and she wouldn't have to share, so she could make it through the next two months, even if her roommate was a nightmare.

"I've never had a roommate," she blurted out, which was one of the talking points she'd been over with Daddy and Sunny before.

"She's real nice," Daddy automatically said. "You've met her via video a couple of times, Rosie-babe. She's not a complete stranger."

"We talked to the landlord," Sunny said.

"I know," Rosie said. Her stomach still bubbled and boiled, and maybe Daddy was right about the sushi in the Texas Panhandle. "Are we going to dinner before we go to the apartment?"

"No," Sunny said. "We've got to get the horses out of the trailer."

"Okay," Rosie said.

"So we have to stop by your training barn," Daddy said. "We'll get Blossom and Wildflower settled. Then we'll call for pizza and go to your place."

He met her eye in the rearview mirror again, his eyebrows up. "Okay? It'll take us ten minutes to move you in, and you'll be fine."

"You're not leaving till tomorrow anyway," Rosie said.

"And we're not leaving until tomorrow anyway," Daddy repeated back to her.

She nodded, her nerves settled, but not soothed. Rosie hadn't spent a whole lot of time crying in her life, and she really only did if she was hurt or angry, but these nerves came from neither pain nor frustration, but pure anxiety.

She picked up her phone and texted Cole: *I am so nervous about moving out.*

He'd left home a couple of years ago to also turn pro in the rodeo. Daddy had managed him for a while, but it was too hard with his little kids.

Now, Cole trained with the same manager as Cash, but their manager didn't work with women, and Rosie had had to find someone for herself.

She knew she'd struck gold with Tucker Hammond. She wasn't going to blow that opportunity. He'd trained two national champions already in his short and young management career.

She'd spoken to both Tarr Olsen and John Richins. They both had only good things to say about Tuck—*he's funny, he's down to earth, he's organized, he's detailed. He's never missed anything.* They'd both been national champions, and when Tarr had been hurt and then retired, Tuck had drifted for the past year or so.

He wouldn't lead her astray, she knew, and her attention

got diverted when her phone brightened with a text from Cole.

First few nights are hard, sissy, he said. *Call me when you're alone, and then you won't be alone.*

She'd always been the wild child out of the pair of them. She spoke her mind; she argued with their parents. She broke more rules. Cole had been steady and silent, but the two of them had been so close—and they still were.

How's Vegas? she asked because she didn't want the spotlight on her anymore.

It's great, Cole said, as he didn't waste words. *When you transition from Texas to Colorado, maybe you should come here for a little bit. Stay with me and Cash for a weekend. We'd love to have you.*

Okay, Rosie said. Daddy would leave her the trailer and the truck—a huge blessing, she knew. She'd never wanted for much of anything, and gratitude filled Rosie so full that her anxiety and worries had no room to stay.

She breathed out, finally feeling more like a human and less like a wound-tight ball. She sighed. She could do this. And when she was alone, she would call someone, and then she wouldn't be alone.

And in the Young family, there were at least sixty people to call, and she smiled to herself, because she'd always loved being a Young.

An hour later, Rosie got out of the truck in front of a duplex just as Tucker Hammond came down the front steps. He wore a smile from ear to ear, and he spread his arms wide and said, "You made it."

He jogged toward her and lifted her right up off her feet as he hugged her. "It's so great to see you in person." He set her back on her feet, and his enthusiasm and joy spread to her, and Rosie couldn't help feeding off of it.

Tucker turned to her daddy as he got out of the truck and said, "Jem Young. So great to see you again. How was the drive?"

"It was tolerable," Daddy said, and Rosie dang near rolled her eyes. She told herself she was not walking into that house as a grumpy-grump, and she turned back to help her sister down. "You help me carry my bag in, okay, Skye?"

"Okay," she said in her cute six-year-old voice, and Rosie loved being with the little kids. The walls of her heart suddenly crashed into each other as she realized what she was leaving in Coral Canyon.

She looked over to Daddy and said, "I won't be able to babysit anymore."

Daddy blinked at her, and Tuck turned to face her too, the smile sliding off his face all at once. It came roaring back, and he said, "Don't you worry, Rosie, you're gonna be babysitting me. And trust me, that's no pleasant job."

He chuckled and went around to the back of the truck and opened the tailgate. "All this is going in?"

Rosie just stood there as Momma and Daddy and Ladd and Tuck, and even Skye started taking things into the house.

When Daddy came out, he said, "Rosie, unfreeze, girl. You're here. This is where you want to be, and it's going to be amazing. Now, come get something out of the back, because I'm not doing all this by myself."

She blinked at him and then turned to follow him to do exactly what he said.

Inside the house, she found her roommate, Ellen, and she said, "Hey, I'm Rosie," in the brightest voice she could muster.

"It's great to meet you in person," she said as she stood up. Her dark eyes roamed down to Rosie's feet and back to her face. "Look at you. You're such a tiny little thing. You're gonna ride the barrels?"

Rosie was barely five-foot-three, but she could command any horse, and she was used to people commenting on her small stature. She didn't like it, but she was used to it. "Yep," she said. "Thank you so much for letting me stay here for a couple of months."

"Yeah, of course," Ellen said. "There's an extra room anyway, and my sister will be back from Europe in March, so it works out perfectly."

Rosie nodded. "Okay, great." She took in the kitchen, which smelled like lemons, deciding she wouldn't be doing a lot of cooking here. Rosie wasn't exactly what someone would call domestic, and she figured she'd be spending most of her time at the barn or with Tucker.

Ellen tracked Daddy and Tucker's movement as they came in with more boxes, the two of them laughing over something she hadn't heard, and went down the hall toward her room. Then she leaned closer to Rosie and asked, "How old is Tucker Hammond?"

Rosie said, "Oh, I don't know, twenty-seven or something."

Ellen giggled, and oh, Rosie knew that sound. Plenty of girls had liked Cole, and they thought if they were friends with Rosie, they'd have a chance of getting closer to him.

That had never worked, but it had never stopped the girls from trying.

"Does he have a girlfriend?" Ellen asked.

Rosie swung her attention away from where Tucker had gone and back to her new roommate. She grinned and nodded. "I think he does."

Ellen's face fell and she shook her head. "Dang it, he sure is handsome."

Rosie would keep that to herself, but it did make her smile. Someone came up the steps, and he had curly hair spilling out from underneath his cowboy hat. Rosie sure thought he was cute, and he raised his hand and knocked on the door.

"Pizza's here," he called.

Rosie grinned over to Ellen and said, "Now *he's* cute, so I'll be getting that." And she went to do exactly that.

thirty-one

Tarr Olson pulled up to the sprawling farmhouse, his truck kicking up a light spray of slush from the January roads. He let out a low whistle as he took in the impressive property.

Of course, Tarr had been here several times now. This just happened to be the first time he'd come alone and with everything he owned in the back of his truck.

He'd quit at the Hammond Family Farm, a place that had welcomed him when he'd needed it most. He'd left friends behind that he missed already, and Tarr had never been too emotionally attached to anyone.

Until Tuck.

The man possessed a huge personality, and it had only taken Tarr a couple of days of being around his family to realize where he'd gotten it from.

He pulled up to the house and parked, then grabbed his

duffel bag from the passenger seat, made sure he had the keys to the place, and made his way inside, boots crunching on the salted walkway. The house sat quiet and empty, just as Tuck and the realtor had said it would be.

"Too quiet," he whispered to himself, because Tarr didn't do so well in the quiet. Tuck had bought the house at the beginning of the year, but he'd had to then furnish an eighty-five-hundred square-foot house, with nine bedrooms, three levels, and multiple common living areas.

He'd bought all the furniture and given the store the code to the front door to get it all set up.

Tarr was no stranger to what money could do, that was for sure. He had plenty in the bank too. Maybe not billions-plenty, but millions-plenty still went a long way.

So he didn't need another job right away, though his gut vibrated at him that he did. Tarr simply didn't like being idle.

He found the guest room on the main floor easily and tossed his bag on the bed. It boasted a gray and white plaid comforter, with big puffy pillows, and white towels stacked on the end of it. His own private bath sat just through the door, and Tarr could probably fit his whole bedroom back at the family farm in the closet.

He should probably stay and unpack before he lost too much of the day, but he wanted to check out the facilities, especially the arena he'd driven by several times. Shrugging back into his coat, Tarr headed outside and made his way across the property, tapping his phone's timer as he went.

Twelve minutes later, he stood in front of the light brown building that housed the arena. It was indeed impressive—

custom-built, well-maintained, with plenty of room for the training they'd do here.

Tarr nodded approvingly as he walked the perimeter. This would be perfect for training with cattle, bulls, and horses.

He had a key, but he'd spent the morning with the realtor, and as the daylight didn't linger in the winter, Tarr thought he better get back and get more of his belongings inside before it got dark.

As he neared the far corner of the huge arena, a movement caught his eye. Tarr squinted through the afternoon light. There, huddled against the fence, sat a dog. As Tarr approached, he found the poor thing soaked to the bone and shivering.

"Hey there, buddy," Tarr said softly, crouching down. The dog—some kind of fifty-pound mutt—looked up at him with doleful eyes. He didn't seem hurt, and he only had a bit of mud around his paws and ankles.

Tarr's heart went out to the pitiful creature, as he'd always had a soft spot for animals. "C'mon, bud," he said. "You can come home with me and I'll get you cleaned up."

The dog whimpered and took a step toward Tarr, so he grinned at it and scrubbed his hand along the animal's jowls. He wore a collar, but no tag, and Tarr figured he could take pictures in the morning and put them up on social media. "You've been taken care of," he said. "At least in the past. Come on, boy. I'm sure I can spare some food for tonight."

Gently, he scooped up the dog and carried it back to the house. That took twice as long as twelve minutes, but every time he thought about putting down the dog, he'd look at him with sad, pathetic eyes, and Tarr would take another step.

In the mudroom, Tarr found some towels he hoped would come clean and got to work drying off the shivering animal.

"There you go," he murmured, rubbing the dog's ears. "That's better, huh?"

Once the dog was reasonably dry, Tarr smiled at him. "I'm gonna call you Jimmy until I know your real name." He straightened and turned to leave the mudroom. "Let's see what's in the fridge."

He'd become an expert at ordering groceries from his time on the road, and he found the microwaveable turkey meal and tossed that in to heat up. "Six minutes, my friend."

He tossed down two of the towels and added, "That's your bed. You stay here while I bring in some boxes." Tarr's foot and ankle had healed well, and he moved easily now, so moving his clothes and few possessions into the bedroom didn't take long.

Tuck had ordered all new pots and pans, silverware, dishes, cups, and more, so Tarr had left all of his at the cabin where he'd been living with Mission. A pang of homesickness hit him that made absolutely no sense, because Tarr was not a Hammond, nor from that farm.

He thought of his only living family—his older brother—in Stephenville, Texas. So very far from him right now. Tarr couldn't remember the last time he'd spoken to Wayne. Probably about when his brother told him he was a coward for joining the rodeo when their daddy needed him at home.

But there had been nothing for Tarr there, and Tucker

Hammond had literally come into his life and saved him from making a mess of his rodeo career before it had truly had a chance to start.

He'd just gotten the last box in his bedroom when Jimmy whined, and he jogged into the kitchen. "I forgot about dinner, didn't I, bud?"

He pulled open the microwave and took out the turkey, the plastic now semi-suctioned back over it. He peeled it back and forked a couple of slices into a bowl he simply wouldn't tell Tuck he'd used to feed a dog. He smiled and smiled as Jimmy lapped up the meat and gravy, and then Tarr ate his part right from the black plastic container he'd used to cook his meal.

"Okay, let's get your picture taken," he said to Jimmy, but before he could lift his phone and aim it at the dog, loud pounding sounded on the front door.

Tarr dang near jumped out of his skin. This house wasn't off a main road. No one would just happen by. Maybe he could just ignore whoever stood on the porch.

"Police," a man called, and the idea of ignoring them disappeared.

Frowning, he hurried out of the kitchen and down the hall past the bathroom and then the double offices to the foyer. "Police?" he muttered. What in the world were the police doing here?

He pulled open the door with a little too much force, forgetting how nice this place was. The huge door gained momentum, and Tarr, despite his strength, couldn't catch it before it hit the wall with a resounding *thud!*

He pressed his eyes closed even as he told himself he had plenty of time to patch a hole in the wall before Tuck got here from San Antonio. Two months, in fact.

He opened his eyes and found a uniformed police officer standing on the porch, looking stern. "Sir," he started. "Have you found a dog this evening?"

"He didn't *find* a dog," a woman said, and Tarr's eyes switched to her. He hadn't seen her there, because she'd been hiding behind the burlier policeman. "He *stole* my dog." Blue ice and fire blared across the space to him, and Tarr sure did like it.

Just like he enjoyed her pajama pants with ice cream cones all over them. She wore an oversized sweatshirt with them, no coat, and her gorgeous blonde hair in waves that fell over her shoulders and down her back.

Tarr's face heated, because he hadn't been out with anyone in a few months now, since Hattie had left the farm to finish college.

She'd been too young for him, and he couldn't help wondering how old this woman was. If he could get her to take the glaring down a notch, perhaps he could learn her name and figure a way to get her phone number before she left.

"I *found* a dog this afternoon," he said, hooking his thumb over his shoulder. "I've got 'im here. He was just eating."

"Eating?" the woman screeched as if the mutt would be on a gluten-free diet. "What did you feed him?" She looked at the officer. "He's now stolen and poisoned my dog."

Tarr blinked in surprise, shock flowing through him.

"Whoa, hold on. I didn't *steal* any dog. I *found* a dog, cold and wet, and I brought him back here, warmed him up, and fed him."

The police officer looked bored as he moved his attention from Tarr to the woman. "Briar?"

The woman folded her arms, but Tarr was halfway to knowing her full name. "Where did you find him?"

"Down by the arena there," he said. "See, my friend just bought the place, and—"

"By the fence?" she asked.

"Yes, ma'am." Perhaps Tarr's Southern gentleman manners would earn him some points with the beautiful-if-surly Briar.

"Yes, sir," she said. "That's where I live."

The officer chuckled and said, "He meant no harm, Briar. Be nice to him, or he might keep Wiggins."

"He will not," she said with plenty of force as the policeman turned and walked away. Legit went down the steps, waving at them over his shoulder without a backward look.

That left Tarr to stare at Briar, who harrumphed as she turned back to face him. "I would like my dog back."

Tarr leaned in the doorway, wondering if a woman like Briar could be impressed by pancakes. Probably not. "You live across the fence? I thought my friend bought this whole place."

"I came with the purchase."

His eyebrows went up, and Briar rolled her eyes. Before she could demand he produce her dog again, he backed up a step. "Come on in, and I'll make coffee. You have to be freezing; you don't even have a coat on."

"Where's my dog?"

Tarr found it a bit odd that he hadn't come running at the sound of his master's voice. "I think he's enjoying a tryptophan nap." He turned and walked into the foyer, leaving the front door open. *Dear God*, he thought. *Please let her come in. I don't want to even imagine the electric bill if we leave the door open for much longer.*

"A what?" she shrieked, her footsteps following him.

A measure of satisfaction flowed through him as the door slammed, and he found Jimmy now licking the black plastic container that had not been on the floor nor empty when Tarr had gone to answer the door.

"You little sneak," he said good-naturedly. He turned back to Briar as she entered the kitchen. "He got up on the counter and ate my dinner."

"Payback for stealing him," she said. She grinned as she crouched down, and Jimmy wagged his whole body as he went to her. Fine. So the turkey had just been a stronger magnet to the canine for a few minutes.

"I'm Tarr Olson," he said. "My friend Tucker Hammond bought the place. You came with it?"

She looked up at him, her hands still stroking down Jimmy's face. Or Wiggins. Whatever the dog's name was. "Yeah, I was helping with all the animals there at the end, and Tuck said he'd need me once he got here."

"Oh, so you've met Tuck." And Tarr was going to have some words with his best friend for not mentioning this woman. Then a terrible thought struck him—maybe she wasn't single.

"We've only texted." She smiled back at Wiggins and stood. "I'm Briar Prescott. I was the vet here for a couple of years, and Tuck said he'd pay me to stay on. Said you guys are going to be training rodeo...something?"

"Yeah," Tarr said with a smile. "We've both got horses, of course, and we'll train with cowboys and cowgirls, and that means we'll have cattle and more horses too."

"Bulls?" she asked.

Tarr shook his head. "Tuck's gonna do the bull riding training off-site." His tongue practically itched to tell her he was a prize-winning National Champion bull rider, but he caught the words before they left his mouth.

"I should probably get this troublemaker home," Briar said, glancing down at Wiggins.

"I can make pancakes or something if you're hungry," he said.

Those electric blue eyes came to his, and Tarr swallowed all of his nerves. He'd never had a problem asking women out, even the prettiest ones, but something about Briar made him nervous.

"And I should probably get your number," he said. "In case Wiggins goes wandering again."

And so much more, he thought.

Briar cocked her head at him as if she could read his mind. "All right," she said slowly. "But I'll have you know that I have security cameras on my place."

He grinned at her. "What does that have to do with me

havin' your number, so I can call you when your naughty dog —who ate my dinner off the counter—gets lost?"

"How much is that microwaveable meal?" she demanded. "My word, I'll pay you back."

Tarr leaned in closer, if only to get a little hint of what her shampoo smelled like. Vanilla. Maybe peaches. All delicious. "How did you know it was a microwaveable meal?" His eyebrows went up, and oh, flirting with her sure was fun.

Her face blanked, and she tossed her hair in the next moment, her emotions cooling completely. "A guess."

"How about dinner, then?" he asked. "Since we're both eating out of the microwave. You can show me what's good in town."

Her eyes rounded, and she seemed to be at war with herself. "I—I can't tonight."

"Sure," he said easily. "Another time then."

She seemed unsettled now, and she pulled out her phone as she walked down the hall. "Give me your number, and I'll text you so you have mine."

That wasn't what Tarr wanted, because she could easily "forget" to text him, and he wouldn't have her number until she did. But he rattled off the number as he followed her into the foyer and then past her to open the door.

He really needed to stop doing that until she was leaving, because electricity wasn't free.

"Okay, uh, thanks for taking care of Wiggins. Sorry about the whole...police...thing."

Tarr chuckled at her awkwardness. "Hey, they got here really fast, so that's good to know."

"Yeah, um, Officer Darby is my uncle."

"Oh, boy." Tarr laughed now. "I hope I don't have to meet him again while he's on duty."

Briar smiled, and the action totally transformed her face into one glowing picture of beauty. "Okay, Tarr, well, 'bye." She went out the front door, Wiggins trotting alongside her.

As he watched them make their way down the sidewalk, Tarr couldn't wipe the grin off his face. "Well, that's one way to meet a woman," he said to himself as her taillights lit up the night. "What other surprises have you got, Lord? Because I'm ready for them."

thirty-two

Opal Hammond stood in front of the mirror in her bedroom, smoothing down her sweater and taking a deep breath. She'd spent the past couple of weeks planning West's second birthday party, wanting everything to be perfect for the darling boy she adored so much. But as she gazed at her reflection, a familiar ache settled in her chest.

"You okay, honeybee?" Tag's voice came from behind her, and his strong arms wrapped around her waist.

Opal leaned back into his embrace, drawing comfort from his steady presence. "I'm fine," she said, but her voice wavered slightly.

Tag turned her gently to face him, his eyes full of concern. "You're in your head."

"I just started my period." She shook her head and closed

her eyes against the worry in his. "It's silly, I know. I just—I want to plan *our* baby's birthday party." Her voice cracked on the last word, but she drew in a long breath. "I'm fine. Really."

Tag cupped her face in his hands, his touch gentle, and she looked up at her strong, tough cowboy husband who knew exactly how to be soft and sweet too. "It's not silly, Opal. Your feelings are valid." He paused, something intense in his dark eyes. "Remember what Pastor Randall said a couple of Sundays ago? About setting too many New Year's Resolutions that we forget to trust in God's timing?"

Opal nodded, feeling a small spark of hope ignite in her heart. "I'm trying to believe that God's plans are perfect," she whispered. A small smile touched her mouth. "I know they are when things are going my way."

Tag chuckled and drew her into his chest. "Ain't that the truth, baby-bee."

She relaxed into his arms, the warmth and care he always provided for her so welcome. "I know you're right," she said. "My faith isn't perfect yet."

"Thank goodness," he teased. "You'd be so boring as a perfect woman." He grinned at her as she stepped back. "Are you gonna look at the stars while I shower?"

"No, I have to finish wrapping the presents."

His eyebrows went up, but he didn't question her further. She'd already spent an hour wrapping presents for West, because she took care of him for a lot of the day, every day, and she'd maybe bought him too many gifts. But, really, could a two-year-old even get too many gifts?

Opal didn't think they could, and certainly not West.

So she left Tag to shower and get ready to head over to Mike and Gerty's for the party while she went down the hall to the airy, light kitchen to finish wrapping his presents in bright green paper with tractors all over it. West adored all things truck and tractor, and she'd also baked a cake and shaped it perfectly into the bright red tractor his momma drove around the farm.

The sugar cookies had been made into neon yellow dump trucks, and Opal had spent all day today going back and forth with treats and presents.

"Only one more trip to go," she said to herself, the words coming out as a sigh. She finished up with the new soccer ball she'd gotten for West, and then finally, the toy truck that would drive Mike and Gerty bonkers, and which Opal already planned to bring back to her house for when she tended to West here.

She already had a bedroom set up for him, so she could babysit him and be in her own space. Then Gerty could come get him after she finished her farm work, or Mikey would come pick up his son once he got home from his office downtown.

"Ready?" Tag asked, and Opal turned toward the laundry basket with all the gifts in it. She put the last one in there and nodded to it.

"Bring that, Mister Muscles."

"How many of these have you already taken to the farmhouse?" He grinned at her and dutifully picked up the laundry basket. It only had four presents in it, as well

LIZ ISAACSON

as the thumping balloons West had loved at Christ-mastime.

Opal decided not to answer her husband, and instead, she took his arm and they left their house and hurried to the truck to make the short half-mile drive to Mike and Gerty's farmhouse.

The crisp air and the sight of the rolling fields helped further calm Opal's nerves. In better weather, Opal walked, but in the dead of winter, she rather liked having all of her fingers and toes.

Despite the feet-deep snow, colorful balloons and a banner that read "Happy 2nd Birthday, West!" had been tied to the front fence at the farmhouse.

"Oh, wow," she said as Tag pulled up next to Mike's truck. "My brother managed to get that blow up truck." Pure delight pulled through her at the big dump truck that had been blown up and placed on the snow, as if it would start plowing it out of the way.

"Your family loves a good blow-up item," Tag teased.

Opal looked over to him. "I did not buy a single thing that needs to be blown up."

"Balloons," Tag said.

"Fine." She turned to get out of the truck. "No party is complete without balloons."

"Absolutely not," Tag agreed as another truck arrived. Opal lifted her hand in a wave to Tarr, who had Bobbie Jo riding in the passenger seat with him. *Interesting*, Opal thought, as Tuck wasn't here right now, and she hadn't been expecting to see his girlfriend without him.

"Ope!" West yelled from the front porch, and she immediately turned her attention to him. "Tag! Ope!" He waved both arms. "I two! Two!"

Opal's heart melted into a puddle of goo as she headed up the sidewalk to him. He practically danced with excitement at the top of the stairs, but he didn't come down as Gerty continually told him to stay put.

When she reached the top step, she swept West into her arms, pressing a kiss to his cheek. "Happy birthday, my sweet boy."

"I two," he said again, pure joy streaming from him. He tried to hold up two chubby fingers but couldn't quite get it without a little help.

Opal smiled over to Gerty, who hugged her with West between them. "So Tarr brought Bobbie Jo." They both looked out as Tarr indicated Bobbie Jo should precede him up the sidewalk.

"Did you know?" Opal asked.

"Yeah," Gerty said just as quietly. "He texted and said they were coming." She pointed and said in a louder voice. "Look, Westy. Tarr has a box shaped like a truck."

"Truck," West said, and he wiggled to get down. Opal set him on his feet, and he did his little dance at the top of the steps while Bobbie Jo and Tarr laughed at him.

"Heya, buddy," Tarr said as he came up the steps. He extended the firetruck-shaped box, which was about the size of a brick, and West took it in both hands.

"Ooh," he said like he'd just been handed a gold bar. "This go wee-ooh-wee-ooh."

Opal giggled, and then turned her attention to Bobbie Jo. "It's good to see you," she said. "How's life in the city?"

"Oh, it's life in the city," Bobbie Jo said with a warm smile. She glanced around the farm, throwing a look toward the barn and stable. "It sure is nice to come out to the country, though."

"It possesses...peace," Opal agreed, and then she opened the door for Bobbie Jo. Warmth and laughter spilled out into the evening, and they all filed inside.

The house bustled with activity—Gerty's grandparents chatted with Boone and Cosette in the living room. Matt and Gloria helped their daughters with something in the corner that looked suspiciously like a ball pit that West would go wild for.

Jane and Cord had arrived with Clint, and Opal wanted to immediately go take the baby from his mother. Steele entertained Hunt and Molly's kids with a magic trick, while Deacon chatted with them near the fireplace.

Bobbie Jo moved that way, and Opal gave a soft smile to her back, noting how seamlessly the woman fit in with her family. She'd have to text Tuck and tell him, and she wondered if her fun-loving, feels-deeply cousin had fallen in love with her yet.

"Looks like everyone's here," Tag commented, following Opal's gaze. "Bobbie Jo seems to be settling in well." He nodded up to the ceiling above the table. "And look, honeybear. Balloons." He whispered the last word as Opal took in the balloon net above the table—somewhere West would never look.

Oh, to be two again and find such happiness in a balloon.

Before Opal could respond, Gerty's voice rang out over the chatter. "Okay, everyone, it's time to eat."

The crowd started to gather around in the kitchen, where Opal's magnificent tractor-shaped cake sat, complete with two glowing candles. West's eyes widened with wonder as Mike held him up to see the cake. Boone waved his hand to lead them all in Happy Birthday, and then all eyes came to West to blow out the candles.

"Dad," he said with awe. "Fire." He turned toward Mike as if this was a real problem. "Hot."

"Yeah, buddy, it's a little hot." He leaned closer, but West pulled back. "You blow 'em out." He grinned at his son. "Watch Daddy." He blew out both candles, and everyone cheered. "You do it."

Gerty quickly relit the candles, and West looked at her with complete trust in his expression. "Go on, baby," she said with so much love in her tone. "Do what Daddy did."

West puffed up his cheeks, and it came as no surprise to Opal that Mike blew out West's candles at the same time he attempted to do so. Both flames extinguished, and the kitchen really erupted with cheers then, including Opal's.

"Okay," Gerty said, sweeping West into her arms. "Let's get a bib on you, and you can have one bite of cake before dinner."

"Cake, cake, cake," West sang happily, and while he sometimes fussed over wearing a bib, tonight, he didn't.

Tag's arm slipped around her waist while others queued up for food and cake. She leaned into her husband, overwhelmed with love for her family and gratitude for this moment. Yes, she still yearned for a child of her own, but right now, surrounded by the warmth and joy of her loved ones, she felt truly blessed.

The party continued with games, present opening, and lots of laughter. As Opal watched West toddle around in his new cowboy boots, showing off for anyone who would look, she silently thanked God for the abundance of love in her life.

Her arms might remain empty for a while yet, but Opal would be okay. She thanked the Lord for His grace and mercy, and she turned to Tag when he said, "You throw an amazing party, baby."

She grinned at him. "I do, don't I?"

"Ope," West said as he came closer. "Truck." He'd just opened the noisy one she'd bought for him, and she reached for it, flipped it over, and pulled the tiny piece of plastic out of the battery so it would blare it's horn.

Then she put it on the floor and said, "You push here, Westy-poo." She touched the steering wheel, and the truck blasted its horn.

"Oh, that one isn't going to last long," Gerty said dryly.

Opal only grinned at her, because she could—as West's aunt. And oh, how she loved being an aunt.

"Will you take him?" Jane asked, pushing Clint into Opal's arms. "I have to run over to Steele's and get something we're going to drop off for his momma on our way home."

Opal was already settling the squishy baby into her arms. "Of course," she said, and now that she had Clint, she had a really good excuse for finding a spot on the couch and staying there.

So she did that, and as she looked down at Clint's sleeping, peaceful face, she knew that whatever God's plan was for her and Tag, it would be perfect...and in His time.

thirty-three

Bobbie Jo stared at the empty suitcase on her bed, her mind swirling with a mix of excitement and anxiety. In just two days, she'd be boarding a plane to San Antonio to spend her birthday weekend with Tuck. It should have been a thrilling prospect, but instead, her stomach churned with uncertainty.

"Bobbie Jo." Cara stuck her head into the room. "Jenny and I are ordering pizza. Do you want that big salad?"

"Yes, please." Bobbie Jo turned toward her. "And the cinnasticks. I can send you some money on CashApp."

Cara grinned and committed to coming into the room. "You don't have anything packed yet."

Bobbie Jo nodded over to the clothes she'd gotten out to go into the suitcase. "Getting there."

Cara sat on the bed, jostling both the clothes and the suitcase. "Are you okay? You look a little stressed."

Bobbie Jo sank onto the other side of the suitcase with a sigh. "Just thinking about this weekend."

"Are you having second thoughts about going?"

"No...maybe? I don't know." Bobbie Jo ran a hand through her hair. "It's just...." She couldn't quite articulate all the nerves running through her mind and body. She missed Tuck something terrible, despite the many texts they'd sent back and forth. He'd called her a couple of times, but neither one of them excelled at talking on the phone.

She didn't think he'd be all that different, though she'd never known him as a rodeo manager. She'd never seen him do the thing he was most passionate about.

"I've never been on an airplane," she admitted, because those fears she could face and try to understand. How she felt about Tuck and if it could be love—she couldn't. "Did you know that?"

"No," Cara said with a smile. "It's not so bad. Didn't he get you a first-class ticket?"

Bobbie Jo nodded, but thinking about the luxury Tuck had arranged for her didn't ease her anxiety. In fact, it only added to it. "And I have a car there, and the directions to both his training barn and the bed and breakfast he booked for me."

Cara got to her feet. "Right, so all you have to do is pack." She picked up one of the flowered blouses and refolded it. "This is so cute." She put it in the suitcase, followed by Bobbie Jo's jeans, which she rolled before placing them inside.

"You don't need to pack for me." Bobbie Jo got to her feet too.

"Are we ordering pizza or not?" Jenny asked as she filled the doorway. "I'm *starving*."

Bobbie Jo turned away from her clothes. It would take her less than ten minutes to pack a few sets of clothes, socks, her boots, a jacket, and her toiletries. She didn't have to do it right now.

"Yeah," she said. "What were you guys getting? Can I order one of those chicken Alfredo ones? I can take the extras to Ben and Troy." Her last day at work this week with her friends was tomorrow, as Tuck had arranged for her to have Friday off.

Tuck had taken care of everything; Tuck had taken very, very good care of Bobbie Jo, and she wished her heart hadn't been attached to a yo-yo. Up and down, up and down, and Bobbie Jo felt certain she loved Tuck in one moment and then that she should end things with him in another.

"We can get that," Jenny said as she tapped on her phone. "I want the Hillbilly. Cara?"

"I can have either of those. Bobbie Jo wanted the salad and the cinnasticks."

"Yep." Jenny tapped and tapped and then said, "Thirty-two minutes," before she lowered her phone. She flopped onto the couch and picked up the remote control. "Bobbie Jo, you pick something."

"I'll do it." Cara swiped the remote out of Jenny's hand. "She's too deep inside her head."

"She is?" Jenny stroked back her dark hair and gathered it into a ponytail. "Bobbie Jo?"

Bobbie Jo sank onto the end of the chaise. "What if I don't fit into his world anymore? He's been in San Antonio, living this exciting rodeo life, and I've just been here." She didn't love her job, but she absolutely had dreams that required funding.

Not if you're with Tucker. She hated the thought as much as she liked it.

"I can guarantee that he's been missing you as much as you've missed him." Jenny nodded and reached for the edge of a nearby blanket.

"Totally," Cara agreed.

"Has he, though?" Bobbie Jo couldn't keep the doubt out of her voice. "He's always been a free spirit." She didn't need to vocalize all of the questions parading through her mind. Tuck had told her right to her face he hadn't wanted to stay in Ivory Peaks, at his family farm. He *liked* life on the road. He loved traveling. The thrill of the rodeo, the lights over the arena, the late-night dinners afterward.

And yet, he'd bought the farm in Deerfield. That huge, gorgeous, perfect-for-goats farm.

Cara sat beside her and put her arm around Bobbie Jo's shoulders, her expression serious. "Bobbie Jo, Tucker bought a whole farm for you. That doesn't exactly scream 'commitment issues' to me."

Bobbie Jo nodded, but the knot in her stomach didn't loosen. "I know. You're right." She put the bravest smile on her face she could muster and gave it to Cara and then Jenny.

"What will you guys do? I can transfer my lease to one of you, and you could get a new roommate."

Jenny's eyebrows went up. "So we're back to marrying him?"

"They're serious," Cara said in Bobbie Jo's defense. "Of course she's going to marry him. Heck, *I'd* marry him just to live on that farm, and I don't even like animals or the outdoors." She giggled and grinned, then got up and headed into the kitchen. "I'm making broth for everyone. It'll settle your nerves."

Bobbie Jo said, "Thanks," in an off-hand way, and Cara had been totally right. She was too far inside her head to pick a movie that night. She just needed the Lord to tell her what to do.

I'll do it, she thought. *If Thou will just guide me.*

She didn't get the feeling or impression that she shouldn't go to San Antonio, and Bobbie Jo had been waiting for that. She told herself that she wanted to support her loving, kind, hard-working boyfriend. She wanted to be there for him, see him train with Rosie Young, and try to figure out how she fit into his life, the farm at Deerfield, all of it.

"You'll see Tuck in a couple of days, and everything you're feeling right now will disappear," Cara called from the kitchen. "You'll see."

Bobbie Jo nodded, feeling a lump form in her throat. "You're right," she said, because she didn't want to talk anymore tonight. She just needed pizza and salad and cinnamon-sugar breadsticks. She'd figure out how she really felt and what to do about it when she came face-to-face with Tuck.

His world felt so...*big* to her. Something she couldn't even imagine.

So you'll see it, and then you'll know it.

The thought sat nicely in her head, soothing her, and Bobbie Jo took a deep breath to relax into it. She'd never liked not knowing what the next day would bring, and since everything with Tuck felt so new, the uncertainty definitely added to her nerves.

He'd driven to San Antonio, and he'd sent her pictures of the journey. His smile covered his whole face and filled his eyes in every one, and Bobbie Jo wanted to live her life with the same enthusiasm he did.

She simply didn't have the same restless spirit, the same gypsy soul, that he did.

Will he truly be happy settling down here? she wondered. *With you? On that farm?*

That plagued her the most, and Bobbie Jo tried to push the questions out of her head. She'd go to San Antonio, and she'd see Tuck in his job, and she'd pay really close attention to how she felt while doing all of that.

* * *

Bobbie Jo called her mother only twenty minutes before she needed to leave for the airport. That way, she'd have an end-time for the conversation.

"Bobbie-Jo-baby." Her mom sounded chipper and joyful,

and Bobbie Jo enjoyed the tone of her voice. It made her stomach calm slightly. "What's goin' on in Colorado?"

"I'm actually heading to San Antonio today," she said, a smile coming to her face. "Tuck's there, working with one of his clients, and…it's my birthday on Sunday, and yeah."

"Daddy and I sent a card," her mom said, ignoring the bit about Tucker and Bobbie Jo's travel all at the same time. "Did you get it?"

"Not yet." Bobbie Jo started to pace in her bedroom, her suitcase packed and ready to go. "Momma, how do you know when you're in love with someone?"

"Oh."

Yeah, that about summed it up.

"I'm afraid." Bobbie Jo sank onto her bed.

"Of what?" Momma's voice stayed calm and even. "You've said nothing but good things about Tucker, baby. Every picture you send is filled with joy."

"Does that mean I love him?"

"What are you afraid of?" Momma asked again.

"Of everything changing," Bobbie Jo blurted out. "Again. Of falling even more in love with him and then having it all fall apart because we want different things. Of not being enough to keep him happy and settled here, or on the farm, or anywhere."

Momma didn't jump right in to refute her, and now that the words had wings and could fly, they didn't flap so hard inside her chest.

"Can I be blunt for a second?" Momma asked.

"Are we ever not blunt with each other?" Bobbie Jo wiped

her tears and contained the sniffle so her mother wouldn't hear it.

"You're borrowing trouble," Momma said firmly. "You're so worried about what *might* happen that you're not giving yourself a chance to enjoy what *is* happening. Tuck loves you. He's made that clear in a hundred different ways. But if you keep waiting for the other shoe to drop, you might end up sabotaging something really beautiful."

Bobbie Jo felt like she'd been hit with a bucket of cold water. "I have to get to the airport."

"Okay," Momma said lightly, all the bluntness gone now. "I know you don't like change, so perhaps think about making a list, the way you did as a teenager. That always seemed to help you."

Light filled Bobbie Jo's mind, and she wished she'd called her momma sooner. "Okay, Momma." She pulled in a sharp breath. "I love you."

"I love you too, baby. Call me when you get to Texas."

The call ended, and Bobbie Jo took a moment to absorb the conversation into her heart, mind, and soul. She had eight minutes before she had to leave, and she dashed into the kitchen and grabbed the pad of paper they used to write down the groceries they needed.

The pen flew over the paper as Bobbie Jo let everything important to her land on the paper.

Family and close friendships
A sense of home and community
Financial independence and security
Time in nature, especially with animals—I want a dog.

Honesty and open communication in relationships

Balance between adventure and stability

Maintaining my own identity even when I'm with Tuck

She ripped off the paper, dropped the pen, and turned to get her backpack and suitcase. She could look at this on the flight to San Antonio, as she didn't have more time right now to analyze anything.

As she drove to the airport, Bobbie Jo thought about the farm. Despite her initial reservations, she couldn't deny the spark of excitement that ran through her when she thought about the potential it held. A home of their own, space for animals, room to grow...it was everything she'd ever wanted.

It was everything she'd had in Oklahoma that she'd lost.

And Tuck had replaced it.

But was the farm everything *Tuck* wanted? Could he really be happy settling down after years of living on the road?

She pushed everything away and focused on following her navigation app to a parking lot she'd never been in. Then getting on a shuttle to get to the terminal. Checking in. Going through security.

She'd never done any of these things before, but the Denver airport had big signs, and she managed to make it to her gate with plenty of time to spare.

She pulled out her phone and found Tuck had texted. *Are you on your way? I'm so excited to see you.*

A smile tugged at the corners of her mouth. *I just got to my gate.* She hesitated, and then decided he'd want to know how she felt too. *I miss you so much. Can't wait to see you.*

Change did scare her. Mightily. But what Bobbie Jo hated worse was feeling like she'd missed out on something she could've had. She didn't want to have any regrets.

So she pulled the wrinkled paper from her pocket and looked at her list.

With more time, and now that she wasn't rushing, Bobbie Jo realized that many of these things aligned with what she knew of Tucker's values. He valued family deeply—he'd bought the farm to create a home for them—and he'd always encouraged her to do what made her happy.

And while his wealth had initially made her uncomfortable, she couldn't deny that it offered a level of financial security she'd never known before.

The areas where they differed—like his comfort with constant travel and change—were things they could potentially work on together. Maybe there was a way to blend her need for stability with his love of adventure.

As for maintaining her own identity within the relationship... well, that was up to her. Tucker had never asked her to change who she was. In fact, he often praised her independence and strength. If she was losing herself, it wasn't because Tucker was taking her identity away.

And sitting right there in the airport, the tension left her body. She still had concerns, still had things she wanted to discuss with Tucker, but the overwhelming fear that had been plaguing her lifted.

Now, she just needed to get to San Antonio and *see him*, see for herself, see if they could blend their two lives into one.

thirty-four

Tuck paced the length of the fence where Rosie rode her horse, his boots kicking up small clouds of dust with each step. The familiar smell of dust, hay, and wood did little to calm his nerves as he glanced at his watch for what felt like the hundredth time in the last hour.

Bobbie Jo's flight should have landed an hour ago. Any minute now, she should be walking through the doors in front of him, and Tuck's heart raced at the thought. Three weeks. It had been three long weeks since he'd seen her, held her, kissed her.

His heartbeat thrashed, because he'd missed Bobbie Jo far more than he'd anticipated. The thrill of traveling? Of being somewhere warm, with horses and training facilities, and even the enormous potential of Rosie winning everything this year—it meant nothing if he had to do it alone.

"You're gonna wear a hole in the ground if you keep that

up," Rosie called from where she'd dropped to the ground and now adjusted the saddle on her horse. Tuck hadn't even noticed she'd stopped looping around the barrels.

Tuck forced a chuckle, trying to mask his anxiety. "Just excited, that's all."

Tarr, who stood at the desk near the door, turned and raised an eyebrow. "Excited? You look like you're about to face down an angry bull."

"Maybe I am," Tuck muttered under his breath, thankfully nowhere near loud enough for Rosie or Tarr to hear. Tarr chuckled anyway, as if he'd heard Tuck.

Frustration built inside Tuck, mostly because Bobbie Jo hadn't arrived yet. She'd texted him only a few moments before taking off and again when she'd landed.

I'm so nervous in the beginning, to *I'm still alive and here in Texas!*

Tuck just wanted to see her. This living-apart wasn't working very well for him, and he hadn't realized how dependent he was on having someone to come home to at night, even if that person was his brother. Or Tarr.

Tuck had not lived alone for much of his life until the past three weeks. He didn't much like the silence in the evenings, and he'd been so happy when Tarr had arrived a few days ago. He wanted to see how things worked with Rosie, so he could be prepared at the training facility in Deerfield.

Not only that, but Tarr had decided to become part of Tuck's management business, and he'd wanted to come meet the other cowboys, cowgirls, their managers and trainers, and start to learn the business for himself. Tuck couldn't be happier about that, as Tarr would live in the huge house in Deerfield, and they'd work the farm and use the training facilities together.

Tuck wanted to expand and grow until they had several managers and their cowboys there, as it could hold probably six or seven people and their trainers. He'd been sketching out plans to add cowboy cabins, so rodeo champions and their trainers-slash-managers could live on-site.

He'd already commissioned new signage for the farm, to clearly designate the public areas for rodeo personnel and then the more private family farm, the house, and anything Bobbie Jo needed for her goats.

Probably a little too forward-thinking, but Tuck couldn't stop himself from envisioning her in the house with him, her on the farm with him, her everywhere with him.

Now, if she could just arrive here, at the training barn where he currently worked, maybe the seething barbs in his throat would go away.

He'd been looking forward to this weekend for weeks, meticulously planning every detail to make Bobbie Jo's birthday special for months. He'd arranged her flights, found a cozy bed and breakfast for her to stay at, and cleared his schedule—and hers—to spend four uninterrupted days with her.

It should feel like he was about to get everything he ever wanted.

So why did he feel like he was about to lose everything?

Tuck ran a hand through his hair, his mind a whirlwind of conflicting thoughts and emotions. He loved Bobbie Jo, of that he was certain. He hadn't told anyone yet. Not Tarr. Not his parents. He hadn't even said it out loud to himself.

But loving her and building a life with her were two very different things, and lately, the gap between those two realities seemed to be widening.

Or maybe that had just happened when he'd left town.

It's not forever, he told himself for at least the dozenth time. He wasn't going to be in San Antonio forever.

"You wanna talk about it?" Tarr asked, his voice low enough that Rosie couldn't hear on the other side of the fence. She'd re-mounted her horse anyway, and she currently loped Blossom around the barrels at the far end.

Tuck sighed, ran his hands through his hair, and leaned against the fence next to his friend. "I don't even know where to start."

"How about with why you look like you're headed to your own funeral instead of a reunion with Bobbie Jo?"

Tuck let out a humorless laugh. "That obvious, huh?"

Tarr just gave him a look that said, *You can't hide from me, Tuck.*

"I just...." Tuck started, then paused, trying to find the right words. "I'm worried, I guess."

"About what?"

"About everything."

"Everything's a lot to worry about," Tarr said. "Want to narrow it down a bit?"

Tuck took a deep breath, the words he'd been holding back since he'd bought the farm seven weeks ago finally spilling out. "What if I can't do this, Tarr? What if I can't be the man Bobbie Jo needs me to be?"

Tarr's eyebrows shot up. "Where's this coming from? Last I checked, you were head over heels for that woman. Bought her the nicest farm in the whole state of Colorado and everything."

"That's only part of the problem." Tuck fixed his eyes on the door, determined not to miss a moment of his weekend with Bobbie Jo. "You're okay here with Rosie for the next few days?"

Tarr glanced into the arena. "Yeah, sure. She's mad her horses like me more than her, but yeah." He grinned, and Tuck finally did too. Tarr had such an easy-going way about him, and it was true that horses and dogs alike loved him more than anyone else.

Tarr looked back to him. "Are you worried she won't come?"

"No," Tuck whispered. "I know she's here. I'm...honestly?" He sighed out all his breath, then drew in as much air as his lungs would hold. "I'm in love with her, Tarr. But it feels like we're on two different pages right now, and I'm scared everything I'm feeling will just come spewing out of my mouth the moment I see her." He rolled his eyes at his own ridiculousness. "You know how I am."

Tarr burst out laughing. "Yeah, I sure do," he said among the chuckles.

"Be serious," Tuck hissed at him. "What if that's not enough?"

"What if what's not enough?" Tarr asked, sobering

slightly. "Tuck, you are *wound up*. Brother, calm down. She's here. She's coming here for you. Do you seriously think she's not in love with you too?"

"I have no idea," Tuck said. "I've always moved faster than her. It took her until like, last week, to come to terms with the farm, for crying out loud."

Frustration had been biting at him since Christmas, and today, a hint of irritation seeped into his bloodstream too. Frustration and irritation with himself, but also with Bobbie Jo. "Maybe we're—I mean, maybe we're just not compatible long-term."

"You're self-sabotaging now."

"What if I go nuts in that house, on that farm?"

"Then you'll take a vacation," Tarr said, folding his arms.

"What if our services take off and I'm on the road more than I'm home?"

"What if?" Tarr challenged. "Maybe she'll go with you. Maybe this isn't a problem at all. Maybe you're just making things up." He raised his eyebrows even as Tuck scoffed.

"Why would I do that?"

"Because you're in love with her," Tarr said, his voice fierce now. "And you're afraid of losing her and losing your heart."

"At least I date," Tuck shot back at him.

"Hey, I've dated," Tarr said.

"Easy relationships," Tuck said, not really wanting to attack his best friend. "Women you knew it wouldn't work out with. Who'd be leaving for college."

Tarr swallowed. "I just happen to have a date with one of our neighbors when I get back."

Shock flowed through Tuck. "What? You didn't tell me that." He searched Tarr's face. "We have neighbors?"

Tarr laughed again and he hauled Tuck into his chest and hugged him. "She actually lives on your farm. Works with the animals." He cleared his throat.

Tuck's mind raced. "Briar? You're going out with *Briar*?"

Tarr lifted his chin. "Yeah," he said. "Yeah, I am."

Several moments of silence passed between them, while Tuck tried to figure out how to respond. "Wow," he finally said. "I'd be careful with her, brother. She's got a...briar-filled tongue."

"That's what I'm hoping." Tarr grinned, though Tuck still reeled. "I mean, I like talking to her so far."

"Wow," Tuck said again.

"Yeah." Tarr exhaled and looked over to the door too. "Are you ready to settle down, Tuck?" His eyes came back to Tuck's, but his gaze danced all over.

"I want to be," Tuck said. "I don't like being here when she's there, I know that." He wanted to say *yes, absolutely, I want to settle down with Bobbie Jo* without hesitation, but the truth was more complicated. He loved Bobbie Jo with every fiber of his being, but the thought of being tied to one place, one routine, for the rest of his life actually terrified him.

"I want to be," he said again. "For her, I want to be."

"It's a start," Tarr said.

"Just gotta start somewhere." Tuck focused on the patch

of sunlight pouring in through the open doorway. "Where is she?"

"She's never been to Texas, bro. Give her some time."

"I don't want to disappoint her," Tuck whispered. "I don't want her to feel like she's always waiting for me to leave."

"Then don't give her a reason to wait," Tarr said simply. "Show her you're committed, not just with grand gestures like buying a farm, but in the little things too. Include her in decisions about your career, about your future, about the future you want with her. Let her see that she's a part of your life, not just along for the ride."

And just like that, Tuck found a way to take a step forward. He found a way to start. "Thanks, brother," he said, clapping Tarr on the shoulder. "I needed that."

Tarr grinned. "Anytime. Now, you might want to go freshen up. Your girl's gonna be here soon, and you look like you've been wrestling with your demons all day."

Tuck laughed, a genuine sound this time. "Yeah, yeah. I'm going." He climbed up on the bottom rung of the fence and called, "Rosie, I'm leaving you in the capable hands of Tarr."

"Okay!" she yelled back. She galloped toward him, expertly bringing her horse to a stop mere inches from the fence. She grinned at him. "Go have fun with Bobbie Jo. I still get to meet 'er, right?"

"Yeah, sure," Tuck said. "I'm just going to go wash up. If she gets here before I come out, promise me you'll be nice."

Rosie's face turned blank as she blinked. "I'm always nice."

Tuck laughed, because one of the first things he did with

his clients was sign them up for public relations classes, and the only note he'd gotten from the instructor after her first one was, *Tell her to be nice. If she can be nice, she'll be fine.*

Even he could admit *be nice* was vague, and he hadn't tackled Rosie's personality with the press yet. He hadn't had to, and he wouldn't for a few more months. But she'd be ready. He'd make sure she was ready.

"Work hard," he said.

"You too." Rosie grinned at him and clicked her tongue at her horse. "Come on, girl. Let's do it a couple more times."

In the locker room, Tuck splashed some water on his face and changed into a fresh shirt. As he looked at himself in the mirror, he tried to see what Bobbie Jo would see when she arrived.

Would she see the man she'd fallen for, the one who promised her the world? Or would she see someone torn between two lives, unable to fully commit to either?

Tuck took a deep breath, straightening his shoulders. "Just don't blurt out that you love her in the first five seconds, okay, cowboy?" He nodded at himself and then turned to head back out to the arena. He wouldn't stay there. He couldn't.

He'd wait for Bobbie Jo out front, with the big Texas sky above him to steal away his nerves. Tuck's heart raced as he hurried to the entrance and outside. She'd be here soon. So soon.

Outside, he scanned the parking lot, only finding truck upon truck. Horse trailers got parked down on the far end, and Tuck knew she hadn't arrived yet, because he'd rented her an SUV. It would stand out among all the vehicles already here.

He sighed and marched over to the corner of the building, looked north, and then turned to go back the way he'd come. Texas in January wasn't the sweltering heat of summer, but the sun did shine down hotly today. Movement on his right caught his attention, and then his brain caught up with the sight of a bright blue SUV pulling into the parking lot.

"She's here," he breathed out, every cell in his body suddenly vibrating at double-speed. Her strawberry blonde hair caught the late afternoon sun, her green eyes lighting up as they landed on him through the windshield.

Maybe Tarr was right; maybe Bobbie Jo loved him too and just hadn't said it out loud yet.

All of Tuck's fears and doubts faded away. Only Bobbie Jo existed, and he couldn't wait to hold her, hear her voice, ask her everything about the past three weeks.

He stepped off the sidewalk, closing the distance between them in a few long strides as she pulled into an available parking space. He opened her door while the engine still ran, and she smiled over to him, that smile that never failed to make his heart skip a beat.

"Hey, cowboy."

Oh, that voice.

She got out of the SUV wearing a pretty sweater in a geometric color pattern and her typical blue jeans, cowgirl boots, and an electric zip in her eyes.

Tuck didn't hesitate. He wrapped his arms around her, pulling her close, breathing in the familiar scent of her shampoo. "I've missed you so so *so* much," he murmured into her hair.

"I've missed you too, Tuck."

As he held her, the words bubbled up inside him, impossible to contain. He pulled back slightly, cupping her face in his hands. "I'm in love with you, sweetheart, and I hate being away from you."

So maybe he hadn't blurted out that he'd loved her within the first five seconds.

But he'd said it within the first ten, and now the words hung in the air between them with Tuck's heart pounding in his chest as he waited for her to say something.

thirty-five

Time seemed to stand still as Tuck's words flowed around her. She could almost see them coated in purple and blue mists of magic.

She smiled, such a calm, peaceful feeling filling her from the soles of her feet, and up through her calves and legs, through her torso and chest, and right through her throat and into the top of her head. Everything buzzed, and Bobbie Jo had no idea how much time had passed.

Loving Tucker Hammond meant opening herself up to a life she'd never imagined possible. It meant trusting that his love for her was stronger than his wanderlust, that they could build a future together despite their differences.

As she looked into his eyes, seeing the vulnerability and hope there, Bobbie Jo had only one thing to say. Only one truth that mattered.

"I love you too, Tucker," she whispered, her voice thick with emotion.

The smile that broke across Tuck's face shone brighter than the Texas sun. He let out a whoop of joy that echoed across the parking lot, and he lifted Bobbie Jo off her feet and spun her around.

She grinned too, gripping his shoulders as the world around them blurred.

"She loves me!" he shouted to no one in particular, his laughter infectious. "Did you hear that, everyone? Bobbie Jo Hanks loves me!"

Bobbie Jo couldn't help but laugh, her earlier nervousness melting away in the face of Tucker's unbridled enthusiasm. The man she'd fallen for—passionate, unafraid to show his emotions, and always, always making her feel like the most important person in the world—finally set her on her feet and gazed at her.

His eyes danced with joy. "I want you all to myself," he said softly. "And that's going to be our whole weekend, okay? But first, I want to show you around and introduce you to everyone. Is that okay?"

Bobbie Jo nodded, grateful for the chance to catch her breath and process the whirlwind of emotions driving through her body. "That sounds perfect."

He grinned and took her hand in his, then turned toward the double-wide doors open over on the right side of the building. "This place is a lot like the one we've got in Deerfield," he said. "We rent time here for our clients, and it's extra if you need the animals. Rosie has her own horses, so we're not incurring those fees right now."

"Is she going to do the break-away roping this year?" Bobbie Jo asked.

Tuck glanced over to her. "Thank you so much for coming. How was your first plane ride?"

"You don't want to talk about work?" she asked, something in her chest tightening slightly.

He pressed a kiss to her temple, then slowed to a stop. He gathered her close, cradled her face in his hands, and bent his head toward hers. "I do, and maybe I was surprised you knew about the break-away roping."

"I listen to you, Tuck," she whispered, a hint of foolishness filling her. "I'm sorry if I ever made you feel like I didn't."

"I know you do."

Her fiery nature reared up. "Doesn't seem like it."

He grinned and then matched his mouth to hers. His smile straightened, and Bobbie Jo rejoiced to be here with him, so close to him, kissing him.

"I love you," he whispered as he broke their kiss and rested his forehead against hers.

"I love you too." She opened her eyes and met his, suddenly shy. She giggled and ducked her head, breaking their gaze. "I've never been in love before."

"Me either." He took her toward the doors again, and Bobbie Jo sure liked walking at his side. They entered the building, and her eyes widened as she took in the vast arena in front of them, the smell of dirt and horses and everything good filling her nostrils.

"Well, howdy, Bobbie Jo," a man said. She turned to see Tarr getting up from a barstool set at a built-in counter, a wide grin on his face. "I hear it's your birthday this weekend." He stepped in to hug her. "Happy birthday. It's great to see you."

"Thanks, Tarr," she replied, accepting his friendly hug. "I—thanks for taking over Rosie this weekend for Tuck." She stepped back and shot a look at him, and his Cheshire Cat grin didn't go unnoticed by his best friend.

Tarr's eyebrows went up, and Tuck simply shook his head and laughed.

"Well, someone has to make sure she doesn't go haywire while lover boy here is busy swooning over you."

Tucker rolled his eyes good-naturedly. "Ignore him. He's just jealous because he doesn't have a beautiful woman flying across the country to see him."

As they bantered, a young woman approached the fence, leading a magnificent chestnut horse. "You must be Bobbie Jo," she said with a smile. "I'm Rosie. I've heard so much about you."

Bobbie Jo left Tuck's side as Tarr leaned in to say something, and she reached up to stroke her hand down the side of the horse's face. "I'm Bobbie Jo." She smiled at the horse and then the young woman, who had to be a decade younger than her. "What's her name?"

"Blossom." Rosie grinned at her and stuck her hand through the slats in the fence. Bobbie Jo shook her hand, immediately warming to the young cowgirl's friendly demeanor.

"It's nice to meet you, Rosie. Tuck's told me a lot about you too. He says you're going to take the rodeo world by storm."

Rosie blushed slightly as she shot a glance over to Tuck. "Well, with Tucker as my manager, I sure hope so. He's been amazing."

Pride swelled in Bobbie Jo's chest as she turned back to her boyfriend too. He looked at her, his eyebrows rising too. "What are you two sayin'?" He pierced Rosie with a glare. "You said you'd be nice."

"I was bein' nice," she said at the same time Bobbie Jo said, "She's nice."

She grinned at Rosie, who gave her a knowing smile in return. "Go on," she said. "We're done for today, and Tarr's promised me a good steak tonight."

"That's right," Tarr said. "You guys go on and get. We'll see you in a few days.

Tuck took Bobbie Jo's hand. "I'm not going to argue with that. Come on, sweetheart."

After a tour of the facility and introductions to the rest of the cowboys and trainers still there, Tucker turned to Bobbie Jo with a soft smile. "Ready to head out? I've got a surprise for you."

"When will the surprises end?" she asked dryly, bumping him with her hip.

He simply grinned and took her hand, leading her back to the SUV. "Did you go to the B-and-B?"

"No, sir," she said. "I came straight here. Well." She got in the car and pulled her seatbelt across her. "I did stop for some

Chick-Fil-A waffle fries in the airport, but I swear I'm starving again."

He laughed, leaned into the SUV, and kissed her sloppily. He then closed the door and went to get behind the wheel. "We'll take your stuff to the bed and breakfast, and then I've got reservations at a place I think you'll really like."

Bobbie Jo nodded, smiled, and rolled down her window. She wanted to feel the sky on her skin and smell how Texas might be different than Colorado. "It's so warm here."

"Different than Ivory Peaks, to be sure," he said.

"And Oklahoma."

"That too." He glanced over to her. "Would you want to live somewhere like this someday?"

Bobbie Jo didn't know what to say or where this conversation might go. The possibility of uprooting her life in Colorado and moving scared her to death. But she took a deep breath and thought of the promise she'd made months ago in the mountains, when she and Tuck had hiked to Promise Rock.

I promise to listen to Thee.

A great promise she'd tried to honor. She'd also promised to be honest with herself and Tuck, and she felt like she'd lived up to both of those.

"Yeah," she said as she lifted her hand out the window and let the pressure of the wind push it up and down. "I'd move here. I'd go anywhere, as long as I was with you."

"Same, sweetheart." He flipped on his blinker and made a turn onto a bigger highway. "But I don't think we'll want to be in Texas come summer." He threw her a smile, and Bobbie Jo felt every joyous piece of it.

As they drove through the Texas countryside, the setting sun painting the sky in brilliant hues of orange and pink, a sense of peace settled over her. She still had some truths to speak, so many fears and doubts to address. But here, with Tucker's hand warm in hers, the future didn't seem quite so daunting.

Several minutes later, he pulled up to a charming bed and breakfast, its white-painted exterior adorned with cheerful flower boxes. "This is where you'll be staying," Tucker explained as he put the SUV in park. "It's twelve minutes from where I'm staying, and I thought you might like something a little more personal than a hotel."

Bobbie Jo's heart swelled, and she leaned her head back against the rest. "It's perfect, Tuck. Thank you."

"Let's go get you settled," he said, and he got out and went around the back to get her luggage. Bobbie Jo collected her backpack and followed him toward the front door. Sometimes, she thought she'd like the anonymity of a hotel, but all of that changed when Tuck turned the key in her room, which sat on the second floor, tucked away from the stairs, and opened the door.

He stepped back and let her go in first, and a great big four-poster bed and a view of the surrounding hills from the window beyond greeted her. The scent of lemons and vanilla filled the air, and Bobbie Jo smiled at the chaise lounger which faced the window.

"This is great," she said, moving over to the window.

Tuck followed her with her bag, and he grunted as he lifted it up onto the luggage rack in the corner. Then he joined her at the window, his arm warm and welcome around her waist.

"The farm scares me," she whispered.

"Me too."

Relief rushed through her for some reason. A smile pulled at her cheeks, and though she tried to resist it, she couldn't fight it off. "Why does it scare you?"

"It's huge, for one," he said.

"You don't have to work it alone."

"And it's so very permanent."

Bobbie Jo tensed and then turned toward him. "That it is."

He squeezed her hands gently, his gaze searching hers. "I can't promise you that I'll never feel the pull of the road, or that I'll suddenly become an expert at domestic life. But I can promise that you'll always be my home, no matter where we are. And I'm willing to work every day to find a balance that makes us both happy."

"Was that a promise you made at Promise Rock?"

"No." He shook his head. "But I promised to listen to God, and He's told me several things over the past few months. He's the one who told me to buy that farm." He exhaled like the beautiful, twenty-million-dollar farm was a nuisance. "And I do love the farm, and I love God, and I love you." He shrugged slightly, both of his powerful shoulders rising an inch or two and then falling.

"So I did it, and I'm trusting that it's the right thing."

Bobbie Jo reached up and ran her hand down the side of his face. "You're the sweetest man alive."

"You're not a good liar."

She grinned. "How many goats can the farm house?"

He chuckled and closed his eyes as he leaned closer. "I don't know, sweetheart. You're gonna have to do that math."

Tears pricked at Bobbie Jo's eyes as his lips touched hers, and she hoped he could feel her love for him in her touch, the way she felt his.

He pulled away and said, "Let's go to dinner."

She followed him downstairs, sure he had every detail of this weekend planned, and that each of them would be utterly fantastic. She wanted to experience them alongside him, not worry about things that may or may not come to fruition.

Her momma had been right. She *had* been borrowing trouble, and for no reason.

Once they were back in the SUV, with Tucker navigating them to the restaurant he'd chosen, he said, "The farm in Deerfield is a blank canvas. We can make it whatever we want it to be. If you want to raise goats, we'll raise goats. If you want to turn it into a sanctuary for three-legged cats, we'll do that too."

She couldn't help but laugh at that, everything about him just so wonderful. "I don't think I want quite that many cats."

"But definitely only the three-legged ones." He grinned at her, sobering very soon afterward. "Whatever you want, sweetheart, whatever makes you happy—that's what I want too. It's not my farm. It's *ours*."

Ours.

"So," Tucker said, his voice taking on a playful tone as it went up in volume. "Now that we've had our serious talk, what do you say we celebrate your birthday properly? I heard a rumor that you've never had Texas barbecue, and well, that's just a crime against humanity."

Bobbie Jo laughed, feeling lighter than she had in weeks. "That sounds perfect, Tuck." She leaned forward as the first stars started to prick the twilight sky. "Could you rope me the stars, Mister Hammond?" She tore her eyes from the twinkling lights and looked over to him. "I heard you're really good with a rope."

"For you, Bobbie Jo, I would try," he whispered, and that made her heart glow with bright, warm, orange embers. He really had ridden into her life as a cowboy on a horse made of storms, and he'd changed everything for the better.

Bobbie Jo wasn't sure she'd ever experienced a change this profound that had been good, and she tipped her head back and prayed: *Thank you, Lord, for this cowboy prince who's rescued me from my life at HMC, from a life of a fear of change, from myself.*

She could still be herself, but she now knew that not every change meant ruin, and that she could be loved by a very, very good man.

thirty-six

Mission trudged through the late-January wind, his boots crunching on the frozen ground as he made his way across the Hammond Family Farm. The cold bit at his exposed skin, and he tugged his coat collar higher, grateful for the warmth of his thick beard—and the scarf Molly had knitted for him for Christmas.

He needed to get to the main barn, the big, red building where most of the administration for the farm took place. Both Matt and Deacon had an office there, and soon enough, Mission would too.

Because he'd accepted the job as foreman of the farm, a position he'd train for over the next few months before he took over when Matt retired in June.

It seemed impossibly far away and yet way too close at the same time.

The thought of the new position still twisted his gut into knots. After weeks of internal struggle and long talks with his grandfather, Mission had finally decided to accept the job. But the weight of responsibility and the ghosts of his past still haunted him, making each step toward the barn feel heavier than the last.

As he reached for the back door to the stable, where he'd at least get the benefit of heat as he walked through the building, a flash of golden hair caught his eye. Kristie Higgins had just reached the corner, her blonde locks whipping in the wind as she turned and disappeared from view. The smaller medical barn where the farm kept its sick animals sat on that side of the stable, and Mission's heart did a little stutter-step at the sight of her, and he immediately chastised himself for the reaction.

He'd been actively avoiding Kris since Opal and Tag's wedding, embarrassed by their awkward dance and subsequent interactions. But now, as if drawn by some unseen force, he found himself changing course to follow her. Why, he had no idea, but the thought had come into his mind, and Mission had enough life experience to listen to such things.

He gained the corner just as she ducked into the medical barn, and now he hesitated. They'd just come out of calving season, and Kris had been out to the farm every couple of days to check their herd. The Hammond Family Farm didn't rely on their cattle sales to pay the bills, but that didn't mean they didn't want the best care for their animals.

And they'd had some sickness running through the

babies this week. Mission wasn't surprised to see the door to the medical barn slamming closed behind Kris, but he was surprised he started walking toward it.

He didn't normally have much to do with the sick animals on the farm; that was Gloria for the horses, and Matt for the cattle.

"Yeah, and you're going to be Matt soon enough," Mission grumbled to himself, and he pushed away from the corner of the barn, where the wind seemed to be the angriest.

He hurried into the medical barn too, cringing as the door slammed closed behind him. The scent of manure and wet cattle filled his nose, and the lowing of sick calves filled the air. The medical barn wasn't a place he particularly liked, and he frowned.

"It stinks in here," he said to himself.

"There are sixteen sick cattle in here," Kris said, and Mission nearly jumped out of his skin.

The beautiful blonde came out of the office on the left, a wry look on her face and pure flint in her eyes. "And this barn is only built to house twelve."

"Why are there so many here then?"

"You tell me, Mister Redbay. I don't own this farm." She wiped her hands on a light blue towel and hung it on a rod right next to the door. "Someone keeps putting them in here."

"It's not me."

"Sure," she said, reaching for the clipboard behind him. He ducked out of the way, as if she might hit him. Knowing her and the way she glared at him, Mission wouldn't put anything past her. "This signature doesn't look anything like Mission to me." She flashed the clipboard at him, rolled her eyes, and walked away.

"What are you doing here?" she tossed over her shoulder. She wore a calf-length white veterinary coat over a pair of black jeans and a black turtleneck, and Mission liked her broad-soled boots too.

"I came to...." He trailed off, lying not really his strong suit. And the truth was, he had no idea why he'd followed her into the medical barn. "I just saw you come in here and though you might need some help."

She paused in front of a calf and bent down to examine it. "From you?"

"Oh, that's right," he said, his mouth running away from him again, the way it had at the wedding. "You don't need help from anyone."

She straightened and turned toward him. She settled her weight on one hip and folded her arms around the clipboard. "This is why you...irritate me."

She hadn't said she didn't like him, but she didn't need to use words to convey that.

"Because I throw your own attitude back to you?" He took a step closer to her, feeling very much like he was about to burn his life to the ground. In four short months, he'd be the foreman of this farm, and he'd have to deal with Kristie Higgins on a much more regular basis. Or find another vet, and she was really good.

As he drew closer, Mission noticed the rosy tint to her cheeks from the cold and the way her blue eyes seemed to match the winter sky, both in color and fierceness. He pushed the observations aside, reminding himself that pretty packaging didn't always mean a friendly interior.

"You're arrogant," she said.

"I'm quiet," he said. "There's a difference."

"You're always looking at everyone like you know better."

"No," he said. "I'm just observing without inserting my voice into every conversation."

She tilted her head at him, a genuine curiosity entering her expression. "I hear that's about to change."

Panic stole through him. "What do you mean?"

"Gloria mentioned that Matt's getting ready to retire and that you might be taking over as foreman."

Mission hadn't told anyone yet, and as far as he knew, Deacon would make the announcement to everyone on the farm in the coming months. He'd never dreamed for a moment he'd have to tell people. He didn't even know if Deacon wanted that.

So he said, "Maybe," and didn't elaborate. He'd learned at a young age to keep his voice out of conversations where it wasn't wanted, and that had simply bled over into staying silent unless he couldn't. It didn't make him arrogant.

Sometimes misunderstood, sure.

Sometimes it was hard for him to make friends.

Sometimes—all the time—he found talking to pretty women downright torturous.

"Mm hm." Kris's eyebrows went up, and unless Mission had completely stopped being able to read people, a playful glint entered her eyes. "Maybe, sure. *Maybe*." She turned away from him again and returned to her examination.

He wasn't sure why he'd come, and he had no idea how to stay. But as she moved down to the next calf, he stepped with her. "What's wrong with 'em?" he finally asked.

"Matt said he suspected some pneumonia," Kris said.

Mission nodded, shoving his hands deeper into his pockets. "Nasty business, calf pneumonia."

"Exactly."

He cleared his throat and went with her down the row of stalls. "How many farms do you work?"

"Two or three," Kris said cooly. "Are you going to fire me when you maybe-take over?"

"No," Mission said. "I think you're a great vet, Kris." He knew he should let her go about her business, but something kept him by her side, and hey, she hadn't kicked him out yet. "I'm sorry for the whole awkward wedding dance thing."

Kris's step faltered for a moment before she took the last step to the next stall. "Oh?" Her cautious tone sent alarms ringing through him. "Which part?"

"The...awkward wedding dance part."

"I think I was the one who marched away from you."

"I remember it that way too."

Kris reached the last stall and started examining the two calves there. One mooed in an absolutely pitiful way, and she smiled at it. "I know, buddy," she said, almost like she'd forgotten Mission stood beside her. "You'll be back with your momma soon enough."

"So maybe I need to apologize," she said.

"Maybe."

"Is this going to be a thing with us?" She straightened and threw him a pretty half-smile.

Us? rang through his mind, but Mission had the willpower to keep it dormant in his throat. He managed to smile as he shrugged one shoulder.

"I don't mean to be short with people," he said.

"No?"

He shook his head, and she finished her work, straightened, and faced him. They'd reached the end of the aisle, and the only way out was back the way they'd come. Mission didn't move, though.

"It's just...I'm not real good with people."

"You don't say."

"Until it all just comes boiling out," he said, feeling reckless and out of control. "And I'm sort of grumpy by then, and it's just—a thing."

"So that's what happened the first time we met."

Confusion ruffled his brow. "I—the first time we met?" He couldn't remember the first time he'd met Kris. "I don't remember...sorry. I don't remember anything."

She cocked one eyebrow, and he suddenly felt like a schoolboy who'd been called to the principal's office. She sighed, a small cloud forming in the cold air. "You said my shoes weren't fit for a farm."

He glanced down at her footwear now. "I can't imagine I said that."

"You're always so gruff, so standoffish."

"I'm *quiet*," he said again, realizing his voice had pitched up in volume and intensity. "However you interpret that is a you-problem, not a me-problem." He turned to walk away. "Lord, why did You lead me out here?" He tossed the heaven-bound question toward the ceiling as he strode away despite Kris's squeak of surprise behind him.

Fine, he'd just been gruff and standoffish in this moment. Didn't mean that was how he always was—or that she had any right to judge him. She wasn't exactly Miss Sunshine.

He spun back to her and said, "You know, you're not always pleasant—" He cut off when he didn't see her anywhere. "Kris?" Mission darted back through the cattle, the lowing suddenly twice as loud. He spotted Kris slumped against the back wall, her face utterly white and her chest rising and falling in short bursts.

He dropped to his knees and skidded the last couple of feet toward her. "Kris." He lifted both hands as if he knew how to check her. But he suddenly wasn't sure he should move her. "Kris, wake up."

She made a terrible noise from somewhere primal inside her, and Mission threw all his caution out the window. He slid his hand behind her neck and held it still, barking, "Kris, wake up. Are you okay?"

Her eyes fluttered open, and it took her several long seconds to focus on him. When she did, she startled, scrambling with those big boots to push herself away from him. But she'd fallen against the wall and had nowhere to go.

"You passed out," he said, and it sounded like an accusation.

"It happens sometimes."

"No," he said. "It does not happen to normal people. What's going on?" He liked the silky quality of her hair and the way she cut through the earthier smells in the barn with her flowery perfume.

"I didn't eat lunch," she admitted, her blue eyes darting all around. Mission had seen this tactic plenty of times—she had more to confess.

"And?"

Her glare fixed on him, and he didn't mind the heat of it so much now. "I have high blood pressure, and I take medication to lower it, and when I don't eat, I crash a little. Sometimes."

"Crash a little." Mission couldn't believe this woman. "Okay." He scooped her into his arms, which elicited another gasp and then a squeal from her. "Let's go get you something to eat."

"Mission." Her voice came out as mostly air. "I'm—I can walk."

"You passed out while standing," he said as he went down the aisle. "I had a meeting in the barn, but I can reschedule it."

"A meeting?" she asked, her tone pitching up in panic. "No, you don't have to cancel it. Not for me."

Mission pushed out into the colder weather and stopped. So not the best place, but the icy air cleared his head somehow. "If not for you, then for who?" he asked.

She studied his face, no answer coming out of the whippish mouth.

"Yeah," he growled. "I don't mind, Kris." That was as

good as Mission could do right now, because he didn't have much experience vocalizing his feelings, especially not for women.

"What was the meeting about?" she asked as Mission started the trek back to his cabin.

He considered how to answer, not wanting to give away too much but wanting to start opening doors for Kris to walk through. "I'm meeting with Matt and Deacon about becoming foreman," he said. "They're going over everything, so I can take over this summer."

"I see," Kris said in a half-formal voice, and he looked at her.

A smile formed on her face, and then her icy exterior cracked. She laughed lightly, the sound floating away into the wide Colorado sky too quickly. "Maybe you can reschedule it."

"Maybe," he said.

She laughed fully now, and Mission sure did like that. For a reason he couldn't name, he didn't even care who saw him carrying this woman across the farm and into his cabin. He had nothing to hide. Not anymore.

And he needed to start living like he didn't belong in the shadows. After all, when he became foreman, he wouldn't be able to stay there for much longer.

The truth was, Mission had been running from the limelight ever since the incident at his last job. The weight of responsibility, the fear of making a mistake that could cost someone their livelihood or worse—it had all become too much. He'd come to the Hammond Family Farm looking for anonymity, a place where he could work hard and keep his head down.

And he'd had it for eighteen years.

But now, here he was, about to step into the spotlight he'd been avoiding for nearly two decades.

"What do you have to eat at your cabin?" she asked.

"Are you going to be picky about that?" he asked. "Because Tarr moved out, and I'm afraid he was a better cook than me."

"I don't believe you, Mission," she said quietly.

"No?"

She shook her head. "Mm, nope. See, men like you...the quiet ones...they know how to take care of themselves."

He finally made it to the steps of his cabin, where he lived alone now that Tarr had moved to work with Tuck on the farm north of the city.

The warmth of the cabin became a welcome relief, and his back and shoulders rejoiced as he laid Kris on the couch in the living room. "Give me ten minutes. I'm gonna get you a drink, and I don't want you to move."

"You're so bossy."

"About this, I am." He gave her a sharp look and went to get her a bottle of water. When he handed it to her, he added, "Small sips."

She twisted off the cap and did what he said. "You seem to have some experience with this."

"My grandfather—" He cut himself off, sure he wasn't about to tell her something personal. At the same time, something inside him yearned, widened, and expanded, desperate to come out. To let someone else in.

He'd had plenty of friends over the years, but cowboys and roommates weren't the same as a pretty woman, and Mission cleared his throat.

"I took care of my grandfather for a bit," he said. "He had some fainting spells." As he returned to the kitchen to put together something quick and simple to eat, his eyes fell on a framed photo on the mantel—a picture of him and his grandfather, taken the day Mission had first arrived at the Hammond Family Farm.

He paused and picked up the frame, studying the faces looking back at him. His own, nearly two decades younger, eyes haunted and posture tense. And beside him, his grandfather, arm around Mission's shoulders, a proud smile on his weathered face.

I'm trying, Granddad, he thought.

You can't outrun your calling forever, boy. Sometimes you've got to stand still and let it catch up to you.

Something his grandfather had said to him just last week.

Mission set the photo back down, a small smile tugging at his lips. Maybe that was what today had become—his calling finally catching up to him.

He moved to the kitchen, very aware of Kris's eyes on his back. She was silent and observant too, blast her.

"Hot dogs?" he asked as he opened the fridge. "I can whip up turkey sandwiches too. Make French fries."

"Anything sounds good," Kris said, and Mission pulled out the sliced meat and cheese, then pulled the loaf of bread off the top of the fridge. He could make a sandwich faster than hot dogs and French fries, and then he could be back on the couch beside her quicker too.

Don't hesitate, he told himself. *Not like you have with so many others. Be kind, but be yourself, and just...see where this goes.*

Mission sure was ready to see where his life went next, even as he stayed right there at the Hammond Family Farm.

thirty-seven

Tarr Olson stared at his reflection in the mirror, adjusting his collar for what felt like the hundredth time. He'd never been this nervous for a date before, but something about Briar Prescott had him all twisted up inside.

It had been a couple of weeks since their first encounter, when he'd "stolen" her dog.

He'd managed to get her to text him, so he'd have her number, by loitering close to the fence that separated the arena from her cabin, which had attracted the attention of Wiggins. Since most dogs and horses loved him to bits and pieces, it hadn't been hard to get Wiggins to come under the fence—which had drawn Briar over too.

He'd even taken the dog home with him a couple of times, and Tarr really needed to get his own dog. As soon as the winter ended, he would. He simply didn't want to deal with a puppy and potty training in the snow.

He'd started texting her after that, and while she'd been reluctant to talk with him, but he'd worn her down with his charm and persistence.

Now, there he stood, getting ready for their first official date. He'd suggested dinner in the nearby town of Federal Heights, wanting to explore the local eateries and get to know Briar better. She'd agreed, albeit with a hint of hesitation that both intrigued and worried him.

Tarr ran a hand through his short, dark hair and took a deep breath. "You've got this," he muttered to himself. "It's just dinner."

But it wasn't just dinner, and he knew it. Something about Briar drew him in like a moth to a flame. Maybe the way she held secrets behind her bright blue eyes, the way she seemed to have built a ten-foot-high brick wall around her life, and yeah, he loved her dog.

Oh, and she sure seemed to see right through him. "You got a date," he told himself, and he turned away from the mirror, determined to make a good, in-person impression tonight.

He grabbed his keys and headed out to his truck, the cool February air nipping at his cheeks. The drive to Briar's place took about eight minutes, as he had to get off the family land, over to the other road, and then wind almost all the way back to the arena.

He could probably walk it faster, and every single turn

seemed to accelerate his pulse in a minuscule way that added up by the time he pulled up in front of her cabin.

A frown pulled his eyebrows down when he saw her waiting on the porch, bundled up in a coat that looked far too big for her petite frame.

Tarr hopped out of the truck and made his way up the path, his boots crunching on the gravel. "Evening, Miss Briar," he called out, tipping his cowboy hat. "You look lovely tonight."

She wore a pair of black leggings with that coat, and he couldn't even see her clothes. She had clipped her hair back, and as he neared, he saw she'd braided it.

Briar rolled her eyes, but he caught the hint of a smile tugging at her lips. "It's just Briar, Tarr. And it's freezing out here. Can we get going?"

"Yes, ma'am," he replied, offering his arm as she came down the steps. "I would've come to the door and knocked."

She hesitated for a moment before linking her arm with his, her eyes hooked into his, and then she blinked, breaking the moment. Tarr had no idea what she thought of him, or anything, because of that high guard that she already had hitched in place.

But his arm tingled with the weight of hers on it, and he smiled to himself as they walked to his truck together. He opened her door for her, and she allowed him to be a gentleman and help her up into the truck. He told himself it didn't matter if he knocked on the door or if she was waiting on the porch, but he hadn't been able to see inside her house, and he could learn a lot from a glimpse of a person's habitat.

As he drove down the lane, he glanced over to her. "So, how long have you been living out here?"

Briar tore her attention from the window, where her breath had been fogging up the glass. "About three years now," she said. "I came out here for the vet position and just... stayed."

Tarr nodded, sensing she had more to tell but not wanting to push. "It's a beautiful area," he said instead. "I can see why you'd want to stick around."

She made no move to ask him anything about himself, and Tarr asked her about her family and got, "I have one brother. He lives in Colorado Springs."

Again, no return question. No further expansion of what she said. Frustration slipped through him, but mostly, Tarr felt stupid.

And he hated feeling like that.

They finally arrived at the restaurant he'd chosen and gotten Briar-approved—a cozy little place called The Rustic Spoon. Tarr had read good things about it online, and Briar had told him she loved their French onion soup.

As they walked in, the warm aroma of home-cooked food enveloped him, and Tarr started to relax.

"Table for two?" the hostess asked with a smile.

"Yes, please." Tarr placed a gentle hand on Briar's back as they followed the hostess to their table. She stiffened slightly at his touch, and he dropped his hand quickly.

Once they had menus and had put in their drink order, yet another awkward silence fell over the table. Tarr cleared his throat, searching for something to say that he hadn't brought up on the way here. "So, uh, what made you want to become a vet?"

Briar looked up from her menu, her blue eyes meeting his. "I've always loved animals," she said, her voice softening. But she didn't go on.

"Do you just want to eat and not talk?" he asked.

Briar blinked at him, her long lashes fluttering rapidly. "What?"

"I've asked you a billion questions, and you give me one-word or one-sentence answers." He leaned forward, his menu forgotten. Maybe they shouldn't even order. "You haven't asked me a single thing about myself."

Fire filled her eyes. "I already know about you."

"You do?" He folded his arms as he leaned back. "How would you know anything about me?"

"You're famous," she said simply. "And I have the Internet."

Tarr glared at her, and he could be dark and dangerous when he had to be. "Nothing on the Internet is true."

"So you're not a National Rodeo Champion?"

"That part's true."

"I'm sure there are some other things that are too." She looked up as the waitress arrived to take their orders. "Hey." She smiled at her, and Tarr had never been jealous of a waitress before. At the same time, he wasn't sure why he wanted to impress Briar. She obviously didn't like him.

Because you won the rodeo?

"I'll have the French onion soup," Briar said, committing them to longer at this table. "And the chicken BLT wrap, please." She handed the other woman her menu and looked over to Tarr with an edge of challenge in her gaze.

As if he could ruin everything by what he ordered.

He scrambled to pick up the menu, his heart racing, as the waitress looked at him, her pen poised. "Uh, I'll have the ribeye."

"Cook?"

"Medium-rare," he said.

"Baked or mashed potatoes?"

"Mashed."

"Any sauces with that?"

Tarr couldn't even find the sauces, so he just closed the menu and said, "I like the herby one. Do you have something like that?"

"The chimichurri?"

"Yes, please."

She took the menu with a smile and a nod. "Be right back."

Briar watched him, and Tarr had no idea if he'd ever pass this woman's tests. "Not a fan of red meat?" he asked, raising an eyebrow.

Briar shrugged, everything about her cool and icy. "I try to eat healthy when I can. Plus, after dealing with livestock all day, sometimes the last thing I want to see is more beef."

Tarr chuckled. "Fair enough. Though I have to say, there's nothing quite like a good steak after a long day of training."

"Yes, let's talk about what exactly you and Tucker plan to do at the farm." The way she said it...she'd clearly been waiting for this to come up. In fact, she wore the most interest in her expression that Tarr had ever seen.

He normally would've loved to talk about the rodeo training and management company he and Tuck were trying to get off the ground. But with Briar, he wasn't so sure.

"Well, we're setting up a training facility for rodeo athletes. Everything from bull riding to barrel racing. Tucker's got connections all over the country, and we're hoping to attract some serious talent."

As he spoke, Briar's expression changed. She leaned away from him, and Tarr had his answer for so many things.

"You don't like the rodeo." He didn't have to ask. Her displeasure screamed from her.

"It's a really dangerous sport. For both the animals and the riders."

All of Tarr's defenses flew up. "We take safety very seriously," he said, his voice taking on a slightly harder edge. "Both for the athletes and the animals. We're not some backyard operation."

Though he sure wasn't going to tell her why he'd retired.

"I didn't mean to imply that you were," Briar replied, holding up her hands as if surrendering. "It's just a concern, that's all."

The tension at the table choked in his throat, and he found himself wishing he could rewind the last few minutes.

Their food arrived, providing a welcome distraction. They ate in relative silence, with only the occasional comment about the quality of the food. Tarr's steak had come a perfect medium-rare, but he found he couldn't fully enjoy it with the weight of their earlier conversation hanging over them.

As they finished their meals, Tarr decided to try and salvage the evening. "So, tell me about Wiggins," he said, forcing a smile. "How long have you had him?"

Briar's face softened at the mention of her dog. "I've had him for about six years now," she said. "Found him wandering around the outskirts of town, half-starved and covered in burrs. Nursed him back to health, and I guess he just decided to stick around."

Tarr grinned. "He's a good boy. Though he does have a taste for microwaveable meals."

That got a laugh out of Briar—finally—and Tarr thought she might say yes to a second date if he asked. He just wasn't sure he wanted to go through another hour like the past one before the single giggle.

He ordered desserts to go, and as the waitress left with his debit card and to get the cheesecakes, he looked across the table to Briar. "I'm sensing you have some rodeo stories of your own."

"Nope," she said way too fast. So that meant yes. "Nothing." She lifted her eyebrows. "Do you?"

"Yeah, tons," he said easily. "I'm sure you read about my injury and subsequent retirement, though, so you're all up to speed."

She'd issued him a challenge, and he'd fired it right back. She blinked again, surprise flowing from her, though she'd clearly read about the accident that had broken Tarr's ankle and sent him and Tuck to the Hammond Family Farm for his recovery.

"Tarr," she said, her voice soft but firm. "I think maybe we should just be neighbors."

"Are you going to quit because Tuck and I are going to train rodeo athletes?"

"No," she said.

"You just don't want to date anyone close to the rodeo."

She lifted her chin. "That's right."

"Then why did you—? Never mind. Don't answer that." He got to his feet as the waitress approached with their desserts, thanking God Above that she'd been quick.

In fact, she glanced over to Briar when she saw him standing. "Okay?"

"Yes," Tarr said. "We're good." He put his rodeo champion smile on his face, and it worked on the waitress. Too bad it wasn't the woman he wanted to charm.

He took the bag with their cheesecakes in it, and he indicated that Briar should go in front of him. He certainly wasn't going to stomp away from her like an angry bull.

The drive back to Briar's cabin happened with country music playing into the silence between them, and part of Tarr wanted to drop her off like she was a high school friend he drove to and from school each day. But his momma would be mortified, and Tarr wanted to be able to both speak to her, sleep at night, and look himself in the eye, so he got out, opened her door, and escorted her all the way up the drive to the porch.

"Well, thanks for trying," he said, though he still

wondered why she'd agreed to go out with him in the first place. Surely she'd looked him up online the moment she'd met him.

"Tarr." She sighed and reached up to fiddle with the barrettes in her hair. "It's...just not a good time for me, you know?"

"I actually don't know," he said. "You've told me absolutely nothing about yourself or your life." He watched her, but she couldn't quite look at him. The injured part of him wailed, and Tarr knew instinctively that she'd been hurt too.

How, he wasn't sure.

When, he had no idea.

By the rodeo? Unclear.

But he hauled her into his chest and hugged her. "Can we be friends too?" he asked into her hair. "Neighbors and friends."

"Yes," she whispered back, and when Wiggins barked with his big voice from inside the house, Briar stepped back. To his surprise, she sniffled and wiped her right eye before turning to the door and opening it.

"Thank you, Tarr," she said as her hound rushed outside.

"Heya, buddy." Tarr crouched down to scrub Wiggins around the ears and jowls. "How are you? Did you have to stay home alone tonight? Did you?" He snuck a glance into Briar's house, but from his lower position, all he could see was the back of the couch as it created a hallway from the front door.

He straightened and nodded to Briar. "I had fun."

She smiled at him, and Tarr couldn't make sense of it. "You did not."

"I didn't hate it. The steak was good." He grinned at her too. "Your food was good. Can't be a total loss."

"Doesn't make it fun." She started into the house, saying, "Come on, Wiggy. Come back inside."

The dog paid her no mind, too busy thumping Tarr with his wagging tail as he stood at his side.

Tarr smiled down at the canine, feeling a mix of amusement and guilt at the dog's clear preference for him. "Go on, buddy," he said to Wiggins. But the dog did not go. He looked up at Tarr with a happy grin on his face.

Tarr faced Briar, who wore an unreadable expression from where she stood halfway in the house and halfway out. "Guess he's still got a soft spot for me."

"It's fine," she said, her voice clipped. "Wiggins, come on. It's time to go inside."

But Wiggins had other ideas. He actually barked at her, then looked up at Tarr, barked at him, and turned. He trotted down the front steps and on toward Tarr's truck. He sat right down outside the passenger door and looked up at it expectantly, like someone would come open it for him, and Tarr would take him home.

Tarr and Briar stared at each other for a moment, and he had no idea what to do. Her expression could've killed him, and finally, Tarr broke the silence. "I could take him for the night? Bring him back in the morning?"

Briar looked torn, glancing between Tarr and Wiggins. Finally, she threw up her hands. "Fine," she said, exasperation clear in her voice. "Go. But I want him back first thing in the morning."

Tarr nodded, trying to hide his smile. "Yes, ma'am. Bright and early." He followed the dog down the steps to the truck and opened the door for him. Wiggins jumped up into the truck and sat on the front passenger seat, only glancing out of the corner of his eye at Tarr as if saying, *I'm in now. Let's go before she calls me back.*

"You're going to get me in trouble," Tarr hissed to the dog, and then he closed the door, waved to Briar as happily as he dared, and got behind the wheel.

As he drove away, Wiggins riding shotgun beside him, Tarr couldn't help but feel a glimmer of hope. Maybe, just maybe, he'd get another chance to win Briar over.

"Yeah, as her *friend*," he said. "Her *neighbor*." He glanced over to Wiggins, who looked at him with adoring eyes. "What do you say, buddy? Think you can help me out with your mom?"

Wiggins let out a soft woof, and Tarr chuckled. "I'll take that as a yes."

He had no idea what had formed her opinions about the rodeo and cowboys like him, but if the rodeo had taught him anything, it was that patience would eventually be rewarded.

thirty-eight

Tuck pulled his bag from the carousel and set it on the wheels. He looped his backpack straps over the handle and pulled his phone out to text Tarr. *On the way out. I'll text you where I am when I get down there.*

We're on the way.

Tuck headed for the ground transportation pickup, his anticipation building with every long stride he took. Bobbie Jo should be riding with Tarr, and Tuck couldn't wait to see her. Another three weeks had passed since he'd seen her in the flesh, and he'd planned a romantic dinner for tomorrow night.

Tonight, he just wanted to shower away this week, get something really greasy to eat, and hold Bobbie Jo on the couch in the house he owned but had never lived in.

"Yet," he muttered as he got on the people mover. *You'll be home in another month.*

Home and settled, with Rosie in one of the cabins. Tarr had spent some time getting it ready and furnished, and Tuck couldn't wait to see the new furniture he'd bought in the house.

The sky blazed with hues of pink and orange, a gorgeous winter sunset happening at only four-thirty in the afternoon. Still, if they could get this tomorrow night, it would make a beautiful backdrop for Valentine's Day.

He texted Tarr the station where he stood, and his best friend's big, black truck came around the corner only a half-minute later. Tuck's eyes locked onto Bobbie Jo, who wore a grin as big as the Rocky Mountains.

Tuck bounced on the balls of his feet and lifted his hand in a wave, as if they couldn't see him standing there. Of course they could. Hardly anyone else stood outside, choosing to wait inside in the warmth instead.

Tarr came to a stop against the curb, and Bobbie Jo spilled from the passenger seat. "Hey, there."

Tuck left his luggage unattended—oops—and swept his lovely girlfriend into his arms. He held her so tightly, like if he pressed her into his chest hard enough, she would become part of him, and he'd be able to take her back to San Antonio with him when he had to leave again.

"I hate being away from you," he whispered as he pulled away. He'd held her long enough that Tarr had gotten out and come around to get Tuck's bag. Bobbie Jo sniffled and indicated the still-open door. "Do you want to ride up front?"

"No, I'm going to make Tarr chauffeur us back to the farm."

"Fine," Tarr drawled as he pulled Tuck into a cowboy-hug. "As long as I don't have to look up into the rearview mirror and see you two kissin'."

Tuck laughed and promised, "Not gonna happen, brother."

"Mm hm." Tarr gave Bobbie Jo a look and moved past them.

Tuck turned into her and slid his hand up the side of her face. "If I can't kiss you in the truck, I better do it now."

"You think so?" Bobbie Jo grinned at him and let her eyes drift closed.

Tuck kissed her gingerly, which somehow became one of the more passionate things he'd done. The cold wind nipped at his ears, reminding him he wasn't alone with Bobbie Jo. He pulled away and whispered, "I love you."

Bobbie Jo gave a soft sigh and then opened her eyes. She turned back to the truck, a vision in a red cable sweater and dark jeans. She wore her cowgirl boots, of course, and her strawberry blonde hair cascaded over her shoulders, catching the last rays of sunlight as she climbed into the truck.

His breath caught in his throat as he followed her, and he reached for her hand the moment he could. "To the farm, please," he said in a mock British voice.

Tarr rolled his eyes and looked in his side mirror to ease his way into the traffic leaving the airport.

"Tell me what you're thinking about HMC," he said in a quiet voice. He didn't mind talking about things in front of Tarr, but sometimes he had to pry things out of Bobbie Jo.

He threw Tarr a look, but his friend didn't seem to have heard them.

"Have you seen that farm you bought?" Bobbie Jo asked, turning toward him. "It's enormous, Tuck. You're going to need a couple of managers for it."

"Great," he said easily, because he didn't need to be reminded that he'd bitten off more than he could chew. "Do you want the job?"

She searched his face. "Are you serious?"

"Bobbie Jo," he said with some disdain in his voice. "Yeah, I'm serious, because when we get married, we're going to live on that farm together, and you can be one of the managers." He ducked his head and created a semi-private pocket for them to talk. "Isn't that what you want? I thought that's what you wanted in Oklahoma."

"It is." She looked away and then brought her attention back to him. "It is, Tuck. Yes, it is."

He smiled at how many times she said it. "And the marriage thing?"

"I want to marry you, Tucker."

"Okay," he said, because those words sounded almost as good as *I love you.* He leaned his head back and slouched down. "I'm tired."

"Yeah?" she asked. "It's been a rough week." She slid over, and Tuck folded himself onto the bench seat and laid his head in her lap. She removed his cowboy hat and laid it on his hip, then stroked his hair, the touch of her fingernails along his scalp sending a thrill through him every time she did it.

"I'll order food while you shower," she said. "And Tarr spilled the beans about your favorite movies, and I've got a Top Three for you to pick from."

"Tarr did what?" Tarr asked from the front seat.

"You told me which movies Tuck likes best when he wants the world to disappear."

Tuck looked up at Bobbie Jo. "What are they?"

"*Up*," she said. "Though I'm secretly hoping you don't pick that one, for full disclosure."

Tuck grinned at her, because no, Bobbie Jo would not like *Up*.

"*Hoosiers*," she said next. "And *Dances With Wolves*."

"I do like all of those," Tuck said.

"So what'll it be tonight?" she asked.

"I promise I won't be tired tomorrow."

"You're fine, Tuck." Bobbie Jo stroked her fingers down the side of his face, along his beard, and leaned down. "I think that's your ninth promise for me."

He closed his eyes and smiled. "Yeah? How far behind are you?"

"I've only made four or five promises."

"Good thing it's not a contest." They settled into silence then, and Tuck drifted to sleep as Tarr drove them from the airport to the farm.

Then Tuck sat up, sighing, as Tarr pulled up to the house, and lights blazed to life with the movement.

"Here you go, Your Majesty," Tarr said with the dryness of the desert.

"This is a really big house," Tuck said.

"You're just noticing?" Bobbie Jo giggled as she got out of the truck, and she reached for Tuck's hand when he slid down too. "Welcome home, Tuck, to your own house."

He grinned, because he'd never slept here, and he couldn't wait to be back here permanently.

The following evening, Tuck bounded up the sidewalk and steps at Bobbie Jo's little blue house, rang the doorbell, and reached to straighten his bowtie. He'd dropped his girlfriend off two hours ago, and he'd spent most of their time apart in transit, barely having time to shower after their day of playing with the three horses Tuck had at his farm.

His, Tarr's, and Briar's. They'd ridden in the arena, brushed down the equines, and gone to lunch. Tuck had planned a picnic breakfast for tomorrow morning before he had to go to the airport and return to San Antonio, and he wished a clock wasn't ticking quite so loudly above his head.

Or maybe that was simply because the sun had gone down already, and it wasn't exactly warm out here on the stoop. Thankfully, the door opened a moment later, and both Cara and Jenny stood there. "Howdy, ladies." Tuck reached up and touched the brim of his cowboy hat, his smile genuine and hopefully gracious at the same time.

Bobbie Jo's roommates scanned him down to his cowboy boots and back to his face. They looked at one another and back to him.

"Do I pass?"

"Mm hm," Cara said as she turned. "Come on in, Tuck."

Jenny held the door for him, and he squeezed past her. "Bobbie Jo's nervous about the dress," Jenny hissed out of the corner of her mouth. "Make a big deal about it, please." With that, she hurried after Cara, bending her head close to her roommate's.

Tuck stared after them. "Bobbie Jo's wearing a dress?" he asked right out loud. He'd been out with her plenty, and she'd never worn a dress. He'd seen her wear skirts and blouses to church, but never a dress.

His mouth suddenly turned dry, and his heartbeat hammered at him not to mess this up. The problem was, he'd had very few valentines, and he didn't even know how to "make a big deal about it."

"Here she is," Cara said from the end of hall, and Bobbie Jo entered his field of view.

She wore a slinky, gorgeous, beautiful red dress, with a low V-neck coming off the wide straps that went over her shoulders.

Tuck couldn't breathe. Not even a little, shallow gasp to give his lungs a chance of making it through the next few minutes.

Bobbie Jo ducked her head, and the lights caught on the diamonds in her ears. The sparkling whiteness told Tuck he needed to get a diamond for her finger—and fast.

She came toward him, looking up as she tucked her curled hair behind her ear, and Tuck rushed at her. "You are stunning," he said, his voice made mostly of air. He took both of her hands in his and spread them wide. "Look at you. This dress is utterly fantastic."

"Is it?" Her voice sounded almost childlike, and she wore such hope in her gaze as she looked at him.

"Absolutely." He leaned forward and finally managed to inhale as his cheek rested against hers. "Mm, you smell amazing. This fabric is so silky. I'm so in love with you."

He pulled back, feeling sparkly and glittery. "Are you ready? Do you need your wallet or anything?"

"Just my phone," she said, her voice a teeny bit hoarse. She turned, and Jenny stood there with her phone. Bobbie Jo took it and tucked it into the left strap of her dress. "It's got a little pocket there for it."

Tuck pulled his eyes away from the flash of bare skin he'd just seen. She had plenty more for him to devour, and he schooled his thoughts as he offered Bobbie Jo his arm. "Let's head out then."

"Where are you two going?" Cara asked as she moved to Bobbie Jo's side.

Jenny came to his. "Masterful job with the dress, Tuck," she whispered.

He didn't know which way to look or what to say, and he found all three women looking at him. His mind fired at him, and he blurted out, "We've got a reservation at Lumière." He rolled the R like a real Frenchman and everything, adding a wide grin to the end of his statement.

Cara gasped, and Jenny squealed, and Bobbie Jo looked between the two of them. "Must be a nice place," she said.

"People get *engaged* there," Cara hissed.

"We're not getting engaged tonight," Bobbie Jo said quickly, swinging her attention to Tuck. Her eyes widened like full moons. "Tuck? Are we?"

"No," he said. "We're not getting engaged tonight."

"Good," she said, relief softening her face. "Because I don't want to get engaged on Valentine's Day."

"How cliche," Tuck said with a scoff, and he took Bobbie Jo's hand and led her to the truck. He helped her up into the passenger seat and tucked her skirt so it wouldn't get caught in the door.

When he got behind the wheel, she looked over to him. "We're really not getting engaged tonight, right?"

"No," Tuck said as he adjusted the heat. "You okay? I left the truck running, but I don't know what's going on over on your side."

She reached for the vents too. "It's great."

"Do you dance in a dress like that?"

"It's more the shoes I have to worry about," she said.

"I promise I won't drop you," he said, grinning at her. "Because I can't wait to hold you in that silky fabric."

She leaned her head back and and turned to gaze at him. "Tuck," she said.

"Mm?"

"I love you."

Happiness exploded through him, and Tuck wanted so badly to have many more Valentine's Days with her. And birthdays. And tons of regular Wednesdays.

And no matter what, he needed to get her a diamond and make her his wife as soon as possible, because then he'd get to come home to her every time he had to leave town. Tuck wanted nothing short of that, and he just needed to get a few things in place before he asked her the most important question of his life.

thirty-nine

B obbie Jo parked against the fence line, not sure where else to go. Tuck had sent her a pin for somewhere on the farm, and it sure seemed to be out in the middle of nowhere. She'd left the house and the private barn and stable behind and parked beside some other outbuildings that looked like they hadn't been used in a while.

"I guess this is it," she muttered to herself as she slid from her car. The early April sun had finally come after a month of rain and mud and muck, and Bobbie Jo couldn't allow her grumpiness to infiltrate her mood. Today, she and Tuck were going to go hiking later that afternoon, back up to Promise Rock, to see how it had changed over the winter and to make brand new promises to themselves, to God, and to each other.

Bobbie Jo breathed in the country air and looked at her phone. "Looks like it's this way," she said as she headed between two buildings, not sure what lay out here on this side of the farm.

It's got to just be fields, she thought. And sure enough, when she reached the end of the long, row building, fields opened up in front of her. Brand new fencing ran along the back of the building, and Bobbie Jo found herself trapped.

She'd have to go over the fence and into the pasture to keep going, or back out and around to get out. No matter what, it sure seemed like Tuck was out here in this field.

She stepped up onto the bottom rung of the fence and shaded her eyes as she looked out over the greening landscape.

As she did, she heard the whine of a machine, and then she made out a four-wheeler coming toward her. Tuck drove it, and he seemed to have a lot of activity around him. Bobbie Jo grinned because seeing him out on a farm did her heart good. He was brilliant with his rodeo cowboys, of course, but Tuck *belonged* on a farm, whether he knew it yet or not.

He waved to her and yelled something that she couldn't make out, and she climbed over the fence and started walking toward him, still trying to figure out what he had going on around him.

When she did, she came to a complete stop, and she only kept breathing because it was a natural function her body did without any direction from her brain.

For Tuck was surrounded by lambs.

There had to be fifty, sixty, seventy, maybe more, and they all trotted alongside and around his four-wheeler as if he were the Pied Piper of Lambs, and they'd been trained to follow that machine engine noise.

He came up to her, killed the engine, and got off laughing. "You found it," he said.

"Barely." She looked around at the pasture, the lambs, the four-wheeler, Tuck. "What is going on out here?"

Tuck bent down and picked up one of the lambs. Bobbie Jo reached out to pat its tawny fur. "You've got a ton of lambs out here. When did you get these?"

"First," he said. "They're not lambs."

Bobbie Jo cocked her eyebrows at him, but his grin was too darn handsome and too darn joyous for her to put on her attitude for long.

"Lambs grow up to be sheep," he said, as if she didn't know. "And *kids* grow up to be goats. These are kids." He smiled down at the one in his arms.

"Yes," she said, "I see that." They crowded around the two of them, some of them making little bleating noises that made everything in Bobbie Jo's life right.

"Where did you get them?" she asked.

"Come on, let's go out here," he said. "I've got lunch set up."

She wanted to argue with him and tell him to answer her questions, but she figured they had time, as they were having lunch today, and then their drive to the trailhead, and *then* their hike. She'd be with him for the next several hours, and she'd needle him until he gave her the answer she wanted.

Tuck climbed on the four-wheeler, and she got on behind

him, wrapped her arms around his torso, and hugged him. "It's good to see you, Tuck," she said.

"Seeing you is my favorite thing ever." He grinned at her over his shoulder and said, "How did Mike take the news of you quitting?"

Bobbie Jo's smile vanished, and Tuck actually twisted to look at her. "You didn't tell him?" A measure of accusation rode in his voice.

"I'm meeting with him next week," she said. "I'm going to tell him then."

"Bobbie Jo," he said. "Who's gonna take care of all these kids?" The teasing quality in his eyes had not disappeared, so Bobbie Jo knew he wasn't really mad.

"Well, it's your farm," she said. "Seems like *you* would be taking care of them."

"I got them for you." He turned around and started the four-wheeler, which made conversation more difficult, and he swung around in a wide arc and headed back out into the pasture.

The kids came with them, and Bobbie Jo enjoyed the ride as some of them did little jumps and kicks as they ran along. Tuck drove toward a stand of trees along the fence line and parked in the shade next to a long rectangular table that he'd set up in the pasture. He'd covered it with a red and white checkered cloth, as if they would have a picnic. Two chairs sat at the table, and it had been covered with food already.

"How'd you get all this out here?" she asked as she dismounted from the four-wheeler.

"There's a service road right on the other side of the trees," he said. "Tarr drove it out."

"Ah, yes, Tarr." Bobbie Jo loved Tarr as Tuck's best friend, and they currently lived together in the huge homestead here on the farm. She and Tuck hadn't talked about where Tarr would live when they got married, but she found she didn't mind all that much. If he simply stayed in the house with them, there would still be seven empty bedrooms, after all.

They hadn't talked too much about when they'd get married or if they'd have a family, despite all of the plans and preparations they'd both been making for Bobbie Jo to be on this farm with Tuck. He'd just bought a bunch of goatlings, for crying out loud.

"So where'd you get the kids?" she asked as he pulled out her chair and she sat down at the picnic table.

"Here and there," he said.

That only made Bobbie Jo roll her eyes as he sat down kitty-corner from her. "Tuck, I'm being serious now," she said, as that sometimes clued him in that she wanted him to answer her.

His smile slipped slightly. "You want kids, right, Bobbie Jo?"

"Like the goat kind?" She searched his face, thinking he meant something else. "Or the human kind?"

He reached over and took her hand in both of his. "I was thinking the human kind." He ducked his head, his cowboy hat covering his face and obscuring his eyes. He pulled his hands away and started serving food, which was pulled pork

429

sandwiches and macaroni and cheese, which meant Tuck had not cooked.

"Where'd you get the food?" she asked.

"You have so many questions." He threw her a glare that made Bobbie Jo laugh.

"Well, if someone would answer them, then I wouldn't have to fire them off like this."

"Jane and Opal made the food," he said. "I got a hundred kids from various goat farms in a few states. You know, Montana, Wyoming, Idaho, a couple places in Utah. They're from all over."

They crowded in around the table, some of them simply lying down in the shade, and some of them acting more like canines as they begged for a piece of pasta. Bobbie Jo smiled at them, then at the sunshine, then the picnic, and then Tuck. He put a plate in front of her, and she said, "I love you, Tucker."

That brought his eyes to hers, and she smiled as brightly as she could. Everything about Tuck softened, and she said, "They're all babies. Did you get any adult goats?"

"They're coming next week," he said. "I just got the ones you showed me, so I hope it's okay."

"It'll be great," Bobbie Jo said brightly. She reached down to pat a little goat and ended up lifting it up onto her lap. It curled into her as if it would take a nap, and Bobbie Jo's soul sang and sang and sang.

"Tuck," she said slowly. "What if I can't sell the goats?"

"There's a big market for them," he said. "Why wouldn't you be able to sell them?"

"That's not what I mean."

"Ah, I see." He finished filling his plate with food. "Then we'll just keep them, Bobbie Jo." He grinned at her and poured them both cups of lemonade. "I don't care what we do with them, sweetheart. If you want five hundred goats as pets, then you'll have five hundred goats as pets."

Bobbie Jo smiled at him again. "You didn't kiss me hello."

"I can't do anything right," Tuck quipped as he leaned forward and touched his lips to hers. Bobbie Jo loved kissing him. She loved being with him. She loved everything about Tucker Hammond.

He cleared his throat as he pulled away. "We might as well get this out of the way. I'm not going to enjoy myself until we do."

Bobbie Jo wanted to ask him what he meant, because he didn't go on. He picked up his fork and started eating, as if eating was the hard thing to do.

"I just want it noted for the record that I didn't ask a question," Bobbie Jo said. "Though there are plenty that could come after what you just said." She picked up her pulled pork sandwich and took a big bite.

Tuck looked over at her, then back to his food, and then he dug in his pocket for something, pulled his hand out, and seemed to melt off of his chair and onto the ground, where he landed on both knees.

He held up a diamond.

Bobbie Jo sucked in a breath, but with the bread and meat in her mouth, she started to cough. Tuck grinned while she scrambled for a napkin and finished eating.

"Tuck," she said from behind the napkin, and he reached up and pulled it away. Bobbie Jo swallowed, thankful that she still could.

"I was going to wait to do this," Tuck said. "Until we got to Promise Rock. But I'm so dang nervous, and I just want to enjoy the day. Of course, if you say no, then I won't enjoy the day at all, and I probably *should* have waited till we got to Promise Rock, because it's such a special place, and I was going to make a promise to you there, and now we're *not* there, and this is just a huge mess."

He ducked his head again, showing her the top of his cowboy hat, and Bobbie Jo giggled.

She gently put the kid back down on the ground, scooted to the edge of her chair, and reached out with both hands to lift Tuck's head back to eye level. She held him there, feeling the pulse in his neck against her fingers as she said, "Today is going to be a great day."

He nodded, his own throat working as he swallowed and swallowed, and Bobbie Jo sure liked that he could be nervous about something. He was fun-loving and loud with his laughter, which she also loved. He'd brought so much color to her life, and yet he got mad and hurt and nervous too, and it just made him so human.

"You're not messing it up," Bobbie Jo said. "Of course, you're not saying anything either."

Tuck finally grinned as he looked down at the diamond and back at her. "Bobbie Jo, I think I might have fallen in love with you the very first day I met you, and I get a little deeper every time I see you or text you or talk to you or even think about you.

"I know you're not a morning person, which is a real bummer, and I know I'm going to be on the road sometimes, which you'll hate. But if there's anything bad that happens in my life, you're the first person I want to tell and the only person I want to celebrate with. This farm is huge and lonely without you, but I know that you'll make it a home, you'll make it ours, and that we could be really happy here together."

He drew in a breath, as if she really might say no, and finished with, "Will you marry me?"

Bobbie Jo grinned and grinned as tears filled her eyes. "Yes," she whispered. "I can't wait to marry you."

* * *

Oh, Bobbie Jo and Tucker are so much fun! I hope you thought so too. If so, **please leave a review for His Ninth Promise by scanning this code on your phone**.

You can read the first two chapters **HIS TENTH DANCE** now! Just keep turning pages.

sneak peek! his tenth dance chapter one:

Mission Redbay left his cabin, already too hot in the navy blue suit coat. One, he never wore clothes like this. Certainly not in the summer, and never around the farm. Maybe to church for a wedding.

And today, Mission wasn't attending a wedding.

"Feels like my own funeral," he muttered as he went down the steps of the new cabin where he'd moved last night.

The foreman's cabin.

Mission didn't have to share as the foreman, and the cabin had been designed and built specifically for a career cowboy and his family. He supposed he had one of those, and blast everything to the stars, an image of the pretty blonde veterinarian he'd once fed a turkey sandwich to entered his mind as his boots touched gravel.

Kristie Higgins.

He'd seen her around the farm, of course. She came at least once a week, but Mission wasn't the one who had to deal with her.

Until today, he thought as the enormity of the farm spread before him. The foreman's cabin sat down at the end of cabin row, where all the cowboys lived. The equipment shed sat across from the last one, and way down by the homestead stood the generational house, where Deacon Hammond, Mission's boss, lived.

Behind the homestead sat the family barn and buildings, and Hunter Hammond and his family took care of that part of the farm.

Other than that family land, the farm looked to Mission for guidance. They had pastures and paddocks for horses and cattle, a large amount of alfalfa acreage, and a dozen commercial buildings for the children's equine therapy unit Molly Hammond administered.

The farm did horseback riding lessons too, and while Mission didn't have to take care of every horse personally, every responsibility of the farm now sat on his shoulders.

No wonder he could barely take the first step across his front lawn and toward the south side of the farm, where the big red barn welcomed students and riders. He had to get over there, though, because the retirement party for Matthew Whettstein, who'd been acting as the foreman for the past twenty-five years, had already started.

"Such big boots to fill," he murmured to himself, imagining himself to be talking to his grandfather. A rare smile touched his lips then, for Granddad should be waiting for him at the party.

A friendly face.

Of course, everyone at the Hammond Family Farm had been nothing but congratulatory and supportive of Mission moving into the foreman position. Deacon had announced it a couple of months ago, and Mission had been meeting with Matt and his teams since then.

He'd already learned far more than he'd even realized he didn't know.

He tugged at the end of his jacket sleeves, half-wanting to go home and throw the jacket in the trashcan. He wouldn't, of course. Because this jacket had come from his grandfather, and Mission loved it beyond measure.

Still, something felt off. Maybe it was the way he'd trimmed his beard this morning. Or the fresh polish on his best boots.

Or maybe it's the jacket.

You have to wear the jacket, he argued with himself. *You're becoming the foreman today.*

And there it sat. The reason the world felt like it had been knocked another twenty-three degrees off center was because Mission was willingly stepping into the spotlight.

Nervous energy thrummed through his veins, and he fisted his fingers to contain the shaking. "It's just a party," he told himself, though Mission couldn't remember the last party he'd been happy to attend.

Which so wasn't true, and Mission pushed against the false narrative happening inside his head. He loved the

Hammond family parties around the fire pit in the backyard, for every holiday, for birthdays, and sometimes just because it was Taco Tuesday, and Molly didn't want to cook.

You're ready for this, he told himself as he made it past the buildings and onto the dirt path that led in front of the generational house. Then he just had to walk past the counselor cabins and between the pastures, and he'd be at the stables. The administration barn stood in front of that, and the party had been set up on the south side, where trees provided shade for bigger outdoor parties such as this one.

Mission breathed in deeply as he took in the pretty blue sky above him, and he tipped his head back and prayed. "Lord." His mind stilled for a moment, and while Mission had known his past indiscretions had been forgiven, he once again felt that cleansing power of God in his life.

"Thank You for this amazing opportunity. Bless me to have a level head and clear thoughts to make good decisions."

It wasn't just him who would pay this time, and Mission's chest threatened to collapse in on itself, trap the air inside, and prevent Mission from ever breathing again.

A bolt of terror moved through him as his swallow reflex abandoned him. Then, his regular faculties returned, and he could exhale and swallow, and everything normalized.

You've got this, boy. You were meant for more than hiding in the shadows.

Granddad's words further buoyed him, and Mission released the tension in his hands in an attempt to find a better way to deal with his nerves. His grandfather had always believed in him, even when Mission himself didn't.

Even when his past mistakes haunted him, threatening to drag him back down.

The June first breeze carried the scent of alfalfa, wildflowers, and something barbecued through the air. As he started down the fences between two pastures, the distant sound of music came from the direction of the big red barn.

His steps slowed as he approached, the knot in his stomach tightening. Only the width of the barn, and the turning of a corner, and Mission would arrive at his own party. Or rather, Matt's party.

He fully committed by striding over the remaining distance and turning the corner before allowing himself to stop. Tents had been erected, with strings of twinkling lights crisscrossing through the rafters. Tables adorned with checkered cloths filled the space, and a long bar holding more food than Mission had ever seen stood against the far wall of the tent.

The Hammonds had gone all out for this celebration, and the thought only added to Mission's anxiety. No one had seen him yet, and he took the moment to collect himself. Deacon stood with Hunter and Mike, two of the most powerful men Mission had ever met. Both Hunt and Mike had stood at the helm of a multi-billion-dollar company, with thousands and thousands of employees, and somehow knowing they'd done that and now stood wearing cowboy hats and laughing with loved ones gave Mission confidence that he could do this job.

Travis Thatcher had brought his whole family, and Tucker, Bobbie Jo, and Tarr had come from the farm where they'd been living and working for the past six months.

Gerty Hammond walked super-slowly beside her toddler, who bent down every other step to exclaim over something, and she chatted with Opal and Taggart Crow, whose clasped hands only reminded Mission of how alone he stood.

Boone and Cosette Whettstein stood with Gloria, but Mission didn't see Matt anywhere. His eyes landed on the other cowboys and cowgirls who worked the farm, as well as several of the counselors at Pony Power.

And then the lovely Kristie Higgins. She wore a pair of blue jeans and a short-sleeved sweater the color of bright purple grapes. Mission's mouth watered slightly, and he told himself it was because he'd loved his grandmother's grape juice growing up.

Not because of Kristie's curves in those clothes.

"You can't go in either?"

The familiar voice made Mission turn. Matt, his mentor and soon-to-be predecessor, stood a few feet away, a knowing smile on his weathered face. The older man was dressed similarly to Mission, though his jacket was made of crushed brown corduroy.

"Just taking it all in," Mission said, working to keep his voice steady.

Matt moved to stand beside him. "It's a lot, isn't it? All this fuss."

"Yeah." Mission let out a breath that had felt trapped. "Matt, I don't know—"

"Don't you dare try to back out now," Matt interrupted, his tone light but with an underlying firmness. "You're ready for this, Mission. More than ready."

Mission met the older man's gaze, seeing the confidence there that he wished he felt himself. "Yeah." He nodded, trying to switch his thoughts again. Why was it so hard to think good things about himself? Other people didn't seem to have the same struggles he did when it came to self-confidence. "You're right."

"I sure am." Matt clapped him on the shoulder. "Now come on. Let's get this show on the road before Deacon sends out a search party."

With a nod, Mission walked with Matt further under the tent and into the party. The noise level increased tenfold as they entered, and it seemed like every eye turned toward them. Mission resisted the urge to rip his jacket off, despite the added heat it brought, and he forced a smile to his face as he approached Deac, Hunt, and Mike.

"Hey," he said.

"There you are." Deacon flashed a quick smile at him, and thankfully, Deacon wasn't one to wear smiles for miles either.

"Hey, Mish." Hunter pulled him into a quick hug, and Mission did the same with Mike, who'd once worked the farm before becoming a CEO and moving to the place he'd bought for his wife. "You ready for this?"

"Ready," Mission said, because he'd been given this role, this promotion. People assumed he deserved it, because it had been given to him. He didn't have to make excuses or be self-depreciating. He was the foreman.

"Hey, man." Tuck arrived and shook his hand, pulling him into a hug as he laughed. "You're going to be so amazing at this."

"Thank you," Mission said, starting to feel a little robotic in his movements and what he said. "Have you seen my granddad?"

"Yeah, I saw him," Tuck said as he turned to survey the crowd gathered under the tent. "I think he asked Cosette for something to drink."

Concern spiked through Mission, but he told himself worrying over his grandfather wouldn't make anyone happy. Granddad didn't need Mission to come pick him up; he could still drive himself. Granddad didn't want to order his groceries online and have them delivered; he wanted to pick out his own bananas and pork chops.

Mission couldn't help worrying over him as he aged, so he looked around, hoping he'd come out of the barn with Cosette, something cold to drink in his hand.

"I could use something to drink too."

"Cosette set up the drinks right around the corner," Matt said. "I'll go with you." He met Mission's eyes, and a swell of gratitude moved through him, because Matt wasn't going to leave Mission alone tonight.

He led the way toward the front corner of the barn, where Kristie happened to be standing. Her golden hair cascaded over her shoulders in soft waves, and she looked his way as he neared.

She smiled, and oh, that rivaled the glory of the early evening sun. Mission wasn't sure if it was the uneven ground or if he'd temporarily gone blind at the nearness of Kristie's beauty, but he stumbled.

Jolt after jolt of electricity struck through him, and he

managed to throw out his hand, hoping to find something to grab onto.

His hand landed on Matt, and his friend said, "Whoa, there," as if Mission were a horse who'd been spooked. Maybe he had been.

His granddad came around the corner then, and Mission detoured toward him when he wanted to go over to Kristie and talk to her. *About what?* he asked himself as he said, "Hey, Granddad."

"There he is." His grandfather's face lit up, and he handed his cup of drink to Matt, who took it like he'd expected to play Mission's butler that evening. "How are you, my boy?"

"I'm great, Granddad." Mission hugged him, leaning and sinking into the embrace. "The drive was okay?"

"Fine."

"I can take you home if it gets too dark."

"I'll be fine." Granddad stepped back, his smile very nearly lifting all the wrinkles in his forehead. "This jacket looks mighty fine on you."

Mission grinned down at the navy blue blazer. "Thanks, Granddad." He looked past him to the corner of the barn. "What do they have to drink over there?"

"Lemonade, ice tea, water, soda pops, all kinds of stuff." He stepped over to Matt and took his drink, then asked him something.

That left Mission to continue to the drink counter by himself. Fine by him. He needed a moment alone right now anyway, after that stumble where he'd nearly gone down in front of Kristie—and everyone else at the party.

He'd barely picked up a red plastic cup when the scent of flowery, fruity perfume met his nose.

"Hey, Mission."

He looked over to Kristie, so many things running through his head. "Hey." Always the example of loquacious.

"I like your jacket."

"Thank you. I—it's my granddad's."

Her face lit up. "Yes, I met him. Very nice guy."

"Yeah." Mission smiled, mostly at the way she'd come to life while talking to him. "He's great."

"Are your parents coming?"

Mission's jaw tightened, and he moved down the table to fill his cup with half lemonade and half iced tea. He could brush off her question, avoid it the way he had for the past thirty years of his life. But something about her made him want to tell her.

"Hey, are you okay?"

Mission lifted his cup to his lips and shook his head.

"I didn't mean...." Kristie looked over her shoulder, then faced him again. She took the cup from him and said, "Come with me."

If she'd have just walked away, Mission could've simply picked up another cup, made another Arnold Palmer, and gone back to the party. No, he wouldn't be able to ever talk to Kristie again, but if she wanted to talk about his parents, that would be fine.

But she took his hand—a gesture that sent another wave of electricity through him—and led him away from the drink counter, the party, and toward the front barn doors. She slipped inside and he followed, the cool air conditioning a welcome relief after the warmer outdoors.

Mission hadn't been this nervous since Deacon had offered him the foreman job. But being in the small lobby of the barn with Kristie? His first instinct was to kiss her. Then she wouldn't be able to ask him anything about his parents. At the same time, he hadn't kissed anyone in a long time, and he really wanted a chance with this woman.

So he couldn't kiss her, because when he crashed doing that, he'd never get a real first date with her.

He stood there, his hand in hers and his heart flopping around inside his chest, anchorless. *Wait,* he told himself. *Wait for her to say something before you blurt out too much.*

sneak peek! his tenth dance chapter two:

Kristie Higgins had hallucinated. Straight-up gone into fantasy-land. Otherwise, how else would she be standing inside the lobby of the administration barn, holding hands with Mission Redbay?

The warmth of his skin against hers sent a shiver through her body, and she quickly released his hand, suddenly aware of how forward she'd been. No fantasy-land. Just her asserting herself in probably an unwelcome way.

She reminded herself that Mission had picked her up off the floor of the barn and carried her across the farm to his house, fed her, and then insisted he drive her back to her van.

Months ago, she told herself. They'd been friendly enough since then, but Kris didn't truly *know* Mission. He made it very difficult for someone to get to know him.

She cleared her throat. "I'm sorry," she said, taking a step back. "I shouldn't—you don't have to tell me anything." She watched his eyes, noting how he didn't look away from her. He didn't flush or duck his head. "I thought maybe you needed a moment."

Mission's dark eyes fired with emotion, which Kris actually liked. He'd been such an enigma, this mystery cowboy that had spent so much time camped out in her head. Seeing him show emotions made him so much more human, more relatable, and she settled her weight on her back leg to put a bit more distance between them.

"It's okay," he said so softly it almost sounded like a hum. "I'm okay."

Kristie nodded, unsure of what to say next. She'd acted on impulse, wanting to comfort this man she barely knew but felt inexplicably drawn to. Now, standing alone with him, a flutter of nervousness assaulted her stomach. "Okay, well, it's your party."

"My parents—it's complicated."

"Most families are."

"Can I tell you another time?"

"Of course. I didn't mean to put you on the spot." She'd simply wondered if his parents would be joining the party when his grandfather had.

"It's fine," he said, but it didn't feel like it was. He turned and looked over his shoulder and then faced her again. Everything about him, from his neatly trimmed beard to the energy in his eyes to that sexy navy jacket, called to her, which surprised her so much. She hadn't liked him much in the past, and now she found herself hoping he'd ask her to dinner.

"I should get back," he said. "I think Deac's gonna make an announcement and everything, as if everyone here doesn't already know tomorrow is my first day as the foreman."

Kris nodded, a twinge of disappointment winging its way through her guts. "Right, of course. Let's go back." She wasn't sure what people would think if they saw her and Mission sneaking out of this barn. Part of her wanted to go down the long hallway and out the back, where she could rejoin the party without all the eyes on her. She didn't normally mind having people look her way, but she knew Mission did, and she didn't want to cause him any issues.

"I'm just going to head to the restroom really quick." She hooked her thumb over her shoulder. "I'll see you out there, okay?"

Mission met her gaze again, and he saw right through her, she knew. "Okay," he said.

Kris held her head high as she walked in the opposite direction, trying not to feel like she was scampering away from the gorgeous cowboy.

Once she made it back outside, Kris stood in the shade of the tent, out of the way but still part of the party. She wasn't a Hammond, but she knew all of them. She'd been coming to Pony Power and the farm for a few years now, and she'd been to Travis and Poppy's farm as well as Mike and Gerty's.

"You okay over here?" a man asked, and Kris turned toward Keith Whettstein. He smiled at her and added, "You won't drive all the way to Blackhorse Bay, will you?"

She grinned at him and leaned in for a hug. "I'm not sure where that is." She glanced over to the woman at his side, and she knew they'd gotten married a couple of years ago, but Kris couldn't remember her name.

"Have you met my wife, Lindsay?" Keith asked.

"I'm not sure." Kris shook her hand, her smile as wide as possible. "So tell me where Blackhorse Bay is."

"It's a big boarding stable about an hour north of here."

"Not as far as Tuck's place," Kris said. "I'd come if you needed me." She glanced back out to the party and then focused on Keith again. "You're telling me a 'big boarding stable' doesn't have a vet on-staff?"

"We have two," Lindsay said. "But one of them is having a baby next month, so we're looking for someone else."

"A full-time position?" Kris met Lindsay's gaze. "I own a roaming veterinary office. I have appointments at various ranches and farms every day, with emergency appointments available same-day."

"My dad says you're great."

"His mom too."

"She is great."

Kris got whipped over to the third voice in the conversation, and now Mission stood there. He gave her a smile and stepped into Keith and Lindsay at the same time. "I sure miss you around here, brother."

Keith laughed, and Kris even heard Mission issue a chuckle. "Maybe I'll come back if I can work for you."

"Nah." Mission shook his head. "You've got such a great gig at Blackhorse." He nodded over to Kris next. "She's a great vet, but you can't steal her from us forever."

The way he spoke about her sent warmth spreading

through her chest. She didn't want to melt into the compliment, but she found herself smiling, ducking her head, and tucking her hair behind her ear.

"Maybe just in a pinch," Keith said. "Bart's been having a hard time finding a full-time vet."

"I can give you my number," Kris said.

"Yeah, sure." Keith smiled at her, and then someone tapped on a live mic.

"Ladies and gentlemen," Deacon said. "Cowboys and cowgirls." He grinned, which Kris didn't see him do often either. She felt nothing for the cowboy standing several yards away, but the moment she looked at Mission, every cell in her body rioted.

The crowd quieted, all eyes turning to Deacon. Kristie glanced at Mission, noticing the way he straightened his posture, his jaw tightening slightly.

"We're here tonight to celebrate two very important things," Deacon continued. "First, the retirement of a man who has been the backbone of this ranch for so many years. Matt Whettstein, would you please c'mon over here?"

Applause erupted as Matt made his way to the center of the tent, his weathered face creased in a broad smile. Deacon clapped him on the back as he reached him, and the two of them spoke to each other, with the mic out to the side so it wasn't broadcasted to the crowd.

Matt stepped back and wiped his eyes, and Deac lifted the mic back to his mouth. "Matt has been more than just a foreman," Deacon said, his voice filled with emotion. "He's been a friend, a mentor, and a part of our family. Heck, he's been here longer than I have." He grinned at Matt as several people laughed and agreed.

Kris didn't know the whole history of the Hammond Family Farm, but she knew Matt had come to the farm as the foreman every summer when Deacon's parents went north.

"Matt, we can't thank you enough for your years of dedication and hard work here at the Hammond Family Farm." Deacon handed him an envelope, which seemed way too small for Matt's big hands. He then passed Matt the mic, and he looked around the crowd for a moment.

"I can't find my wife."

"Right here," Gloria called from back by the front of the barn.

Matt nodded, his throat working as he swallowed several times. "It's been my honor to work for the Hammond family for so long. Some of them know this, and my kids definitely know this, but this job saved me. It saved my kids' lives, and it provided a new start for Gloria and I that we both needed so badly."

He glanced around and nodded to various people, including Travis Thatcher, Cord Behr, Hunter, Deacon, his own brother, Mike, Gray and Elise, and finally, Mission.

He said nothing, and yet the air carried an emotional charge that had Kris tearing up. Why, she had no idea. Perhaps seeing such camaraderie and loyalty and love simply reminded her that the world still had good people living in it.

"The Hammond family has become my family, and I can't wait to spend more free time with some of you." He grinned then, and he extended his arm toward Mission.

"And I know I'm leaving the ranch in extremely good hands."

Mission marched over to Matt, his legs barely bending as he did. He looked like he might start yelling at any moment, and then he stepped into Matt and hugged him. He softened then, and again, the two men talked without anyone else being able to hear them.

Deacon took the mic back, and Matt stood next to Mission, his arm around the man's shoulders. "Which brings me to our second celebration," Deacon said. "As one chapter ends, another begins. I'm thrilled to be the Hammond who gets to announce that Mission Redbay is the new foreman here at the farm, and we're all really excited to keep working with him."

He extended the mic to Mission, who looked at it like it had turned into a rattlesnake. Kris ducked her head to hide her smile, because the thought of Mission making a speech was laughable.

Mission simply leaned over and said, "Thanks, everyone. I'm going to do my best." Then he straightened and looked right at her. She grinned and grinned, and she started to clap along with everyone else.

The applause swelled up and up, a few cowboys adding whoops and hollers to the noise, and Mission's face turned an adorable shade of red Kris would like to see again.

His words had been sincere, if simple, and Kris whooped as the applause started to die down.

"Please, everyone, eat as much as you can," Deacon said. "We have so much food."

Mission got surrounded by friends and the cowboys he worked with, and since Kris wasn't on the staff here at the farm, she felt slightly removed from everyone. Thankfully, one of the counselors at Pony Power, a woman named Hannah, looped her arm through Kris's and said, "Come get something to eat with me."

"Yes, I'm starving," Kris said, grateful to have a friend to go with.

"How are things at the office?" Hannah asked.

"Good." Kris worked out of a home office to schedule her appointments at the farms and ranches where she worked. "I'm taking tomorrow off, in fact. I'm going to go through the files in my office and get everything put away."

"You'll be happy about that." Hannah grinned and picked up a plate.

"Yeah." Kris kept her smile on her face as she moved down the table behind her friend, but she seriously wondered if her life's happiness had come to her cleaning up her client files in the spare bedroom of her house.

Holy cow, she thought. Because it had.

As she sat at one of the checkered-cloth covered tables, she couldn't help but keep glancing at Mission. He seemed more at ease now, laughing with some of the other ranch hands and accepting handshakes from what seemed like the same people as before.

"Mind if I join you?"

Kristie looked up to see Mission's grandfather standing beside her table, a plate of food shaking in in his hands.

She jumped to her feet and took his plate. "Of course not,"

she said, pulling out the chair in front of him. "Please, sit with us."

"Mission can have that spot," the older man said as he went around the chair and sat. Kris put his plate in front of him and glanced over to Mission. She found he'd moved to the buffet, and he'd have his food in only a few minutes. Surely he'd know to come sit with his grandfather, and Kris's pulse rioted at the thought of eating with him.

"I'm Ted," he said, extending a hand. "Mission's grandfather."

"Kristie." She shook his hand. "We met near the drinks."

"Yes, yes." Ted looked at her with pleasant, dark brown eyes. "Kristie," he repeated thoughtfully. "Are you a veterinarian?"

"Yes, sir." She smiled at him. "How did you know that?"

"My grandson's mentioned you," Ted said.

Kris blinked, not sure what to make of that. "Oh, I didn't realize he talked about me."

Ted chuckled and picked up his fork. "Don't worry, it's all good things. Though between me and you, I think—"

"Grandad," Mission said as he sank into the chair between Kris and Ted. "I hope you're not tellin' stories you shouldn't." He turned away from Kris to look at his grandfather, then cut her a look out of the corner of his eye.

Kris's heartbeat skipped over beats as she thought about what Ted would've said. Or maybe that was the scent of Mission's cologne—a mix of cedar wood, something spicy, and a touch of delicious male.

"I was just telling Kristie here that I think you're sweet on her."

Kris sucked in a breath, and Hannah coughed once, then started to laugh. Mission sat there, his face absolutely stoic. He seemed to have frozen; his chest didn't even rise and fall.

After a few seconds, where both she and Hannah stared at Mission and his grandfather simply ate a few bites of his cole slaw, Mission turned toward Ted. "You know what? I kind of am."

Kris pulled in another breath, surprised she still had room in her lungs for more air. She and Mission had texted plenty of times in the past six months, but always about work. And moving forward, she expected to keep dealing with Gloria, but she'd have to copy him on the important things, because that was what she'd done with Matt.

He turned toward her, glancing over to Hannah before clearing his throat and meeting her eye. "I've been thinkin' about asking you to dinner."

"You've been thinking about it?" she asked, surprised her voice worked at all. "Or you're doing it?"

The heat in his eyes turned into a glare. "I'm hoping you'll be free for dinner soon," he said. "With me. Dinner with me." He looked over to his granddad. "See what you made me do?"

Kris smiled, especially when Ted bickered back with him. Her curiosity about their relationship soared, and her pulse roared at her. She'd hoped he'd ask her out in the barn, and now he'd finally done it.

But she'd been hurt before, and getting involved with someone she worked with had never turned out well for her.

Suddenly, everything felt exactly as Mission had said in the barn—complicated.

Mission turned back to her, his expression now a mix of hope, nerves, and irritation, and Kris knew her next words could change everything between them, and she cast a look over to Hannah, who nodded encouragingly.

Then she opened her mouth and prayed the right thing would come out.

* * *

Holy brown cows! What is Kristie going to say to Mission? And will it be enough to soothe his ego so they can try for happily-ever-after?

Preorder **HIS TENTH DANCE** so you don't miss a moment of life in Ivory Peaks with the Hammond family!

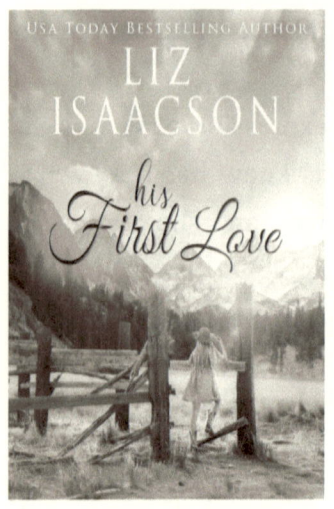

His First Love (Book 1): She broke up with him a decade ago. He's back in town after finishing a degree at MIT, ready to start his job at the family company. Can Hunter and Molly find their way through their pasts to build a future together?

His Second Chance (Book 2): They broke up over twenty years ago. She's lost everything when she shows up at the farm in Ivory Peaks where he works. Can Matt and Gloria heal from their pasts to find a future happily-ever-after with each other?

His Third Try (Book 3): He moved to Ivory Peaks with his daughter to start over after a devastating break-up. She's never had a meaningful relationship with a man, especially a cowboy. Can Boone and Cosette help each other heal enough to build a happily-ever-after...and a family?

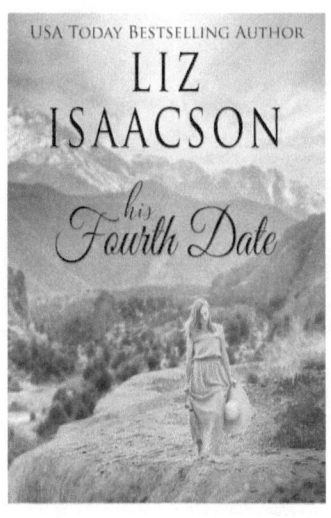

His Fourth Date (Book 4): Their relationship has been nothing but loose goats, a leaking roof, and her complete humiliation after he pays her mortgage so she won't lose her farm. Travis wants to go back in time and start over with Poppy, but he doesn't know how. Can a small town speed-dating event get their second chance off on the right foot?

His Fifth Kiss (Book 5): They once had a few summers together. Now, Michael Hammond is back in town after a devastating injury overseas. He's looking to reset and recover...not to fall in love. But with Gertrude Whettstein also back at the farm, can Gerty and Mike make their second chance romance into a happily-ever-after?

His Sixth Sweetheart (Book 6): She's had a crush on him for decades. He's finally in a place where he feels ready to date the boss's daughter. Can Cord and Jane take their relationship to the next level without getting burned?

His Seventh Stop (Book 7): He's a seasoned cowboy on a delivery mission. She's a resilient hobby farm owner braving the winter storm. Can Keith and Lindsay forge a bond in the heart of a tempest and find love in the calm that follows?

His Eighth Ride (Book 8): Tag has secretly admired Opal from afar. He even went so far as to ask her out, but the timing was all off, and now he's just awkward around his best friend's little sister. Can their unexpected reunion mend the fences between them and finally lead them to the forever love they've been waiting for?

His Ninth Promise (Book 9): At home on the Hammond Family Farm, where gypsy souls and rodeo dreams collide, Tucker's heart has been beating for Bobbie Jo. But with her heart set on a distant love and Tucker searching for something more, their paths seemed destined to cross but never converge. Can he stick it out for another ride if the promise is coming home to Bobbie Jo?

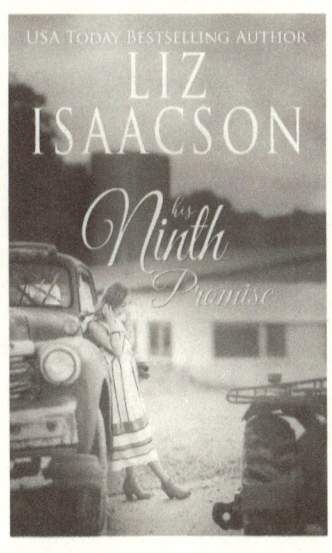

His Tenth Dance (Book 10): Mission has carried the weight of his past for a long time, and letting someone in feels like a risk. But maybe, just maybe, Kristie is worth it. When his granddad tells her about his secret crush, sparks fly between them, walls come down, and love might just get a second chance to take the lead... if Kristie and Mission are willing to take a leap of faith.

Her Cowboy Billionaire Birthday Wish (Book 1): All the maid at Whiskey Mountain Lodge wants for her birthday is a handsome cowboy billionaire. And Colton can make that wish come true—if only he hadn't escaped to Coral Canyon after being left at the altar...

Her Cowboy Billionaire Butler (Book 2): She broke up with him to date another man...who broke her heart. He's a former CEO with nothing to do who can't get her out of his head. Can Wes and Bree find a way toward happily-ever-after at Whiskey Mountain Lodge?

Her Cowboy Billionaire Best Friend's Brother (Book 3): She's best friends with the single dad cowboy's brother and has watched two friends find love with the sexy new cowboys in town. When Gray Hammond comes to Whiskey Mountain Lodge with his son, will Elise finally get her own happily-ever-after with one of the Hammond brothers?

Her Cowboy Billionaire Beast (Book 4): A cowboy billionaire beast, his new manager, and the Christmas traditions that soften his heart and bring them together.

Her Cowboy Billionaire Bad Boy (Book 5): A cowboy billionaire cop who's a stickler for rules, the woman he pulls over when he's not even on duty, and the personal mandates he has to break to keep her in his life...

Her Cowboy Billionaire Best Friend (Book 1): Graham Whittaker returns to Coral Canyon a few days after Christmas—after the death of his father. He takes over the energy company his dad built from the ground up and buys a high-end lodge to live in —only a mile from the home of his once-best friend, Laney McAllister. They were best friends once, but Laney's always entertained feelings for him, and spending so much time with him while they make Christmas memories puts her heart in danger of getting broken again...

Her Cowboy Billionaire Boss (Book 2): Since the death of his wife a few years ago, Eli Whittaker has been running from one job to another, unable to find somewhere for him and his son to settle. Meg Palmer is Stockton's nanny, and she comes with her boss, Eli, to the lodge, her long-time crush on the man no different in Wyoming than it was on the beach. When she confesses her feelings for him and gets nothing in return, she's crushed, embarrassed, and unsure if she can stay in Coral Canyon for Christmas. Then Eli starts to show some feelings for her too...

Her Cowboy Billionaire Boyfriend (Book 3): Andrew Whittaker is the public face for the Whittaker Brothers' family energy company, and with his older brother's robot about to be announced, he needs a press secretary to help him get everything ready and tour the state to make the announcements. When he's hit by a protest sign being carried by the company's biggest opponent, Rebecca Collings, he learns with a few clicks that she has the background they need. He offers her the job of press secretary when she thought she was going to be arrested, and not only because the spark between them in so hot Andrew can't see straight.

Can Becca and Andrew work together and keep their relationship a secret? Or will hearts break in this classic romance retelling reminiscent of *Two Weeks Notice*?

Her Cowboy Billionaire Bodyguard (Book 4): Beau Whittaker has watched his brothers find love one by one, but every attempt he's made has ended in disaster. Lily Everett has been in the spotlight since childhood and has half a dozen platinum records with her two sisters. She's taking a break from the brutal music industry and hiding out in Wyoming while her ex-husband continues to cause trouble for her. When she hears of Beau Whittaker and what he offers his clients, she wants to meet him. Beau is instantly attracted to Lily, but he tried a relationship with his last client that left a scar that still hasn't healed...

Can Lily use the spirit of Christmas to discover what matters most? Will Beau open his heart to the possibility of love with someone so different from him?

Her Cowboy Billionaire Bull Rider (Book 5): Todd Christopherson has just retired from the professional rodeo circuit and returned to his hometown of Coral Canyon. Problem is, he's got no family there anymore, no land, and no job. Not that he needs a job--he's got plenty of money from his illustrious career riding bulls.

Then Todd gets thrown during a routine horseback ride up the canyon, and his only support as he recovers physically is the beautiful Violet Everett. She's no nurse, but she does the best she can for the handsome cowboy. **Will she lose her heart to the billionaire bull rider? Can Todd trust that God led him to Coral Canyon...and Vi?**

Her Cowboy Billionaire Bachelor (Book 6): Rose Everett isn't sure what to do with her life now that her country music career is on hold. After all, with both of her sisters in Coral Canyon, and one about to have a baby, they're not making albums anymore.

Liam Murphy has been working for Doctors Without Borders, but he's back in the US now, and looking to start a new clinic in Coral Canyon, where he spent his summers.

When Rose wins a date with Liam in a bachelor auction, their relationship blooms and grows quickly. **Can Liam and Rose find a solution to their problems that doesn't involve one of them leaving Coral Canyon with a broken heart?**

Her Cowboy Billionaire Blind Date (Book 7): Her sons want her to be happy, but she's too old to be set up on a blind date...isn't she?

Amanda Whittaker has been looking for a second chance at love since the death of her husband several years ago. Finley Barber is a cowboy in every sense of the word. Born and raised on a racehorse farm in Kentucky, he's since moved to Dog Valley and started his own breeding stable for champion horses. He hasn't dated in years, and everything about Amanda makes him nervous.

Will Amanda take the leap of faith required to be with Finn? Or will he become just another boyfriend who doesn't make the cut?

Her Cowboy Billionaire Best Man (Book 8): When Celia Abbott-Armstrong runs into a gorgeous cowboy at her best friend's wedding, she decides she's ready to start dating again.

But the cowboy is Zach Zuckerman, and the Zuckermans and Abbotts have been at war for generations.

Can Zach and Celia find a way to reconcile their family's differences so they can have a future together?

Tex (Book 1): He's back in town after a successful country music career. She owns a bordering farm to the family land he wants to buy...and she outbids him at the auction. Can Tex and Abigail rekindle their old flame, or will the issue of land ownership come between them?

Otis (Book 2): He's finished with his last album and looking for a soft place to fall after a devastating break-up. She runs the small town bookshop in Coral Canyon and needs a new boyfriend to get her old one out of her life for good. Can Georgia convince Otis to take another shot at real love when their first kiss was fake?

Morris (Book 3): Morris Young is just settling into his new life as the manager of Country Quad when he attends a wedding. He sees his ex-wife there—apparently Leighann is back in Coral Canyon—along with a little boy who can't be more or less than five years old... Could he be Morris's? And why is his heart hoping for that, and for a reconciliation with the woman who left him because he traveled too much?

Trace (Book 4): He's been accused of only dating celebrities. She's a simple line dance instructor in small town Coral Canyon, with a soft spot for kids...and cowboys. Trace could use some dance lessons to go along with his love lessons... Can he and Everly fall in love with the beat, or will she dance her way right out of his arms?

Blaze (Book 5): He's dark as night, a single dad, and a retired bull riding champion. With all his money, his rugged good looks, and his ability to say all the right things, Faith has no chance against Blaze Young's charms. But she's his complete opposite, and she just doesn't see how they can be together...

...so she ends things with him.

Gabe (Book 6): He's a father's rights advocate lawyer with a sweet little girl. She's fighting for her own daughter. Can Gabe and Hilde find happily-ever-after when they're at such odds with one another?

Jem (Book 7): He's still healing from his vices, and Jem has dedicated everything he has to his two kids. At least he's not mourning his divorce anymore, and in fact, he might be ready to move on. She's his former best friend, and once he breaks his wrist, his nurse. Can Sunny somehow rope this cowboy's heart?

Luke (Book 8): He swore off women when his ex told him he might not be their daughter's father. But a paternity test confirmed he is, and Luke Young has dedicated his life to his little girl and his brothers' band. There hasn't been time for a girlfriend anyway. He's tried here and there, and the women in small-town Coral Canyon are certainly interested in him.

But he's been thinking about his massage therapist for a while now. Can he ask Sterling out when all they've ever been is professional? Oh, and there's the fact that she's seen practically every inch of his body... Awkward, right?

Bryce (Book 9): Bryce Young has been broken and drifting for years. After giving up his son for adoption, he left Coral Canyon and hasn't returned...until now.

Harry (Book 10): He's a country music star who doesn't live in town. She's a Missing Persons Investigator with strong ties to her community... and she's not so sure about Harry's T-shirts... But Belle knows her heart sings whenever she sees Harry - if only that were more often.

about liz

Liz Isaacson writes inspirational romance, usually set in Texas, or Wyoming, or anywhere else horses and cowboys exist. She lives in Utah, where she writes full-time, takes her two dogs to the park everyday, and eats a lot of veggies while writing. Find her on her website, along with all of her pen names, at feelgoodfictionbooks.com.